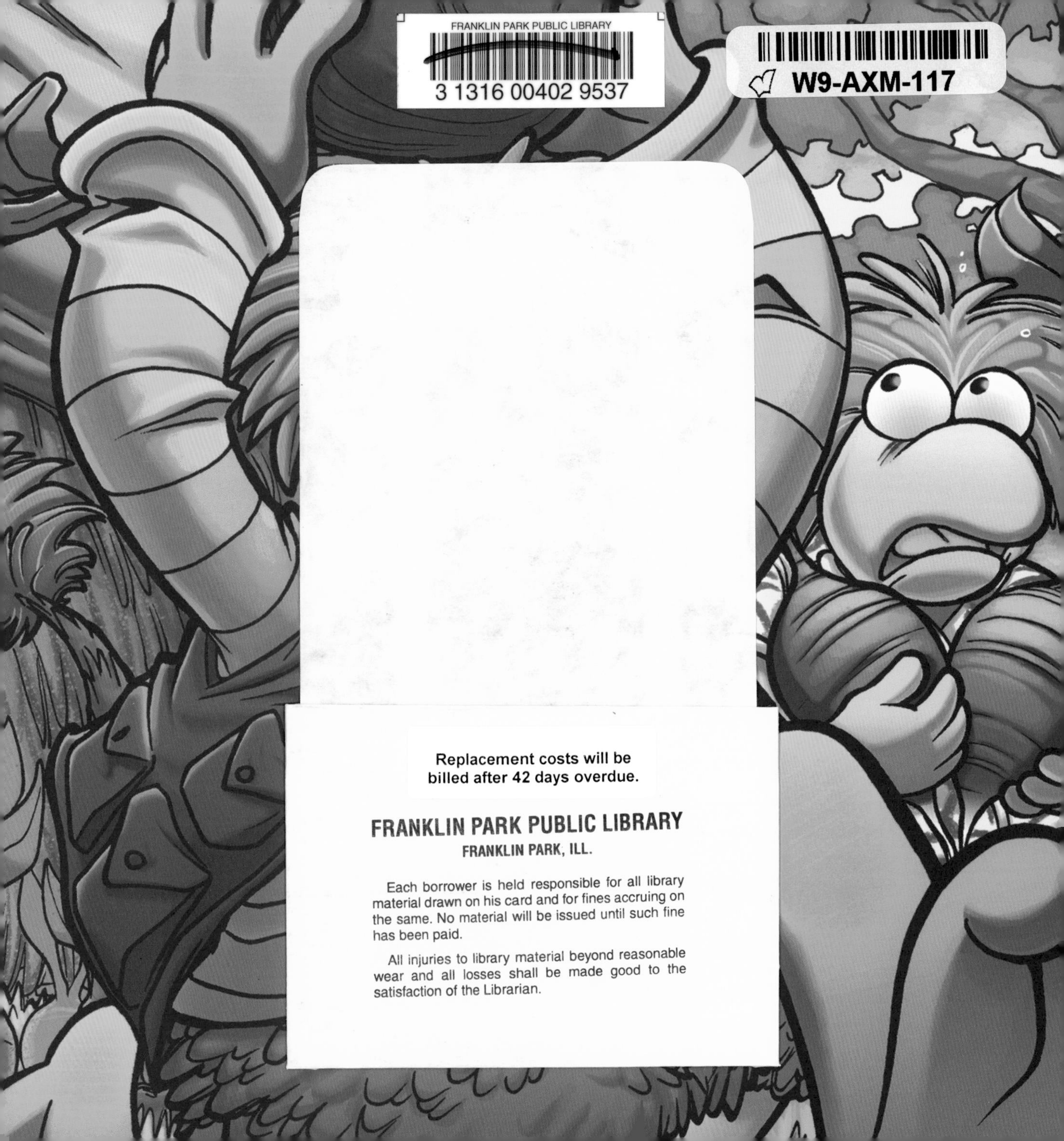

Jim Henson's FRAGGLE ROCK™

Tails and Tales

The Jim Henson Company
www.henson.com

Archaia Entertainment LLC
www.archaia.com

Jim Henson's FRAGGLE ROCK™

Tails and Tales

Written by
Tim Beedle
Jason M. Burns
Katie Cook
Jake T. Forbes
Joe LeFavi
Paul Morrissey
Grace Randolph
Katie Strickland

Lettered by
Deron Bennett
Dave Lanphear

Volume Cover by
David Petersen

Illustrated by
Heidi Arnhold
Nichol Ashworth
Ross Campbell
Lindsay Cibos
Katie Cook
Joanna Estep
Chandra Free
Cory Godbey
Hendry Iwanaga
Lizzy John
Chris Lie
Mark Simmons
Fandy Soegiarto

Special Thanks to **Brian Henson**, **Lisa Henson**, **Jim Formanek**, **Nicole Goldman**, **Maryanne Pittman**, **Melissa Segal**, **Hillary Howell**, **Jill Peterson** and the entire Henson team!

ARCHAIA™
NEW STORIES. NEW WORLDS.

Jim Henson™
THE JIM HENSON COMPANY

Published by **Archaia**

Archaia Entertainment LLC
1680 Vine Street, Suite 912
Los Angeles, California, 90028, USA
www.archaia.com

FRAGGLE ROCK VOLUME TWO. July 2011. FIRST PRINTING

10 9 8 7 6 5 4 3 2 1

ISBN: 1-936393-13-1
ISBN 13: 978-1-936393-13-8

Table of Contents

J-GN
FRAGGLE ROCK
402-9537

Wabbish

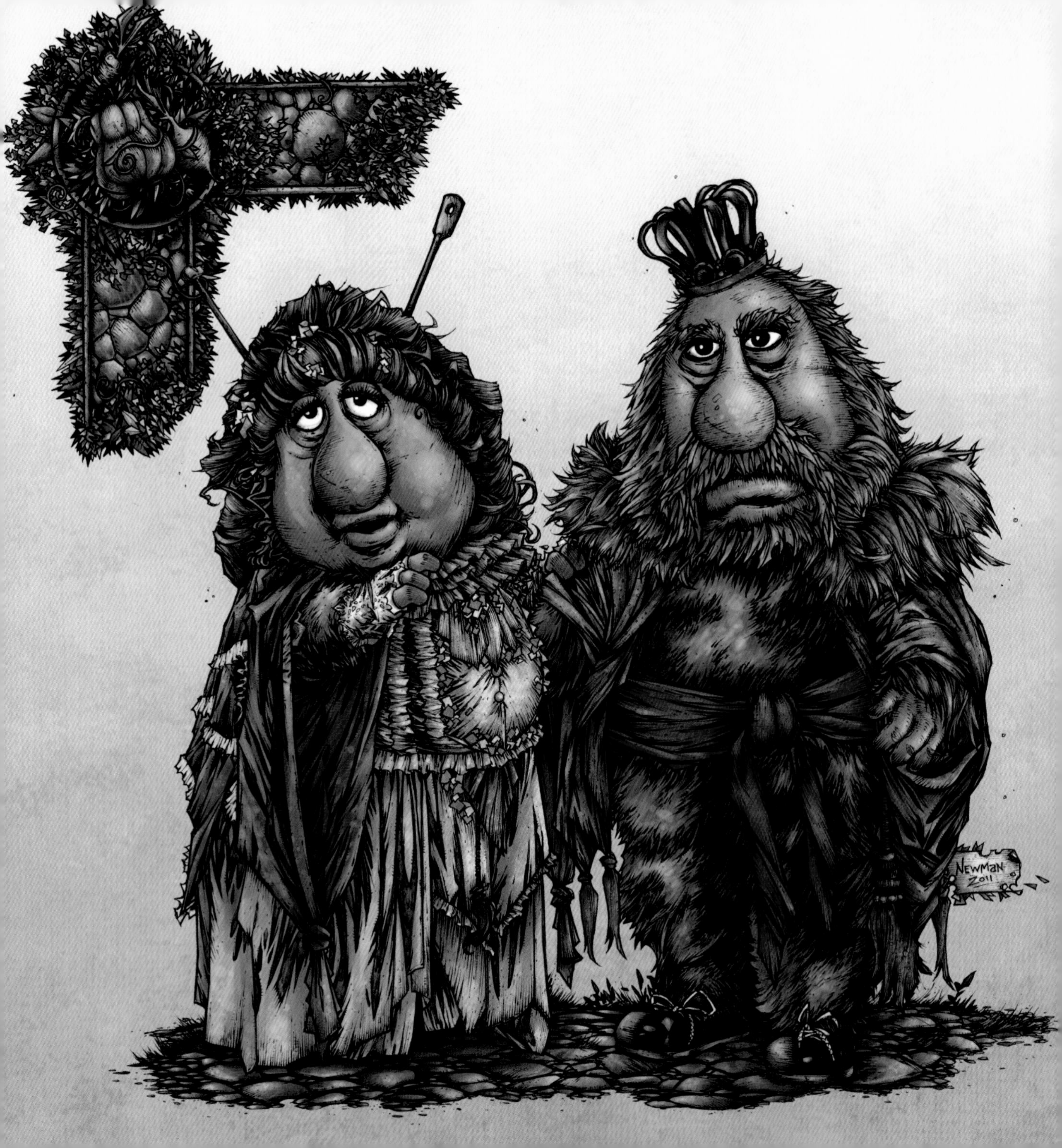
NEWMAN
2011

Foreword

"I'd like to do a show that stops war."

It was a weekend in 1981; Jim Henson, in the midst of shooting **The Dark Crystal**, had called a group of his creative team together to discuss an idea for a new television series aimed at 7 to 12 year-olds. Of course, Jim was not so naive as to think a television series could really stop war. But he thought we should try. We would do a television series that was great fun, but beneath all the singing, parties and adventures would be the theme of harmony. The stories would revolve around conflicts between characters, species and the environment. The Fraggles would find ways to resolve these conflicts, all the while having the time of their lives. They would be forces for good.

When I was about 10, our family went camping and I made friends with the other kids in the campground. We went exploring and discovered a "cave" made from giant boulders that had fallen against each other, leaving irregular spaces in between. We slithered through the crevices "deep underground"… okay, maybe it was only a few feet, but the wonder of our "cave" adventure has never left me. Fraggle Rock is a vast series of magical underground caverns. A backdrop for endless adventures of the body, mind and heart.

We performed the Fraggles as ageless; each is a mixture of child and adult. I think we carry our history within us, like rings in a tree. The most hard-boiled executive has a child buried deep within, and the most innocent child has flickers of great wisdom. That's what our work is about: we're miners in the cavern of the heart. We try to unearth the child within the adult and the adult within the child.

Those of us who worked on **Fraggle Rock** consider it one of our favorite projects. It changed our lives; in my case it led to having children. When they started school, I noticed that raising children brought out the best in the parents. We tried to show our kids how to respect others and our environment. We became our best selves.

It was my great good fortune to work with Jim Henson for 17 years. Under his playful, gentle guidance, everyone grew. He respected all opinions and encouraged everyone in the room to contribute ideas—then he used what he felt would work best. Our producer, Larry Mirkin, expressed this most elegantly: he said, "We are all working in service of the best idea." It was creative utopia.

I am thrilled that The Jim Henson Company remains the custodian of **Fraggle Rock**, for the Henson family understands what **Fraggle Rock** means. In the pages of this book you will find even more Fraggle adventures to share with your children. So put in a load of laundry, curl up with your child, grab some Doozer sticks, and enjoy the magical world of **Fraggle Rock**. Maybe war won't disappear, but learning about harmony will only make the world better.

—**Dave Goelz**
Puppeteer of Boober, Travelling Matt, Philo,
The World's Oldest Fraggle & Large Marvin

The Residents of Fraggle Rock

Gobo

Gobo is the natural leader of the Fraggle Five. He is an explorer, spending his days charting the unexplored (and explored-but-forgotten) regions of Fraggle Rock. He is highly respected by other Fraggles, although they occasionally find him a little pompous. He is also somewhat egocentric, which can make it hard for him to admit mistakes. As a leader, Gobo often provides his friends with direction, although, since he's a Fraggle, it's sometimes a fairly silly one.

Red

Red Fraggle is a nonstop whirligig of activity. To her fellow Fraggles, Red is often seen as a flash of crimson racing to her next athletic pursuit. She is Fraggle Rock champion in Tug-of-War, Diving while Singing Backwards, the Blindfolded One-Legged Radish Relay, and a number of other traditional Fraggle sports. She is outgoing, enthusiastic, and athletic, but take note--her impetuosity can get her into real trouble.

Uncle Travelling Matt

Gobo's Uncle Travelling Matt is the greatest living Fraggle explorer--the Fraggle equivalent of an astronaut. After completing his exploration of Fraggle Rock, he ventured forth into our world, a place the Fraggles call "Outer Space." He sends his observations back to Gobo on postcards in care of Doc.

Boober

According to Boober Fraggle, there are only two things certain in this world: death and laundry. Boober is terrified by the former and fascinated by the latter. He is also paranoid and superstitious. According to Boober, anything that can go wrong surely will, and when it does, it will inevitably happen to him. But Boober's negative attitude has a big plus--he can see real trouble coming a mile away, a useful attribute in a land of eternal optimists!

Mokey

Mokey is an artist, poet and philosopher. She seems to be in touch with some sort of higher Fraggle consciousness. Mokey is fascinated by the beauty and intricacy of the world around her, and is always seeking new ways to share this feeling with others. Mokey may have her head in the clouds, but she's also very courageous and resourceful. Her job is to brave the Gorg garden to gather the radishes the Fraggles eat.

Wembley

Wembley is indecision personified. He only owns two shirts, and both have a banana-tree motif. If he had any other clothes, he'd never be able to get dressed in the morning! Wembley has an uncanny ability to find merit on both sides of any issue. He is steadfast in his admiration for his best friend and roommate, Gobo. It was Gobo who encouraged Wembley to apply for his job with the Fraggle Rock Volunteer Fire Department. Wembley is the siren.

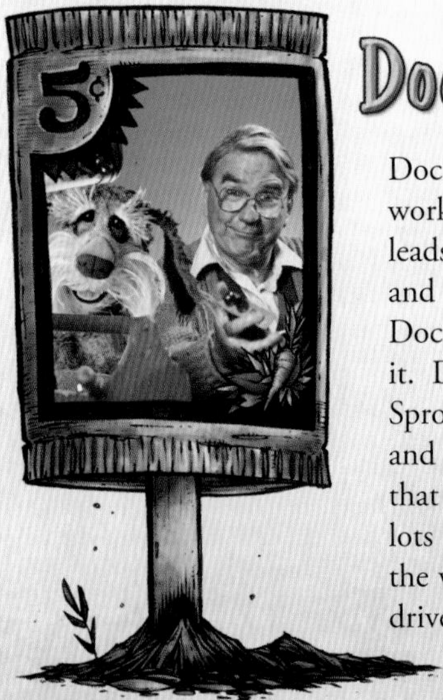
5¢

Doc & Sprocket

Doc, the man who inhabits the workshop that contains the hole that leads to Fraggle Rock, is an inventor and a tinkerer. If it's a wee bit odd, Doc has probably already invented it. Doc doesn't know about Fraggles. Sprocket is Doc's extremely intelligent and expressive dog. Sprocket knows that the Fraggles exist. He's seen them lots of times...but he just doesn't have the words to tell Doc about them. This drives Sprocket crazy!

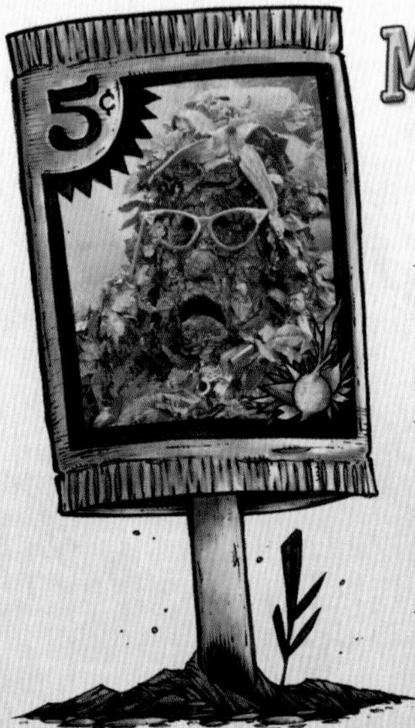
5¢

Marjory the Trash Heap

A matronly, sentient pile compost who acts as an oracle the Fraggles. She sees all and kn all, but at times her offerings wisdom go awry in the hands of Fraggles. Nevertheless, Marjo advice is usually beneficial. S likes to encourage the Fraggles just to find temporary soluti to their problems, but to beco more self-reliant and work to l in harmony with the other spec around them.

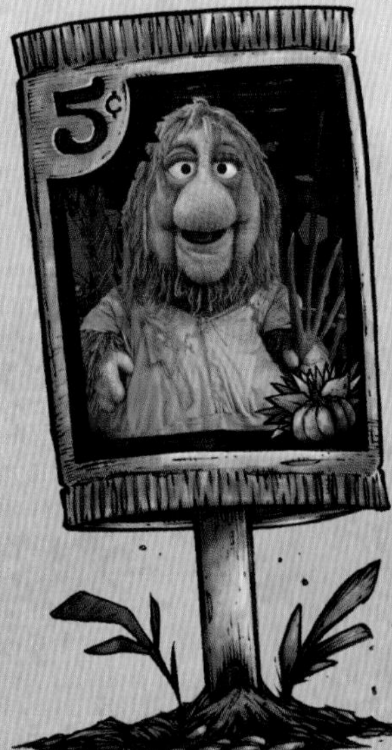
5¢

Junior Gorg

Sweet, loveable, galumphing Junior is the apple of his mother's eye and the bane of the Fraggles' existence! All he wants to do is "get those Fwaggles." The Fraggles raid the Gorg garden for radishes, and the garden is Junior's pride and joy. But the Fraggles are never really in any danger. Junior isn't very bright or coordinated, and really wouldn't hurt a fly.

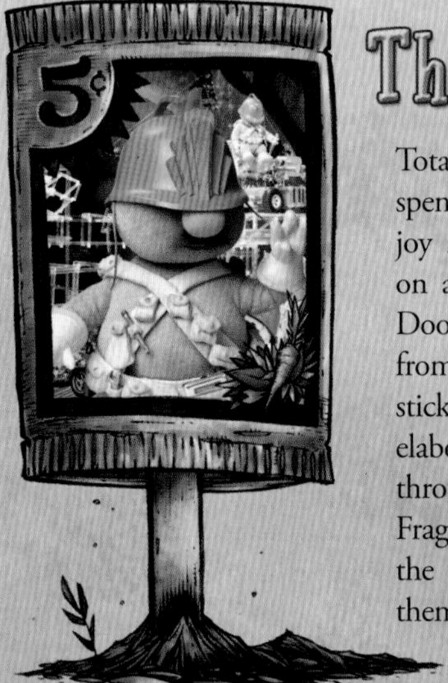
5¢

The Doozers

Totally unlike the Fraggles, Dooz spend their lives working. The great joy in a Doozer's life is to get up, p on a hard hat and take a place on t Doozer work crew. Doozers mine radish from the Gorg garden and make Doo sticks with them, with which they bu elaborate crystalline Doozer constructio throughout Fraggle Rock--which t Fraggles then eat with relish. This plea the Doozers immensely, since it allo them more room to build.

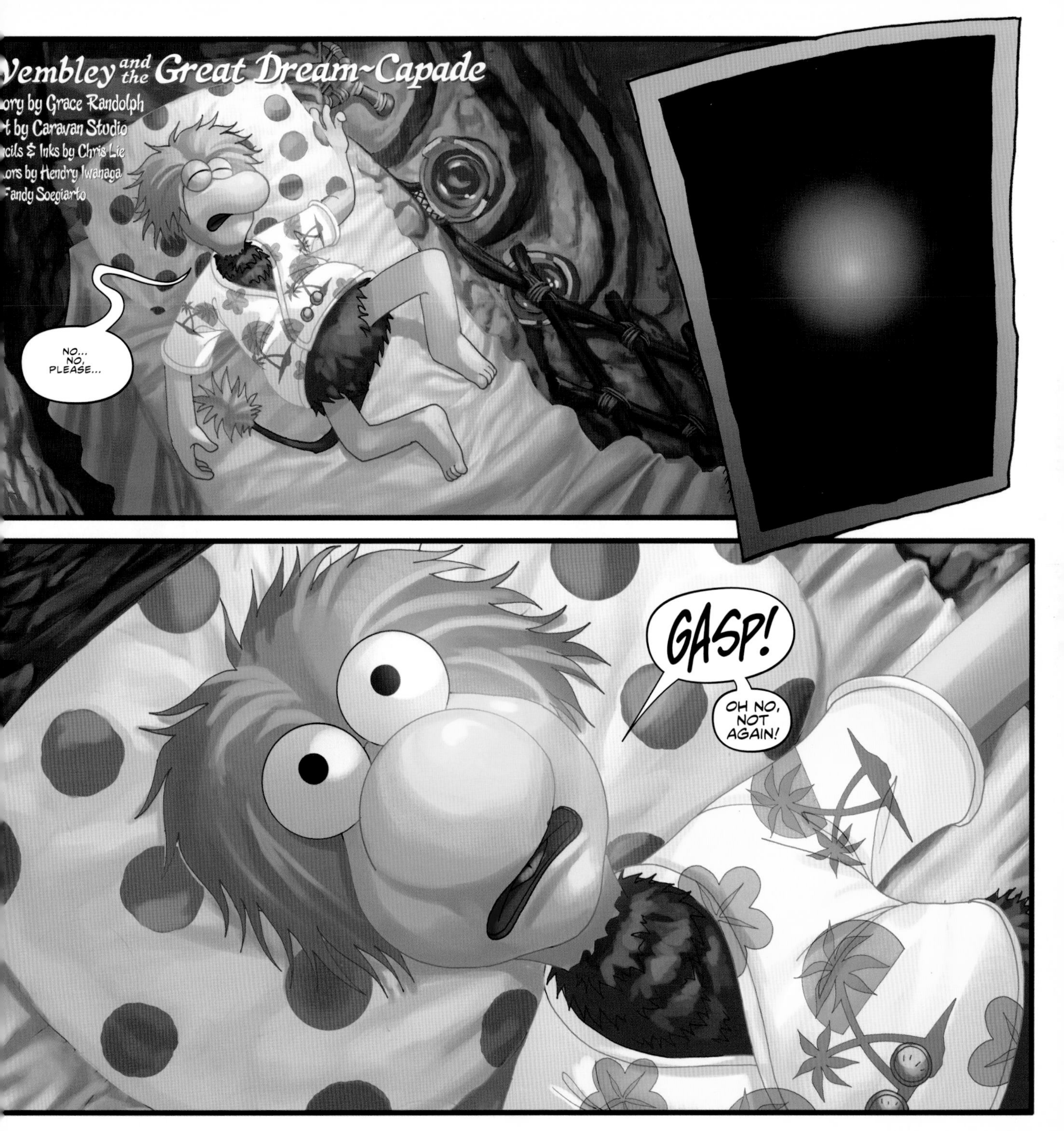
Vembley and the Great Dream~Capade
ory by Grace Randolph
t by Caravan Studio
cils & Inks by Chris Lie
ors by Hendry Iwanaga
Fandy Soegiarto
NO... NO, PLEASE...
GASP!
OH NO, NOT AGAIN!

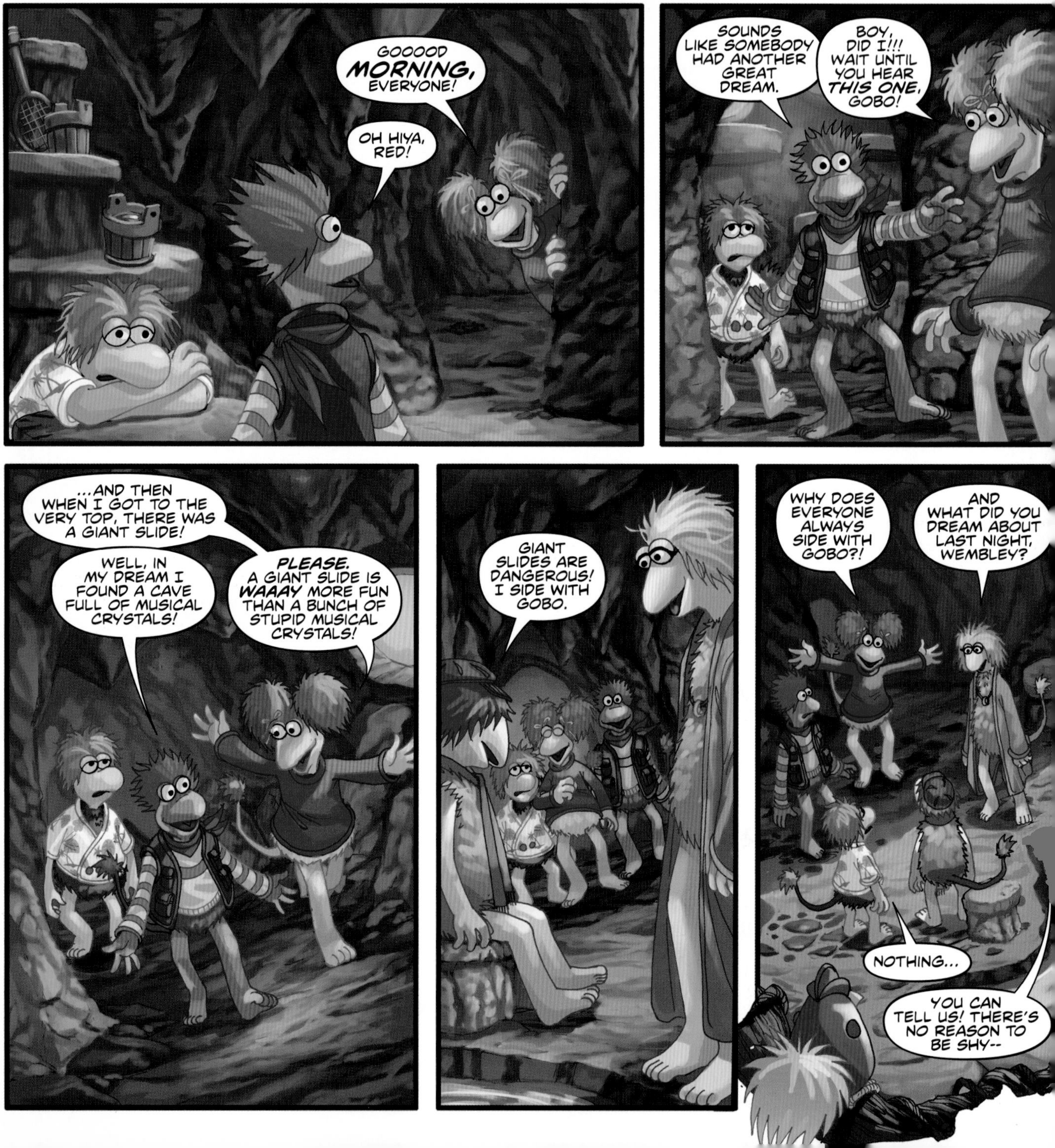
GOOOOD MORNING, EVERYONE!
OH HIYA, RED!
SOUNDS LIKE SOMEBODY HAD ANOTHER GREAT DREAM.
BOY, DID I!!! WAIT UNTIL YOU HEAR THIS ONE, GOBO!
...AND THEN WHEN I GOT TO THE VERY TOP, THERE WAS A GIANT SLIDE!
WELL, IN MY DREAM I FOUND A CAVE FULL OF MUSICAL CRYSTALS!
PLEASE. A GIANT SLIDE IS WAAAY MORE FUN THAN A BUNCH OF STUPID MUSICAL CRYSTALS!
GIANT SLIDES ARE DANGEROUS! I SIDE WITH GOBO.
WHY DOES EVERYONE ALWAYS SIDE WITH GOBO?!
AND WHAT DID YOU DREAM ABOUT LAST NIGHT, WEMBLEY?
NOTHING...
YOU CAN TELL US! THERE'S NO REASON TO BE SHY--

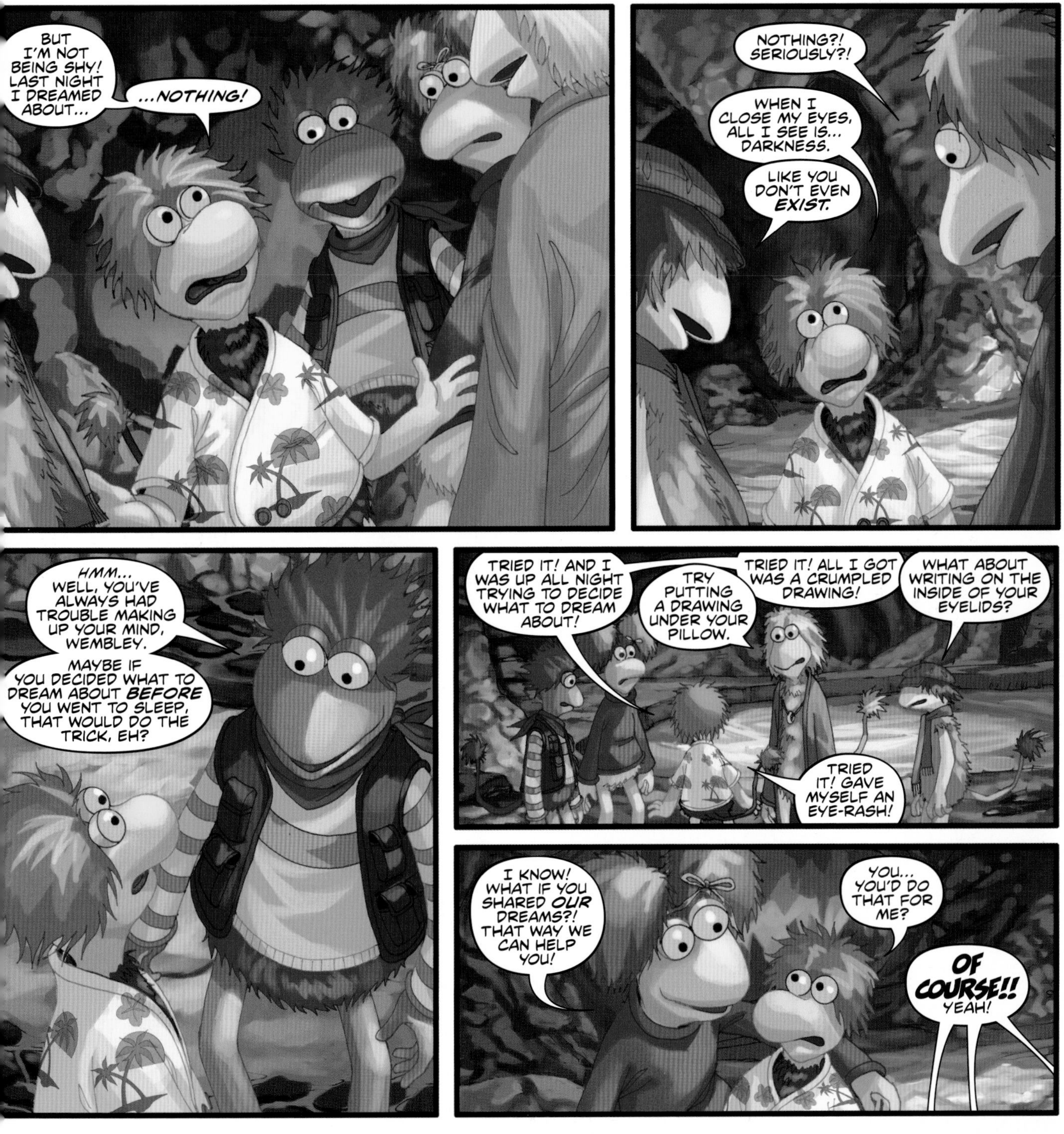

BUT I'M NOT BEING SHY! LAST NIGHT I DREAMED ABOUT...
...*NOTHING!*
NOTHING?! SERIOUSLY?!
WHEN I CLOSE MY EYES, ALL I SEE IS... DARKNESS.
LIKE YOU DON'T EVEN ***EXIST.***
HMM... WELL, YOU'VE ALWAYS HAD TROUBLE MAKING UP YOUR MIND, WEMBLEY.
MAYBE IF YOU DECIDED WHAT TO DREAM ABOUT ***BEFORE*** YOU WENT TO SLEEP, THAT WOULD DO THE TRICK, EH?
TRIED IT! AND I WAS UP ALL NIGHT TRYING TO DECIDE WHAT TO DREAM ABOUT!
TRY PUTTING A DRAWING UNDER YOUR PILLOW.
TRIED IT! ALL I GOT WAS A CRUMPLED DRAWING!
WHAT ABOUT WRITING ON THE INSIDE OF YOUR EYELIDS?
TRIED IT! GAVE MYSELF AN EYE-RASH!
I KNOW! WHAT IF YOU SHARED ***OUR*** DREAMS?! THAT WAY WE CAN HELP YOU!
YOU... YOU'D DO THAT FOR ME?
OF COURSE!! YEAH!

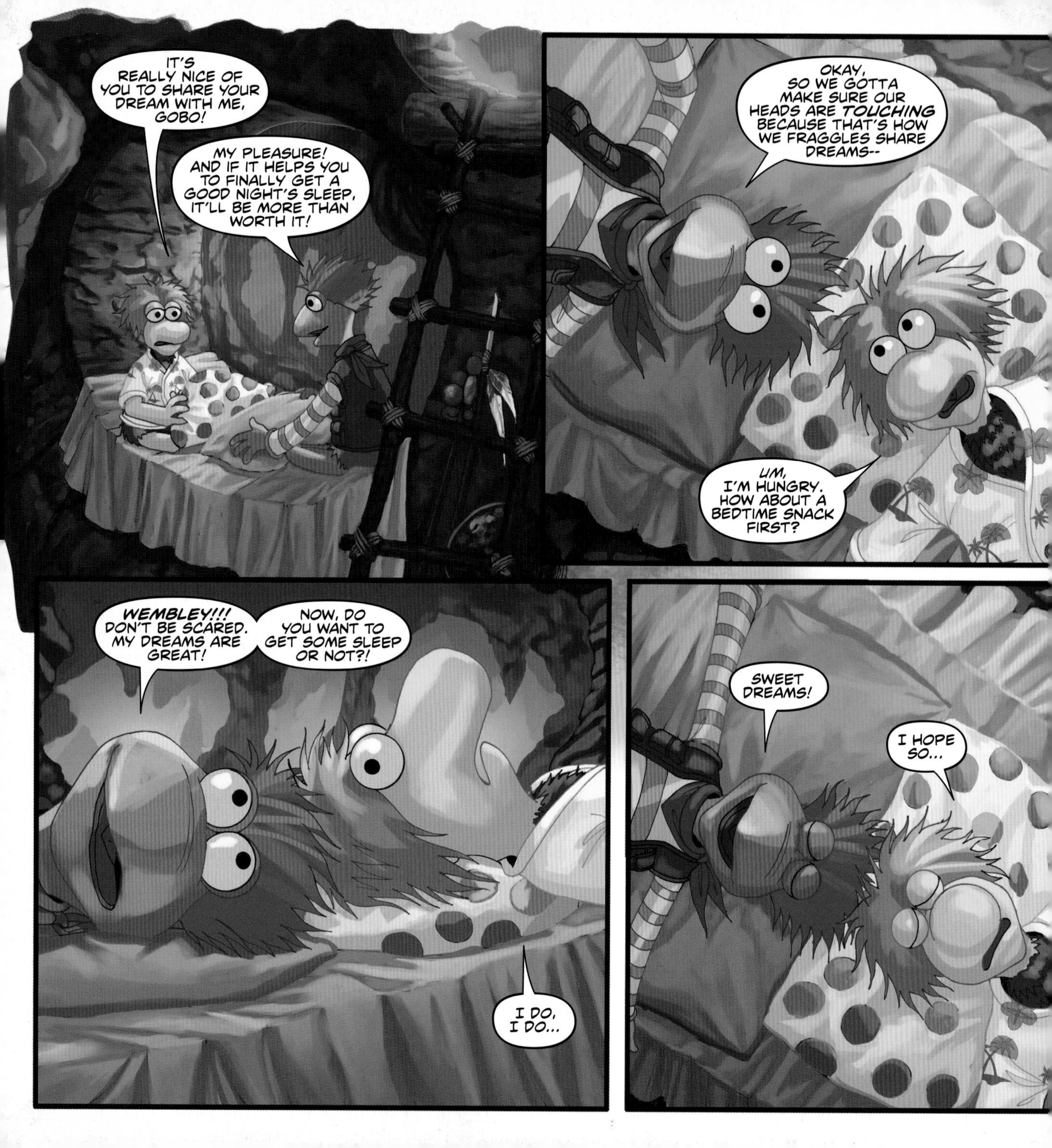
IT'S REALLY NICE OF YOU TO SHARE YOUR DREAM WITH ME, GOBO!
MY PLEASURE! AND IF IT HELPS YOU TO FINALLY GET A GOOD NIGHT'S SLEEP, IT'LL BE MORE THAN WORTH IT!
OKAY, SO WE GOTTA MAKE SURE OUR HEADS ARE *TOUCHING* BECAUSE THAT'S HOW WE FRAGGLES SHARE DREAMS--
UM, I'M HUNGRY. HOW ABOUT A BEDTIME SNACK FIRST?
WEMBLEY!!! DON'T BE SCARED. MY DREAMS ARE GREAT!
NOW, DO YOU WANT TO GET SOME SLEEP OR NOT?!
I DO, I DO...
SWEET DREAMS!
I HOPE SO...

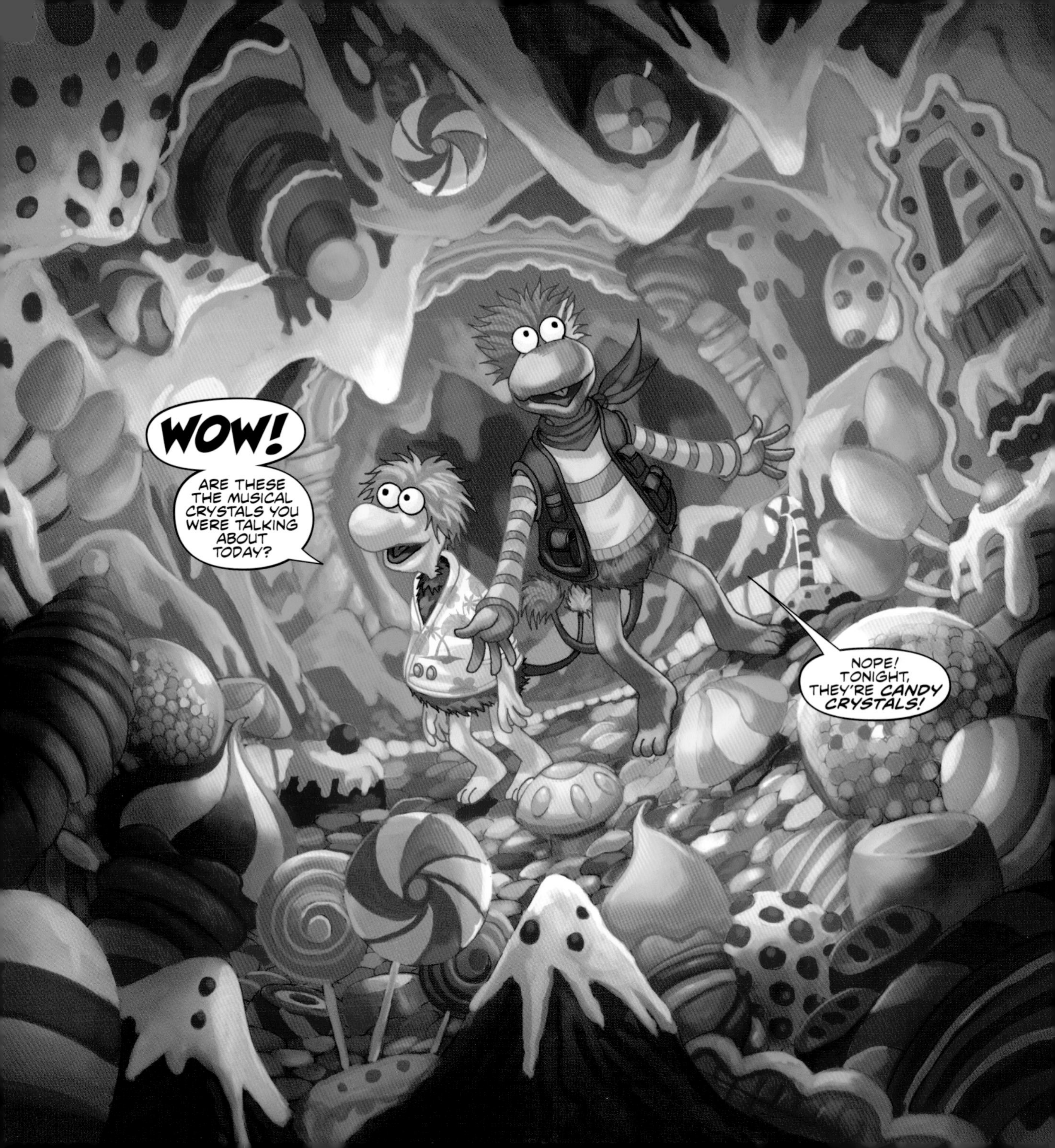
WOW!
ARE THESE THE MUSICAL CRYSTALS YOU WERE TALKING ABOUT TODAY?
NOPE! TONIGHT, THEY'RE CANDY CRYSTALS!

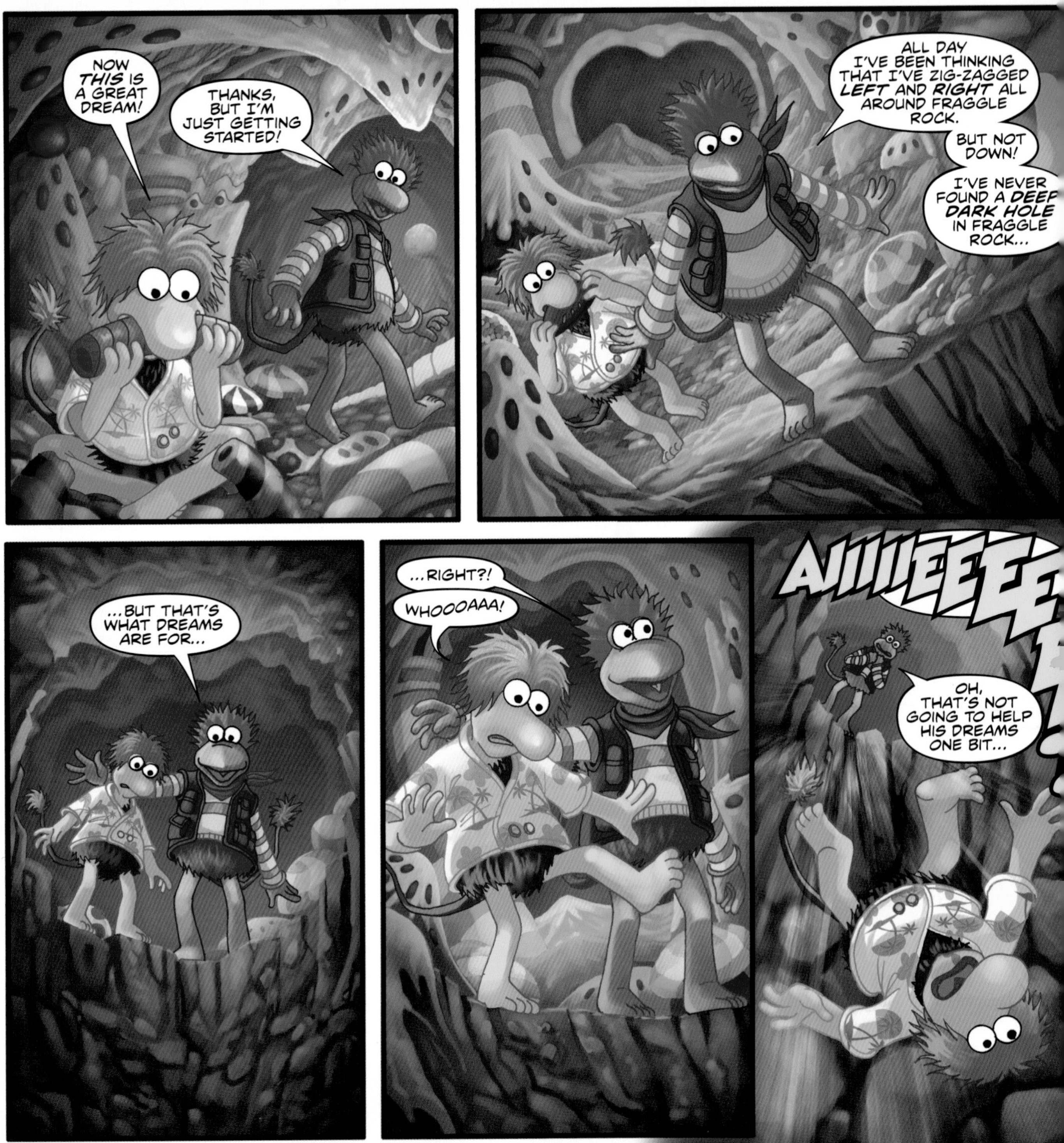
NOW THIS IS A GREAT DREAM!
THANKS, BUT I'M JUST GETTING STARTED!
ALL DAY I'VE BEEN THINKING THAT I'VE ZIG-ZAGGED LEFT AND RIGHT ALL AROUND FRAGGLE ROCK.
BUT NOT DOWN!
I'VE NEVER FOUND A DEEP DARK HOLE IN FRAGGLE ROCK...
...BUT THAT'S WHAT DREAMS ARE FOR...
...RIGHT?!
WHOOOAAA!
AIIIIEEEE
OH, THAT'S NOT GOING TO HELP HIS DREAMS ONE BIT...

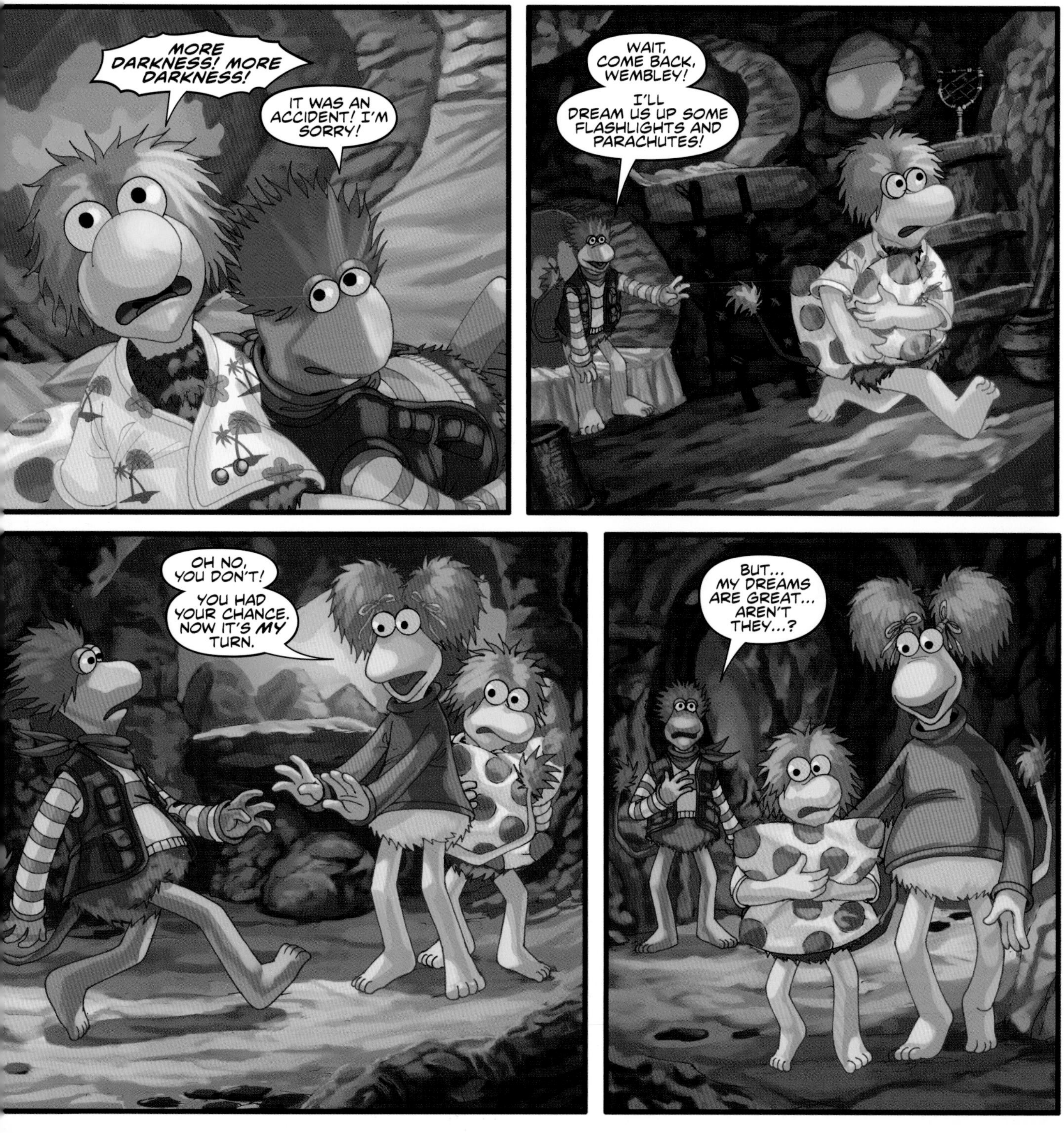
MORE DARKNESS! MORE DARKNESS!
IT WAS AN ACCIDENT! I'M SORRY!
WAIT, COME BACK, WEMBLEY!
I'LL DREAM US UP SOME FLASHLIGHTS AND PARACHUTES!
OH NO, YOU DON'T!
YOU HAD YOUR CHANCE. NOW IT'S *MY* TURN.
BUT... MY DREAMS ARE GREAT... AREN'T THEY...?

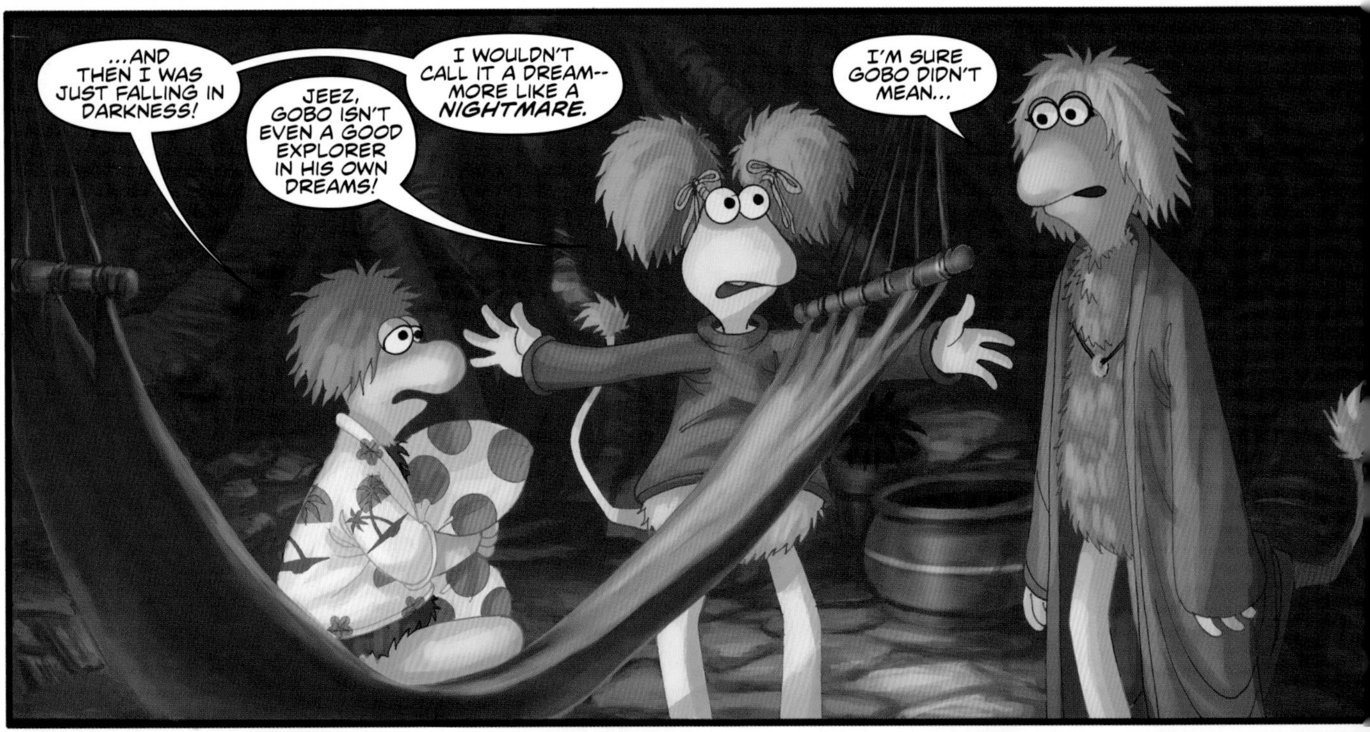
...AND THEN I WAS JUST FALLING IN DARKNESS!
I WOULDN'T CALL IT A DREAM-- MORE LIKE A *NIGHTMARE*.
JEEZ, GOBO ISN'T EVEN A GOOD EXPLORER IN HIS OWN DREAMS!
I'M SURE GOBO DIDN'T MEAN...

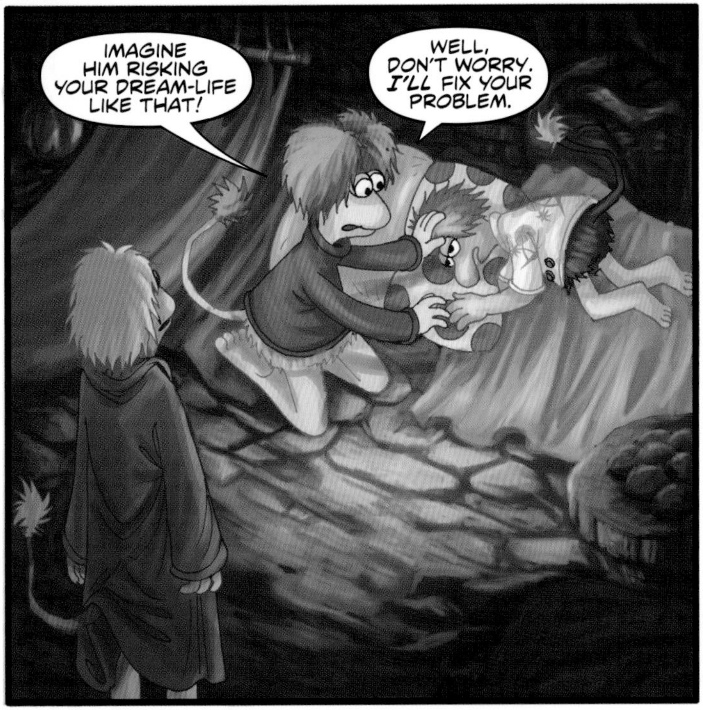
IMAGINE HIM RISKING YOUR DREAM-LIFE LIKE THAT!
WELL, DON'T WORRY. *I'LL* FIX YOUR PROBLEM.

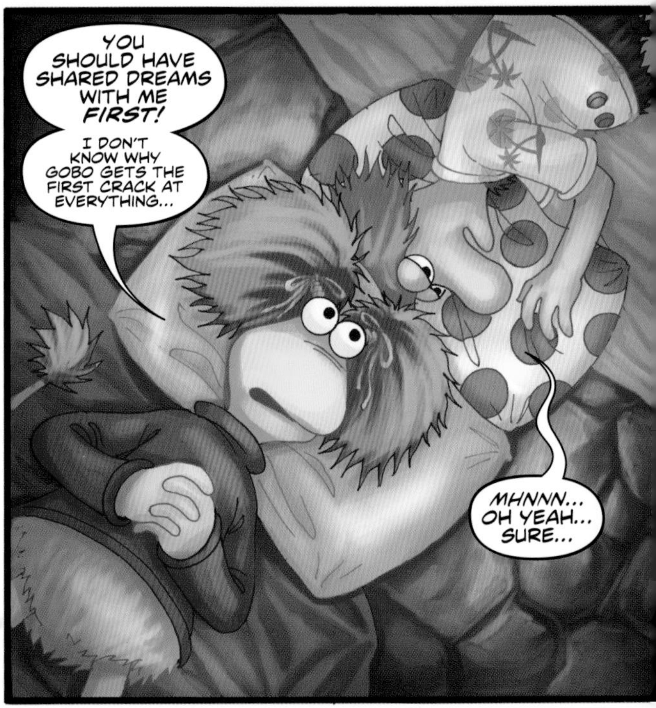
YOU SHOULD HAVE SHARED DREAMS WITH ME *FIRST!*
I DON'T KNOW WHY GOBO GETS THE FIRST CRACK AT EVERYTHING...
MHNNN... OH YEAH... SURE...

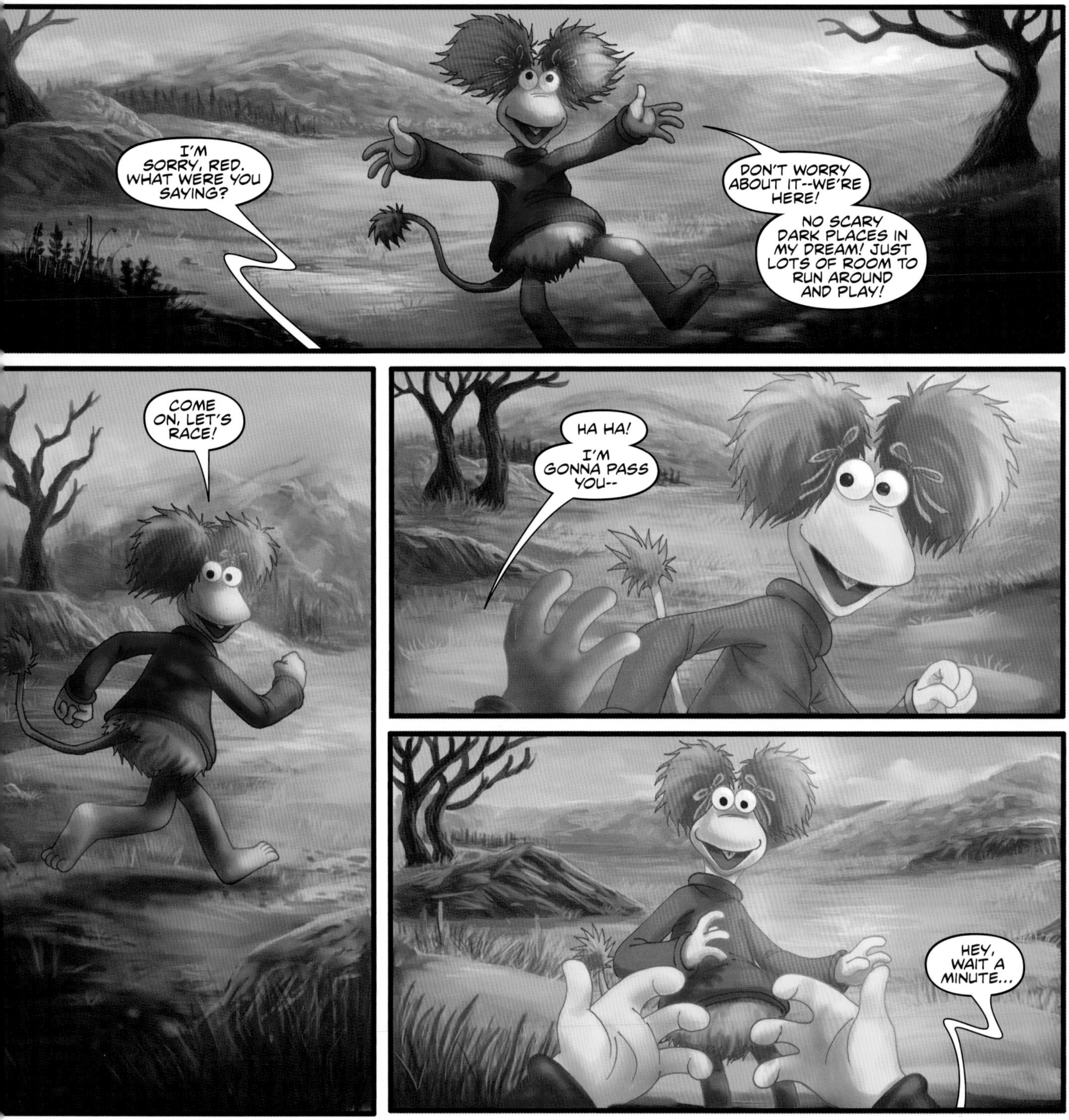
I'M SORRY, RED. WHAT WERE YOU SAYING?
DON'T WORRY ABOUT IT--WE'RE HERE!
NO SCARY DARK PLACES IN MY DREAM! JUST LOTS OF ROOM TO RUN AROUND AND PLAY!
COME ON, LET'S RACE!
HA HA!
I'M GONNA PASS YOU--
HEY, WAIT A MINUTE...

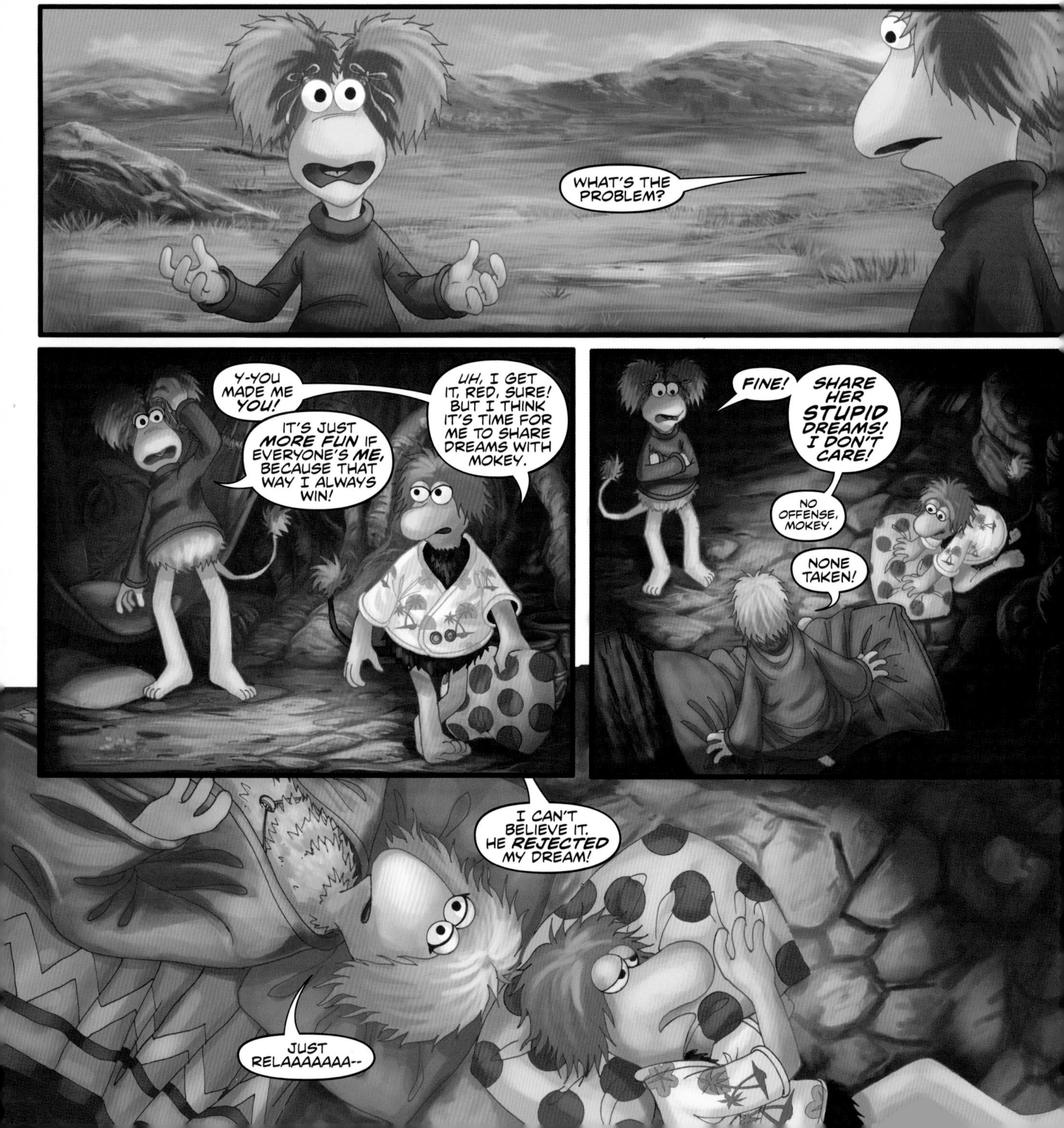
WHAT'S THE PROBLEM?
Y-YOU MADE ME YOU!
IT'S JUST MORE FUN IF EVERYONE'S ME, BECAUSE THAT WAY I ALWAYS WIN!
UH, I GET IT, RED, SURE! BUT I THINK IT'S TIME FOR ME TO SHARE DREAMS WITH MOKEY.
FINE!
SHARE HER STUPID DREAMS! I DON'T CARE!
NO OFFENSE, MOKEY.
NONE TAKEN!
I CAN'T BELIEVE IT. HE REJECTED MY DREAM!
JUST RELAAAAAAA--

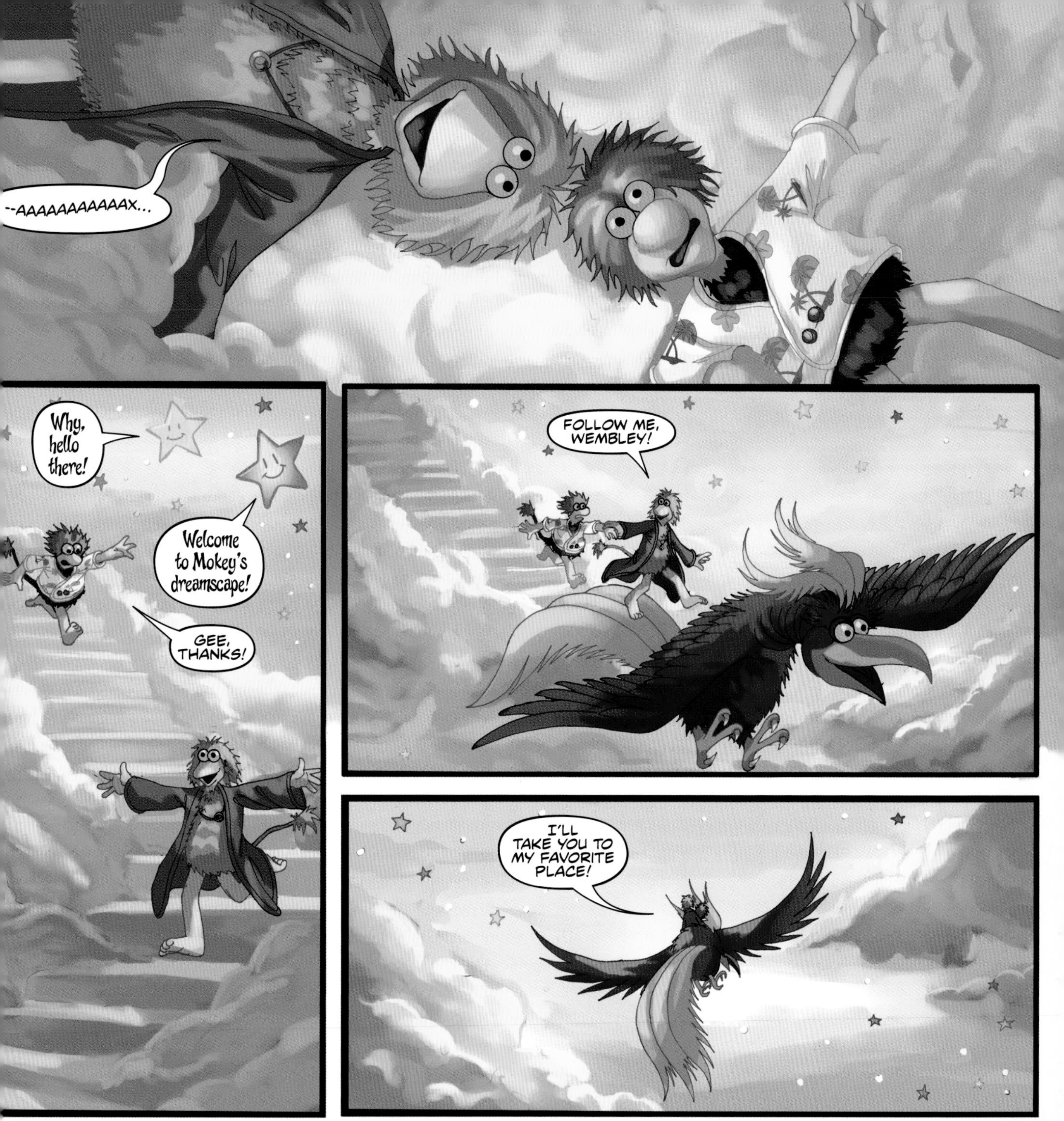

--AAAAAAAAAAAX...
Why, hello there!
Welcome to Mokey's dreamscape!
GEE, THANKS!
FOLLOW ME, WEMBLEY!
I'LL TAKE YOU TO MY FAVORITE PLACE!

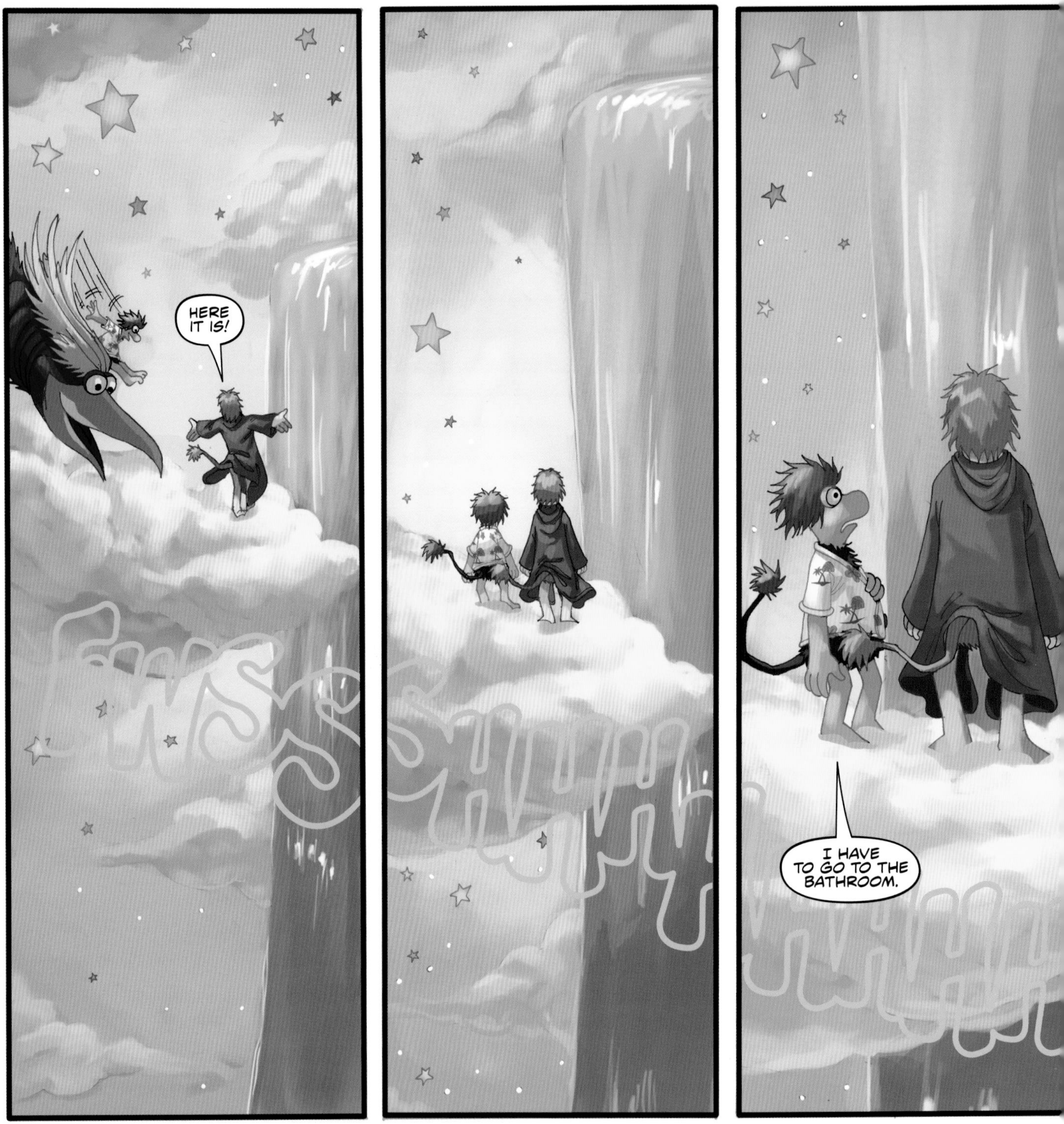
HERE IT IS!
I HAVE TO GO TO THE BATHROOM.

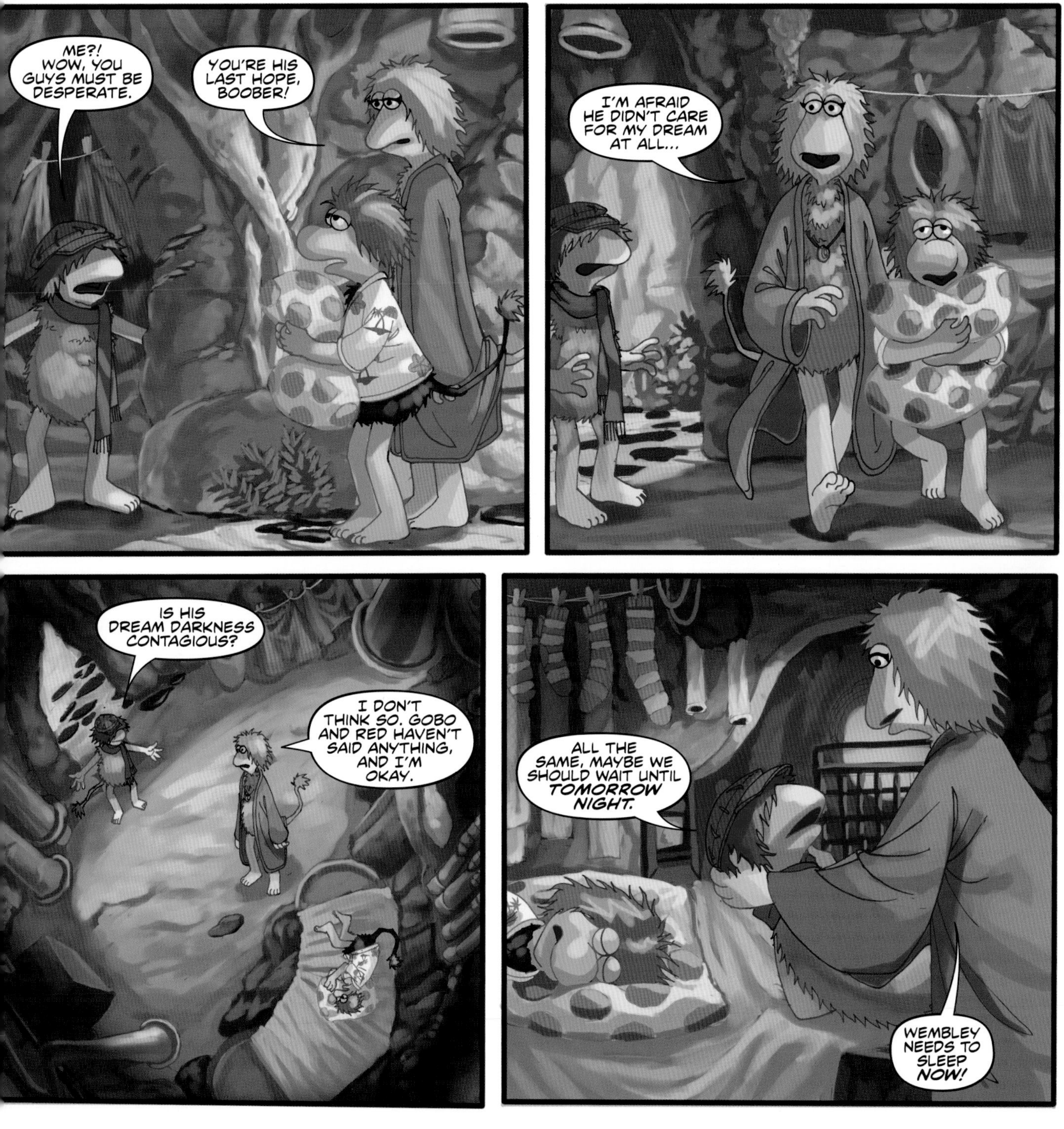
ME?! WOW, YOU GUYS MUST BE DESPERATE.
YOU'RE HIS LAST HOPE, BOOBER!
I'M AFRAID HE DIDN'T CARE FOR MY DREAM AT ALL...
IS HIS DREAM DARKNESS CONTAGIOUS?
I DON'T THINK SO. GOBO AND RED HAVEN'T SAID ANYTHING, AND I'M OKAY.
ALL THE SAME, MAYBE WE SHOULD WAIT UNTIL TOMORROW NIGHT.
WEMBLEY NEEDS TO SLEEP NOW!

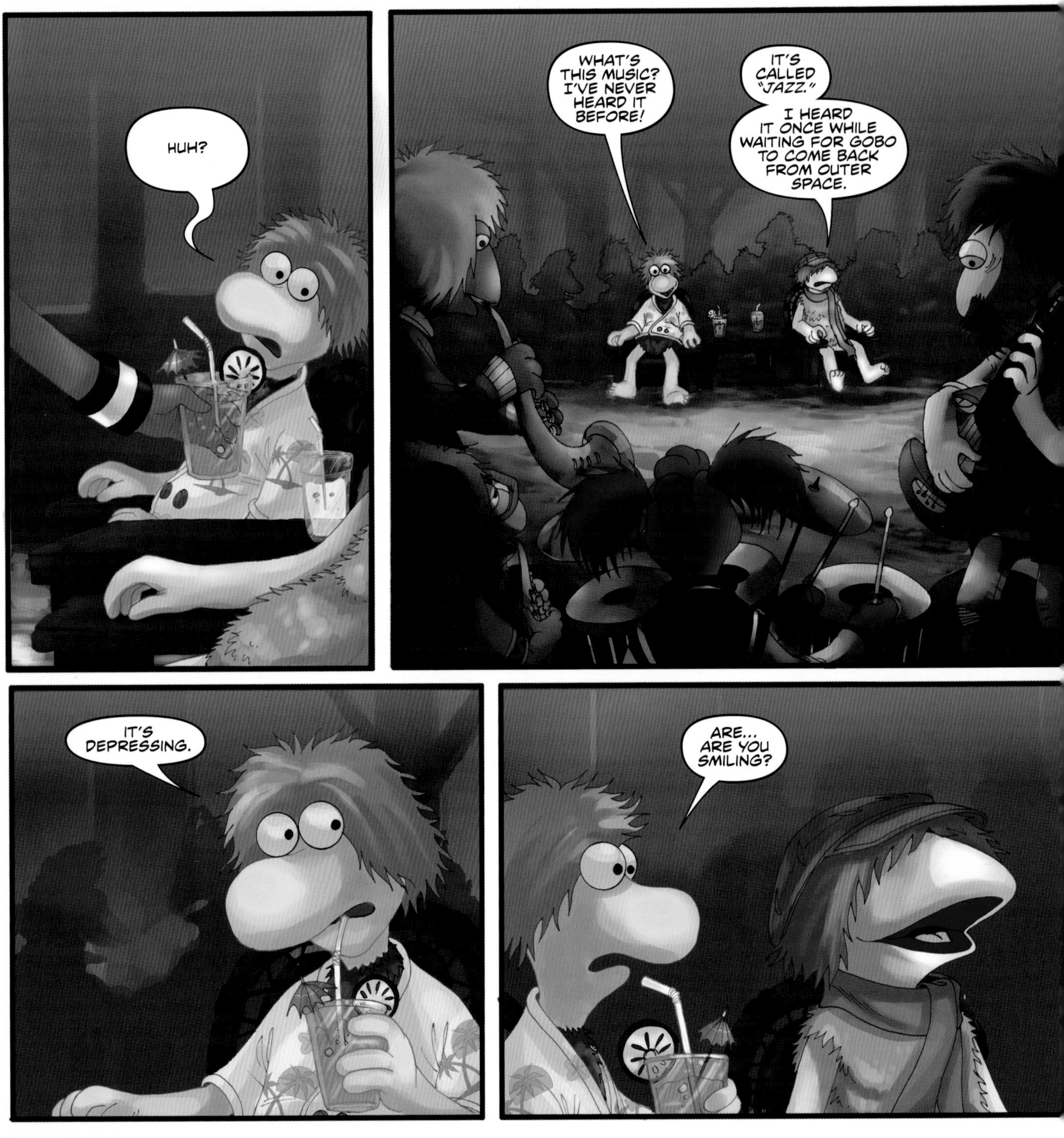
HUH?
WHAT'S THIS MUSIC? I'VE NEVER HEARD IT BEFORE!
IT'S CALLED "JAZZ."
I HEARD IT ONCE WHILE WAITING FOR GOBO TO COME BACK FROM OUTER SPACE.
IT'S DEPRESSING.
ARE... ARE YOU SMILING?

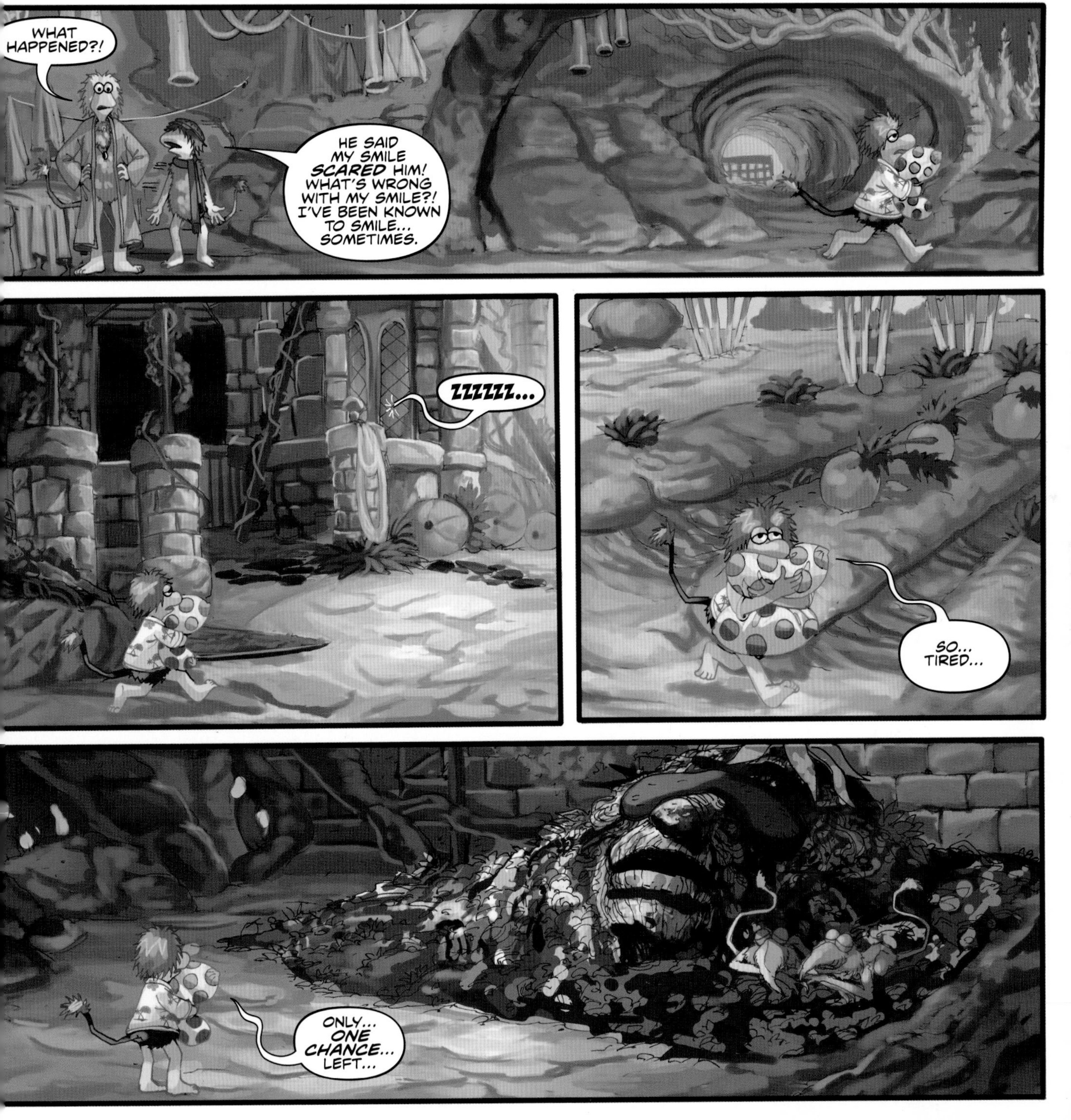
WHAT HAPPENED?!
HE SAID MY SMILE SCARED HIM! WHAT'S WRONG WITH MY SMILE?! I'VE BEEN KNOWN TO SMILE... SOMETIMES.
ZZZZZZ...
SO... TIRED...
ONLY... ONE CHANCE... LEFT...

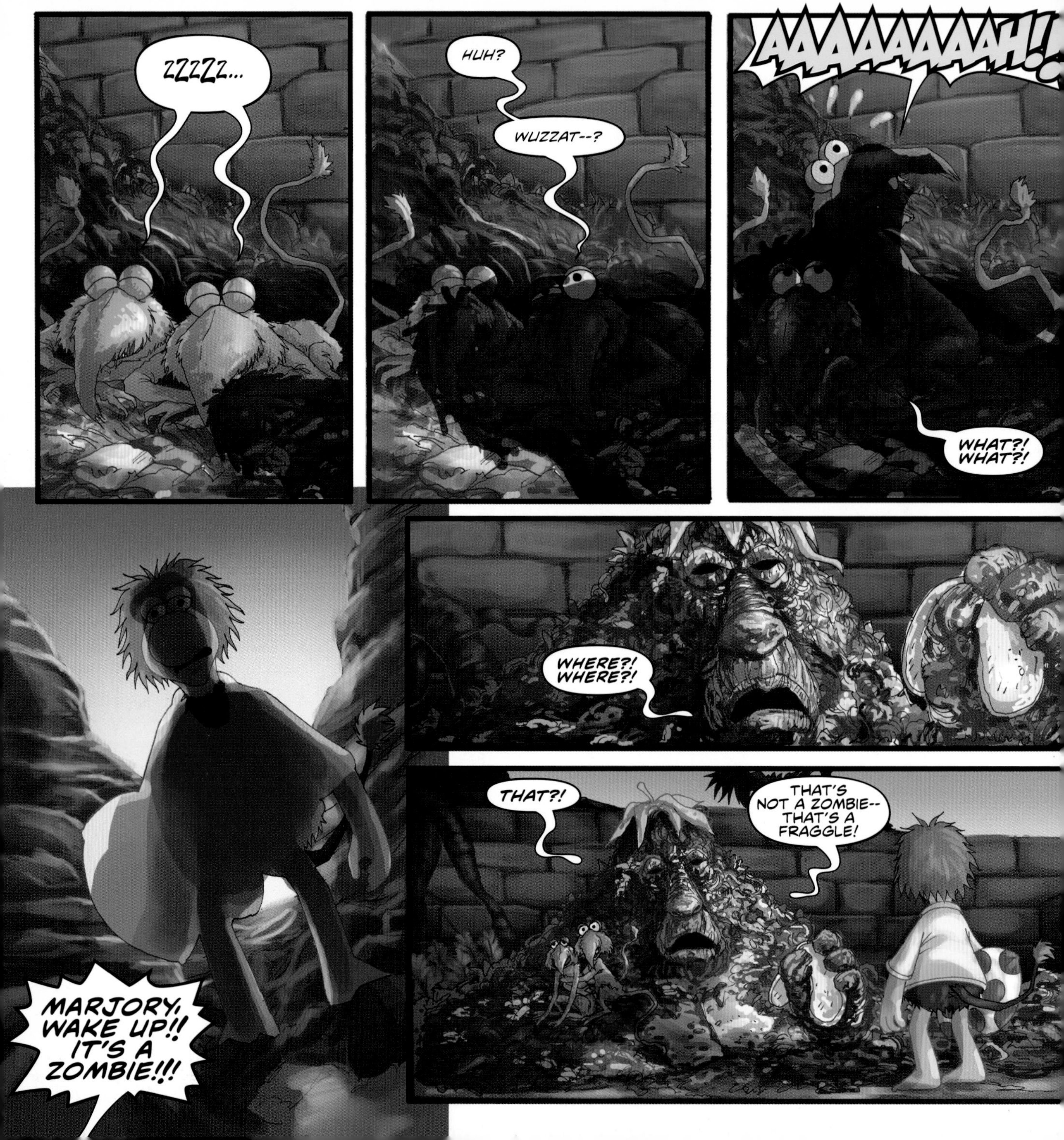
ZZZZZ...
HUH?
WUZZAT--?
AAAAAAAAH!
WHAT?! WHAT?!
MARJORY, WAKE UP!! IT'S A ZOMBIE!!!
WHERE?! WHERE?!
THAT?!
THAT'S NOT A ZOMBIE-- THAT'S A FRAGGLE!

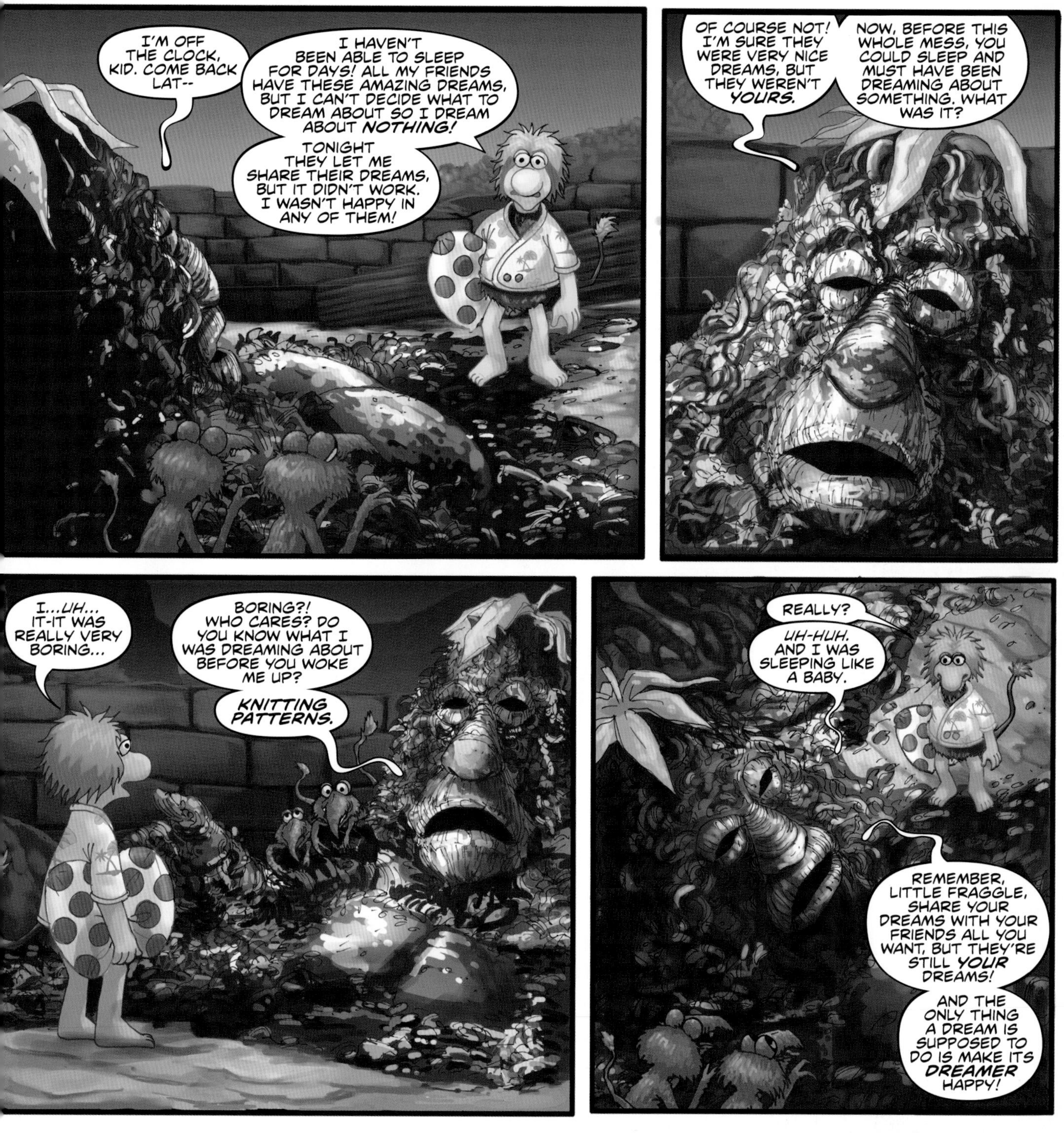

I'M OFF THE CLOCK, KID. COME BACK LAT--
I HAVEN'T BEEN ABLE TO SLEEP FOR DAYS! ALL MY FRIENDS HAVE THESE AMAZING DREAMS, BUT I CAN'T DECIDE WHAT TO DREAM ABOUT SO I DREAM ABOUT NOTHING!
TONIGHT THEY LET ME SHARE THEIR DREAMS, BUT IT DIDN'T WORK. I WASN'T HAPPY IN ANY OF THEM!
OF COURSE NOT! I'M SURE THEY WERE VERY NICE DREAMS, BUT THEY WEREN'T YOURS.
NOW, BEFORE THIS WHOLE MESS, YOU COULD SLEEP AND MUST HAVE BEEN DREAMING ABOUT SOMETHING. WHAT WAS IT?
I...UH... IT-IT WAS REALLY VERY BORING...
BORING?! WHO CARES? DO YOU KNOW WHAT I WAS DREAMING ABOUT BEFORE YOU WOKE ME UP?
KNITTING PATTERNS.
REALLY?
UH-HUH. AND I WAS SLEEPING LIKE A BABY.
REMEMBER, LITTLE FRAGGLE, SHARE YOUR DREAMS WITH YOUR FRIENDS ALL YOU WANT, BUT THEY'RE STILL YOUR DREAMS!
AND THE ONLY THING A DREAM IS SUPPOSED TO DO IS MAKE ITS DREAMER HAPPY!

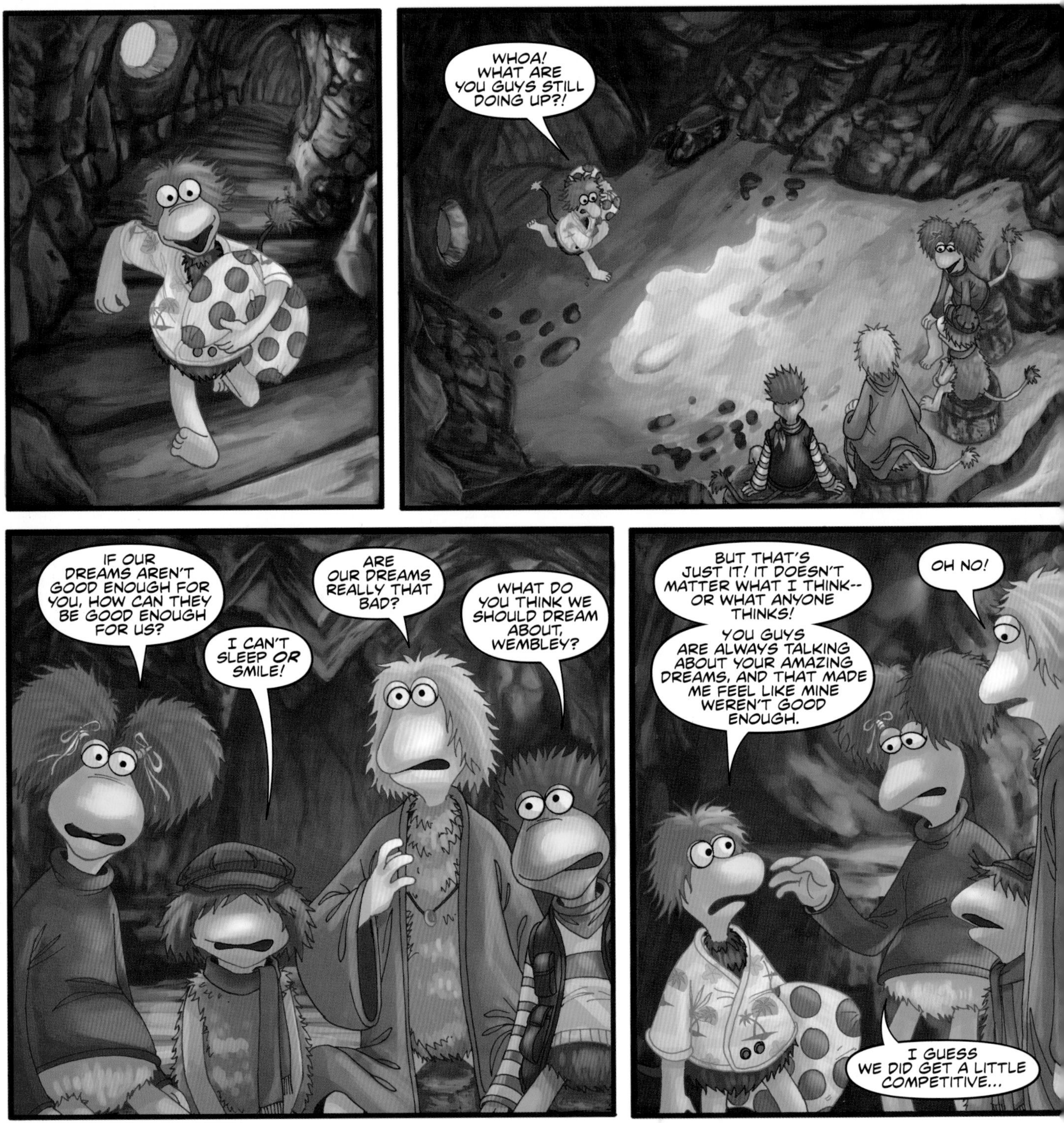
WHOA! WHAT ARE YOU GUYS STILL DOING UP?!
IF OUR DREAMS AREN'T GOOD ENOUGH FOR YOU, HOW CAN THEY BE GOOD ENOUGH FOR US?
I CAN'T SLEEP OR SMILE!
ARE OUR DREAMS REALLY THAT BAD?
WHAT DO YOU THINK WE SHOULD DREAM ABOUT, WEMBLEY?
BUT THAT'S JUST IT! IT DOESN'T MATTER WHAT I THINK-- OR WHAT ANYONE THINKS!
YOU GUYS ARE ALWAYS TALKING ABOUT YOUR AMAZING DREAMS, AND THAT MADE ME FEEL LIKE MINE WEREN'T GOOD ENOUGH.
OH NO!
I GUESS WE DID GET A LITTLE COMPETITIVE...

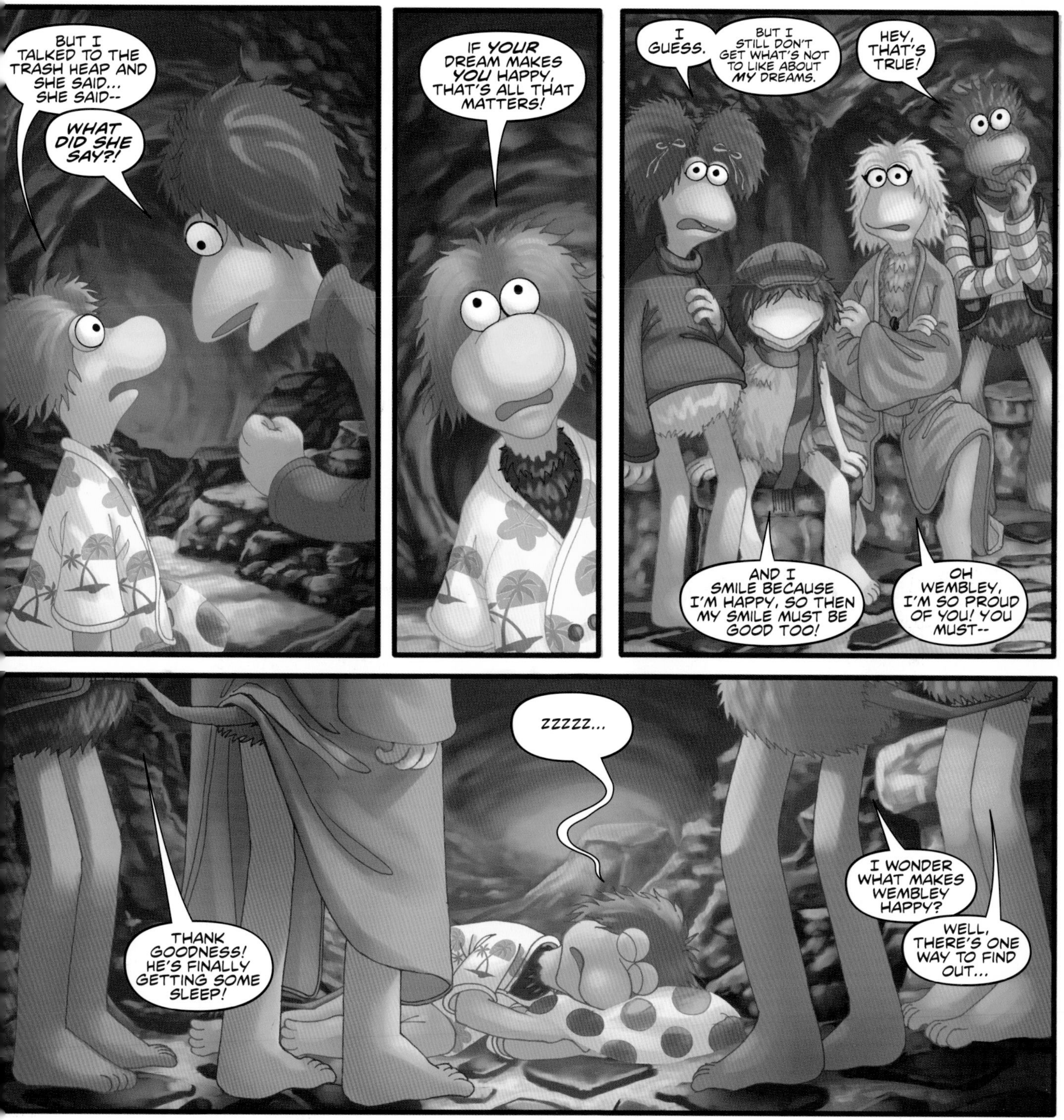

BUT I TALKED TO THE TRASH HEAP AND SHE SAID... SHE SAID--
WHAT DID SHE SAY?!
IF YOUR DREAM MAKES YOU HAPPY, THAT'S ALL THAT MATTERS!
I GUESS.
BUT I STILL DON'T GET WHAT'S NOT TO LIKE ABOUT MY DREAMS.
HEY, THAT'S TRUE!
AND I SMILE BECAUSE I'M HAPPY, SO THEN MY SMILE MUST BE GOOD TOO!
OH WEMBLEY, I'M SO PROUD OF YOU! YOU MUST--
ZZZZZ...
THANK GOODNESS! HE'S FINALLY GETTING SOME SLEEP!
I WONDER WHAT MAKES WEMBLEY HAPPY?
WELL, THERE'S ONE WAY TO FIND OUT...

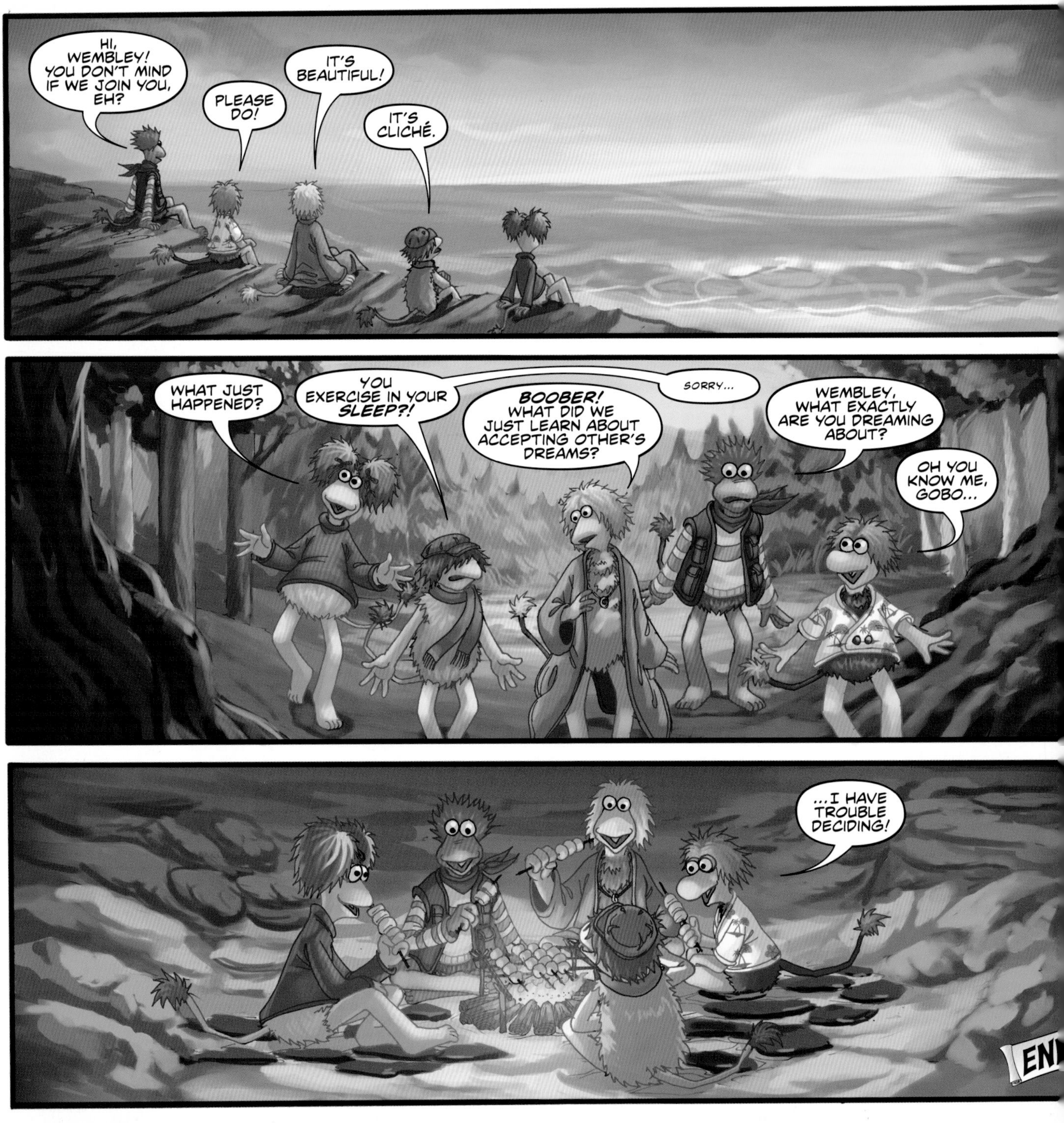
HI, WEMBLEY! YOU DON'T MIND IF WE JOIN YOU, EH?
PLEASE DO!
IT'S BEAUTIFUL!
IT'S CLICHÉ.
WHAT JUST HAPPENED?
YOU EXERCISE IN YOUR *SLEEP?!*
SORRY...
BOOBER! WHAT DID WE JUST LEARN ABOUT ACCEPTING OTHER'S DREAMS?
WEMBLEY, WHAT EXACTLY ARE YOU DREAMING ABOUT?
OH YOU KNOW ME, GOBO...
...I HAVE TROUBLE DECIDING!

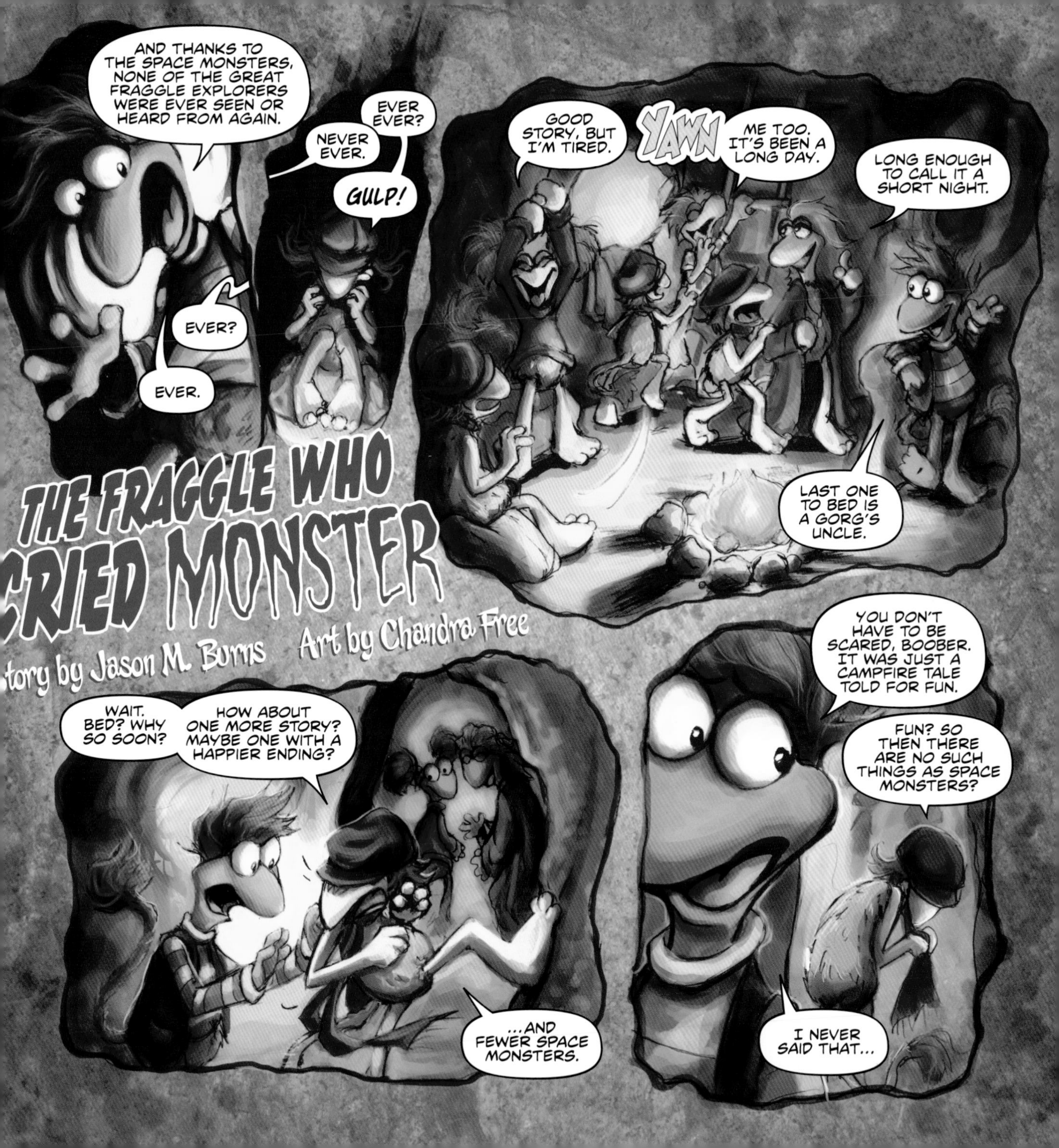

AND THANKS TO THE SPACE MONSTERS, NONE OF THE GREAT FRAGGLE EXPLORERS WERE EVER SEEN OR HEARD FROM AGAIN.
EVER?
EVER.
NEVER EVER.
EVER EVER?
GULP!
THE FRAGGLE WHO CRIED MONSTER
tory by Jason M. Burns
Art by Chandra Free
GOOD STORY, BUT I'M TIRED.
YAWN
ME TOO. IT'S BEEN A LONG DAY.
LONG ENOUGH TO CALL IT A SHORT NIGHT.
LAST ONE TO BED IS A GORG'S UNCLE.
WAIT. BED? WHY SO SOON?
HOW ABOUT ONE MORE STORY? MAYBE ONE WITH A HAPPIER ENDING?
...AND FEWER SPACE MONSTERS.
YOU DON'T HAVE TO BE SCARED, BOOBER. IT WAS JUST A CAMPFIRE TALE TOLD FOR FUN.
FUN? SO THEN THERE ARE NO SUCH THINGS AS SPACE MONSTERS?
I NEVER SAID THAT...

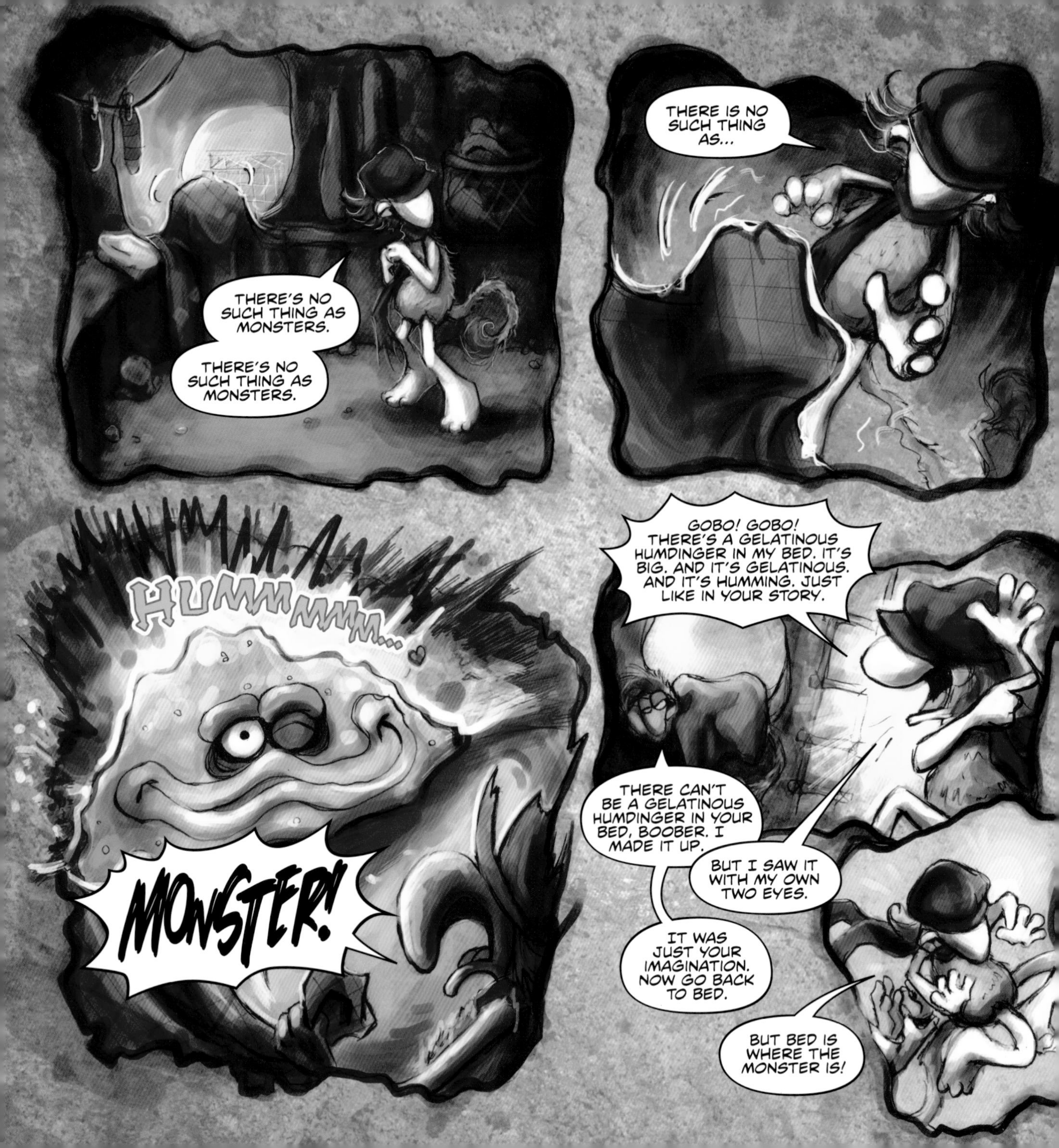

THERE'S NO SUCH THING AS MONSTERS.
THERE'S NO SUCH THING AS MONSTERS.
THERE IS NO SUCH THING AS...
HUMMMMMMM...
MONSTER!
GOBO! GOBO! THERE'S A GELATINOUS HUMDINGER IN MY BED. IT'S BIG. AND IT'S GELATINOUS. AND IT'S HUMMING. JUST LIKE IN YOUR STORY.
THERE CAN'T BE A GELATINOUS HUMDINGER IN YOUR BED, BOOBER. I MADE IT UP.
BUT I SAW IT WITH MY OWN TWO EYES.
IT WAS JUST YOUR IMAGINATION. NOW GO BACK TO BED.
BUT BED IS WHERE THE MONSTER IS!

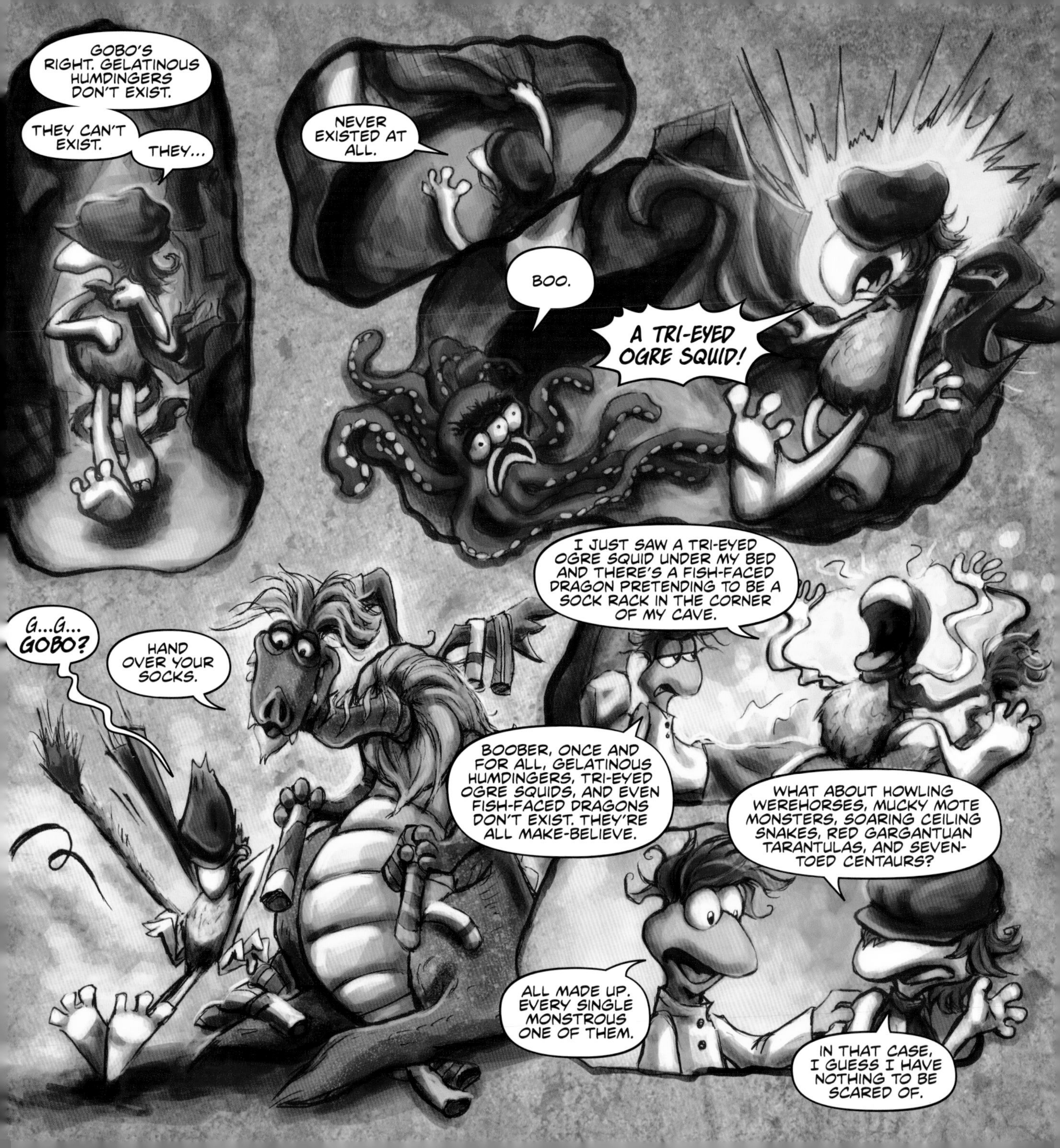
GOBO'S RIGHT. GELATINOUS HUMDINGERS DON'T EXIST.
THEY CAN'T EXIST.
THEY...
NEVER EXISTED AT ALL.
BOO.
A TRI-EYED OGRE SQUID!
I JUST SAW A TRI-EYED OGRE SQUID UNDER MY BED AND THERE'S A FISH-FACED DRAGON PRETENDING TO BE A SOCK RACK IN THE CORNER OF MY CAVE.
G...G... GOBO?
HAND OVER YOUR SOCKS.
BOOBER, ONCE AND FOR ALL, GELATINOUS HUMDINGERS, TRI-EYED OGRE SQUIDS, AND EVEN FISH-FACED DRAGONS DON'T EXIST. THEY'RE ALL MAKE-BELIEVE.
WHAT ABOUT HOWLING WEREHORSES, MUCKY MOTE MONSTERS, SOARING CEILING SNAKES, RED GARGANTUAN TARANTULAS, AND SEVEN-TOED CENTAURS?
ALL MADE UP. EVERY SINGLE MONSTROUS ONE OF THEM.
IN THAT CASE, I GUESS I HAVE NOTHING TO BE SCARED OF.

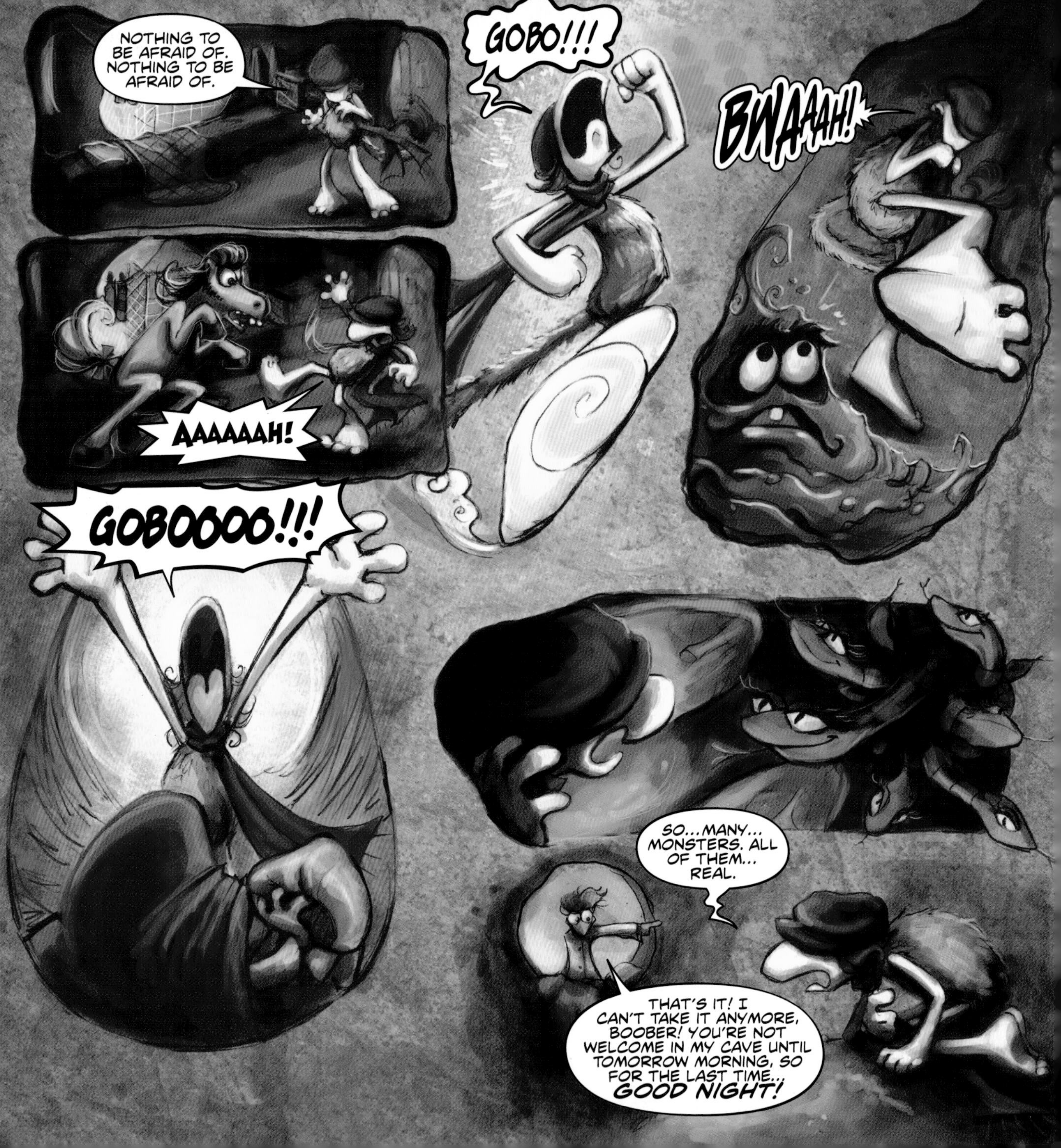
NOTHING TO BE AFRAID OF. NOTHING TO BE AFRAID OF.
AAAAAAH!
GOBO!!!
BWAAAH!
GOBOOOO!!!
SO... MANY... MONSTERS. ALL OF THEM... REAL.
THAT'S IT! I CAN'T TAKE IT ANYMORE, BOOBER! YOU'RE NOT WELCOME IN MY CAVE UNTIL TOMORROW MORNING, SO FOR THE LAST TIME... GOOD NIGHT!

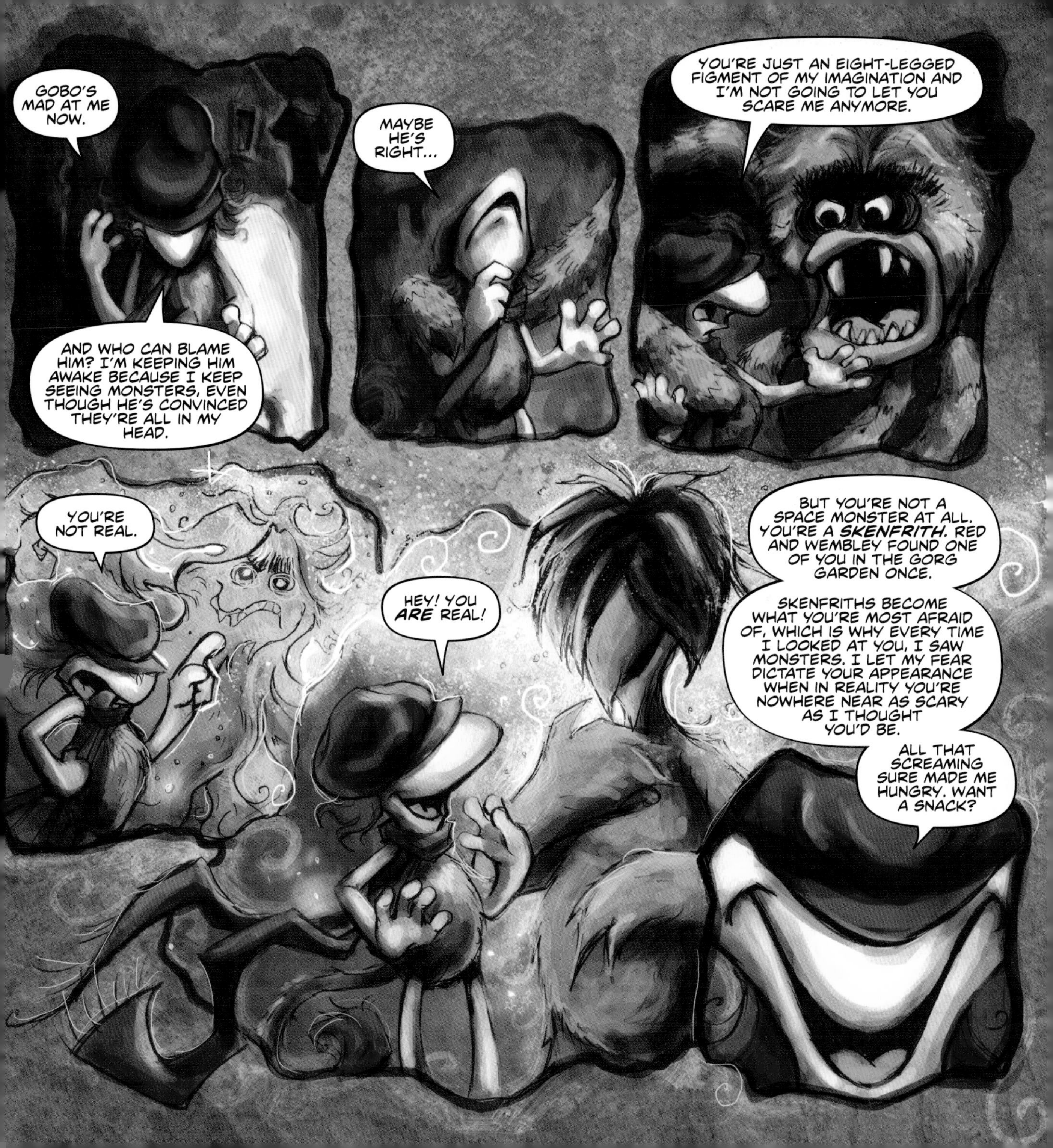
GOBO'S MAD AT ME NOW.
AND WHO CAN BLAME HIM? I'M KEEPING HIM AWAKE BECAUSE I KEEP SEEING MONSTERS, EVEN THOUGH HE'S CONVINCED THEY'RE ALL IN MY HEAD.
MAYBE HE'S RIGHT...
YOU'RE JUST AN EIGHT-LEGGED FIGMENT OF MY IMAGINATION AND I'M NOT GOING TO LET YOU SCARE ME ANYMORE.
YOU'RE NOT REAL.
HEY! YOU **ARE** REAL!
BUT YOU'RE NOT A SPACE MONSTER AT ALL. YOU'RE A ***SKENFRITH.*** RED AND WEMBLEY FOUND ONE OF YOU IN THE GORG GARDEN ONCE.
SKENFRITHS BECOME WHAT YOU'RE MOST AFRAID OF, WHICH IS WHY EVERY TIME I LOOKED AT YOU, I SAW MONSTERS. I LET MY FEAR DICTATE YOUR APPEARANCE WHEN IN REALITY YOU'RE NOWHERE NEAR AS SCARY AS I THOUGHT YOU'D BE.
ALL THAT SCREAMING SURE MADE ME HUNGRY. WANT A SNACK?

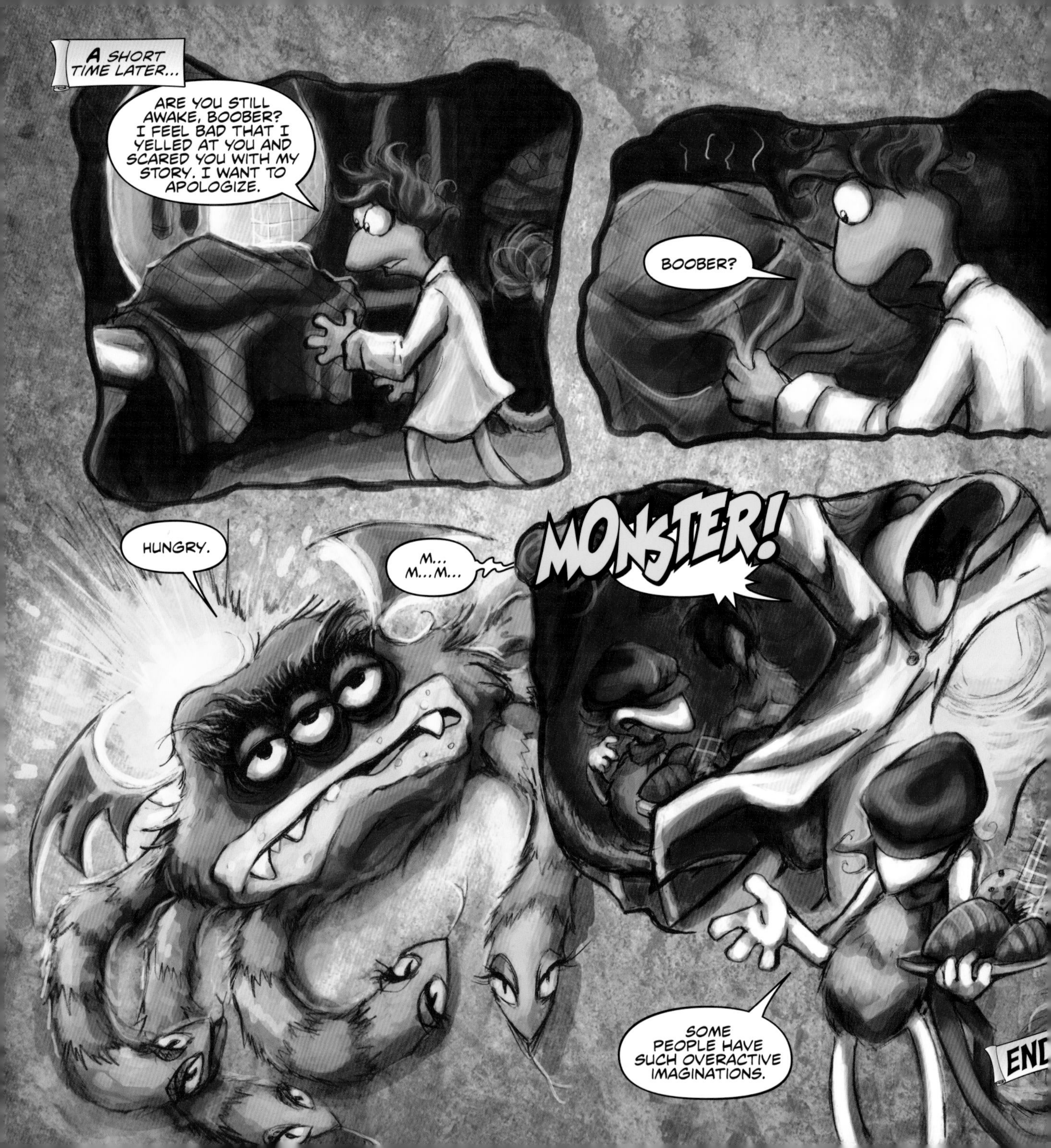
A SHORT TIME LATER...
ARE YOU STILL AWAKE, BOOBER? I FEEL BAD THAT I YELLED AT YOU AND SCARED YOU WITH MY STORY. I WANT TO APOLOGIZE.
BOOBER?
HUNGRY.
M... M...M...
MONSTER!
SOME PEOPLE HAVE SUCH OVERACTIVE IMAGINATIONS.
END

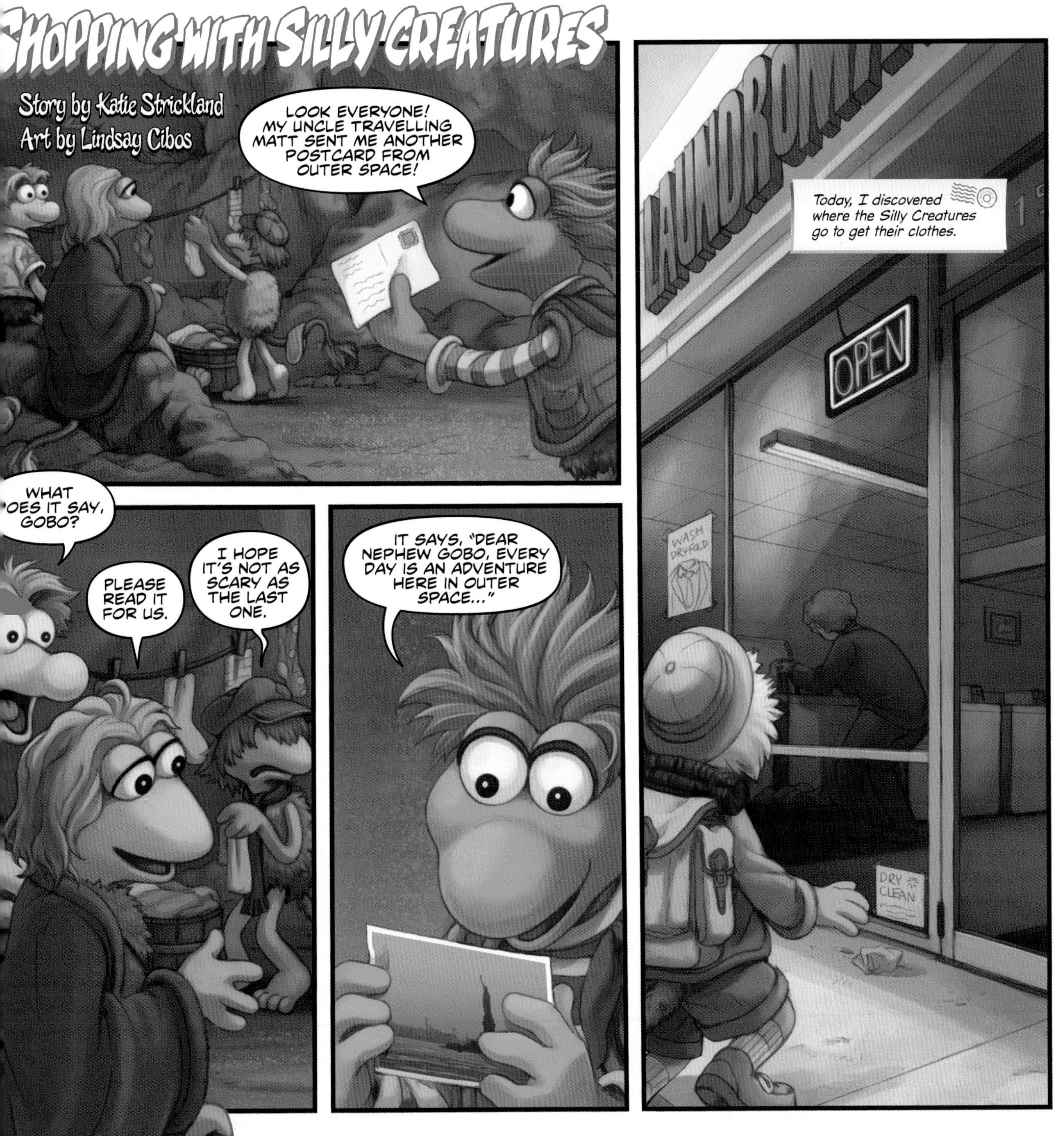
SHOPPING WITH SILLY CREATURES
Story by Katie Strickland
Art by Lindsay Cibos
LOOK EVERYONE! MY UNCLE TRAVELLING MATT SENT ME ANOTHER POSTCARD FROM OUTER SPACE!
WHAT OES IT SAY, GOBO?
PLEASE READ IT FOR US.
I HOPE IT'S NOT AS SCARY AS THE LAST ONE.
IT SAYS, "DEAR NEPHEW GOBO, EVERY DAY IS AN ADVENTURE HERE IN OUTER SPACE..."
LAUNDROM
Today, I discovered where the Silly Creatures go to get their clothes.
OPEN
WASH DRY-FOLD
DRY CLEAN

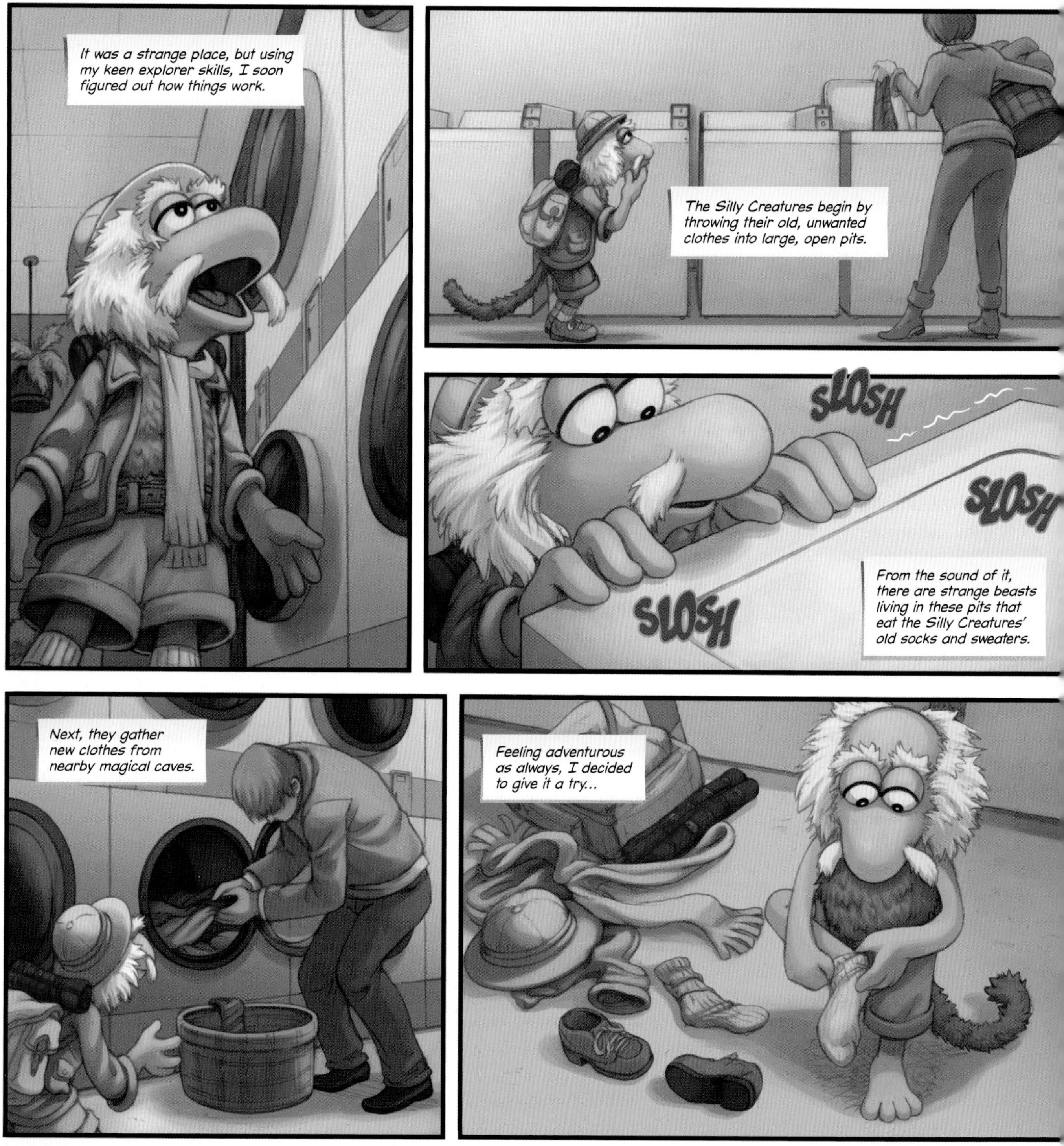
It was a strange place, but using my keen explorer skills, I soon figured out how things work.
The Silly Creatures begin by throwing their old, unwanted clothes into large, open pits.
SLOSH
SLOSH
SLOSH
From the sound of it, there are strange beasts living in these pits that eat the Silly Creatures' old socks and sweaters.
Next, they gather new clothes from nearby magical caves.
Feeling adventurous as always, I decided to give it a try...

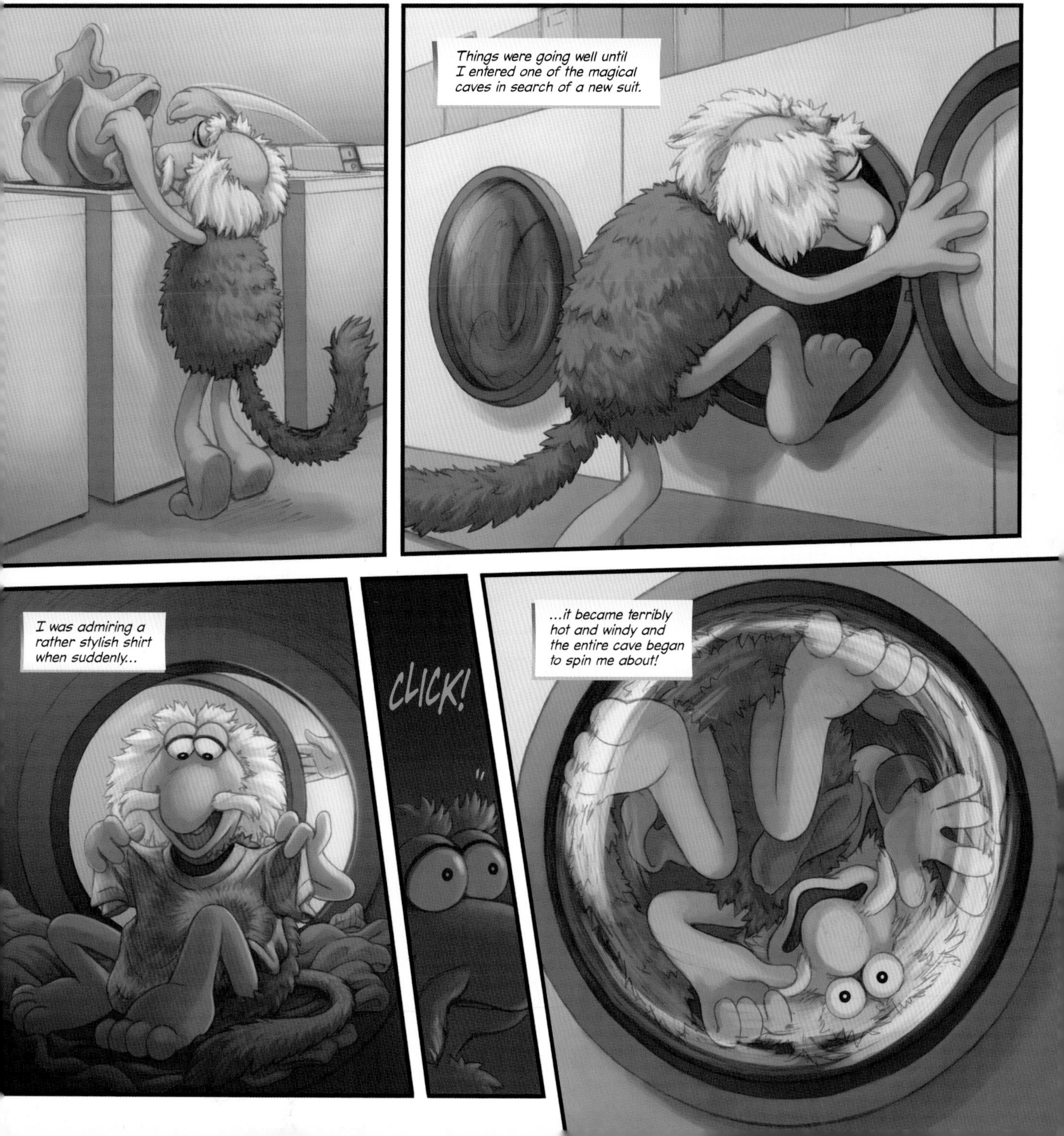
Things were going well until I entered one of the magical caves in search of a new suit.
I was admiring a rather stylish shirt when suddenly...
CLICK!
...it became terribly hot and windy and the entire cave began to spin me about!

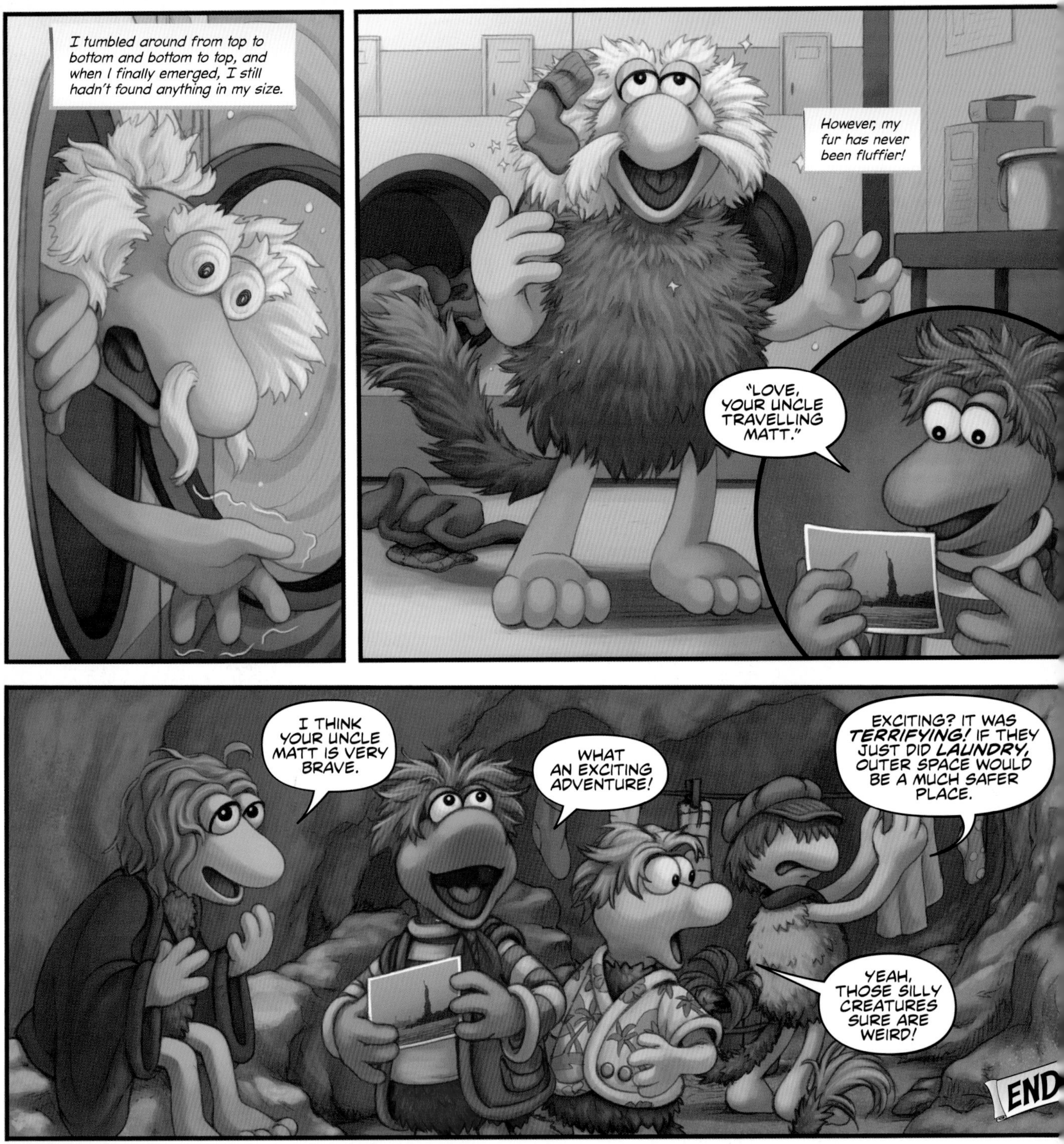
I tumbled around from top to bottom and bottom to top, and when I finally emerged, I still hadn't found anything in my size.
However, my fur has never been fluffier!
"LOVE, YOUR UNCLE TRAVELLING MATT."
I THINK YOUR UNCLE MATT IS VERY BRAVE.
WHAT AN EXCITING ADVENTURE!
EXCITING? IT WAS *TERRIFYING!* IF THEY JUST DID *LAUNDRY,* OUTER SPACE WOULD BE A MUCH SAFER PLACE.
YEAH, THOSE SILLY CREATURES SURE ARE WEIRD!
END

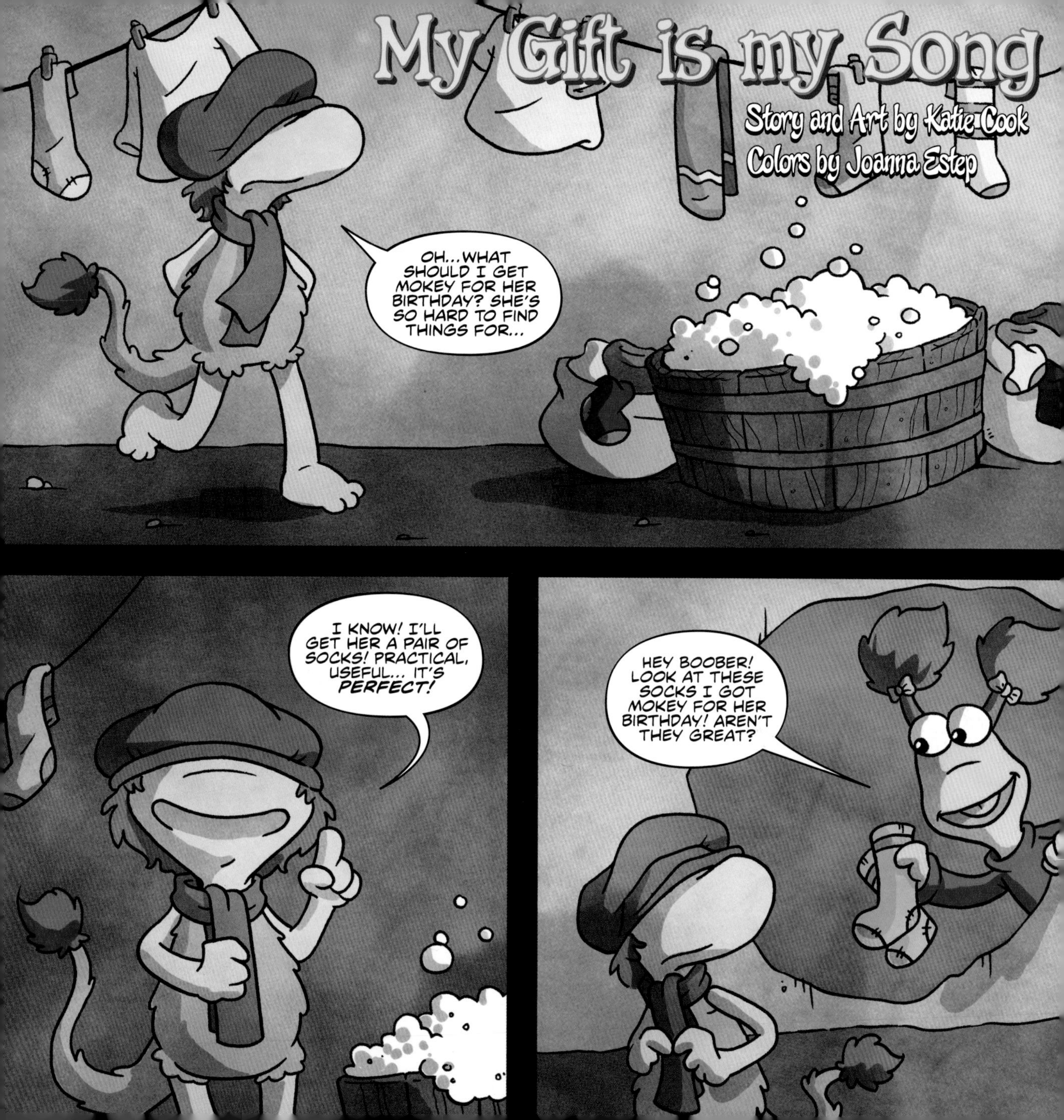
My Gift is my Song
Story and Art by Katie Cook
Colors by Joanna Estep
OH...WHAT SHOULD I GET MOKEY FOR HER BIRTHDAY? SHE'S SO HARD TO FIND THINGS FOR...
I KNOW! I'LL GET HER A PAIR OF SOCKS! PRACTICAL, USEFUL... IT'S *PERFECT!*
HEY BOOBER! LOOK AT THESE SOCKS I GOT MOKEY FOR HER BIRTHDAY! AREN'T THEY GREAT?

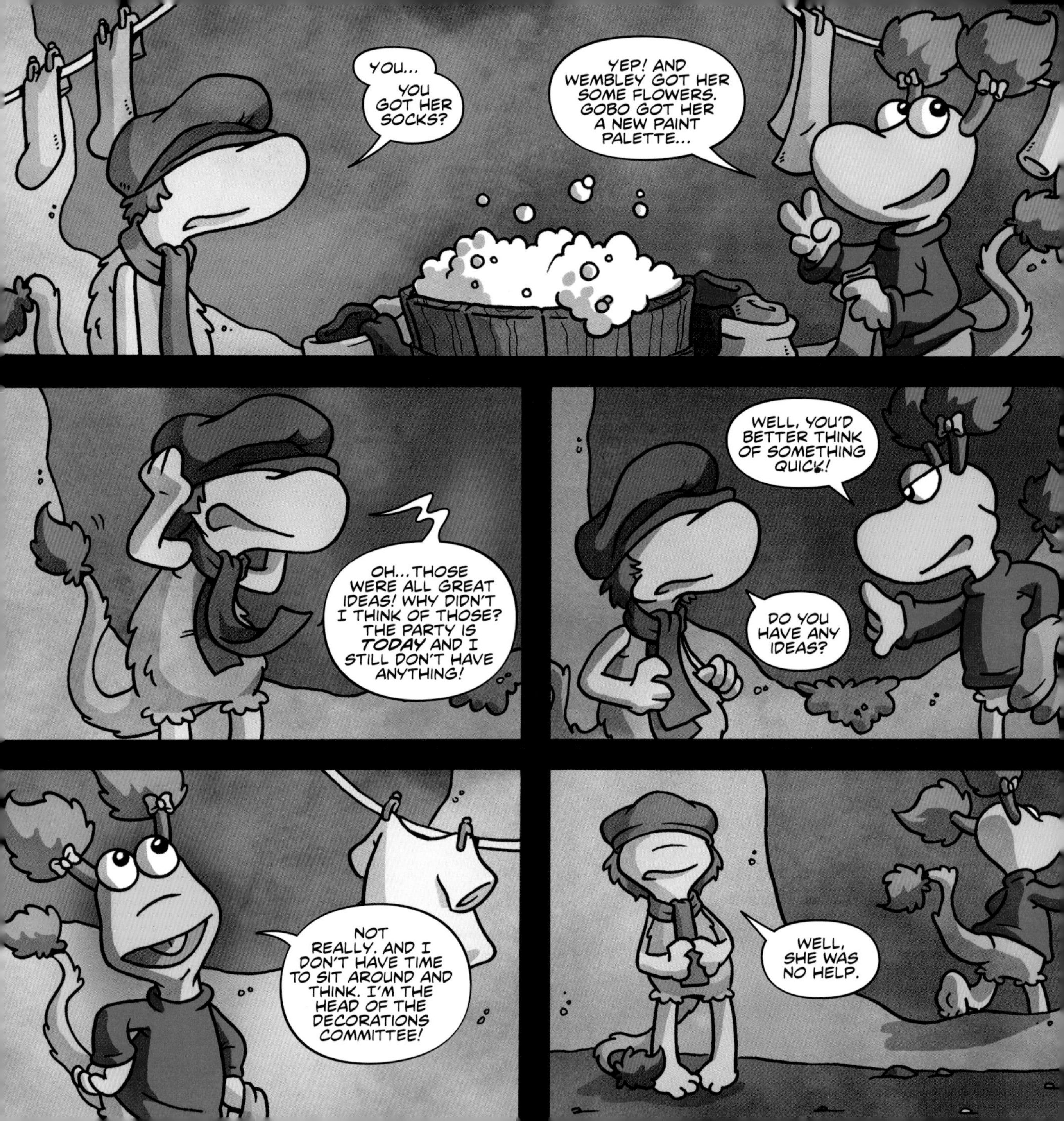
YOU... YOU GOT HER SOCKS?
YEP! AND WEMBLEY GOT HER SOME FLOWERS. GOBO GOT HER A NEW PAINT PALETTE...
OH...THOSE WERE ALL GREAT IDEAS! WHY DIDN'T I THINK OF THOSE? THE PARTY IS *TODAY* AND I STILL DON'T HAVE ANYTHING!
WELL, YOU'D BETTER THINK OF SOMETHING QUICK!
DO YOU HAVE ANY IDEAS?
NOT REALLY. AND I DON'T HAVE TIME TO SIT AROUND AND THINK. I'M THE HEAD OF THE DECORATIONS COMMITTEE!
WELL, SHE WAS NO HELP.

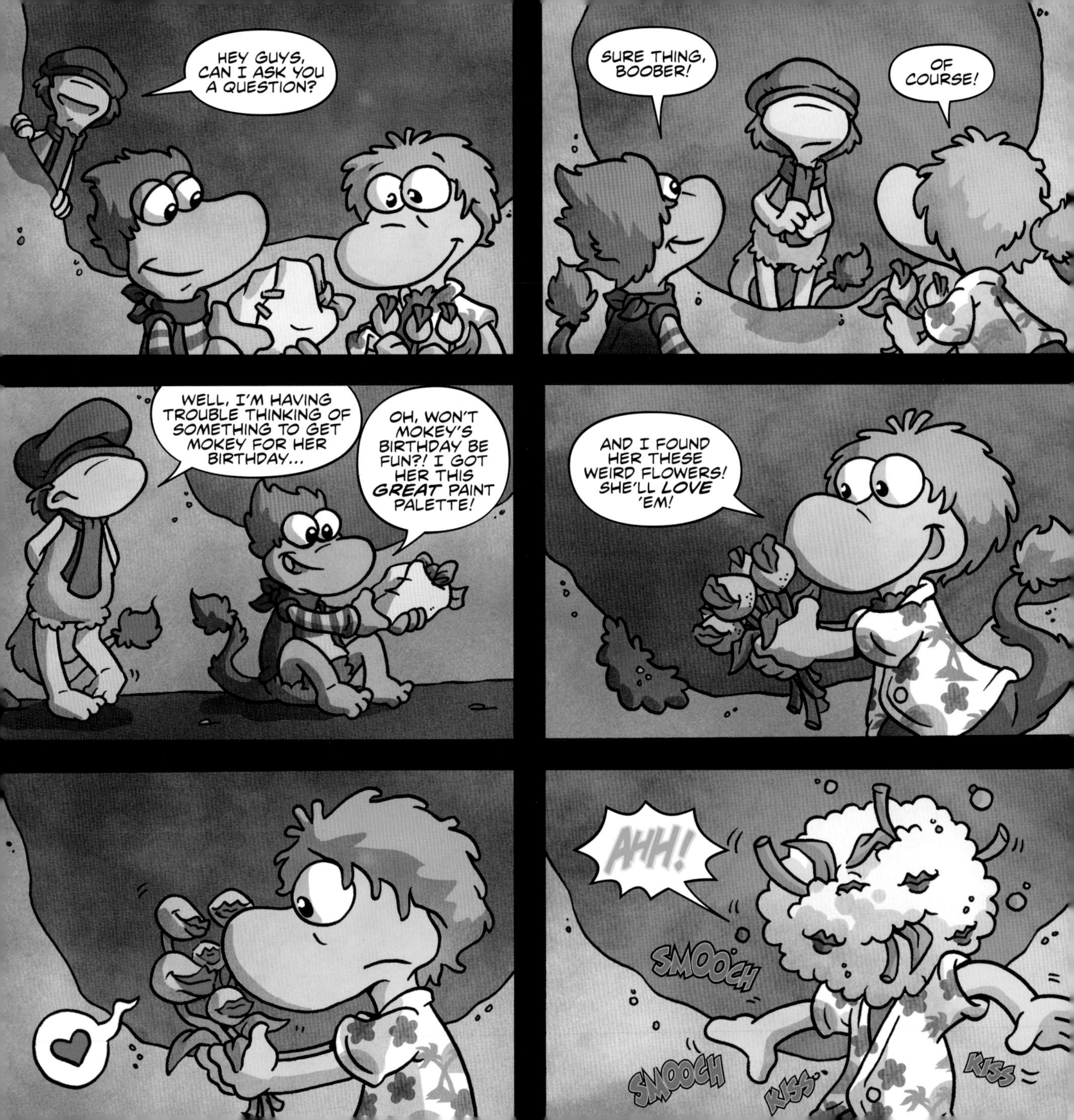
HEY GUYS, CAN I ASK YOU A QUESTION?
SURE THING, BOOBER!
OF COURSE!
WELL, I'M HAVING TROUBLE THINKING OF SOMETHING TO GET MOKEY FOR HER BIRTHDAY...
OH, WON'T MOKEY'S BIRTHDAY BE FUN?! I GOT HER THIS *GREAT* PAINT PALETTE!
AND I FOUND HER THESE WEIRD FLOWERS! SHE'LL *LOVE* 'EM!
AHH!
SMOOCH
SMOOCH
KISS
KISS

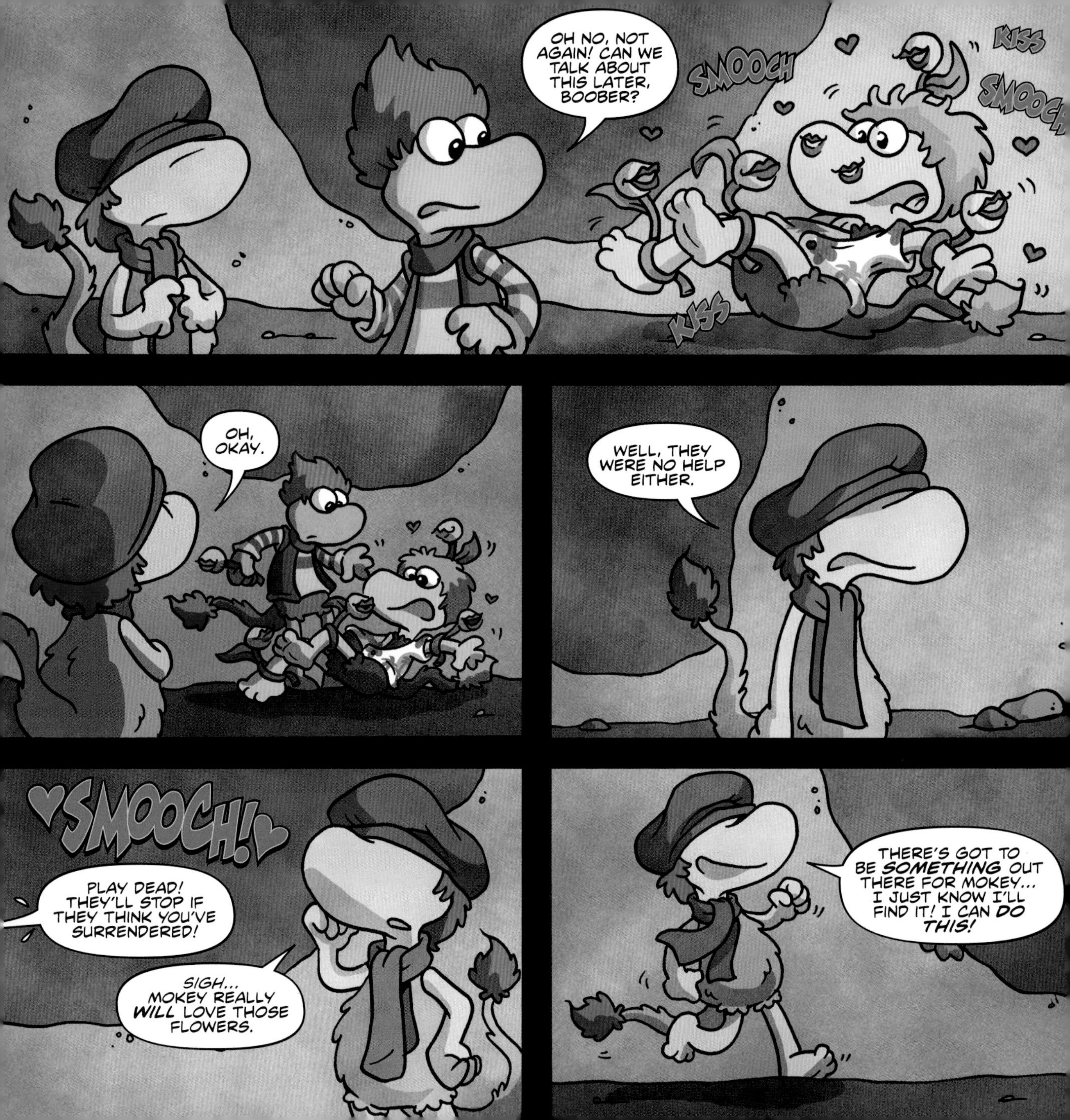
OH NO, NOT AGAIN! CAN WE TALK ABOUT THIS LATER, BOOBER?
SMOOCH
KISS
SMOOCH
KISS
OH, OKAY.
WELL, THEY WERE NO HELP EITHER.
♥SMOOCH!♥
PLAY DEAD! THEY'LL STOP IF THEY THINK YOU'VE SURRENDERED!
SIGH... MOKEY REALLY **WILL** LOVE THOSE FLOWERS.
THERE'S GOT TO BE **SOMETHING** OUT THERE FOR MOKEY... I JUST KNOW I'LL FIND IT! I CAN **DO THIS!**

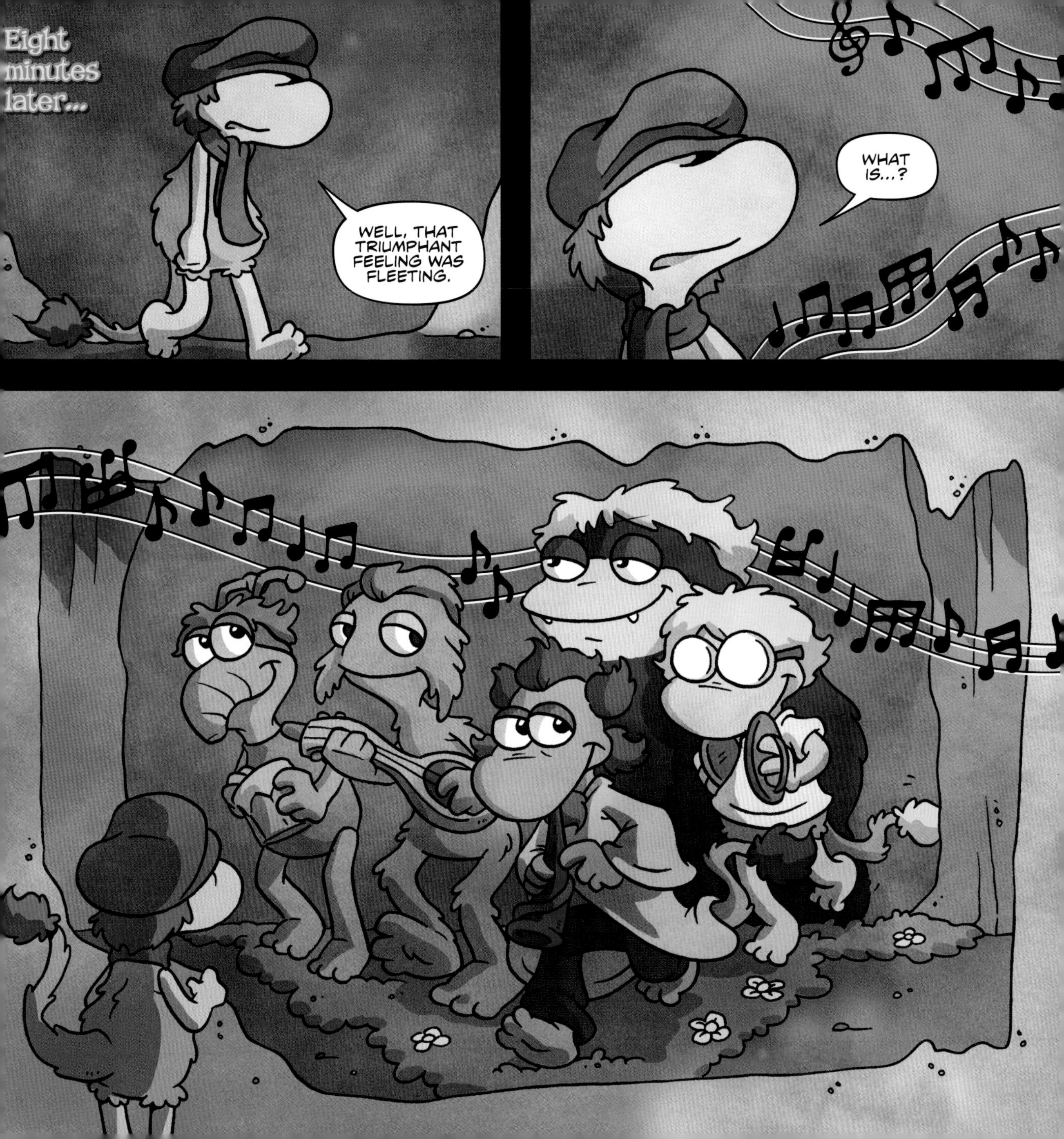
Eight minutes later...
WELL, THAT TRIUMPHANT FEELING WAS FLEETING.
WHAT IS...?

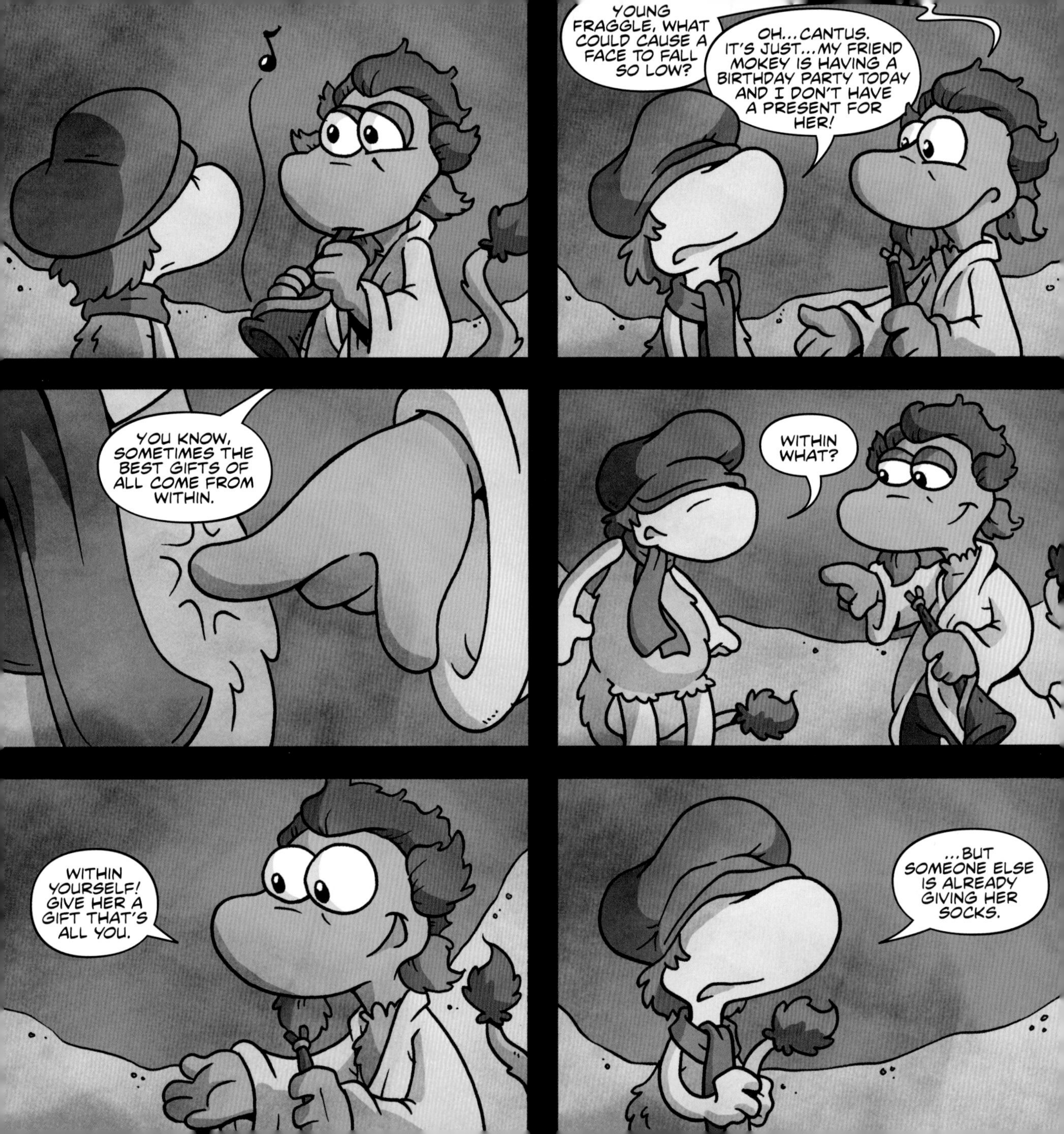
YOUNG FRAGGLE, WHAT COULD CAUSE A FACE TO FALL SO LOW?
OH...CANTUS. IT'S JUST...MY FRIEND MOKEY IS HAVING A BIRTHDAY PARTY TODAY AND I DON'T HAVE A PRESENT FOR HER!
YOU KNOW, SOMETIMES THE BEST GIFTS OF ALL COME FROM WITHIN.
WITHIN WHAT?
WITHIN YOURSELF! GIVE HER A GIFT THAT'S ALL YOU.
...BUT SOMEONE ELSE IS ALREADY GIVING HER SOCKS.

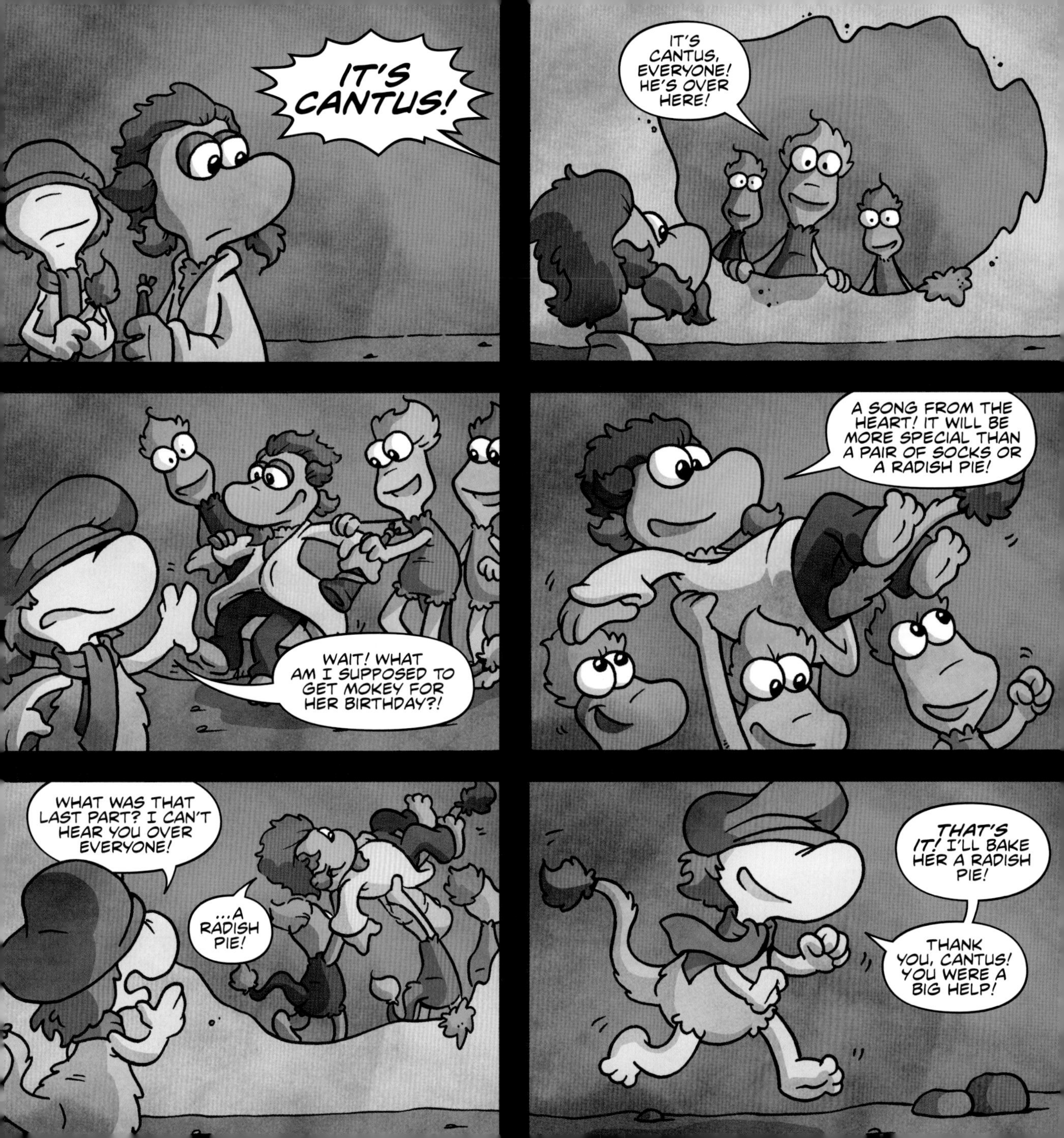
IT'S CANTUS!
IT'S CANTUS, EVERYONE! HE'S OVER HERE!
WAIT! WHAT AM I SUPPOSED TO GET MOKEY FOR HER BIRTHDAY?!
A SONG FROM THE HEART! IT WILL BE MORE SPECIAL THAN A PAIR OF SOCKS OR A RADISH PIE!
WHAT WAS THAT LAST PART? I CAN'T HEAR YOU OVER EVERYONE!
...A RADISH PIE!
THAT'S IT! I'LL BAKE HER A RADISH PIE!
THANK YOU, CANTUS! YOU WERE A BIG HELP!

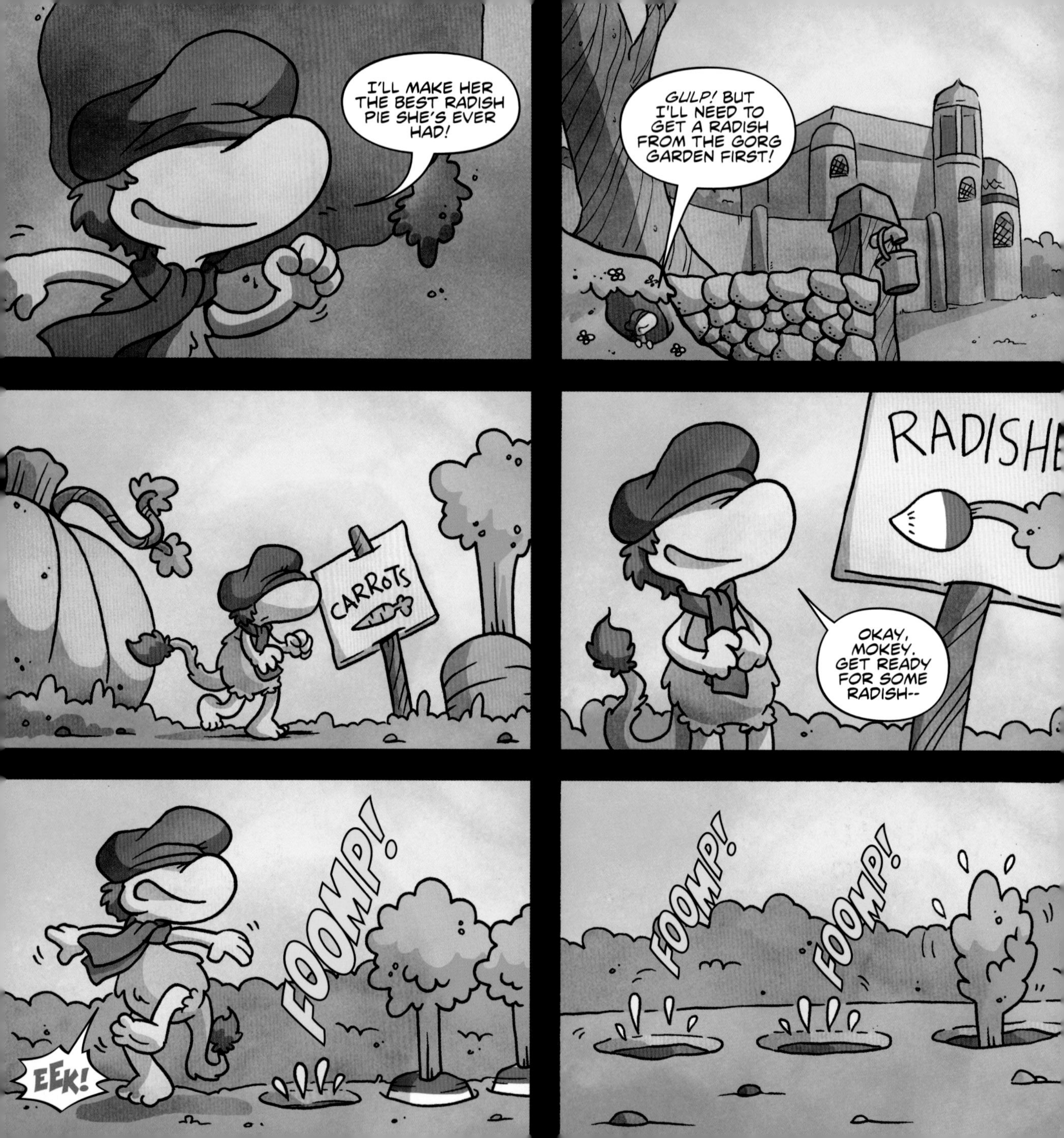
I'LL MAKE HER THE BEST RADISH PIE SHE'S EVER HAD!
GULP! BUT I'LL NEED TO GET A RADISH FROM THE GORG GARDEN FIRST!
CARROTS
RADISHE
OKAY, MOKEY. GET READY FOR SOME RADISH--
FOOMP!
EEK!
FOOMP!
FOOMP!

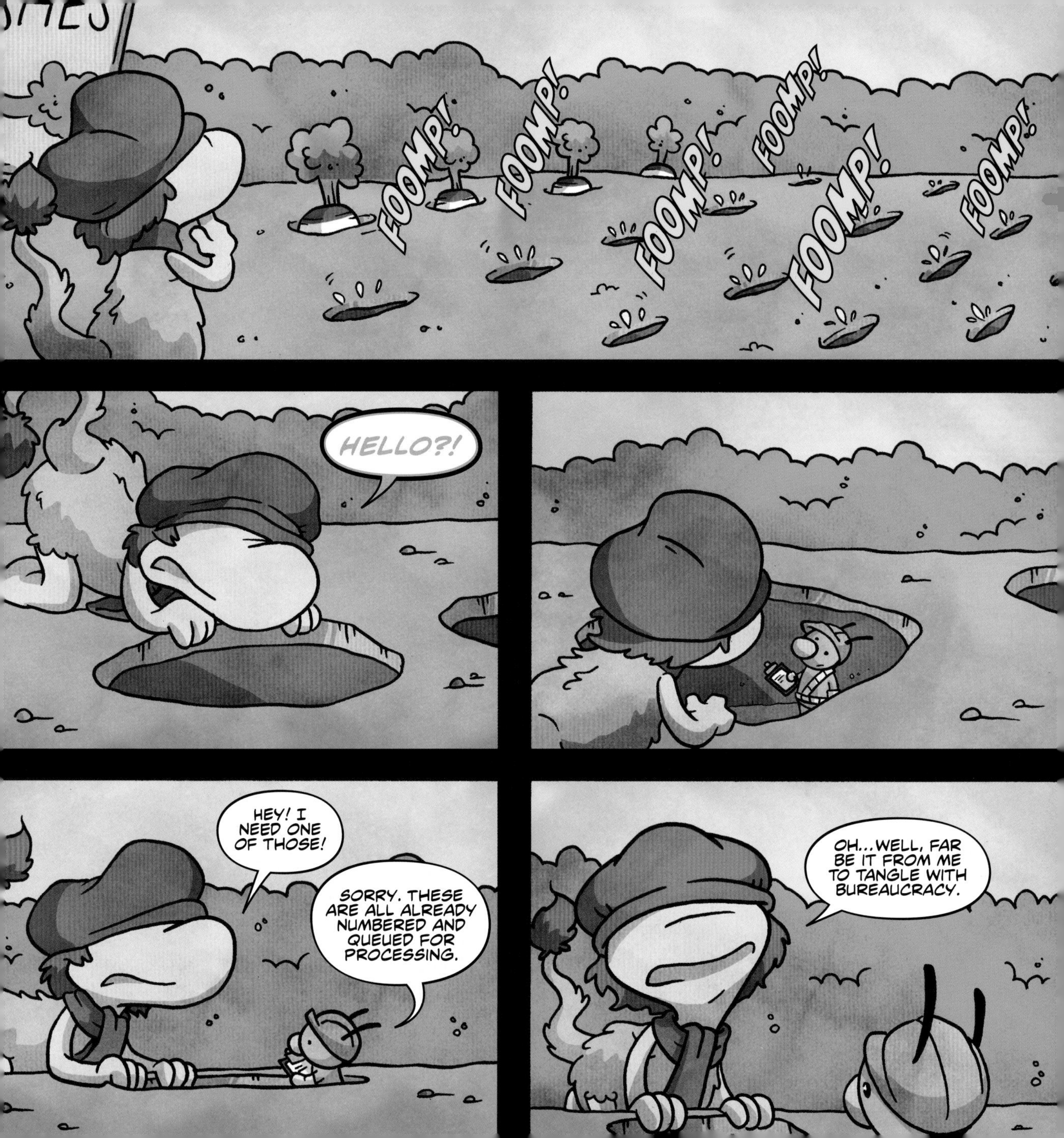
FOOMP!
FOOMP!
FOOMP!
FOOMP!
FOOMP!
FOOMP!
FOOMP!
HELLO?!
HEY! I NEED ONE OF THOSE!
SORRY. THESE ARE ALL ALREADY NUMBERED AND QUEUED FOR PROCESSING.
OH...WELL, FAR BE IT FROM ME TO TANGLE WITH BUREAUCRACY.

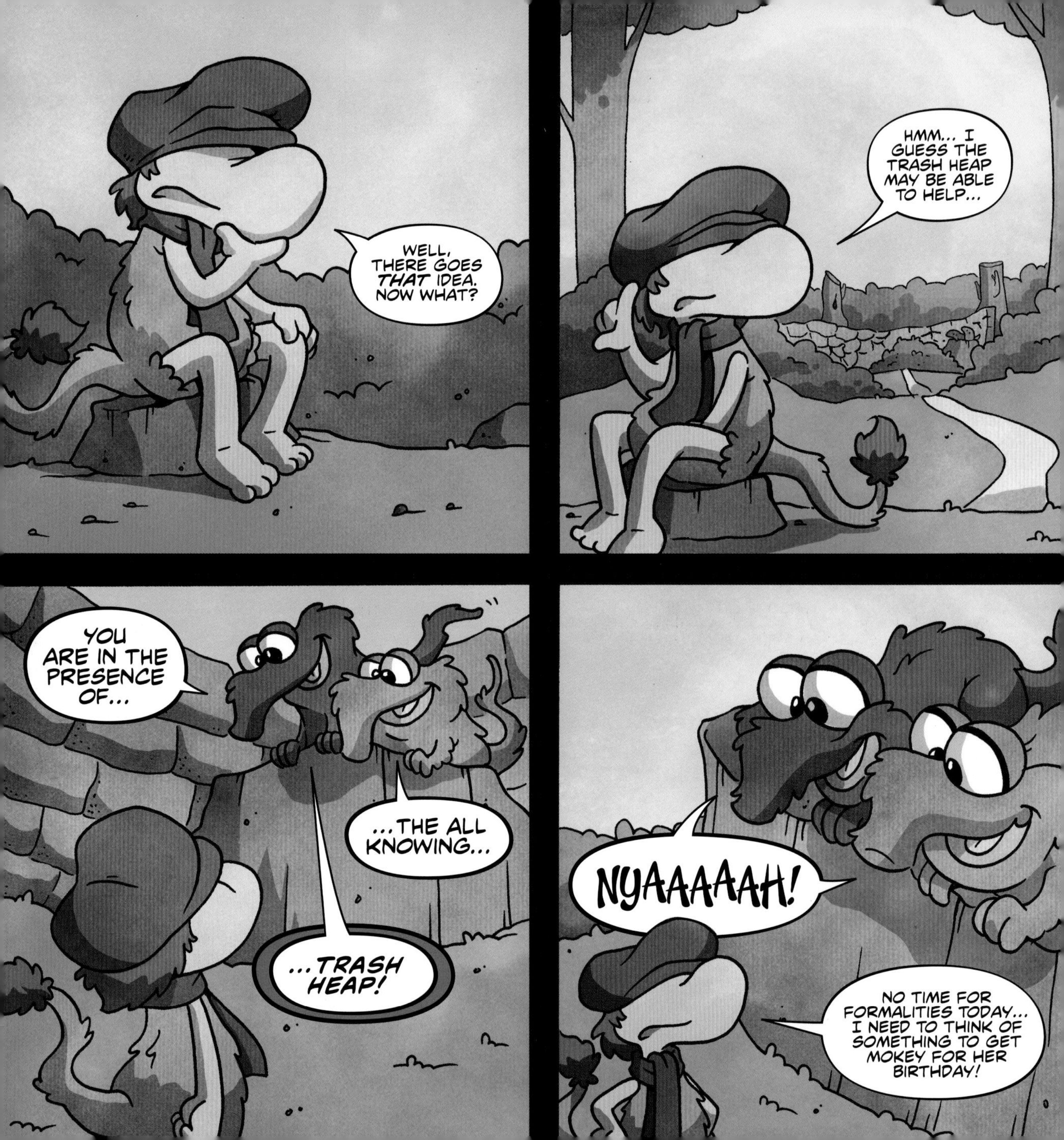
WELL, THERE GOES *THAT* IDEA. NOW WHAT?
HMM... I GUESS THE TRASH HEAP MAY BE ABLE TO HELP...
YOU ARE IN THE PRESENCE OF...
...THE ALL KNOWING...
...*TRASH HEAP!*
NYAAAAAH!
NO TIME FOR FORMALITIES TODAY... I NEED TO THINK OF SOMETHING TO GET MOKEY FOR HER BIRTHDAY!

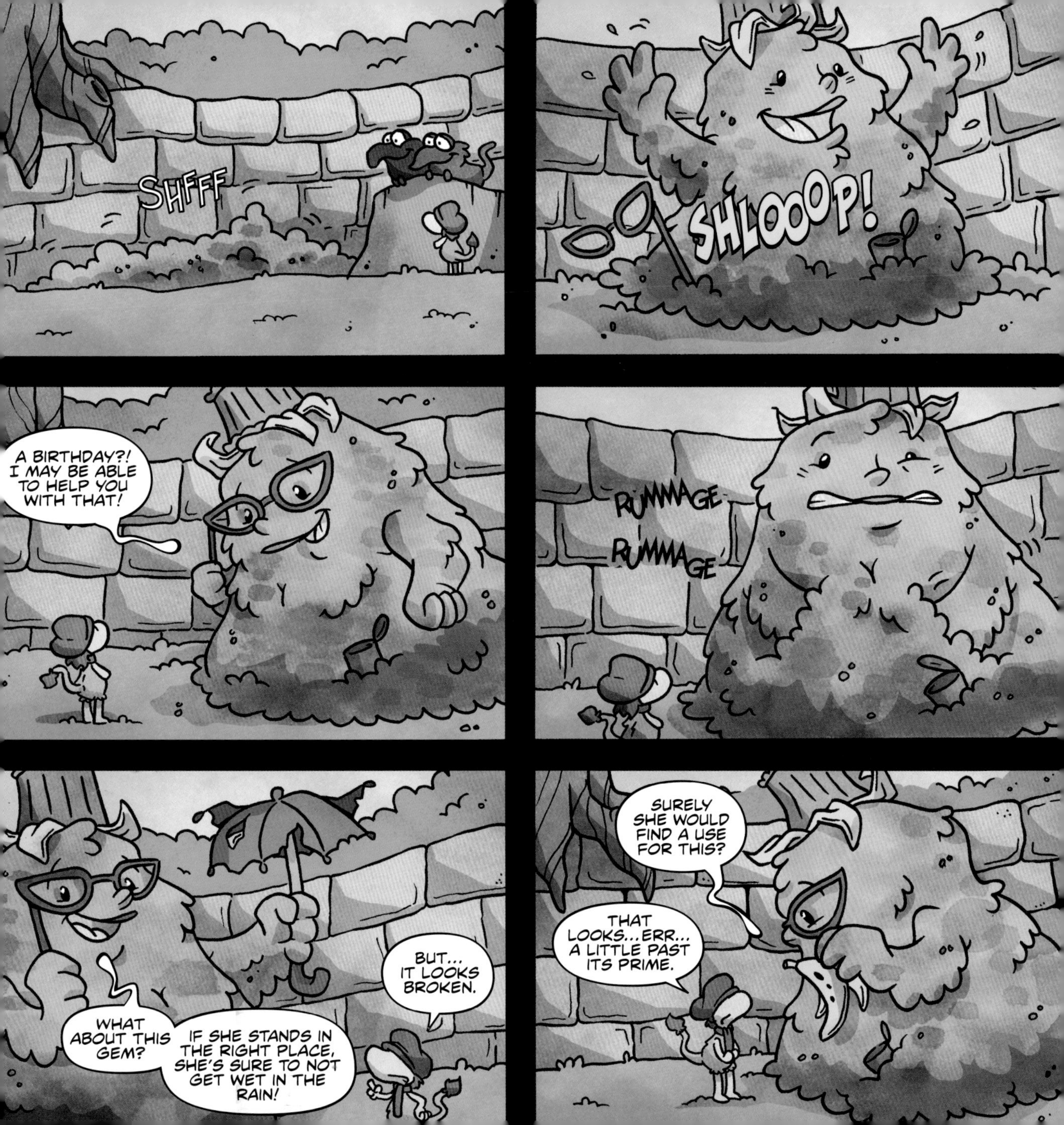
SHFFF
SHLOOOP!
A BIRTHDAY?! I MAY BE ABLE TO HELP YOU WITH THAT!
RUMMAGE RUMMAGE
WHAT ABOUT THIS GEM?
IF SHE STANDS IN THE RIGHT PLACE, SHE'S SURE TO NOT GET WET IN THE RAIN!
BUT... IT LOOKS BROKEN.
SURELY SHE WOULD FIND A USE FOR THIS?
THAT LOOKS...ERR... A LITTLE PAST ITS PRIME.

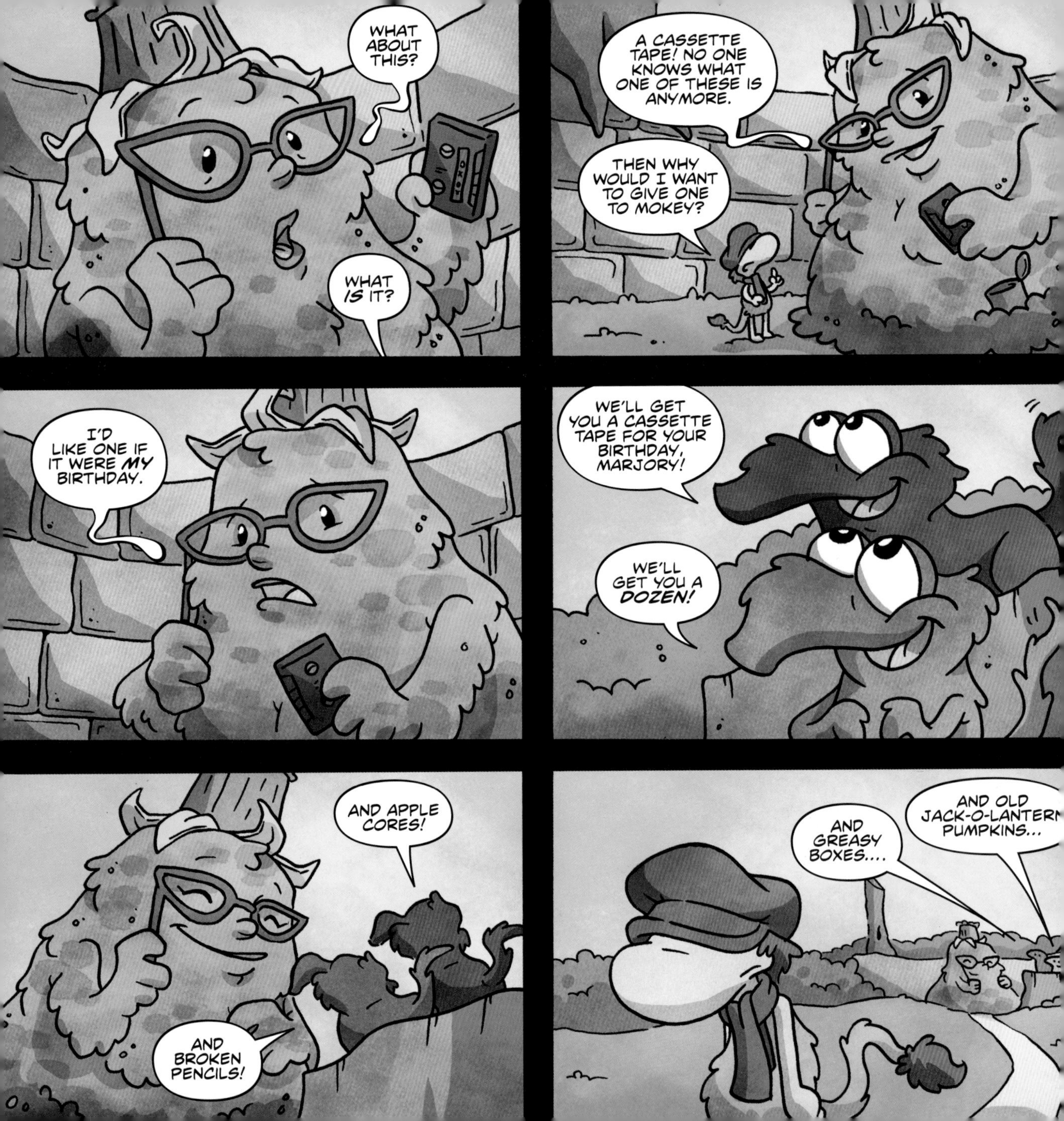

WHAT ABOUT THIS?
WHAT *IS* IT?
A CASSETTE TAPE! NO ONE KNOWS WHAT ONE OF THESE IS ANYMORE.
THEN WHY WOULD I WANT TO GIVE ONE TO MOKEY?
I'D LIKE ONE IF IT WERE *MY* BIRTHDAY.
WE'LL GET YOU A CASSETTE TAPE FOR YOUR BIRTHDAY, MARJORY!
WE'LL GET YOU A *DOZEN!*
AND APPLE CORES!
AND BROKEN PENCILS!
AND GREASY BOXES....
AND OLD JACK-O-LANTERN PUMPKINS...

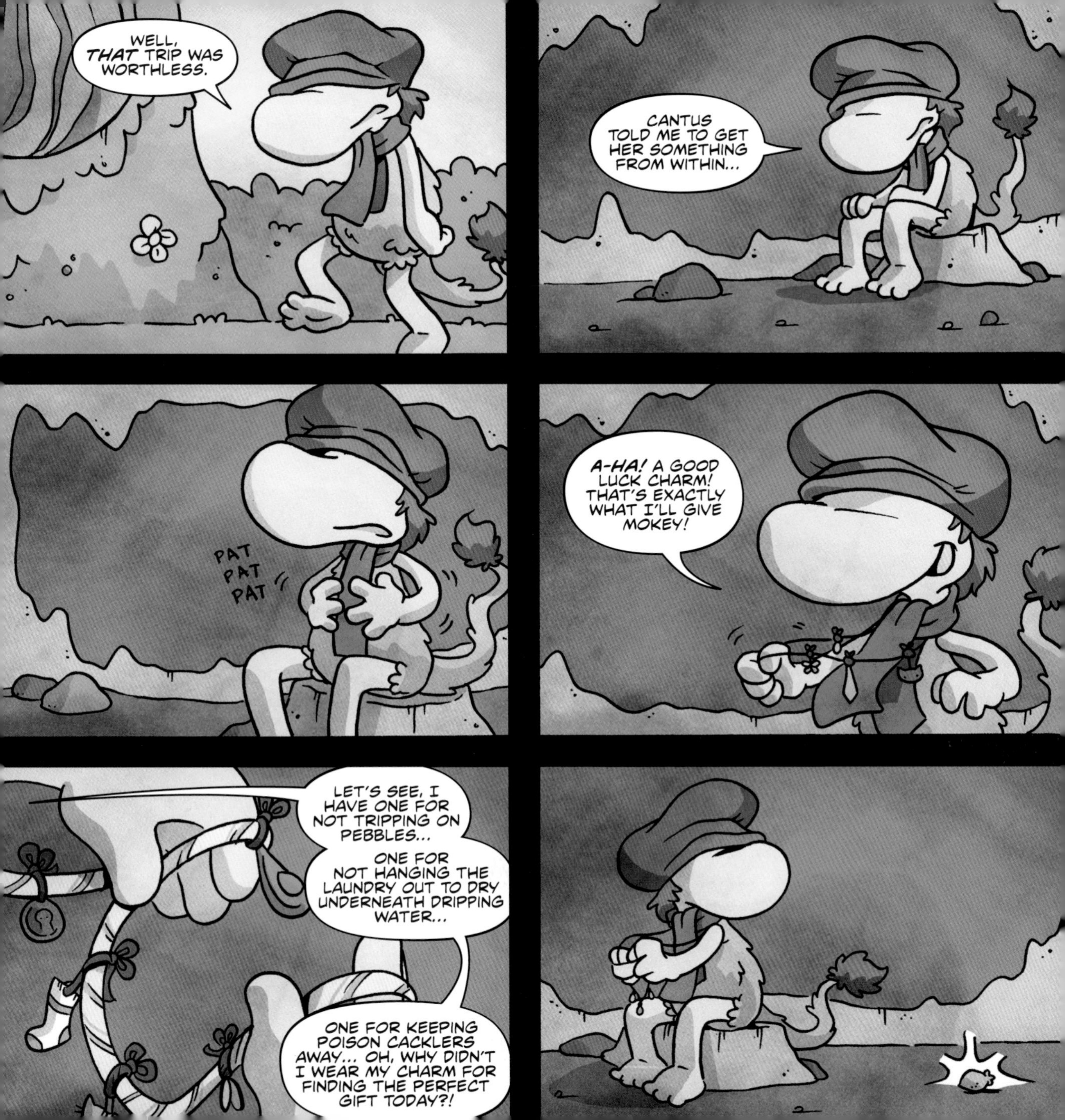
WELL, *THAT* TRIP WAS WORTHLESS.
CANTUS TOLD ME TO GET HER SOMETHING FROM WITHIN...
PAT PAT PAT
A-HA! A GOOD LUCK CHARM! THAT'S EXACTLY WHAT I'LL GIVE MOKEY!
LET'S SEE, I HAVE ONE FOR NOT TRIPPING ON PEBBLES...
ONE FOR NOT HANGING THE LAUNDRY OUT TO DRY UNDERNEATH DRIPPING WATER...
ONE FOR KEEPING POISON CACKLERS AWAY... OH, WHY DIDN'T I WEAR MY CHARM FOR FINDING THE PERFECT GIFT TODAY?!

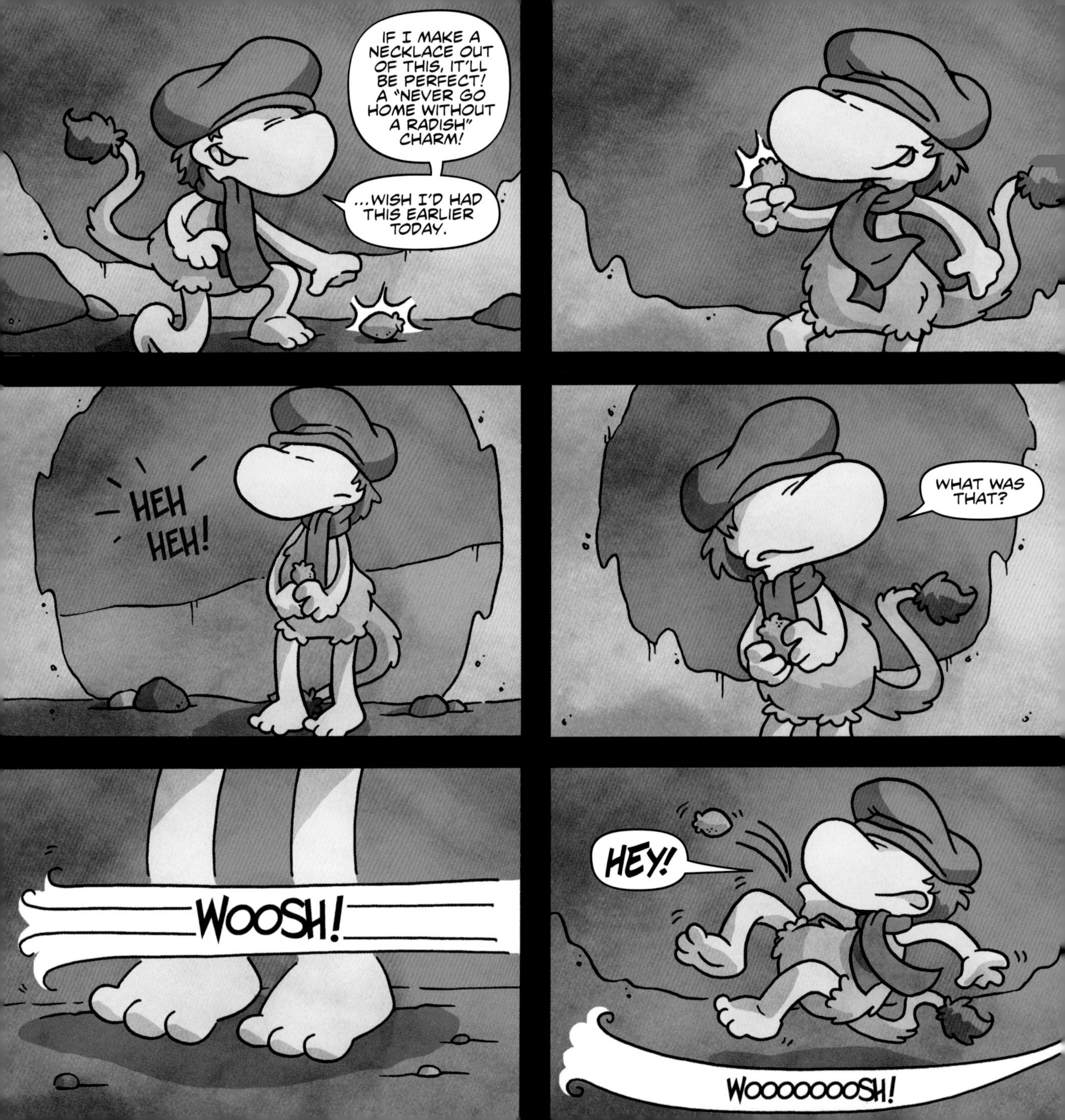
IF I MAKE A NECKLACE OUT OF THIS, IT'LL BE PERFECT! A "NEVER GO HOME WITHOUT A RADISH" CHARM!
...WISH I'D HAD THIS EARLIER TODAY.
HEH HEH!
WHAT WAS THAT?
WOOSH!
HEY!
WOOOOOOOSH!

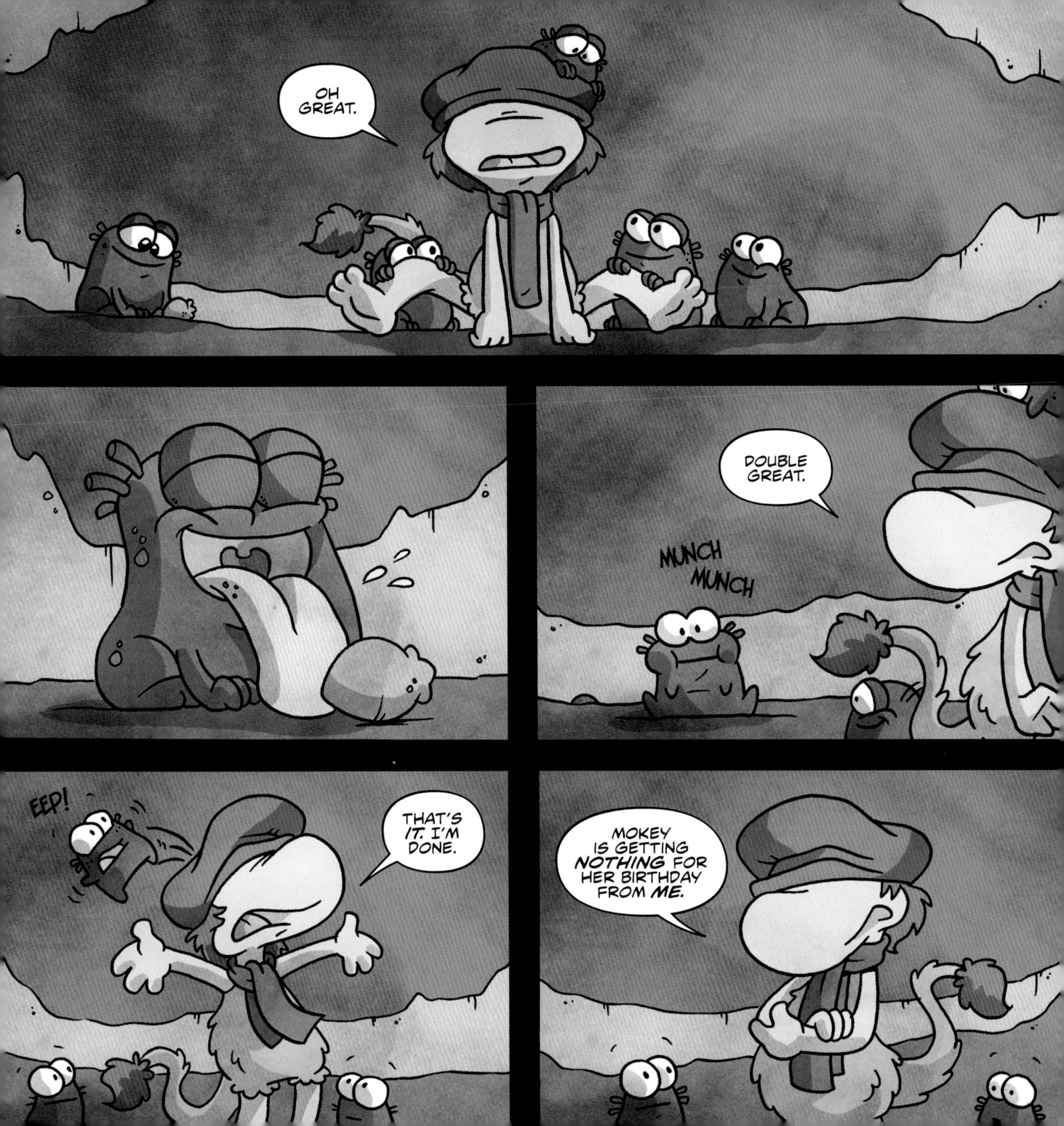
OH GREAT.
DOUBLE GREAT.
MUNCH MUNCH
EEP!
THAT'S *IT.* I'M DONE.
MOKEY IS GETTING ***NOTHING*** FOR HER BIRTHDAY FROM ***ME.***

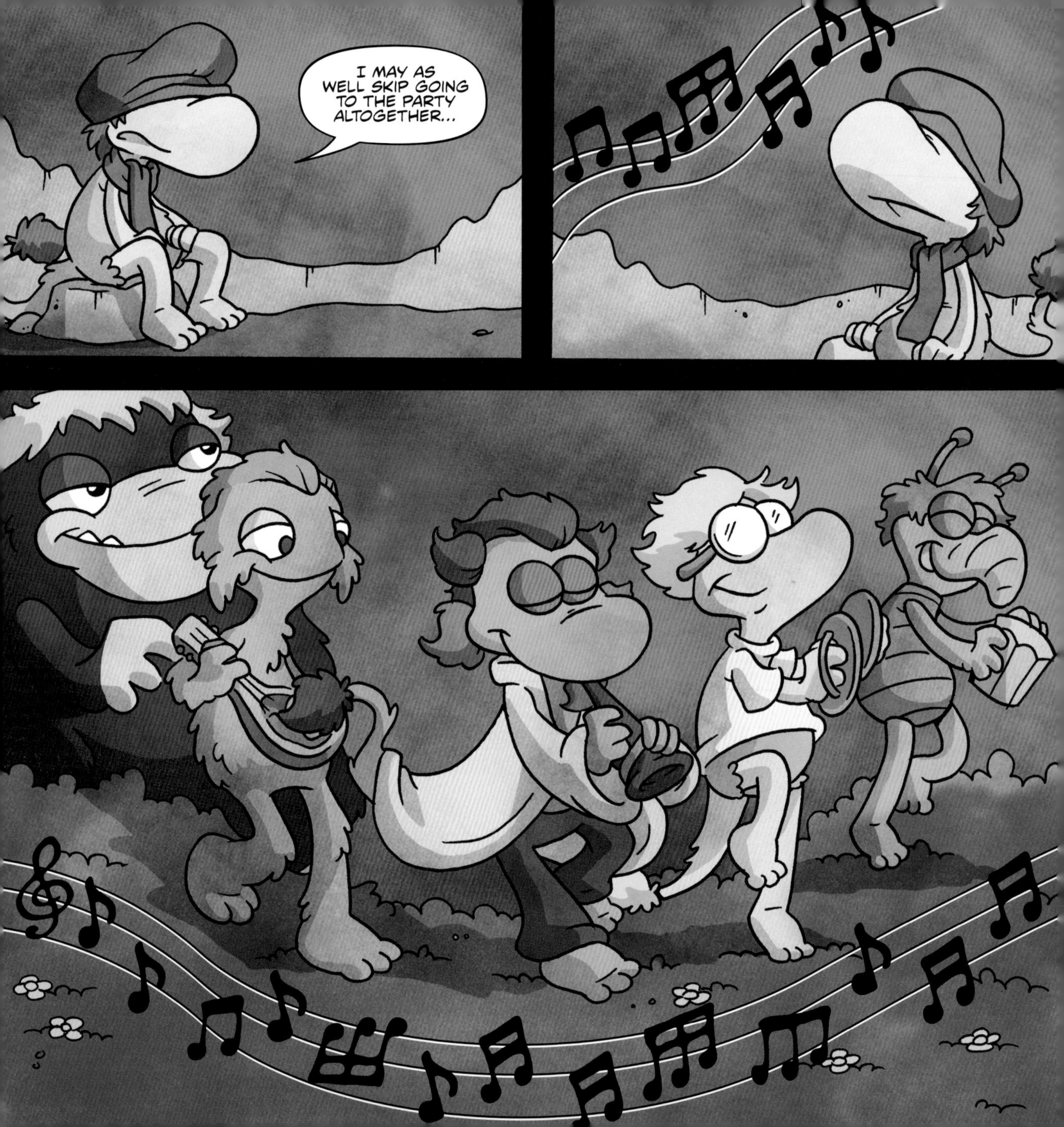
I MAY AS WELL SKIP GOING TO THE PARTY ALTOGETHER...

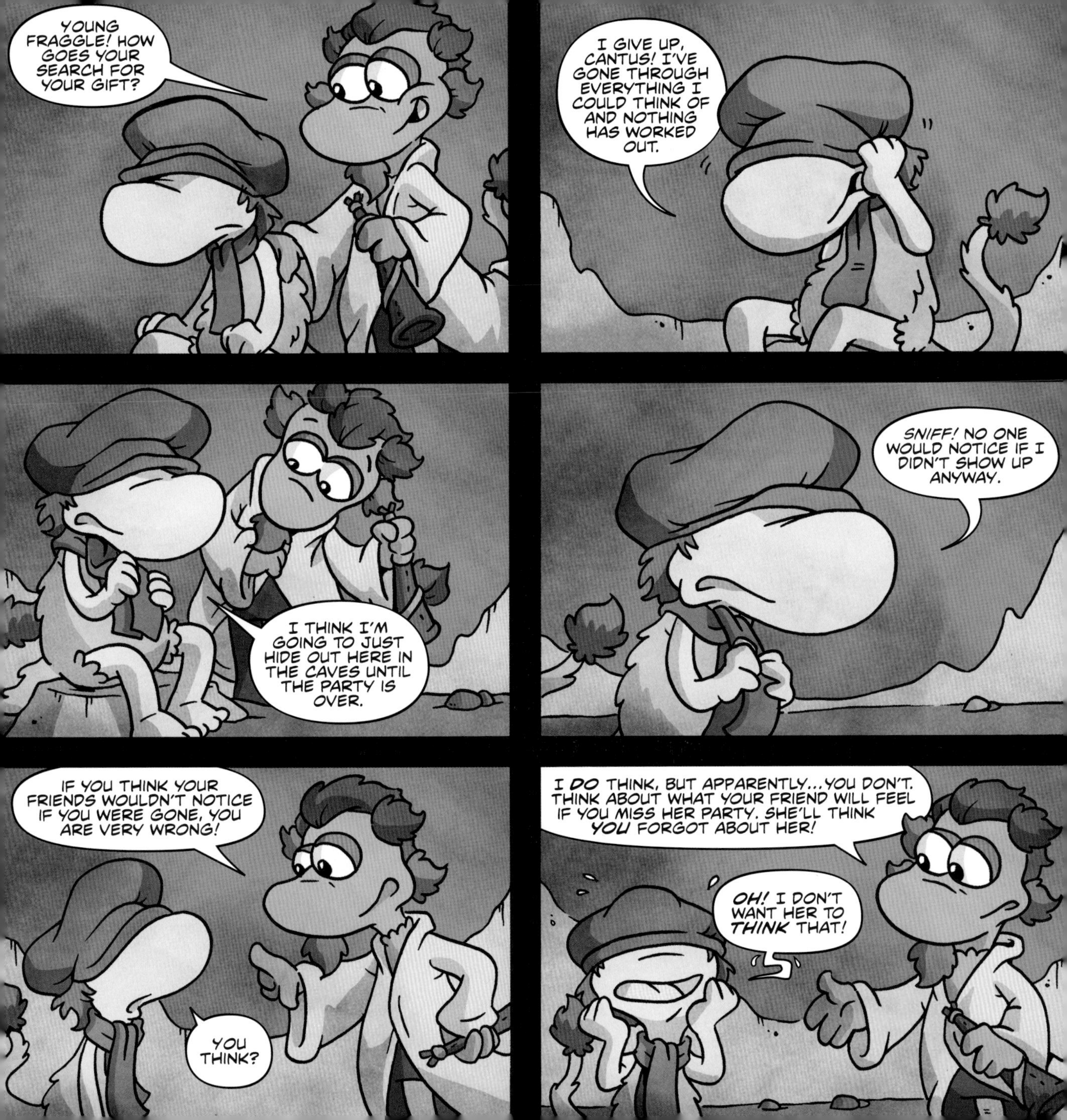
YOUNG FRAGGLE! HOW GOES YOUR SEARCH FOR YOUR GIFT?
I GIVE UP, CANTUS! I'VE GONE THROUGH EVERYTHING I COULD THINK OF AND NOTHING HAS WORKED OUT.
I THINK I'M GOING TO JUST HIDE OUT HERE IN THE CAVES UNTIL THE PARTY IS OVER.
SNIFF! NO ONE WOULD NOTICE IF I DIDN'T SHOW UP ANYWAY.
IF YOU THINK YOUR FRIENDS WOULDN'T NOTICE IF YOU WERE GONE, YOU ARE VERY WRONG!
YOU THINK?
I ***DO*** THINK, BUT APPARENTLY... YOU DON'T. THINK ABOUT WHAT YOUR FRIEND WILL FEEL IF YOU MISS HER PARTY. SHE'LL THINK ***YOU*** FORGOT ABOUT HER!
OH! I DON'T WANT HER TO ***THINK*** THAT!

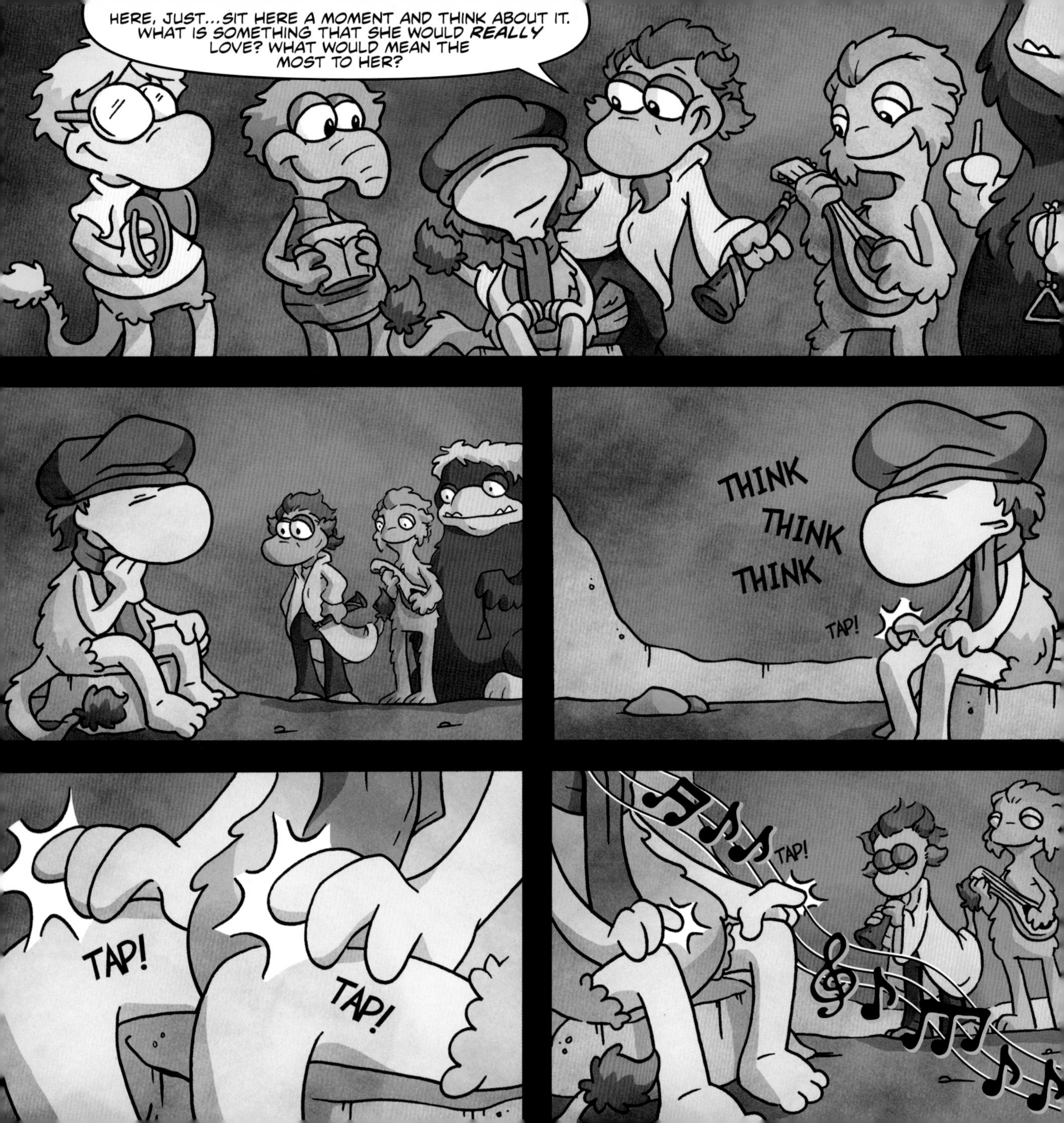
HERE, JUST...SIT HERE A MOMENT AND THINK ABOUT IT. WHAT IS SOMETHING THAT SHE WOULD *REALLY* LOVE? WHAT WOULD MEAN THE MOST TO HER?
THINK
THINK
THINK
TAP!
TAP!
TAP!
TAP!

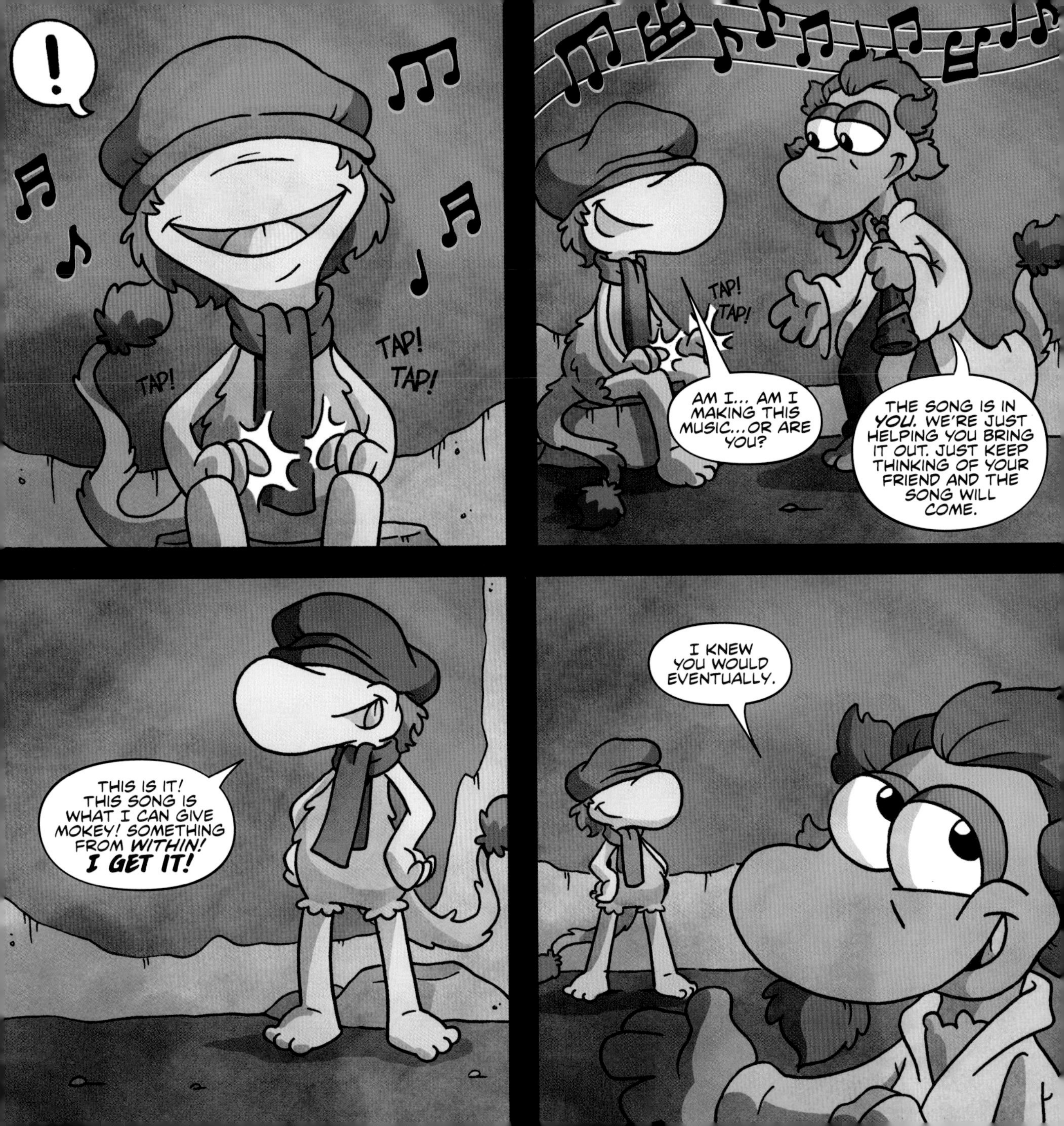
!
TAP!
TAP!
TAP!
TAP!
TAP!
AM I... AM I MAKING THIS MUSIC...OR ARE YOU?
THE SONG IS IN *YOU.* WE'RE JUST HELPING YOU BRING IT OUT. JUST KEEP THINKING OF YOUR FRIEND AND THE SONG WILL COME.
THIS IS IT! THIS SONG IS WHAT I CAN GIVE MOKEY! SOMETHING FROM *WITHIN!* ***I GET IT!***
I KNEW YOU WOULD EVENTUALLY.

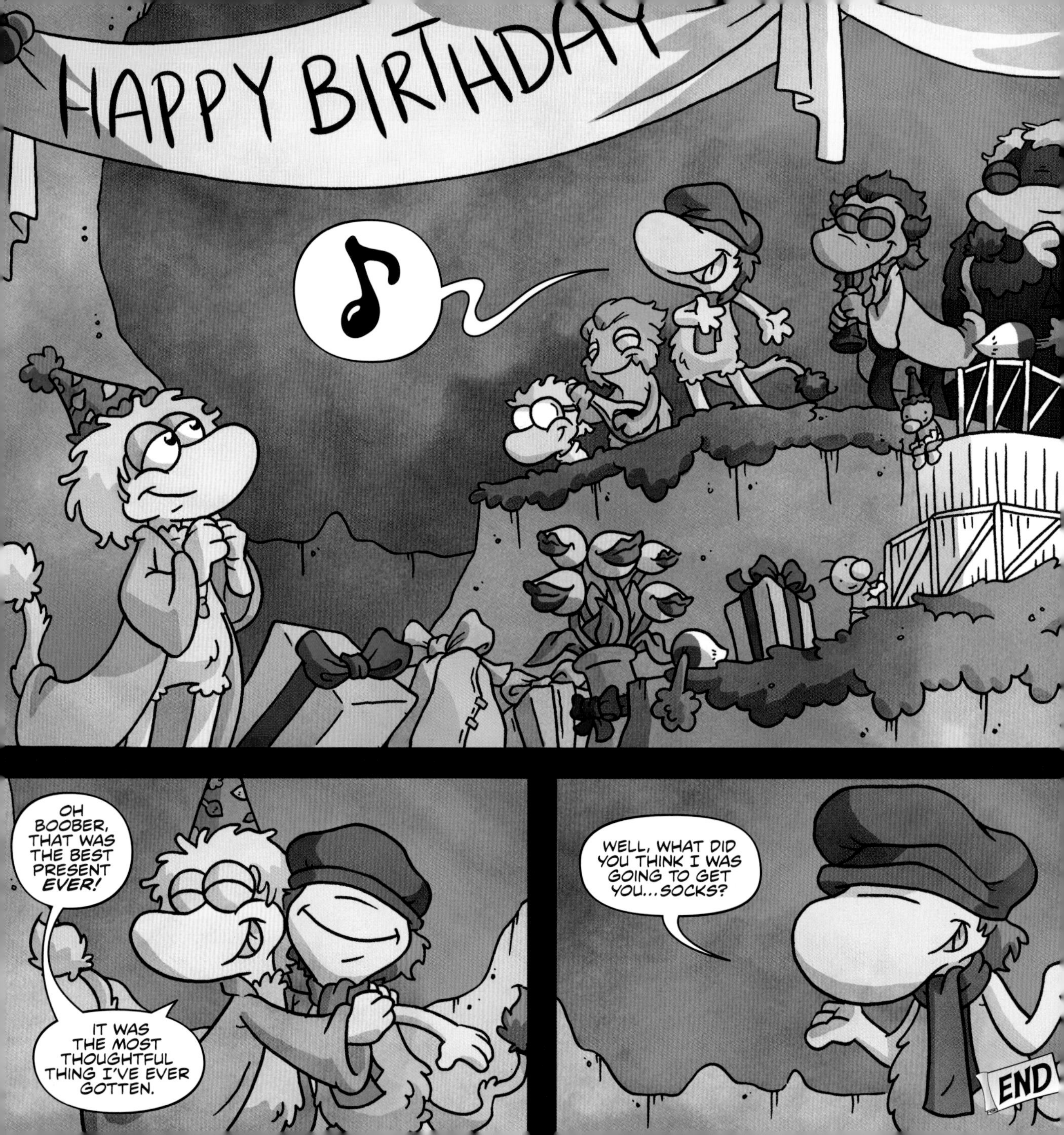
HAPPY BIRTHDAY
OH BOOBER, THAT WAS THE BEST PRESENT *EVER!*
IT WAS THE MOST THOUGHTFUL THING I'VE EVER GOTTEN.
WELL, WHAT DID YOU THINK I WAS GOING TO GET YOU...SOCKS?
END

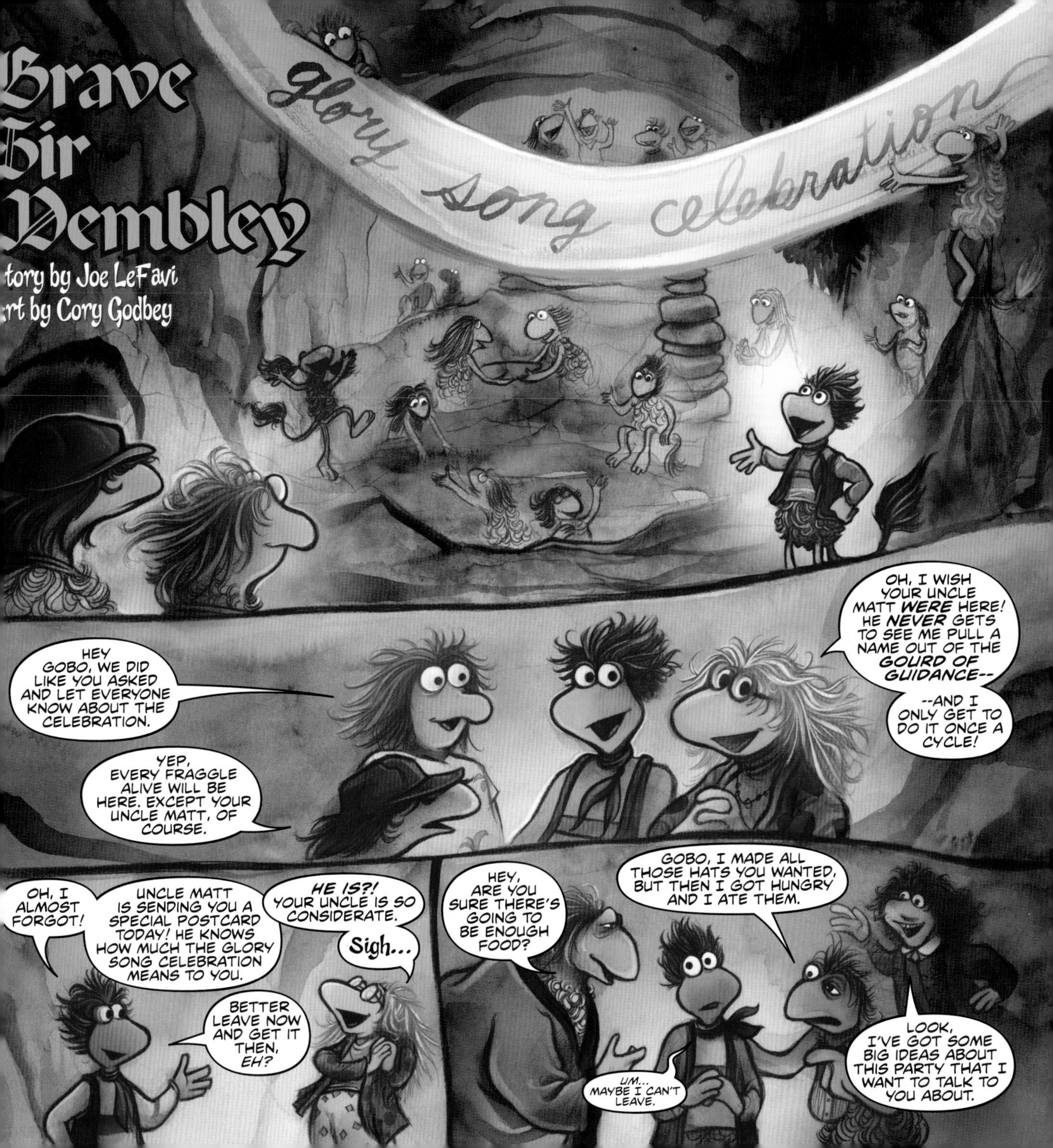
rave
ir
embley
tory by Joe LeFavi
rt by Cory Godbey
glory song celebration
HEY GOBO, WE DID LIKE YOU ASKED AND LET EVERYONE KNOW ABOUT THE CELEBRATION.
YEP, EVERY FRAGGLE ALIVE WILL BE HERE. EXCEPT YOUR UNCLE MATT, OF COURSE.
OH, I WISH YOUR UNCLE MATT *WERE* HERE! HE *NEVER* GETS TO SEE ME PULL A NAME OUT OF THE *GOURD OF GUIDANCE*--
--AND I ONLY GET TO DO IT ONCE A CYCLE!
OH, I ALMOST FORGOT!
UNCLE MATT IS SENDING YOU A SPECIAL POSTCARD TODAY! HE KNOWS HOW MUCH THE GLORY SONG CELEBRATION MEANS TO YOU.
HE IS?! YOUR UNCLE IS SO CONSIDERATE.
Sigh...
BETTER LEAVE NOW AND GET IT THEN, EH?
HEY, ARE YOU SURE THERE'S GOING TO BE ENOUGH FOOD?
GOBO, I MADE ALL THOSE HATS YOU WANTED, BUT THEN I GOT HUNGRY AND I ATE THEM.
LOOK, I'VE GOT SOME BIG IDEAS ABOUT THIS PARTY THAT I WANT TO TALK TO YOU ABOUT.
UM... MAYBE I CAN'T LEAVE.

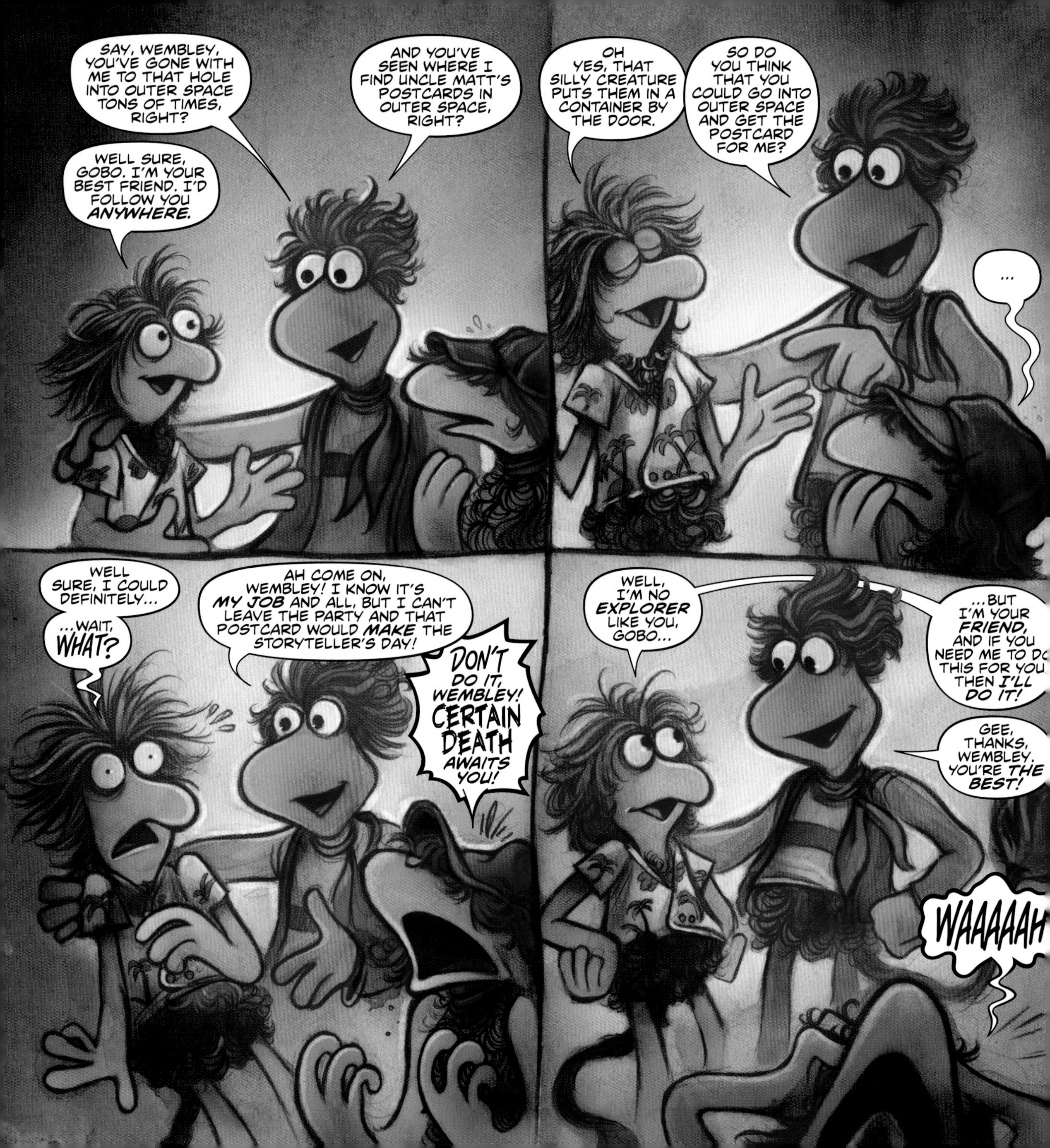

SAY, WEMBLEY, YOU'VE GONE WITH ME TO THAT HOLE INTO OUTER SPACE TONS OF TIMES, RIGHT?
WELL SURE, GOBO. I'M YOUR BEST FRIEND. I'D FOLLOW YOU ANYWHERE.
AND YOU'VE SEEN WHERE I FIND UNCLE MATT'S POSTCARDS IN OUTER SPACE, RIGHT?
OH YES, THAT SILLY CREATURE PUTS THEM IN A CONTAINER BY THE DOOR.
SO DO YOU THINK THAT YOU COULD GO INTO OUTER SPACE AND GET THE POSTCARD FOR ME?
...
WELL SURE, I COULD DEFINITELY...
...WAIT, WHAT?
AH COME ON, WEMBLEY! I KNOW IT'S MY JOB AND ALL, BUT I CAN'T LEAVE THE PARTY AND THAT POSTCARD WOULD MAKE THE STORYTELLER'S DAY!
DON'T DO IT, WEMBLEY! CERTAIN DEATH AWAITS YOU!
WELL, I'M NO EXPLORER LIKE YOU, GOBO...
...BUT I'M YOUR FRIEND, AND IF YOU NEED ME TO DO THIS FOR YOU THEN I'LL DO IT!
GEE, THANKS, WEMBLEY. YOU'RE THE BEST!
WAAAAAH

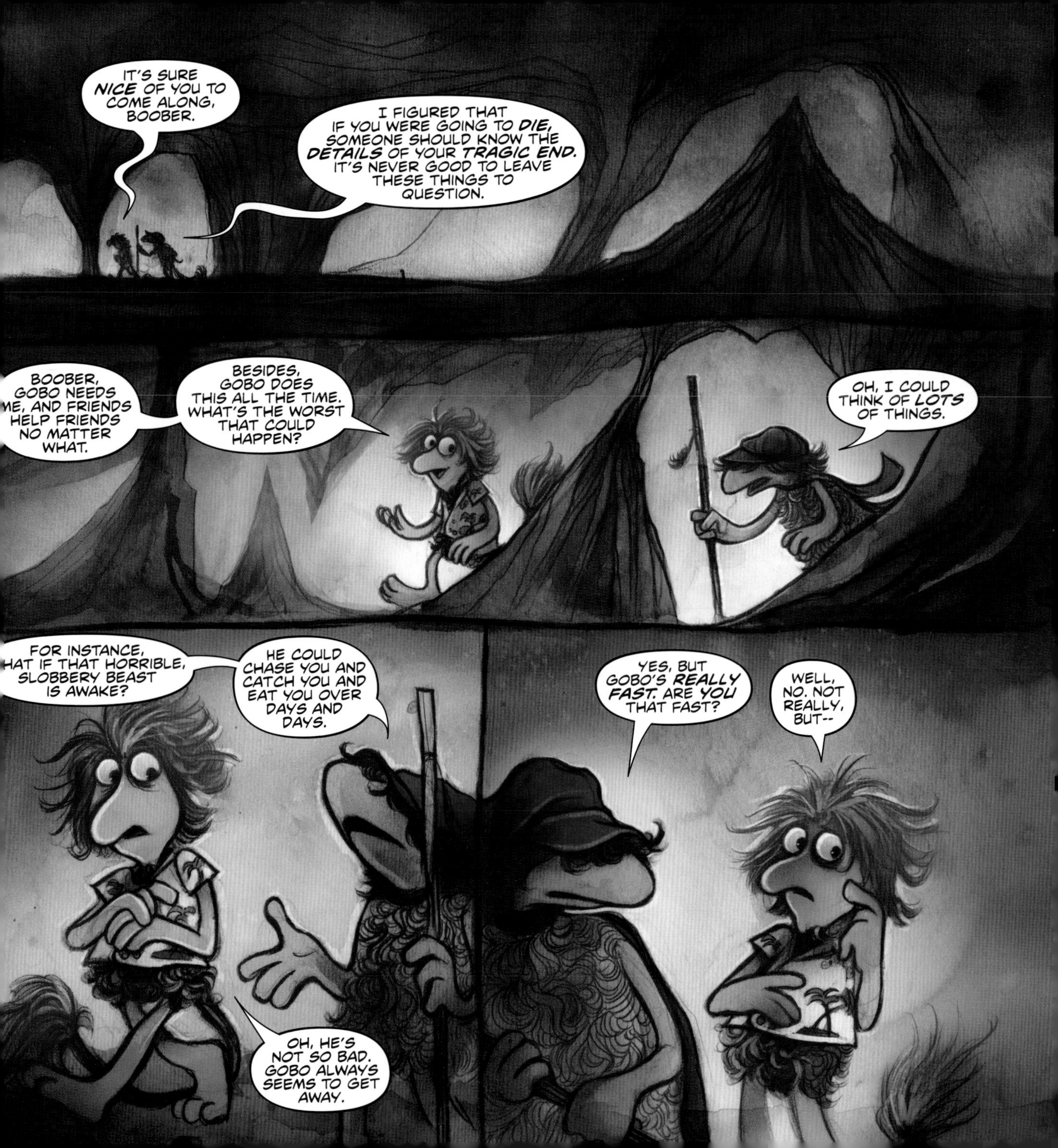
IT'S SURE NICE OF YOU TO COME ALONG, BOOBER.
I FIGURED THAT IF YOU WERE GOING TO DIE, SOMEONE SHOULD KNOW THE DETAILS OF YOUR TRAGIC END. IT'S NEVER GOOD TO LEAVE THESE THINGS TO QUESTION.
BOOBER, GOBO NEEDS ME, AND FRIENDS HELP FRIENDS NO MATTER WHAT.
BESIDES, GOBO DOES THIS ALL THE TIME. WHAT'S THE WORST THAT COULD HAPPEN?
OH, I COULD THINK OF LOTS OF THINGS.
FOR INSTANCE, HAT IF THAT HORRIBLE, SLOBBERY BEAST IS AWAKE?
HE COULD CHASE YOU AND CATCH YOU AND EAT YOU OVER DAYS AND DAYS.
OH, HE'S NOT SO BAD. GOBO ALWAYS SEEMS TO GET AWAY.
YES, BUT GOBO'S REALLY FAST. ARE YOU THAT FAST?
WELL, NO. NOT REALLY, BUT--

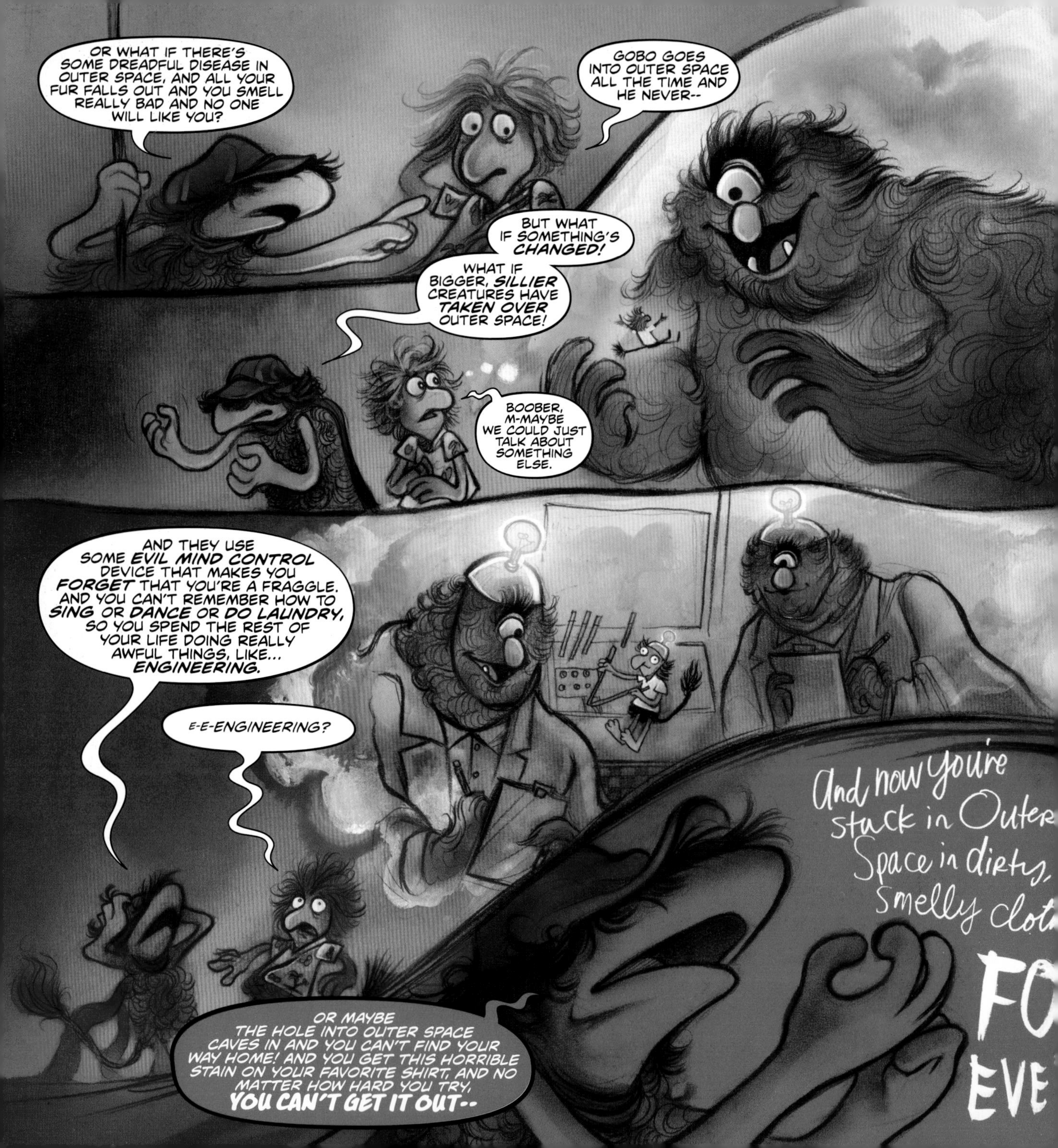
OR WHAT IF THERE'S SOME DREADFUL DISEASE IN OUTER SPACE, AND ALL YOUR FUR FALLS OUT AND YOU SMELL REALLY BAD AND NO ONE WILL LIKE YOU?
GOBO GOES INTO OUTER SPACE ALL THE TIME AND HE NEVER--
BUT WHAT IF SOMETHING'S CHANGED!
WHAT IF BIGGER, SILLIER CREATURES HAVE TAKEN OVER OUTER SPACE!
BOOBER, M-MAYBE WE COULD JUST TALK ABOUT SOMETHING ELSE.
AND THEY USE SOME EVIL MIND CONTROL DEVICE THAT MAKES YOU FORGET THAT YOU'RE A FRAGGLE. AND YOU CAN'T REMEMBER HOW TO SING OR DANCE OR DO LAUNDRY, SO YOU SPEND THE REST OF YOUR LIFE DOING REALLY AWFUL THINGS, LIKE... ENGINEERING.
E-E-ENGINEERING?
OR MAYBE THE HOLE INTO OUTER SPACE CAVES IN AND YOU CAN'T FIND YOUR WAY HOME! AND YOU GET THIS HORRIBLE STAIN ON YOUR FAVORITE SHIRT, AND NO MATTER HOW HARD YOU TRY, YOU CAN'T GET IT OUT--
And now you're stuck in Outer Space in dirty, smelly clot
FO
EVE

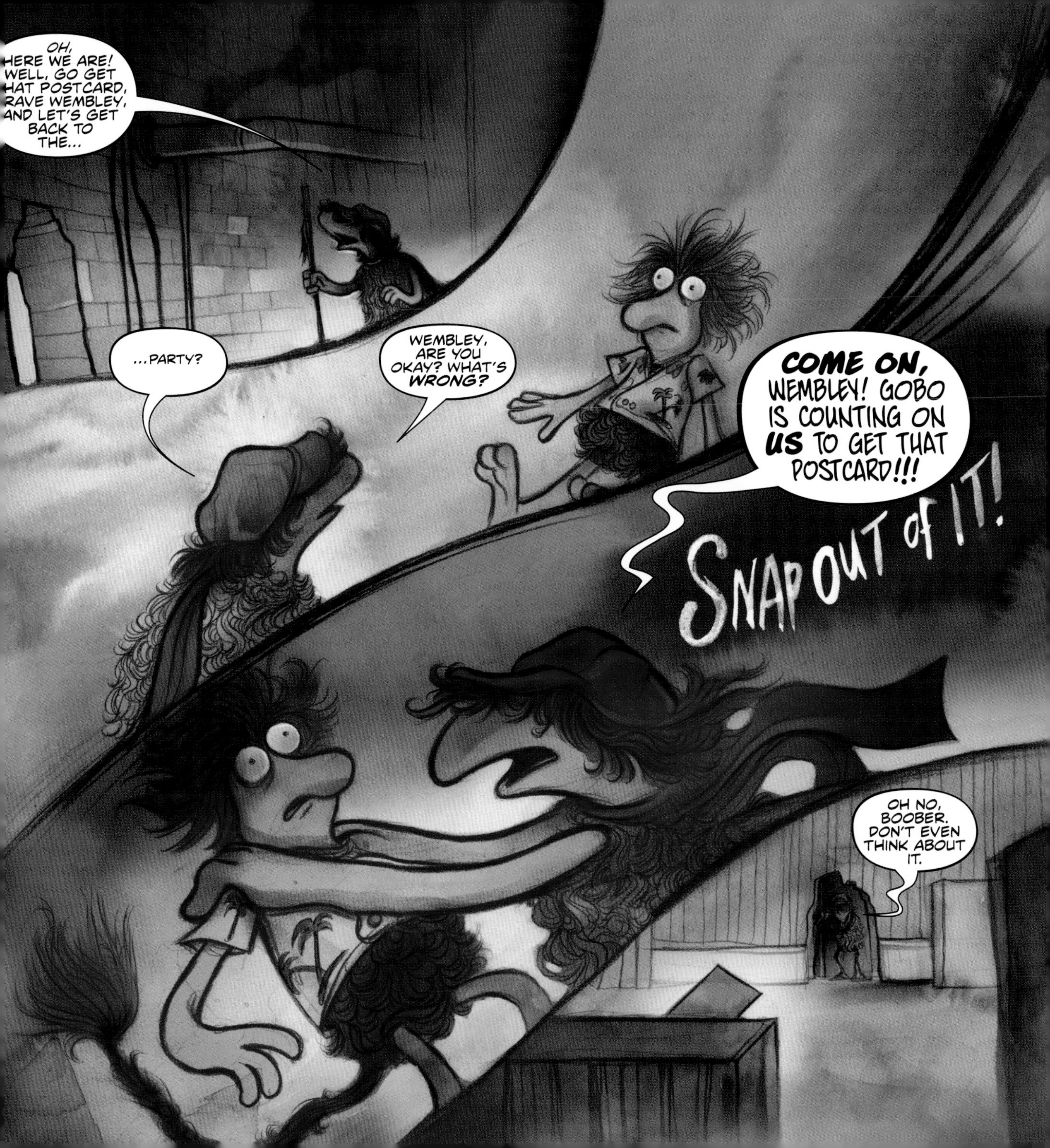
OH, HERE WE ARE! WELL, GO GET HAT POSTCARD, RAVE WEMBLEY, AND LET'S GET BACK TO THE...
...PARTY?
WEMBLEY, ARE YOU OKAY? WHAT'S WRONG?
COME ON, WEMBLEY! GOBO IS COUNTING ON US TO GET THAT POSTCARD!!!
SNAP OUT OF IT!
OH NO, BOOBER. DON'T EVEN THINK ABOUT IT.

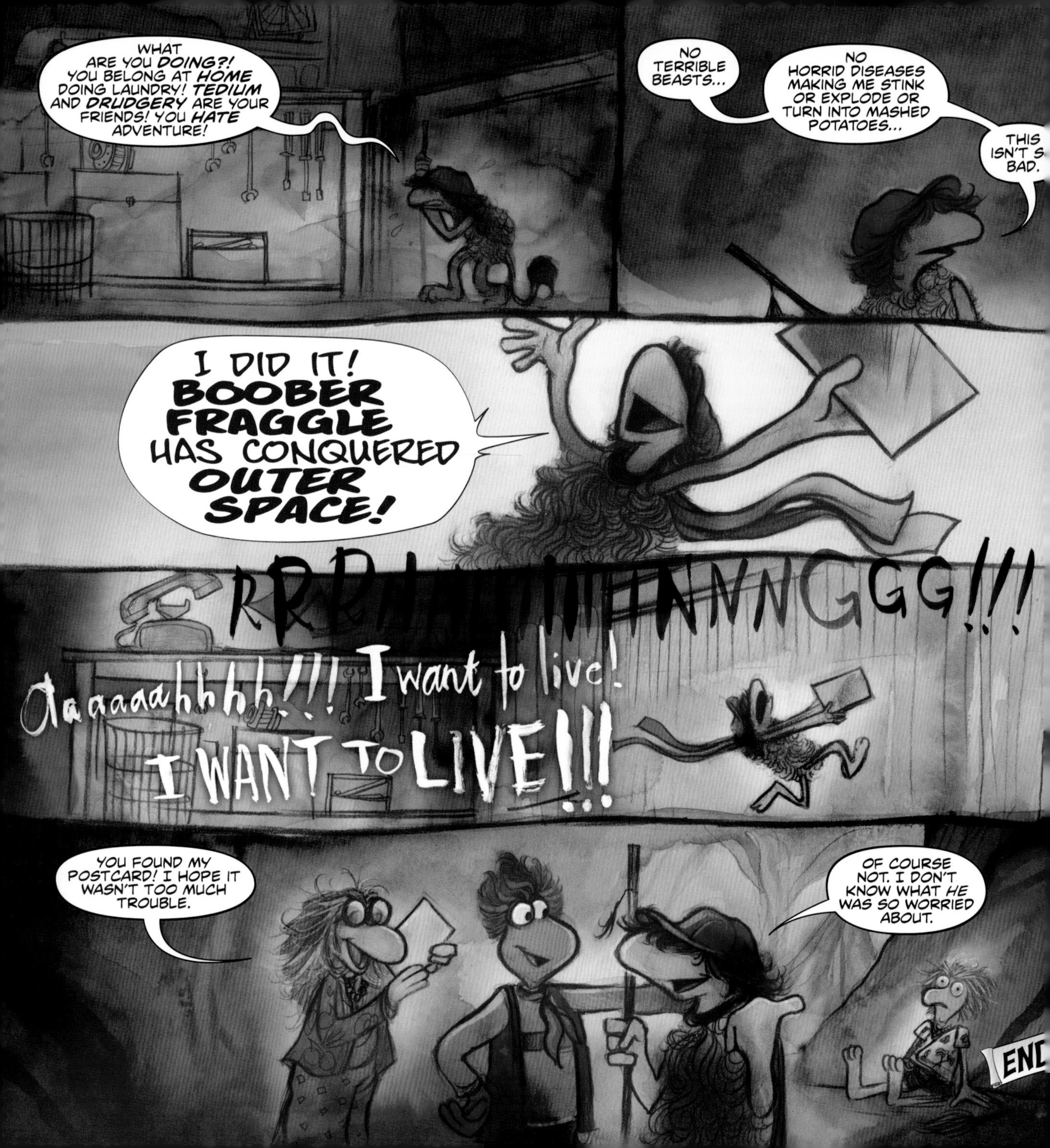
WHAT ARE YOU DOING?! YOU BELONG AT HOME DOING LAUNDRY! TEDIUM AND DRUDGERY ARE YOUR FRIENDS! YOU HATE ADVENTURE!
NO TERRIBLE BEASTS...
NO HORRID DISEASES MAKING ME STINK OR EXPLODE OR TURN INTO MASHED POTATOES...
THIS ISN'T S BAD.
I DID IT! BOOBER FRAGGLE HAS CONQUERED OUTER SPACE!
RRRIIIIIIIINNNNGGG!!!
Aaaaaahhhh!!! I want to live!
I WANT TO LIVE!!!
YOU FOUND MY POSTCARD! I HOPE IT WASN'T TOO MUCH TROUBLE.
OF COURSE NOT. I DON'T KNOW WHAT HE WAS SO WORRIED ABOUT.
END

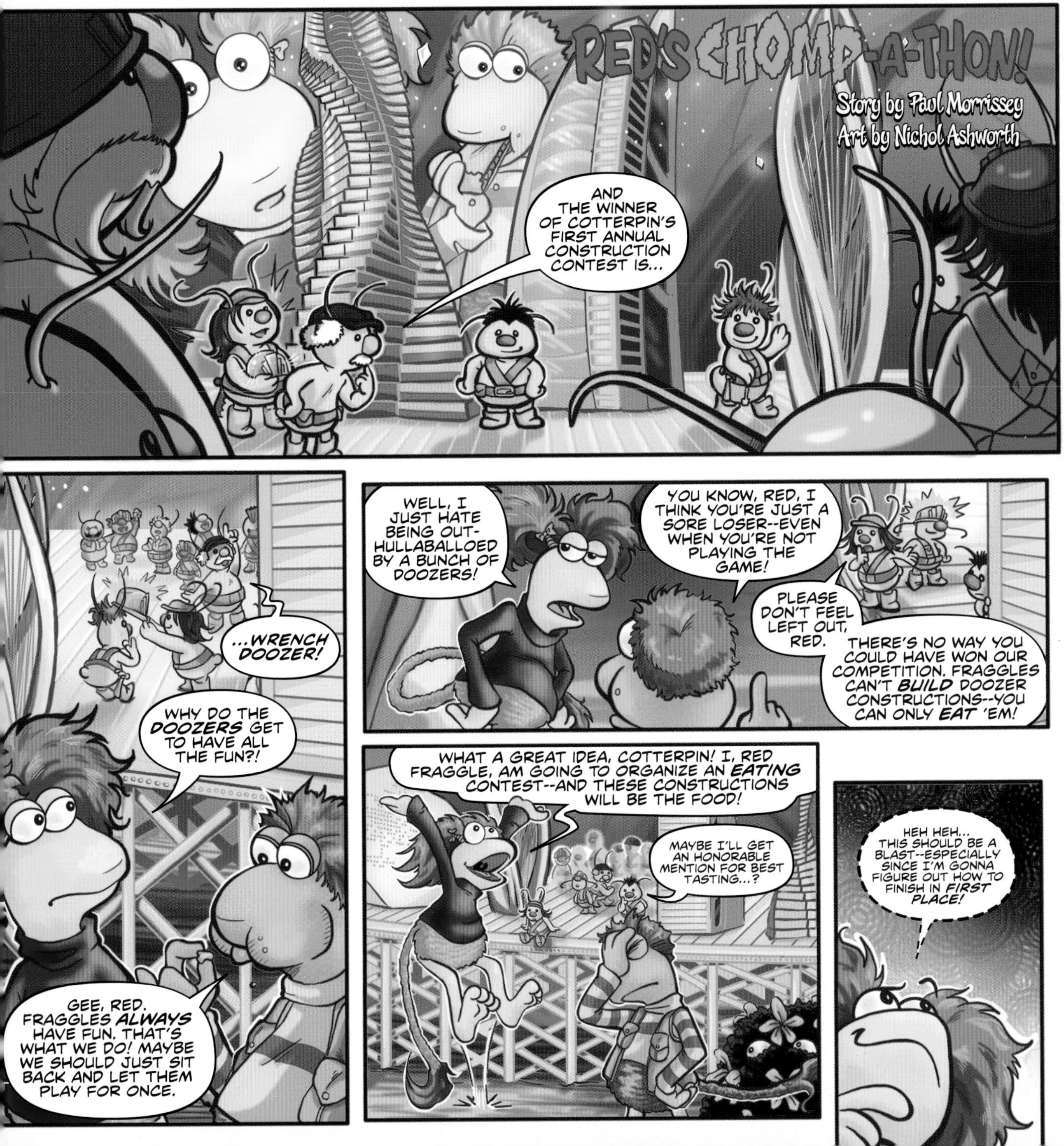
RED'S CHOMP-A-THON!
Story by Paul Morrissey
Art by Nichol Ashworth
AND THE WINNER OF COTTERPIN'S FIRST ANNUAL CONSTRUCTION CONTEST IS...
...WRENCH DOOZER!
WHY DO THE DOOZERS GET TO HAVE ALL THE FUN?!
GEE, RED. FRAGGLES ALWAYS HAVE FUN. THAT'S WHAT WE DO! MAYBE WE SHOULD JUST SIT BACK AND LET THEM PLAY FOR ONCE.
WELL, I JUST HATE BEING OUT-HULLABALLOOED BY A BUNCH OF DOOZERS!
YOU KNOW, RED, I THINK YOU'RE JUST A SORE LOSER--EVEN WHEN YOU'RE NOT PLAYING THE GAME!
PLEASE DON'T FEEL LEFT OUT, RED.
THERE'S NO WAY YOU COULD HAVE WON OUR COMPETITION. FRAGGLES CAN'T BUILD DOOZER CONSTRUCTIONS--YOU CAN ONLY EAT 'EM!
WHAT A GREAT IDEA, COTTERPIN! I, RED FRAGGLE, AM GOING TO ORGANIZE AN EATING CONTEST--AND THESE CONSTRUCTIONS WILL BE THE FOOD!
MAYBE I'LL GET AN HONORABLE MENTION FOR BEST TASTING...?
HEH HEH... THIS SHOULD BE A BLAST--ESPECIALLY SINCE I'M GONNA FIGURE OUT HOW TO FINISH IN FIRST PLACE!

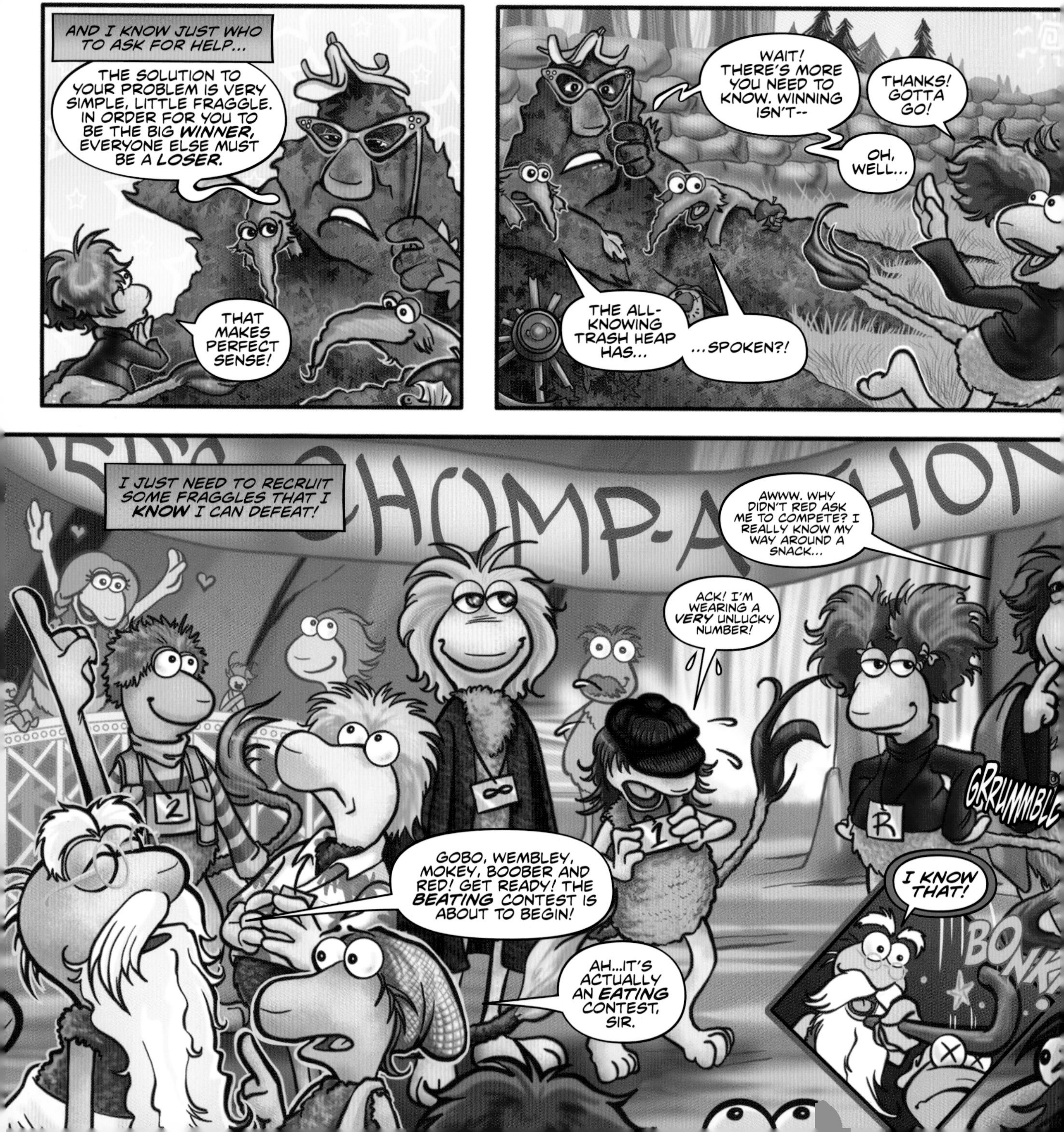

AND I KNOW JUST WHO TO ASK FOR HELP...
THE SOLUTION TO YOUR PROBLEM IS VERY SIMPLE, LITTLE FRAGGLE. IN ORDER FOR YOU TO BE THE BIG *WINNER*, EVERYONE ELSE MUST BE A *LOSER*.
THAT MAKES PERFECT SENSE!
WAIT! THERE'S MORE YOU NEED TO KNOW. WINNING ISN'T--
THANKS! GOTTA GO!
OH, WELL...
THE ALL-KNOWING TRASH HEAP HAS...
...SPOKEN?!
I JUST NEED TO RECRUIT SOME FRAGGLES THAT I *KNOW* I CAN DEFEAT!
AWWW. WHY DIDN'T RED ASK ME TO COMPETE? I REALLY KNOW MY WAY AROUND A SNACK...
ACK! I'M WEARING A *VERY* UNLUCKY NUMBER!
GOBO, WEMBLEY, MOKEY, BOOBER AND RED! GET READY! THE *BEATING* CONTEST IS ABOUT TO BEGIN!
AH...IT'S ACTUALLY AN *EATING* CONTEST, SIR.
I KNOW THAT!

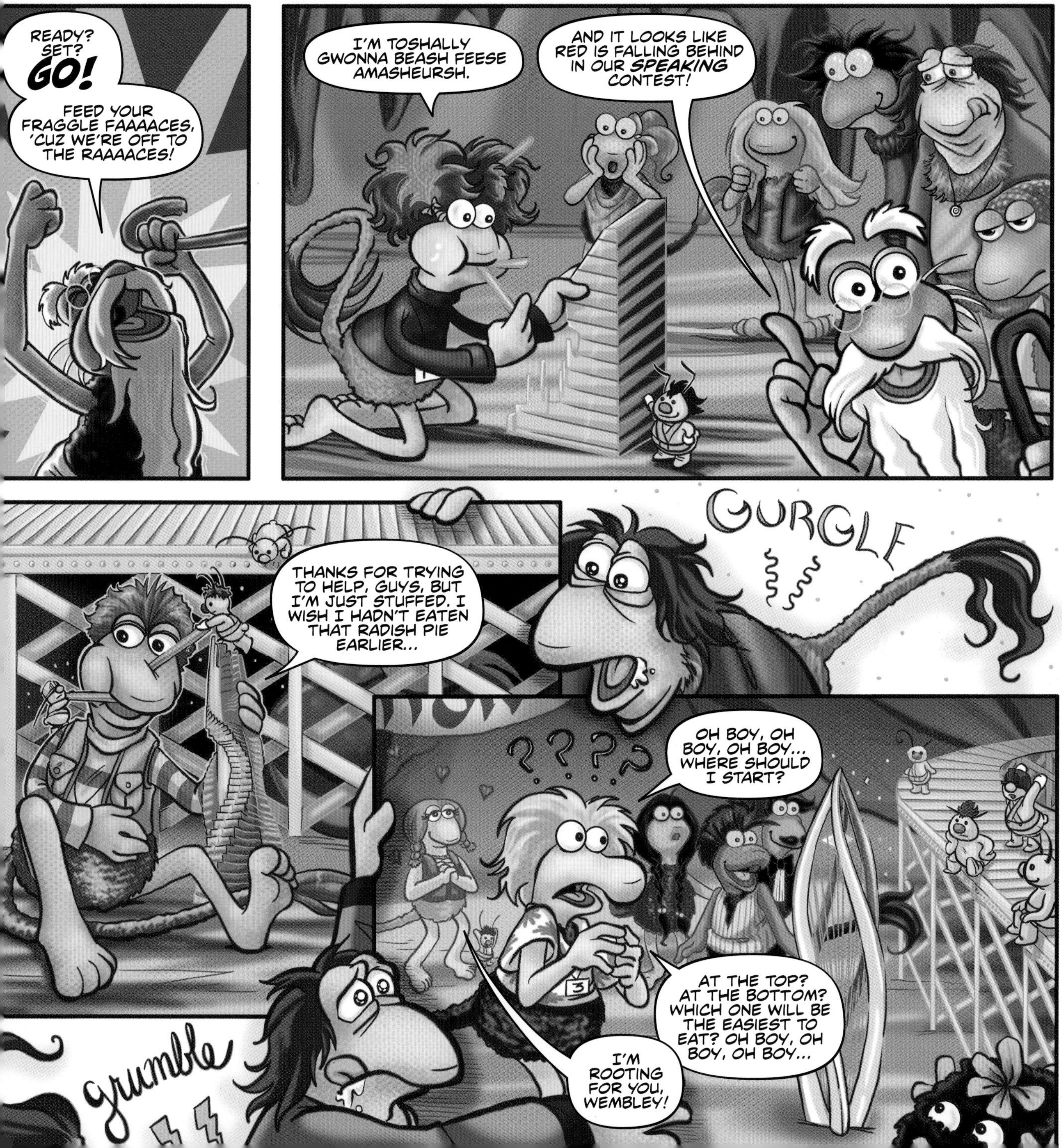
READY? SET? GO!
FEED YOUR FRAGGLE FAAAACES, 'CUZ WE'RE OFF TO THE RAAAACES!
I'M TOSHALLY GWONNA BEASH FEESE AMASHEURSH.
AND IT LOOKS LIKE RED IS FALLING BEHIND IN OUR SPEAKING CONTEST!
THANKS FOR TRYING TO HELP, GUYS, BUT I'M JUST STUFFED. I WISH I HADN'T EATEN THAT RADISH PIE EARLIER...
GURGLE
OH BOY, OH BOY, OH BOY... WHERE SHOULD I START?
AT THE TOP? AT THE BOTTOM? WHICH ONE WILL BE THE EASIEST TO EAT? OH BOY, OH BOY, OH BOY...
I'M ROOTING FOR YOU, WEMBLEY!
grumble

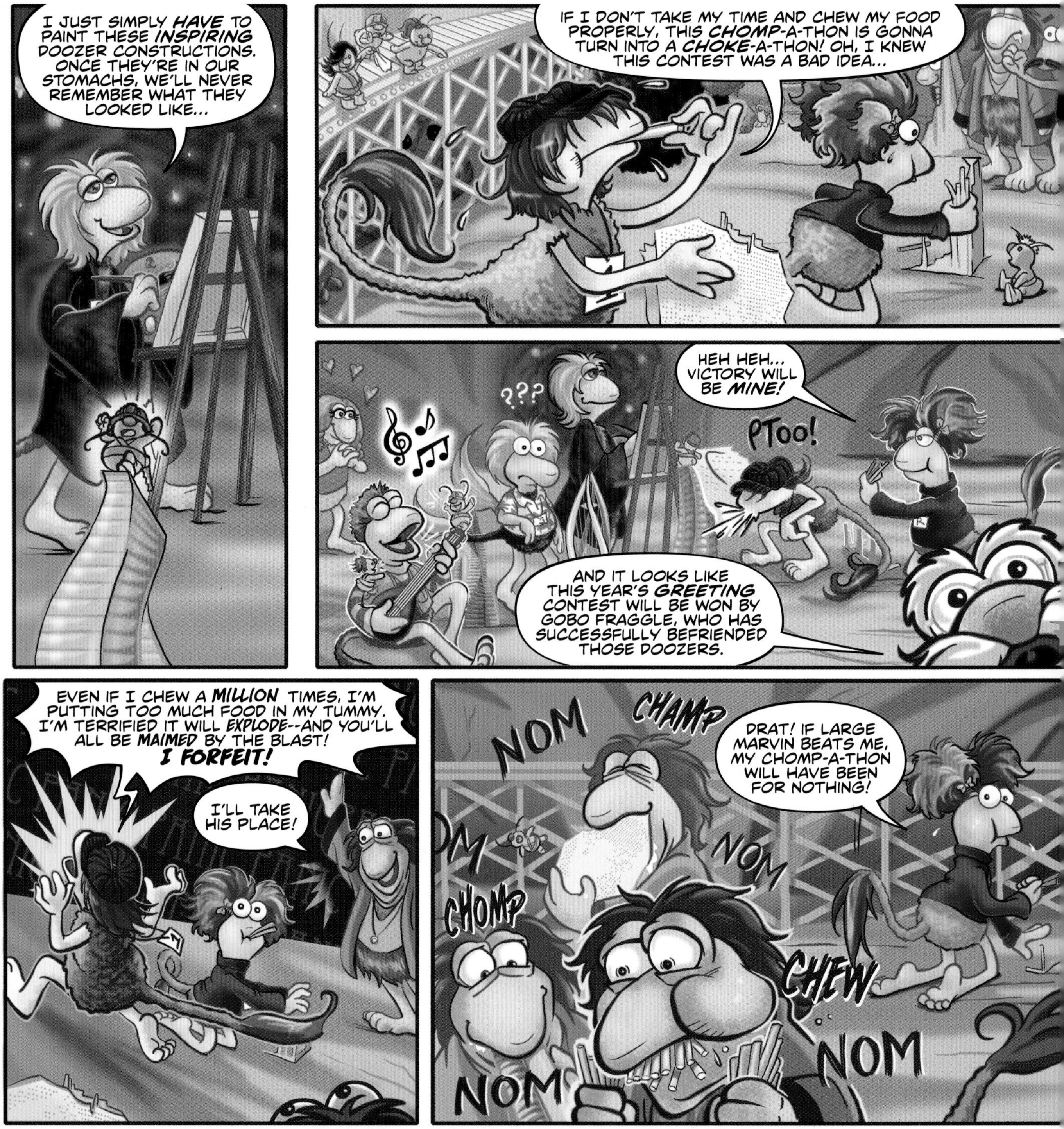
I JUST SIMPLY HAVE TO PAINT THESE INSPIRING DOOZER CONSTRUCTIONS. ONCE THEY'RE IN OUR STOMACHS, WE'LL NEVER REMEMBER WHAT THEY LOOKED LIKE...
IF I DON'T TAKE MY TIME AND CHEW MY FOOD PROPERLY, THIS CHOMP-A-THON IS GONNA TURN INTO A CHOKE-A-THON! OH, I KNEW THIS CONTEST WAS A BAD IDEA...
???
HEH HEH... VICTORY WILL BE MINE!
PTOO!
AND IT LOOKS LIKE THIS YEAR'S GREETING CONTEST WILL BE WON BY GOBO FRAGGLE, WHO HAS SUCCESSFULLY BEFRIENDED THOSE DOOZERS.
EVEN IF I CHEW A MILLION TIMES, I'M PUTTING TOO MUCH FOOD IN MY TUMMY. I'M TERRIFIED IT WILL EXPLODE--AND YOU'LL ALL BE MAIMED BY THE BLAST!
I FORFEIT!
I'LL TAKE HIS PLACE!
NOM
CHAMP
DRAT! IF LARGE MARVIN BEATS ME, MY CHOMP-A-THON WILL HAVE BEEN FOR NOTHING!
NOM
CHOMP
CHEW
NOM
NOM

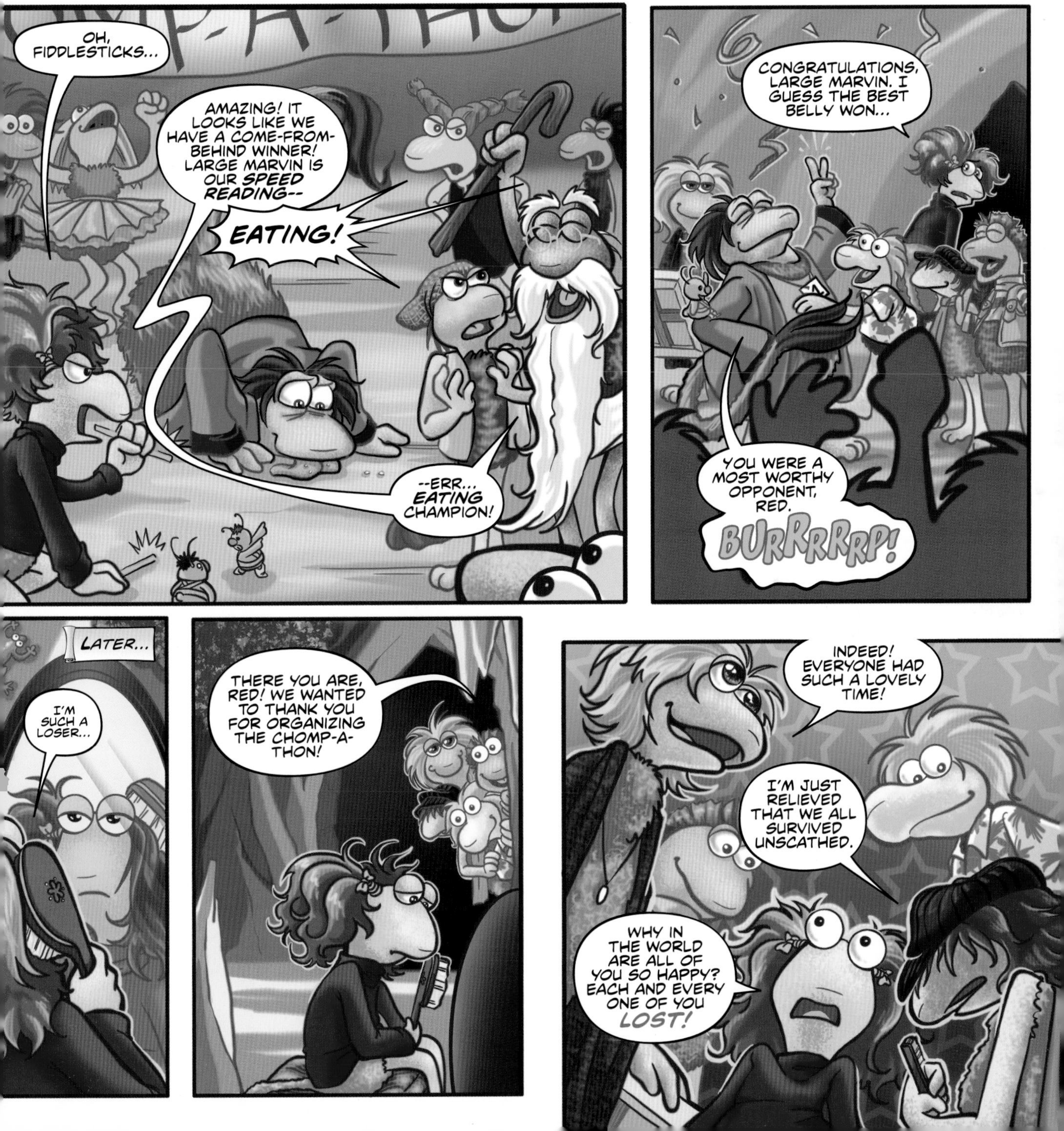
OH, FIDDLESTICKS...
AMAZING! IT LOOKS LIKE WE HAVE A COME-FROM-BEHIND WINNER! LARGE MARVIN IS OUR SPEED READING--
EATING!
--ERR... EATING CHAMPION!
CONGRATULATIONS, LARGE MARVIN. I GUESS THE BEST BELLY WON...
YOU WERE A MOST WORTHY OPPONENT, RED.
BURRRRRP!
LATER...
I'M SUCH A LOSER...
THERE YOU ARE, RED! WE WANTED TO THANK YOU FOR ORGANIZING THE CHOMP-A-THON!
INDEED! EVERYONE HAD SUCH A LOVELY TIME!
I'M JUST RELIEVED THAT WE ALL SURVIVED UNSCATHED.
WHY IN THE WORLD ARE ALL OF YOU SO HAPPY? EACH AND EVERY ONE OF YOU LOST!

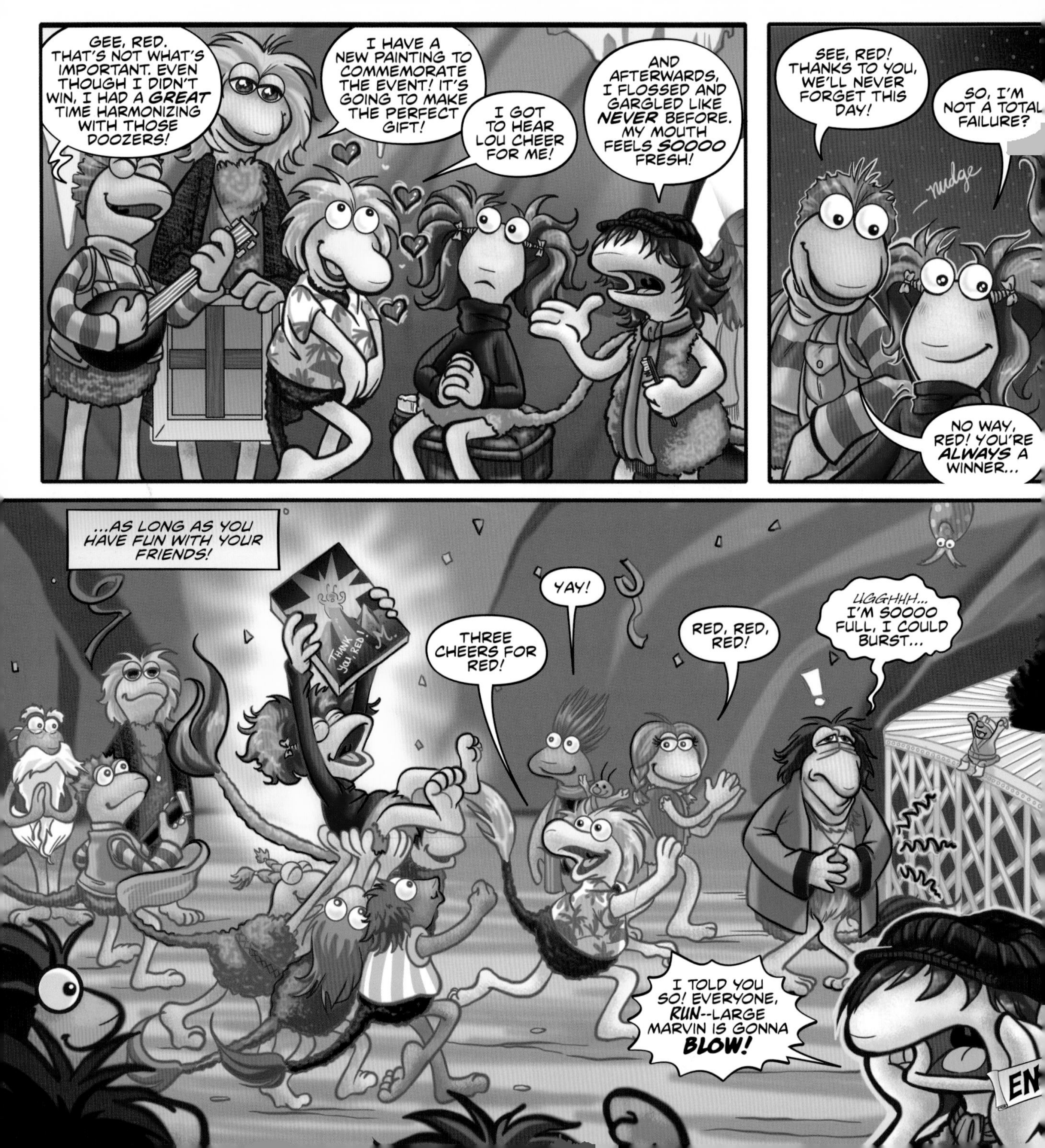
GEE, RED. THAT'S NOT WHAT'S IMPORTANT. EVEN THOUGH I DIDN'T WIN, I HAD A **GREAT** TIME HARMONIZING WITH THOSE DOOZERS!
I HAVE A NEW PAINTING TO COMMEMORATE THE EVENT! IT'S GOING TO MAKE THE PERFECT GIFT!
I GOT TO HEAR LOU CHEER FOR ME!
AND AFTERWARDS, I FLOSSED AND GARGLED LIKE **NEVER** BEFORE. MY MOUTH FEELS **SOOOO** FRESH!
SEE, RED! THANKS TO YOU, WE'LL NEVER FORGET THIS DAY!
nudge
SO, I'M NOT A TOTAL FAILURE?
NO WAY, RED! YOU'RE **ALWAYS** A WINNER...
...AS LONG AS YOU HAVE FUN WITH YOUR FRIENDS!
THANK YOU, RED! M.
THREE CHEERS FOR RED!
YAY!
RED, RED, RED!
UGGHHH... I'M SOOOO FULL, I COULD BURST...
!
I TOLD YOU SO! EVERYONE, **RUN**--LARGE MARVIN IS GONNA **BLOW!**

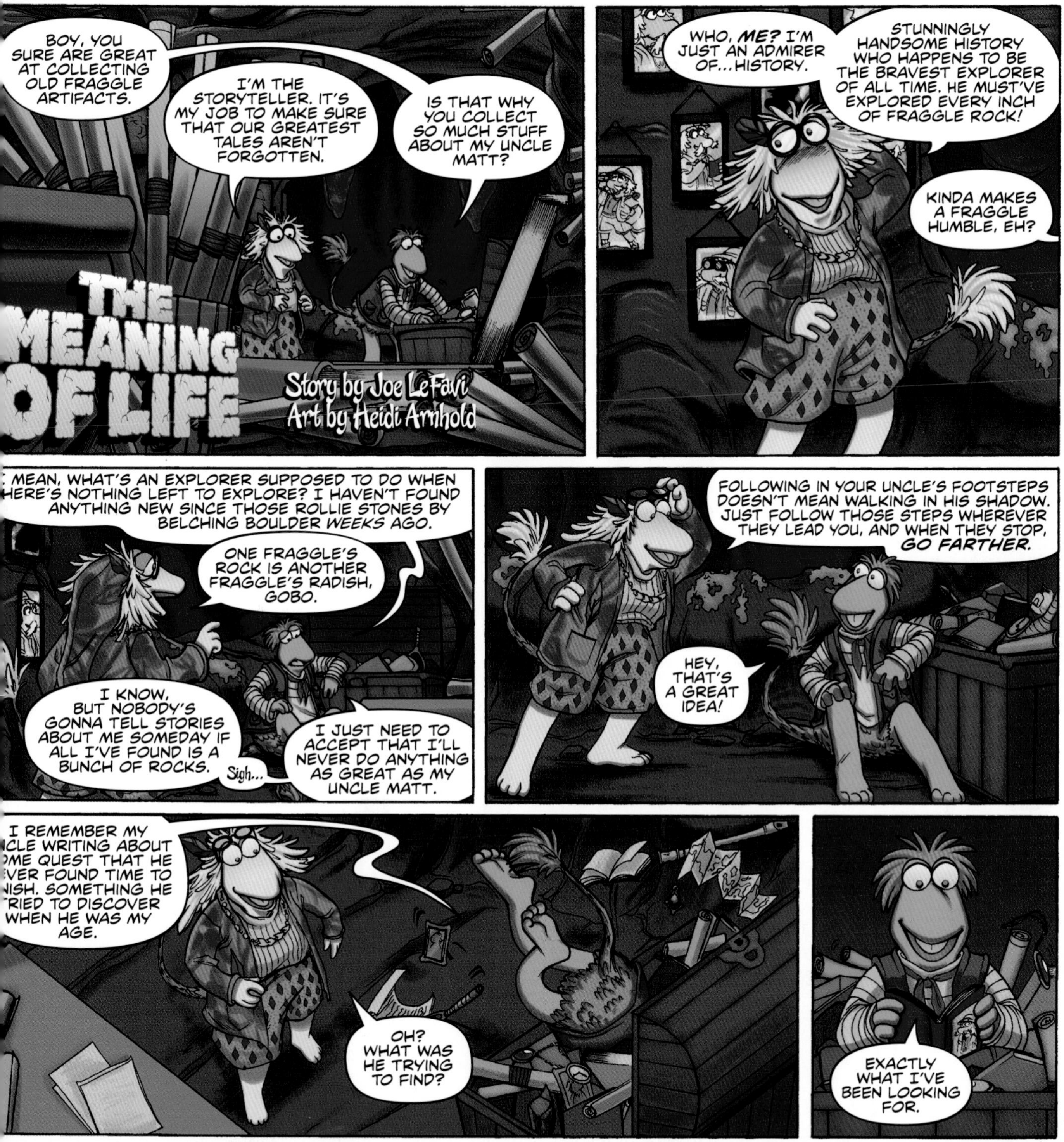
BOY, YOU SURE ARE GREAT AT COLLECTING OLD FRAGGLE ARTIFACTS.
I'M THE STORYTELLER. IT'S MY JOB TO MAKE SURE THAT OUR GREATEST TALES AREN'T FORGOTTEN.
IS THAT WHY YOU COLLECT SO MUCH STUFF ABOUT MY UNCLE MATT?
THE MEANING OF LIFE
Story by Joe LeFavi
Art by Heidi Arnhold
WHO, ME? I'M JUST AN ADMIRER OF... HISTORY.
STUNNINGLY HANDSOME HISTORY WHO HAPPENS TO BE THE BRAVEST EXPLORER OF ALL TIME. HE MUST'VE EXPLORED EVERY INCH OF FRAGGLE ROCK!
KINDA MAKES A FRAGGLE HUMBLE, EH?
MEAN, WHAT'S AN EXPLORER SUPPOSED TO DO WHEN HERE'S NOTHING LEFT TO EXPLORE? I HAVEN'T FOUND ANYTHING NEW SINCE THOSE ROLLIE STONES BY BELCHING BOULDER WEEKS AGO.
ONE FRAGGLE'S ROCK IS ANOTHER FRAGGLE'S RADISH, GOBO.
I KNOW, BUT NOBODY'S GONNA TELL STORIES ABOUT ME SOMEDAY IF ALL I'VE FOUND IS A BUNCH OF ROCKS.
Sigh...
I JUST NEED TO ACCEPT THAT I'LL NEVER DO ANYTHING AS GREAT AS MY UNCLE MATT.
FOLLOWING IN YOUR UNCLE'S FOOTSTEPS DOESN'T MEAN WALKING IN HIS SHADOW. JUST FOLLOW THOSE STEPS WHEREVER THEY LEAD YOU, AND WHEN THEY STOP, GO FARTHER.
HEY, THAT'S A GREAT IDEA!
I REMEMBER MY CLE WRITING ABOUT ME QUEST THAT HE VER FOUND TIME TO NISH. SOMETHING HE TRIED TO DISCOVER WHEN HE WAS MY AGE.
OH? WHAT WAS HE TRYING TO FIND?
EXACTLY WHAT I'VE BEEN LOOKING FOR.

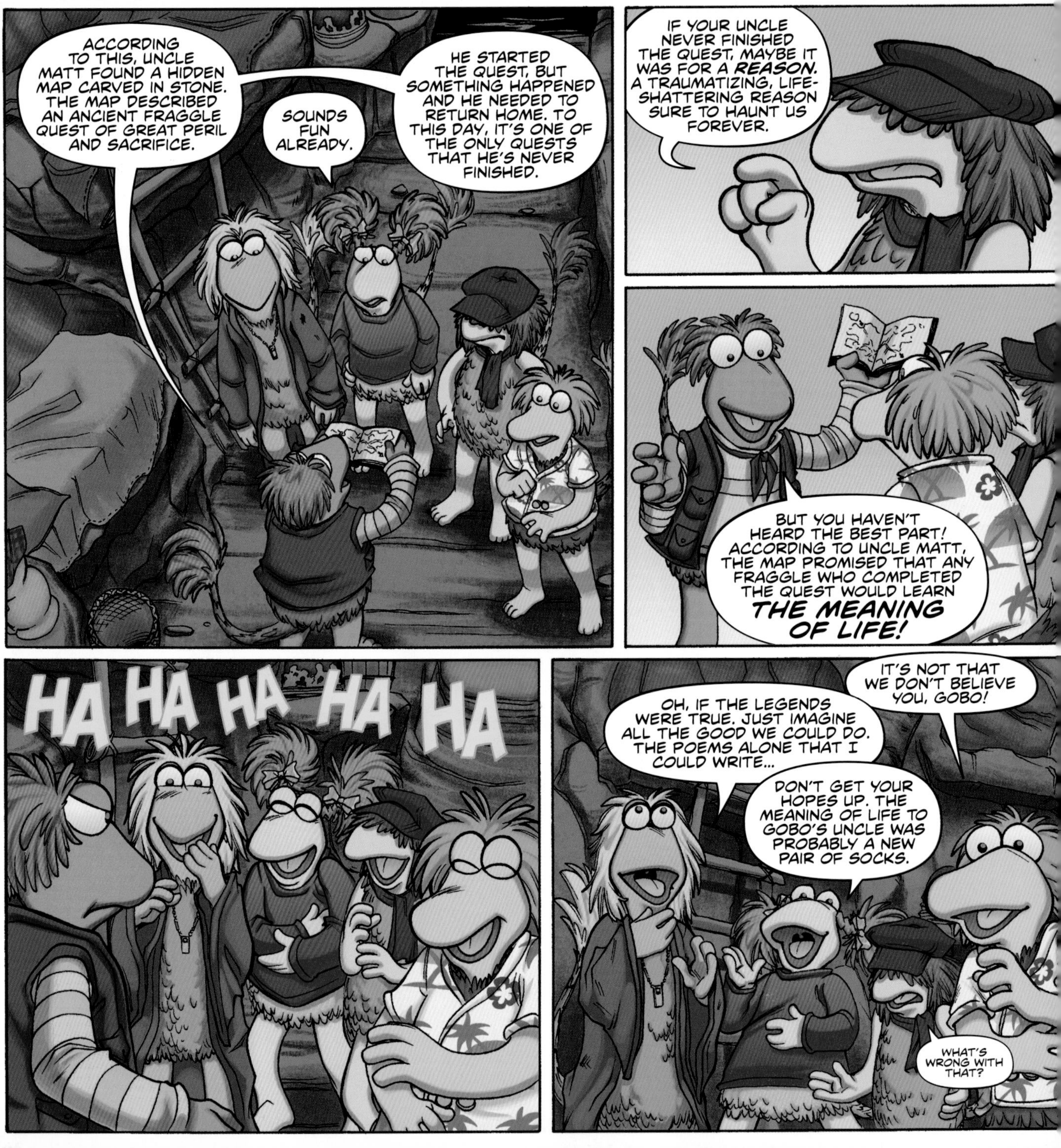
ACCORDING TO THIS, UNCLE MATT FOUND A HIDDEN MAP CARVED IN STONE. THE MAP DESCRIBED AN ANCIENT FRAGGLE QUEST OF GREAT PERIL AND SACRIFICE.
HE STARTED THE QUEST, BUT SOMETHING HAPPENED AND HE NEEDED TO RETURN HOME. TO THIS DAY, IT'S ONE OF THE ONLY QUESTS THAT HE'S NEVER FINISHED.
SOUNDS FUN ALREADY.
IF YOUR UNCLE NEVER FINISHED THE QUEST, MAYBE IT WAS FOR A *REASON.* A TRAUMATIZING, LIFE-SHATTERING REASON SURE TO HAUNT US FOREVER.
BUT YOU HAVEN'T HEARD THE BEST PART! ACCORDING TO UNCLE MATT, THE MAP PROMISED THAT ANY FRAGGLE WHO COMPLETED THE QUEST WOULD LEARN ***THE MEANING OF LIFE!***
HA HA HA HA HA
IT'S NOT THAT WE DON'T BELIEVE YOU, GOBO!
OH, IF THE LEGENDS WERE TRUE. JUST IMAGINE ALL THE GOOD WE COULD DO. THE POEMS ALONE THAT I COULD WRITE...
DON'T GET YOUR HOPES UP. THE MEANING OF LIFE TO GOBO'S UNCLE WAS PROBABLY A NEW PAIR OF SOCKS.
WHAT'S WRONG WITH THAT?

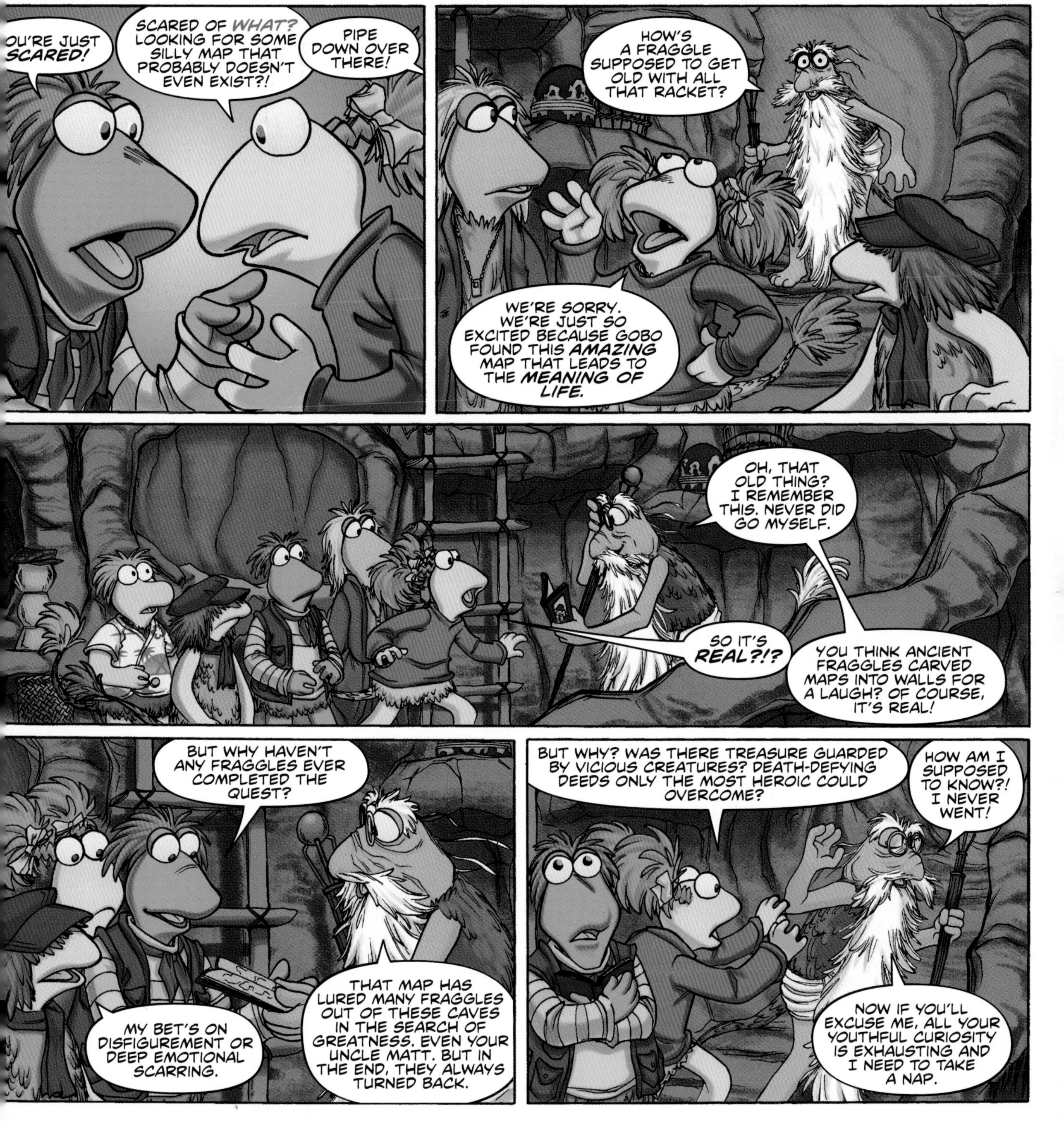
OU'RE JUST SCARED!
SCARED OF WHAT? LOOKING FOR SOME SILLY MAP THAT PROBABLY DOESN'T EVEN EXIST?!
PIPE DOWN OVER THERE!
HOW'S A FRAGGLE SUPPOSED TO GET OLD WITH ALL THAT RACKET?
WE'RE SORRY. WE'RE JUST SO EXCITED BECAUSE GOBO FOUND THIS AMAZING MAP THAT LEADS TO THE MEANING OF LIFE.
OH, THAT OLD THING? I REMEMBER THIS. NEVER DID GO MYSELF.
SO IT'S REAL?!?
YOU THINK ANCIENT FRAGGLES CARVED MAPS INTO WALLS FOR A LAUGH? OF COURSE, IT'S REAL!
BUT WHY HAVEN'T ANY FRAGGLES EVER COMPLETED THE QUEST?
THAT MAP HAS LURED MANY FRAGGLES OUT OF THESE CAVES IN THE SEARCH OF GREATNESS. EVEN YOUR UNCLE MATT. BUT IN THE END, THEY ALWAYS TURNED BACK.
MY BET'S ON DISFIGUREMENT OR DEEP EMOTIONAL SCARRING.
BUT WHY? WAS THERE TREASURE GUARDED BY VICIOUS CREATURES? DEATH-DEFYING DEEDS ONLY THE MOST HEROIC COULD OVERCOME?
HOW AM I SUPPOSED TO KNOW?! I NEVER WENT!
NOW IF YOU'LL EXCUSE ME, ALL YOUR YOUTHFUL CURIOSITY IS EXHAUSTING AND I NEED TO TAKE A NAP.

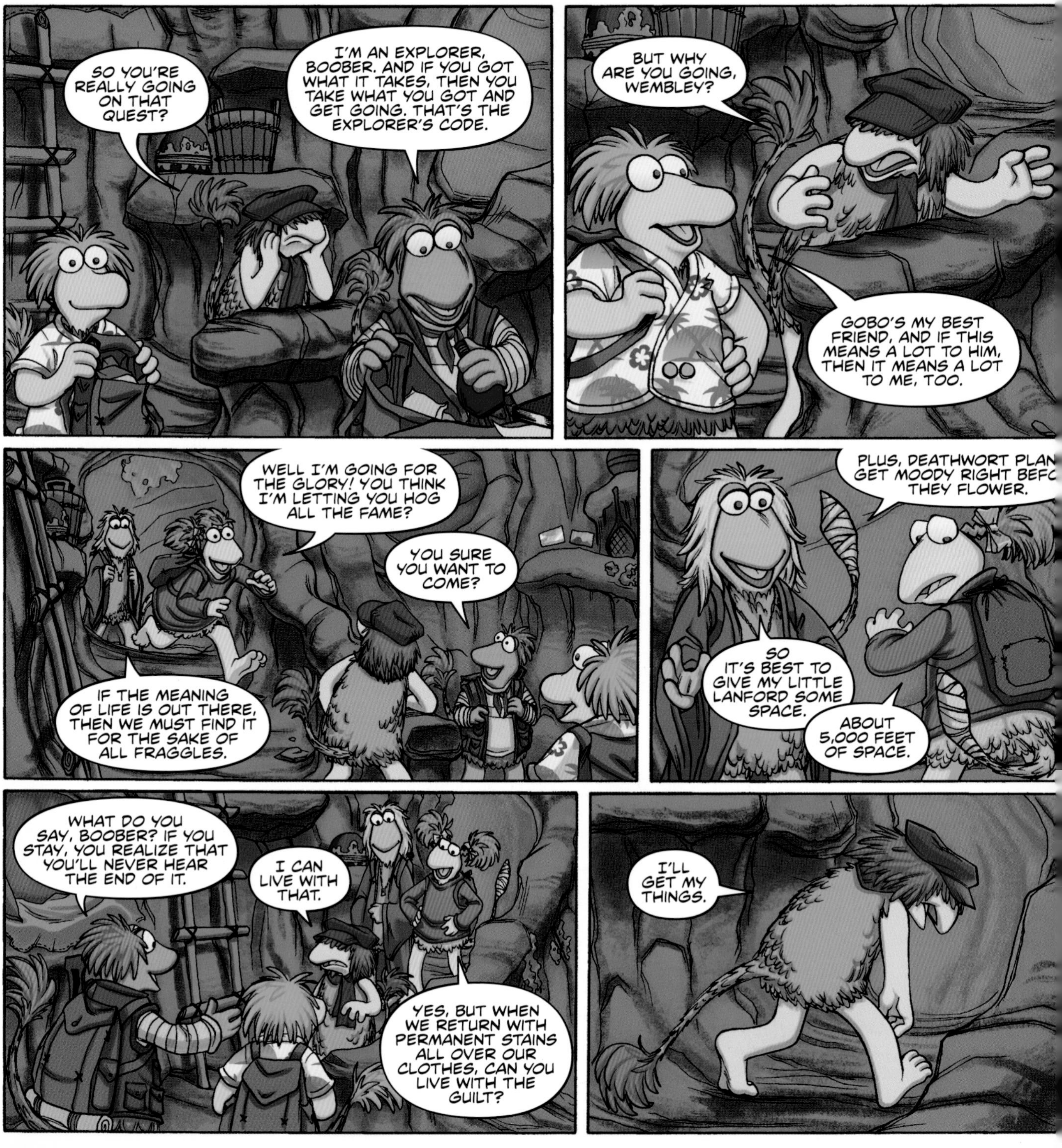
SO YOU'RE REALLY GOING ON THAT QUEST?
I'M AN EXPLORER, BOOBER. AND IF YOU GOT WHAT IT TAKES, THEN YOU TAKE WHAT YOU GOT AND GET GOING. THAT'S THE EXPLORER'S CODE.
BUT WHY ARE YOU GOING, WEMBLEY?
GOBO'S MY BEST FRIEND, AND IF THIS MEANS A LOT TO HIM, THEN IT MEANS A LOT TO ME, TOO.
WELL I'M GOING FOR THE GLORY! YOU THINK I'M LETTING YOU HOG ALL THE FAME?
IF THE MEANING OF LIFE IS OUT THERE, THEN WE MUST FIND IT FOR THE SAKE OF ALL FRAGGLES.
YOU SURE YOU WANT TO COME?
PLUS, DEATHWORT PLAN GET MOODY RIGHT BEFO THEY FLOWER.
SO IT'S BEST TO GIVE MY LITTLE LANFORD SOME SPACE.
ABOUT 5,000 FEET OF SPACE.
WHAT DO YOU SAY, BOOBER? IF YOU STAY, YOU REALIZE THAT YOU'LL NEVER HEAR THE END OF IT.
I CAN LIVE WITH THAT.
YES, BUT WHEN WE RETURN WITH PERMANENT STAINS ALL OVER OUR CLOTHES, CAN YOU LIVE WITH THE GUILT?
I'LL GET MY THINGS.

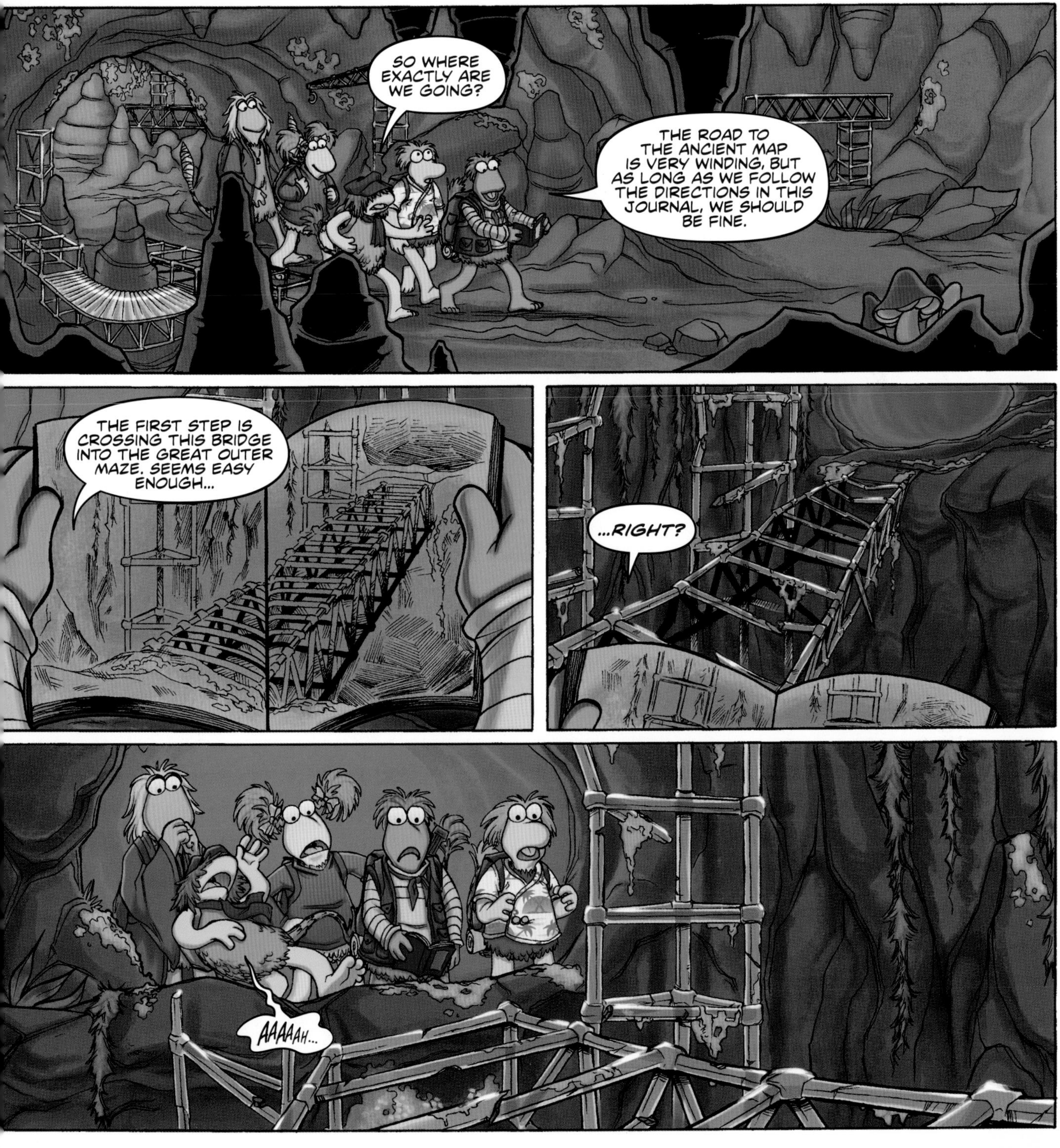
SO WHERE EXACTLY ARE WE GOING?
THE ROAD TO THE ANCIENT MAP IS VERY WINDING, BUT AS LONG AS WE FOLLOW THE DIRECTIONS IN THIS JOURNAL, WE SHOULD BE FINE.
THE FIRST STEP IS CROSSING THIS BRIDGE INTO THE GREAT OUTER MAZE. SEEMS EASY ENOUGH...
...RIGHT?
AAAAAH...

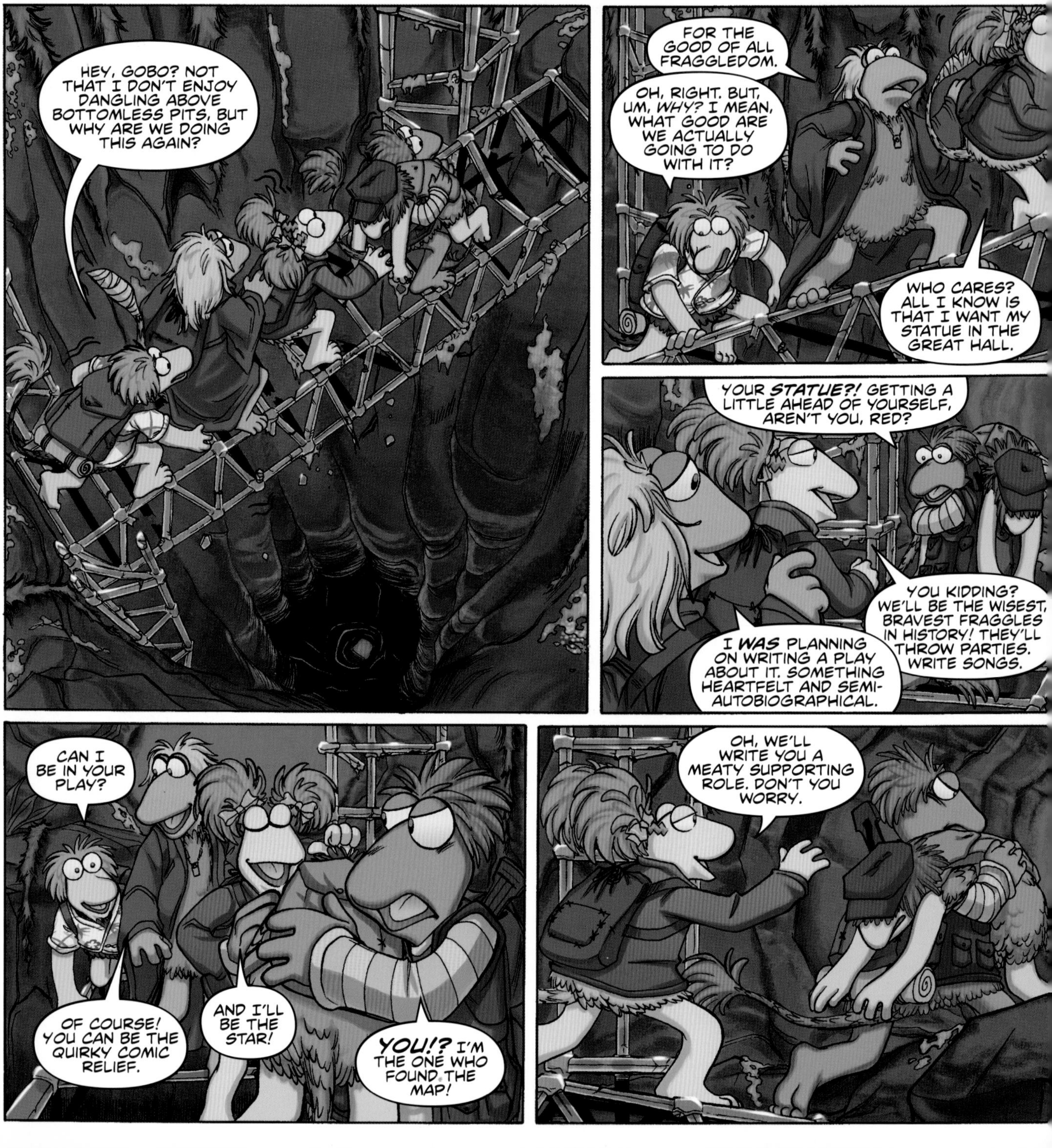
HEY, GOBO? NOT THAT I DON'T ENJOY DANGLING ABOVE BOTTOMLESS PITS, BUT WHY ARE WE DOING THIS AGAIN?
FOR THE GOOD OF ALL FRAGGLEDOM.
OH, RIGHT. BUT, UM, WHY? I MEAN, WHAT GOOD ARE WE ACTUALLY GOING TO DO WITH IT?
WHO CARES? ALL I KNOW IS THAT I WANT MY STATUE IN THE GREAT HALL.
YOUR STATUE?! GETTING A LITTLE AHEAD OF YOURSELF, AREN'T YOU, RED?
YOU KIDDING? WE'LL BE THE WISEST, BRAVEST FRAGGLES IN HISTORY! THEY'LL THROW PARTIES. WRITE SONGS.
I WAS PLANNING ON WRITING A PLAY ABOUT IT. SOMETHING HEARTFELT AND SEMI-AUTOBIOGRAPHICAL.
CAN I BE IN YOUR PLAY?
OF COURSE! YOU CAN BE THE QUIRKY COMIC RELIEF.
AND I'LL BE THE STAR!
YOU!? I'M THE ONE WHO FOUND THE MAP!
OH, WE'LL WRITE YOU A MEATY SUPPORTING ROLE. DON'T YOU WORRY.

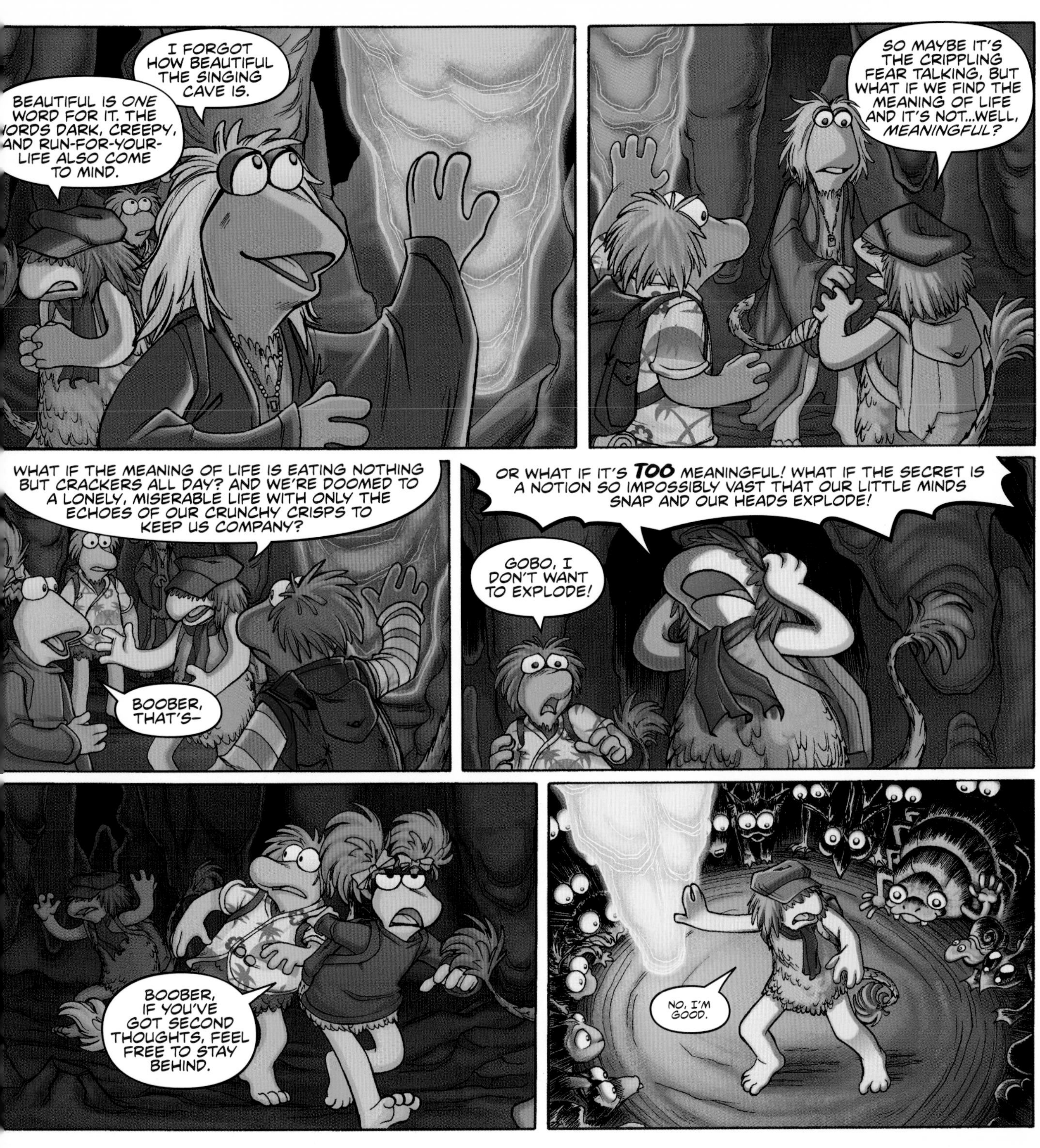

I FORGOT HOW BEAUTIFUL THE SINGING CAVE IS.
BEAUTIFUL IS ONE WORD FOR IT. THE WORDS DARK, CREEPY, AND RUN-FOR-YOUR-LIFE ALSO COME TO MIND.
SO MAYBE IT'S THE CRIPPLING FEAR TALKING, BUT WHAT IF WE FIND THE MEANING OF LIFE AND IT'S NOT...WELL, MEANINGFUL?
WHAT IF THE MEANING OF LIFE IS EATING NOTHING BUT CRACKERS ALL DAY? AND WE'RE DOOMED TO A LONELY, MISERABLE LIFE WITH ONLY THE ECHOES OF OUR CRUNCHY CRISPS TO KEEP US COMPANY?
BOOBER, THAT'S–
OR WHAT IF IT'S TOO MEANINGFUL! WHAT IF THE SECRET IS A NOTION SO IMPOSSIBLY VAST THAT OUR LITTLE MINDS SNAP AND OUR HEADS EXPLODE!
GOBO, I DON'T WANT TO EXPLODE!
BOOBER, IF YOU'VE GOT SECOND THOUGHTS, FEEL FREE TO STAY BEHIND.
NO, I'M GOOD.

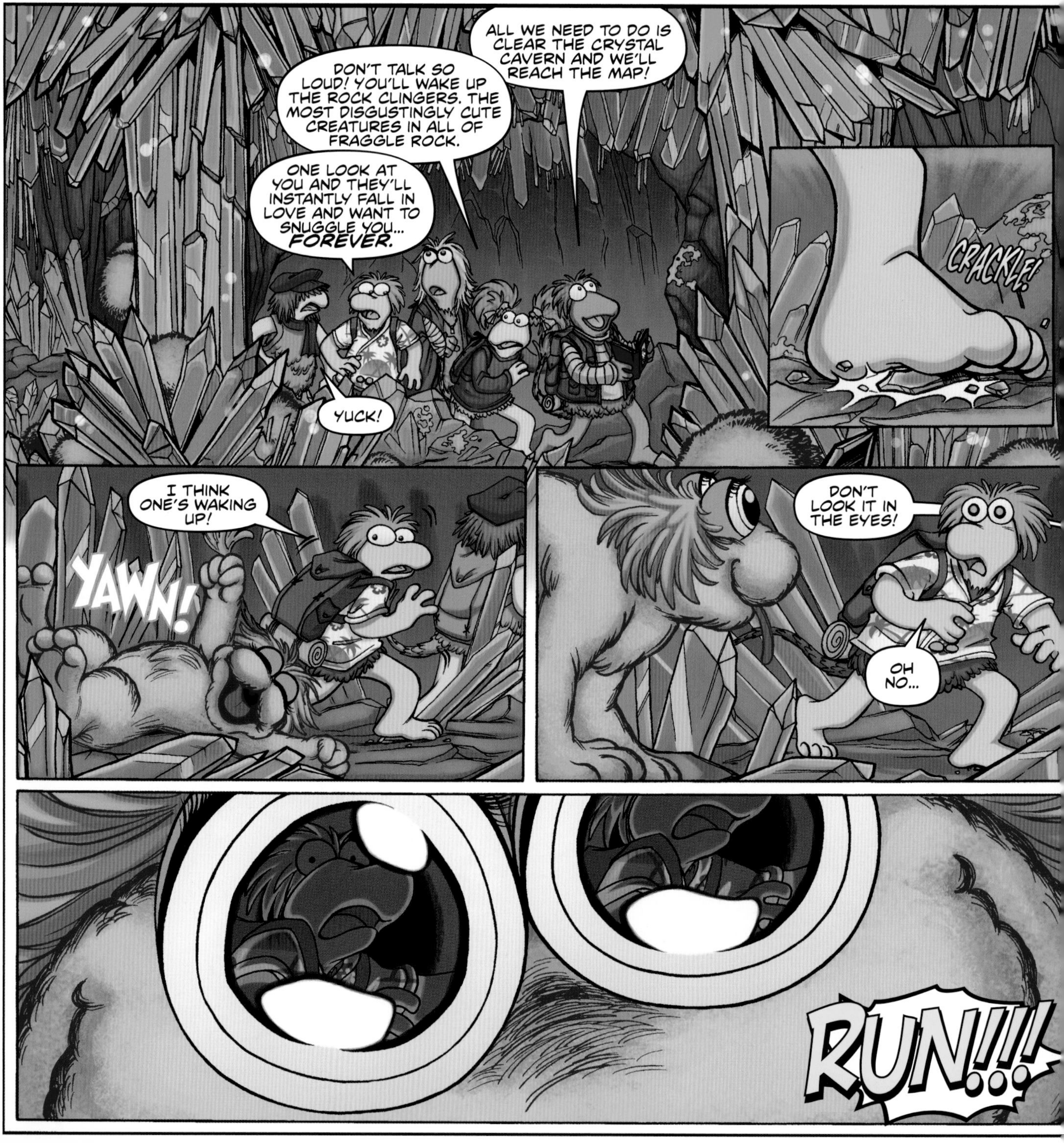
ALL WE NEED TO DO IS CLEAR THE CRYSTAL CAVERN AND WE'LL REACH THE MAP!
DON'T TALK SO LOUD! YOU'LL WAKE UP THE ROCK CLINGERS. THE MOST DISGUSTINGLY CUTE CREATURES IN ALL OF FRAGGLE ROCK.
ONE LOOK AT YOU AND THEY'LL INSTANTLY FALL IN LOVE AND WANT TO SNUGGLE YOU... FOREVER.
YUCK!
CRACKLE!
I THINK ONE'S WAKING UP!
YAWN!
DON'T LOOK IT IN THE EYES!
OH NO...
RUN!!!!

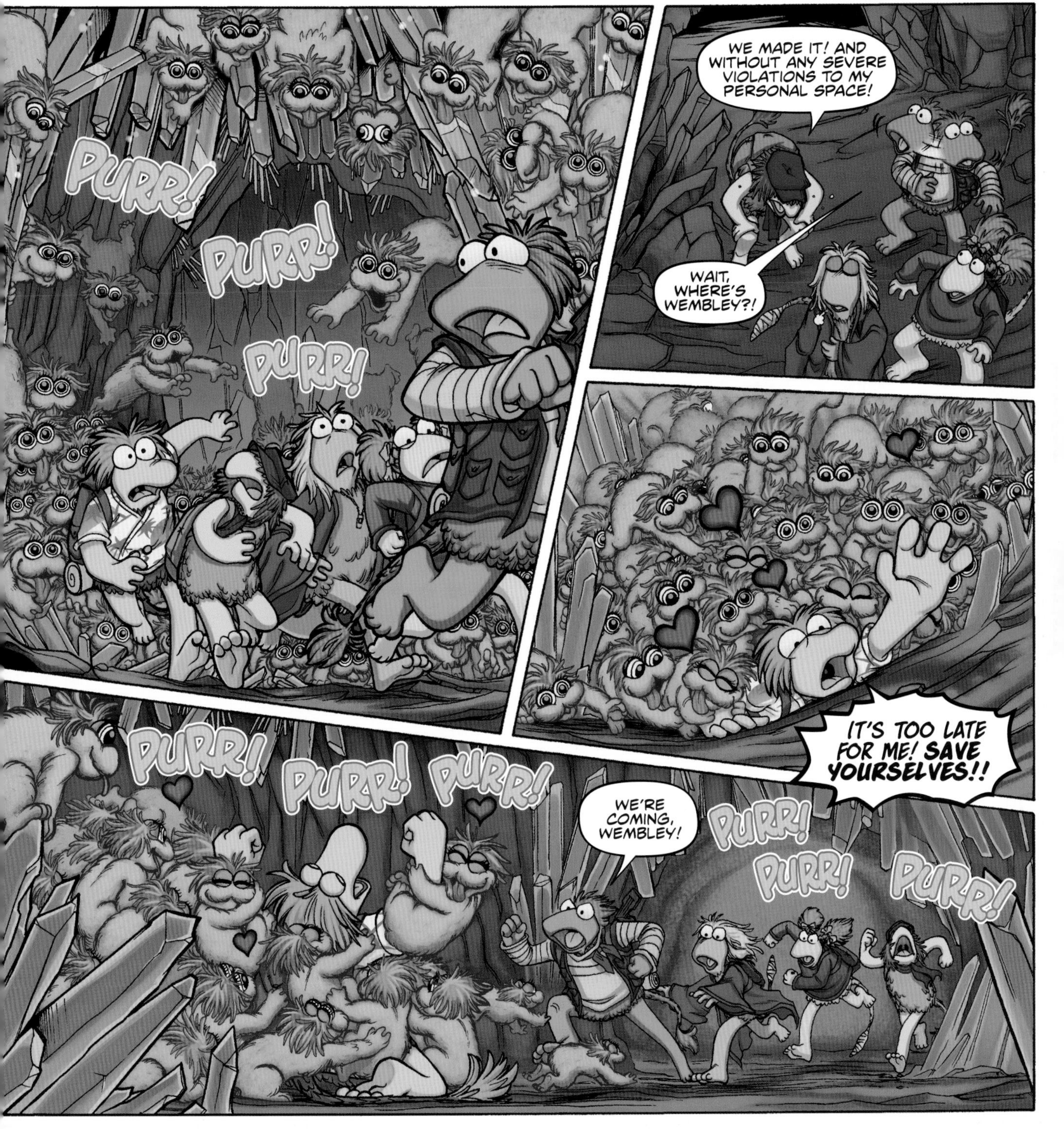
PURR!
PURR!
PURR!
WE MADE IT! AND WITHOUT ANY SEVERE VIOLATIONS TO MY PERSONAL SPACE!
WAIT, WHERE'S WEMBLEY?!
IT'S TOO LATE FOR ME! SAVE YOURSELVES!!
PURR!
PURR!
PURR!
WE'RE COMING, WEMBLEY!
PURR!
PURR!
PURR!

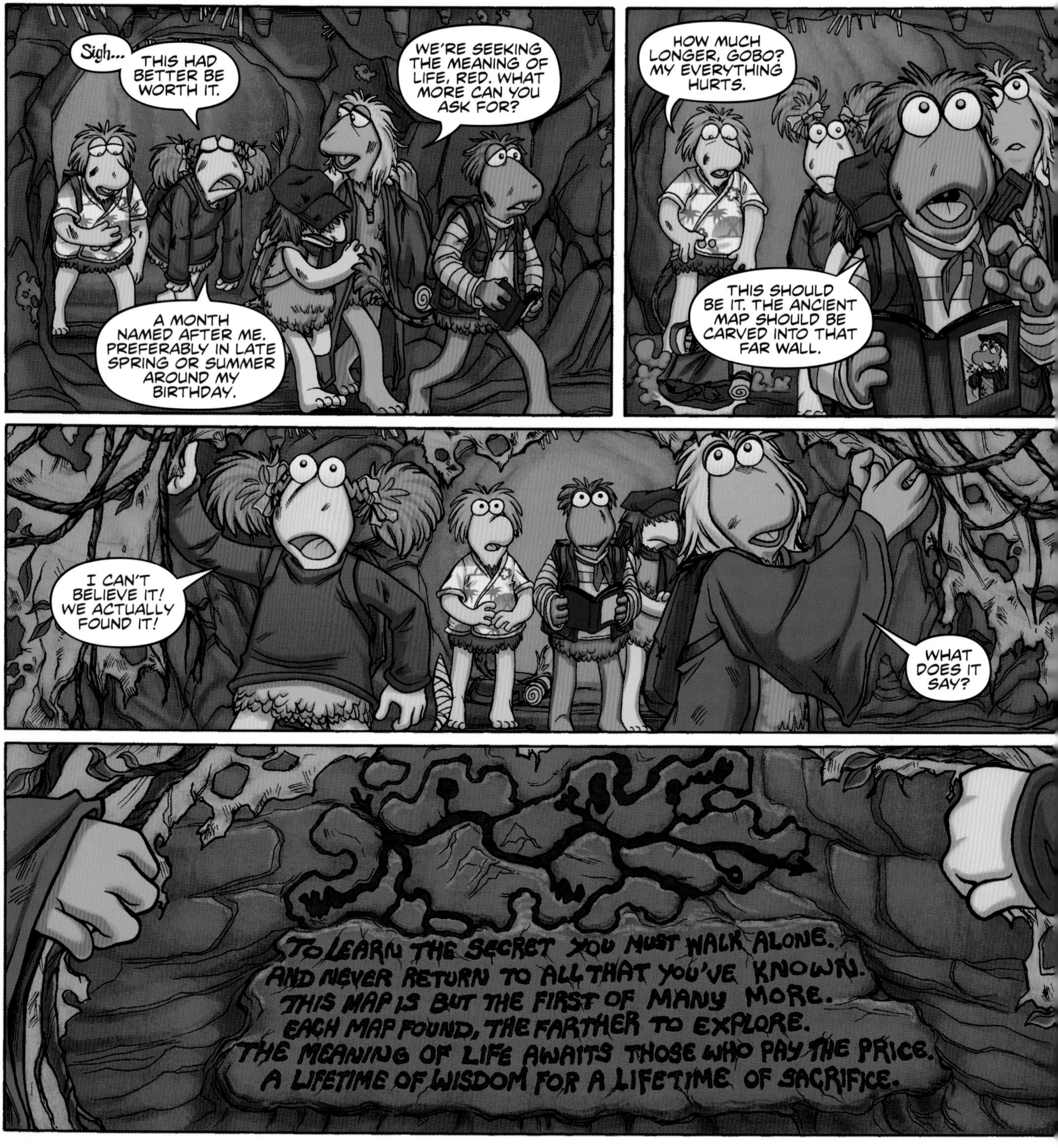
Sigh...
THIS HAD BETTER BE WORTH IT.
WE'RE SEEKING THE MEANING OF LIFE, RED. WHAT MORE CAN YOU ASK FOR?
A MONTH NAMED AFTER ME. PREFERABLY IN LATE SPRING OR SUMMER AROUND MY BIRTHDAY.
HOW MUCH LONGER, GOBO? MY EVERYTHING HURTS.
THIS SHOULD BE IT. THE ANCIENT MAP SHOULD BE CARVED INTO THAT FAR WALL.
I CAN'T BELIEVE IT! WE ACTUALLY FOUND IT!
WHAT DOES IT SAY?
TO LEARN THE SECRET YOU MUST WALK ALONE.
AND NEVER RETURN TO ALL THAT YOU'VE KNOWN.
THIS MAP IS BUT THE FIRST OF MANY MORE.
EACH MAP FOUND, THE FARTHER TO EXPLORE.
THE MEANING OF LIFE AWAITS THOSE WHO PAY THE PRICE.
A LIFETIME OF WISDOM FOR A LIFETIME OF SACRIFICE.

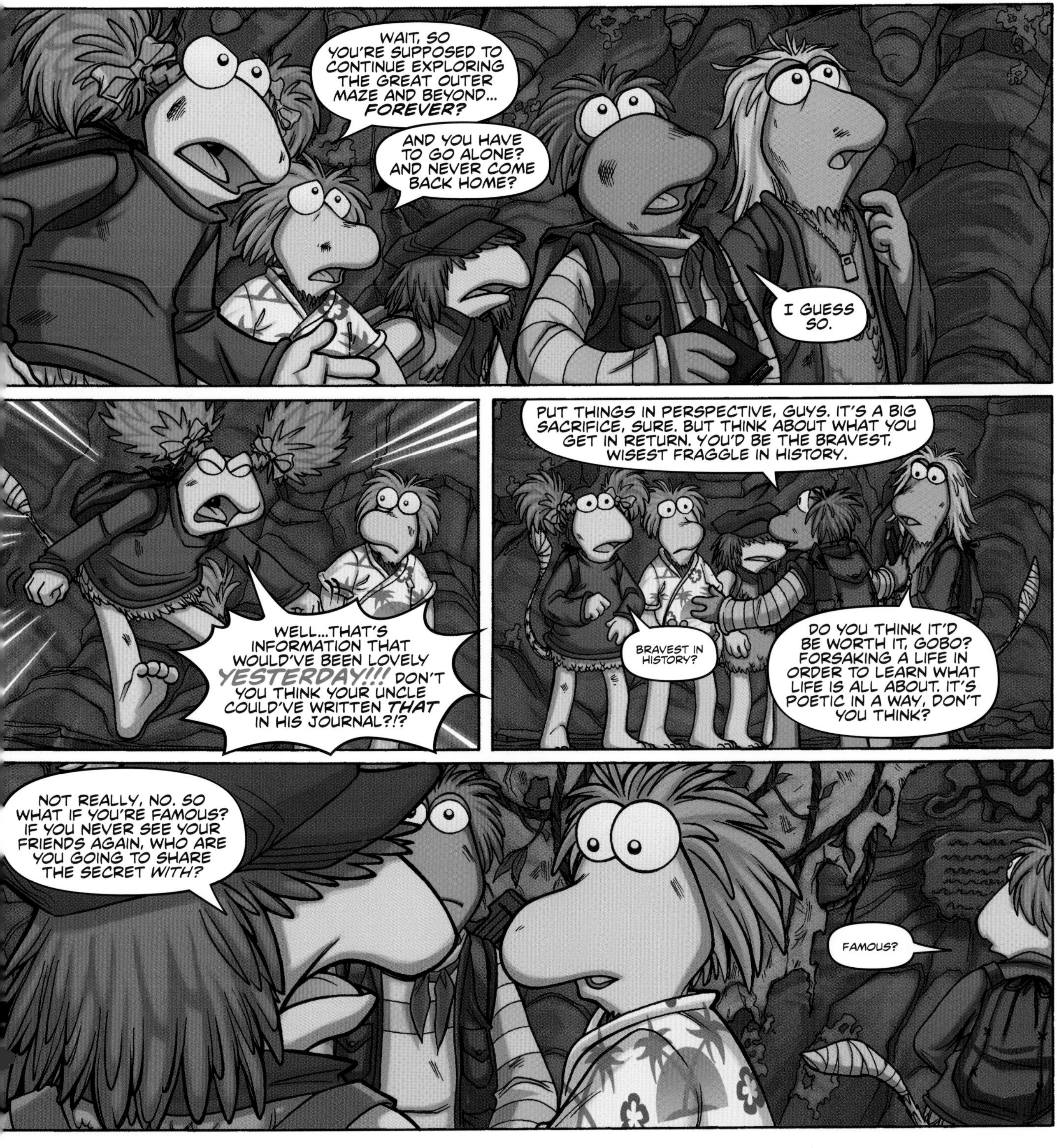

WAIT, SO YOU'RE SUPPOSED TO CONTINUE EXPLORING THE GREAT OUTER MAZE AND BEYOND... FOREVER?
AND YOU HAVE TO GO ALONE? AND NEVER COME BACK HOME?
I GUESS SO.
WELL...THAT'S INFORMATION THAT WOULD'VE BEEN LOVELY YESTERDAY!!! DON'T YOU THINK YOUR UNCLE COULD'VE WRITTEN THAT IN HIS JOURNAL?!?
PUT THINGS IN PERSPECTIVE, GUYS. IT'S A BIG SACRIFICE, SURE. BUT THINK ABOUT WHAT YOU GET IN RETURN. YOU'D BE THE BRAVEST, WISEST FRAGGLE IN HISTORY.
BRAVEST IN HISTORY?
DO YOU THINK IT'D BE WORTH IT, GOBO? FORSAKING A LIFE IN ORDER TO LEARN WHAT LIFE IS ALL ABOUT. IT'S POETIC IN A WAY, DON'T YOU THINK?
NOT REALLY, NO. SO WHAT IF YOU'RE FAMOUS? IF YOU NEVER SEE YOUR FRIENDS AGAIN, WHO ARE YOU GOING TO SHARE THE SECRET WITH?
FAMOUS?

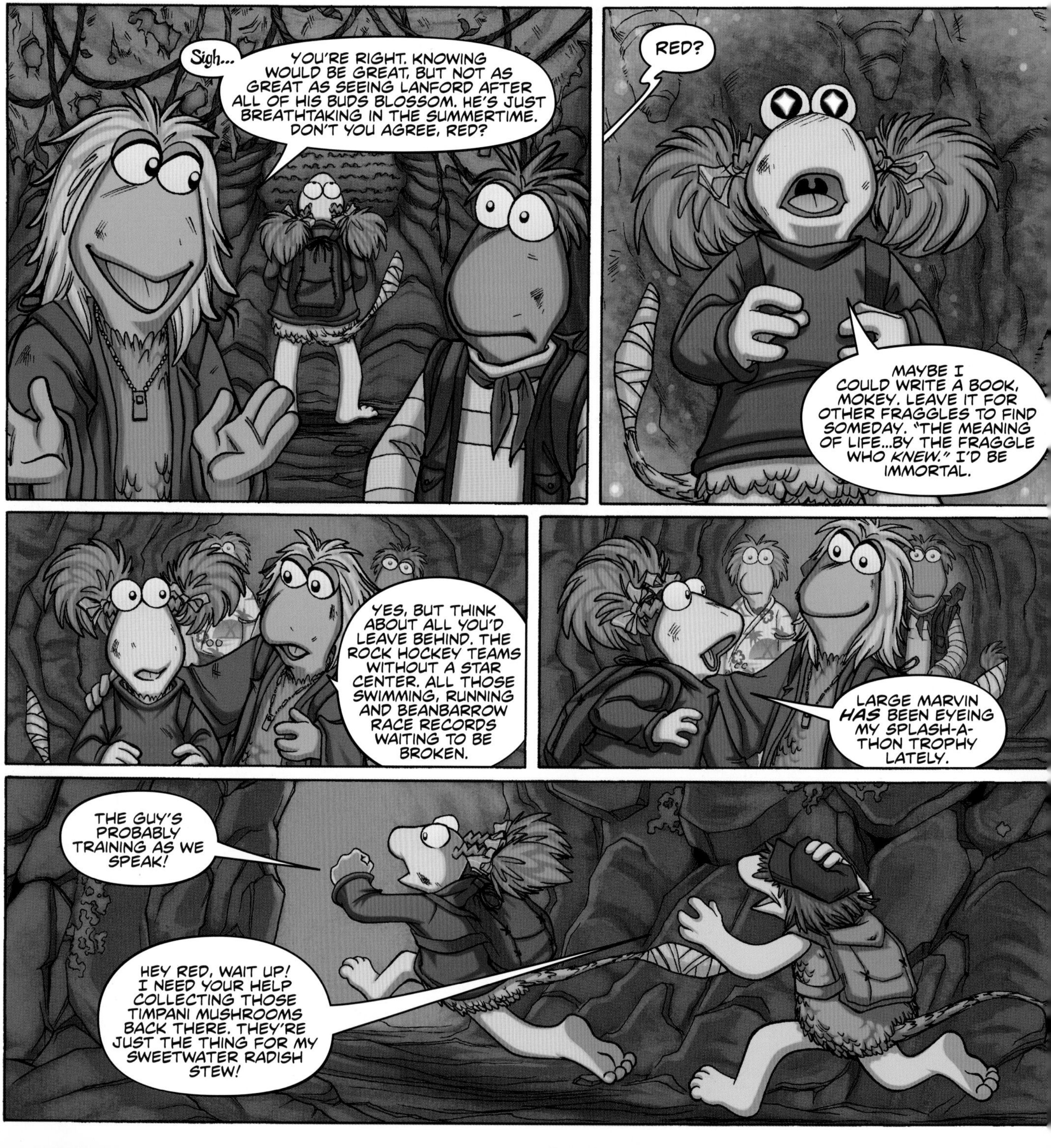
Sigh...
YOU'RE RIGHT. KNOWING WOULD BE GREAT, BUT NOT AS GREAT AS SEEING LANFORD AFTER ALL OF HIS BUDS BLOSSOM. HE'S JUST BREATHTAKING IN THE SUMMERTIME. DON'T YOU AGREE, RED?
RED?
MAYBE I COULD WRITE A BOOK, MOKEY. LEAVE IT FOR OTHER FRAGGLES TO FIND SOMEDAY. "THE MEANING OF LIFE...BY THE FRAGGLE WHO KNEW." I'D BE IMMORTAL.
YES, BUT THINK ABOUT ALL YOU'D LEAVE BEHIND. THE ROCK HOCKEY TEAMS WITHOUT A STAR CENTER. ALL THOSE SWIMMING, RUNNING AND BEANBARROW RACE RECORDS WAITING TO BE BROKEN.
LARGE MARVIN HAS BEEN EYEING MY SPLASH-A-THON TROPHY LATELY.
THE GUY'S PROBABLY TRAINING AS WE SPEAK!
HEY RED, WAIT UP! I NEED YOUR HELP COLLECTING THOSE TIMPANI MUSHROOMS BACK THERE. THEY'RE JUST THE THING FOR MY SWEETWATER RADISH STEW!

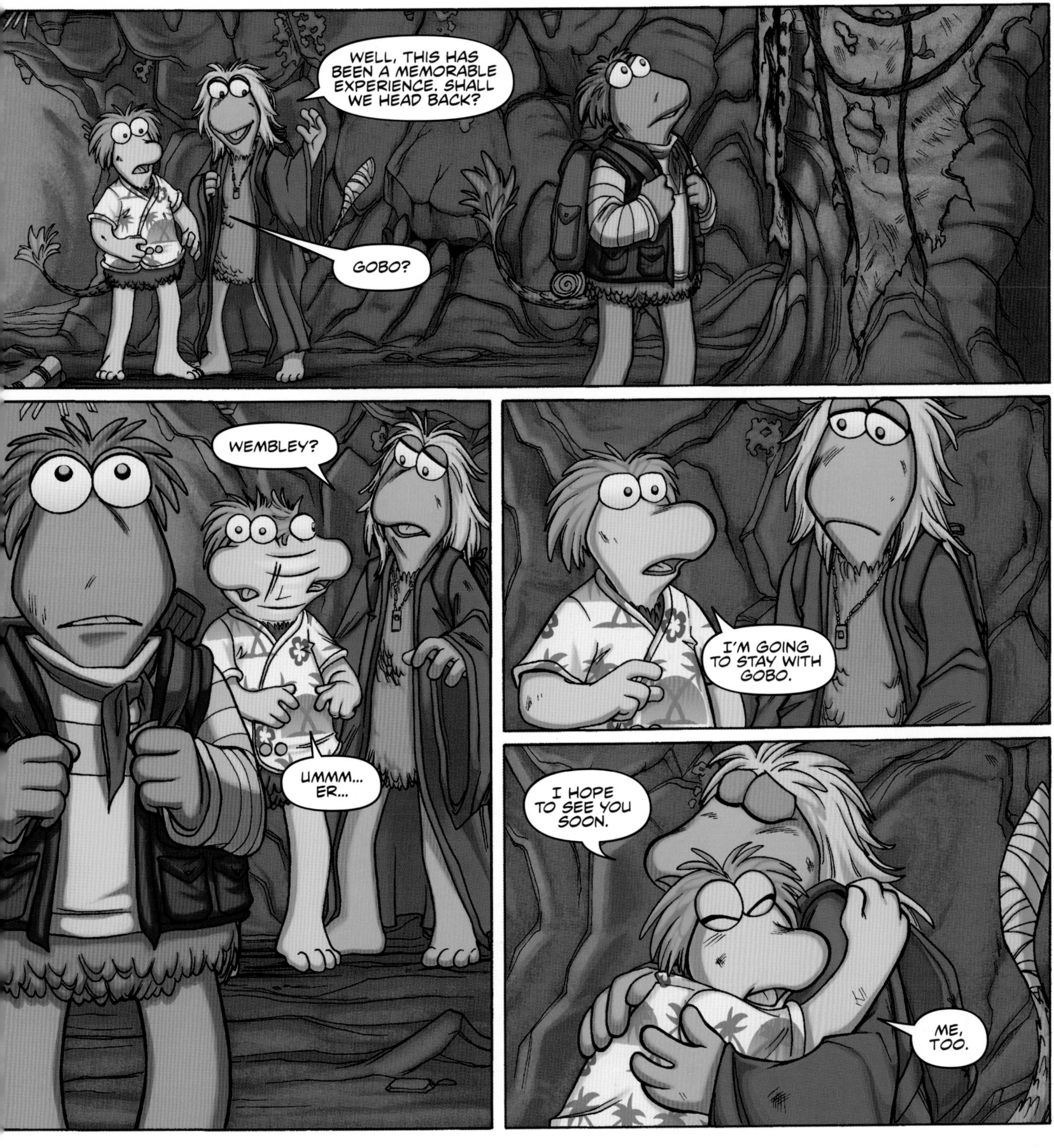
WELL, THIS HAS BEEN A MEMORABLE EXPERIENCE. SHALL WE HEAD BACK?
GOBO?
WEMBLEY?
UMMM... ER...
I'M GOING TO STAY WITH GOBO.
I HOPE TO SEE YOU SOON.
ME, TOO.

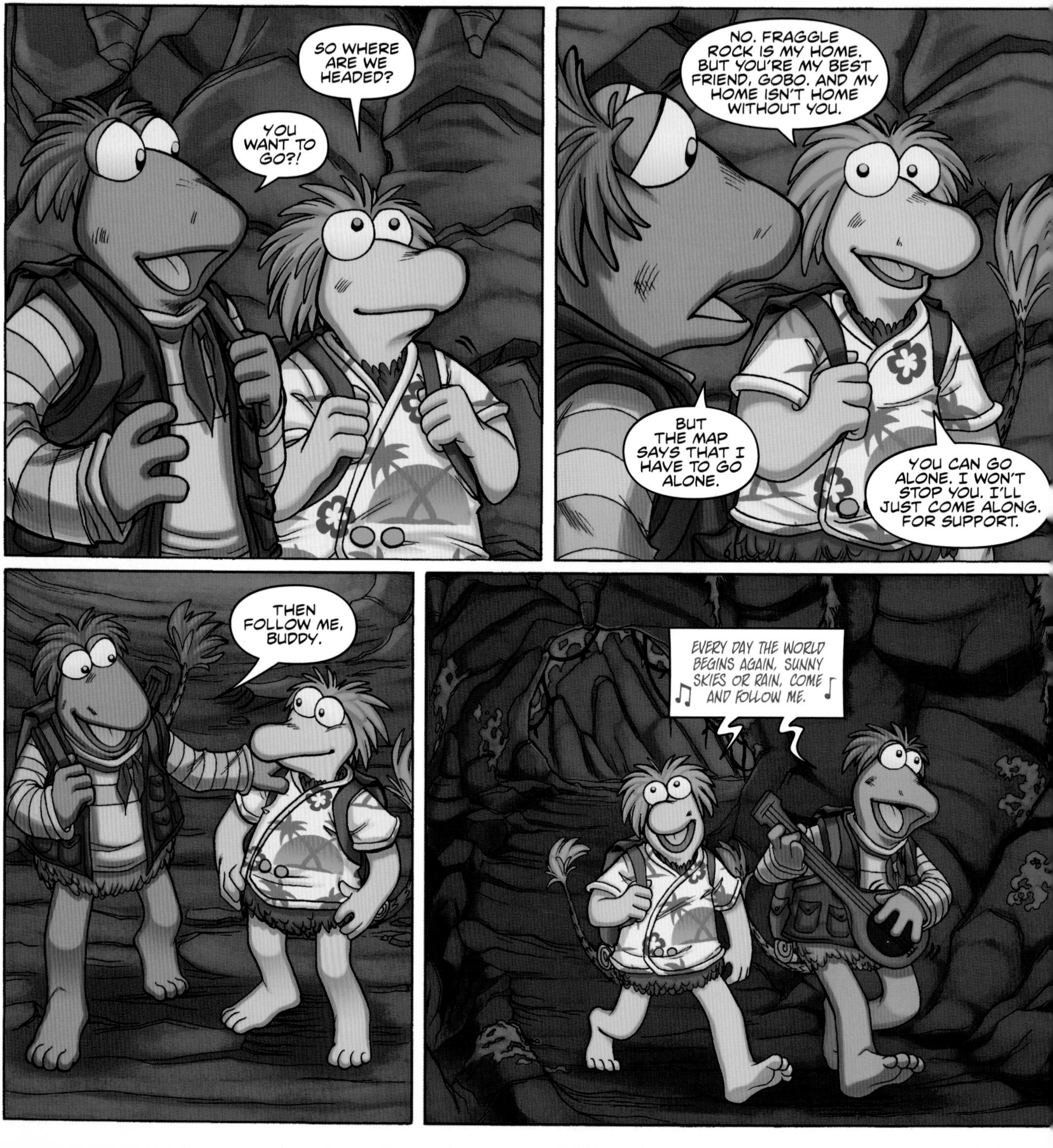
SO WHERE ARE WE HEADED?
YOU WANT TO GO?!
NO. FRAGGLE ROCK IS MY HOME. BUT YOU'RE MY BEST FRIEND, GOBO. AND MY HOME ISN'T HOME WITHOUT YOU.
BUT THE MAP SAYS THAT I HAVE TO GO ALONE.
YOU CAN GO ALONE. I WON'T STOP YOU. I'LL JUST COME ALONG. FOR SUPPORT.
THEN FOLLOW ME, BUDDY.
♫ EVERY DAY THE WORLD BEGINS AGAIN, SUNNY SKIES OR RAIN, COME AND FOLLOW ME. ♪

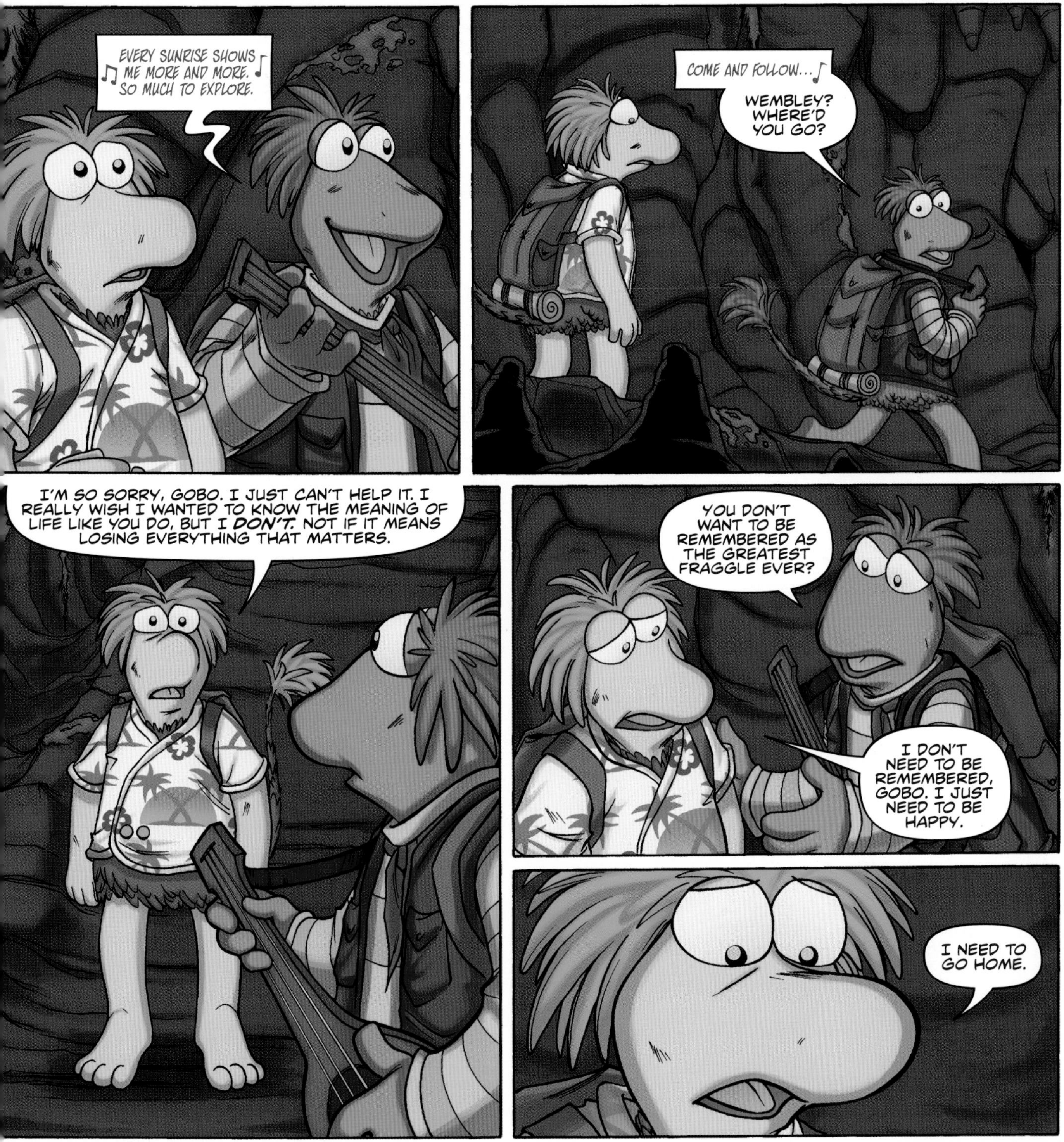
EVERY SUNRISE SHOWS ME MORE AND MORE. SO MUCH TO EXPLORE.
COME AND FOLLOW...
WEMBLEY? WHERE'D YOU GO?
I'M SO SORRY, GOBO. I JUST CAN'T HELP IT. I REALLY WISH I WANTED TO KNOW THE MEANING OF LIFE LIKE YOU DO, BUT I DON'T. NOT IF IT MEANS LOSING EVERYTHING THAT MATTERS.
YOU DON'T WANT TO BE REMEMBERED AS THE GREATEST FRAGGLE EVER?
I DON'T NEED TO BE REMEMBERED, GOBO. I JUST NEED TO BE HAPPY.
I NEED TO GO HOME.

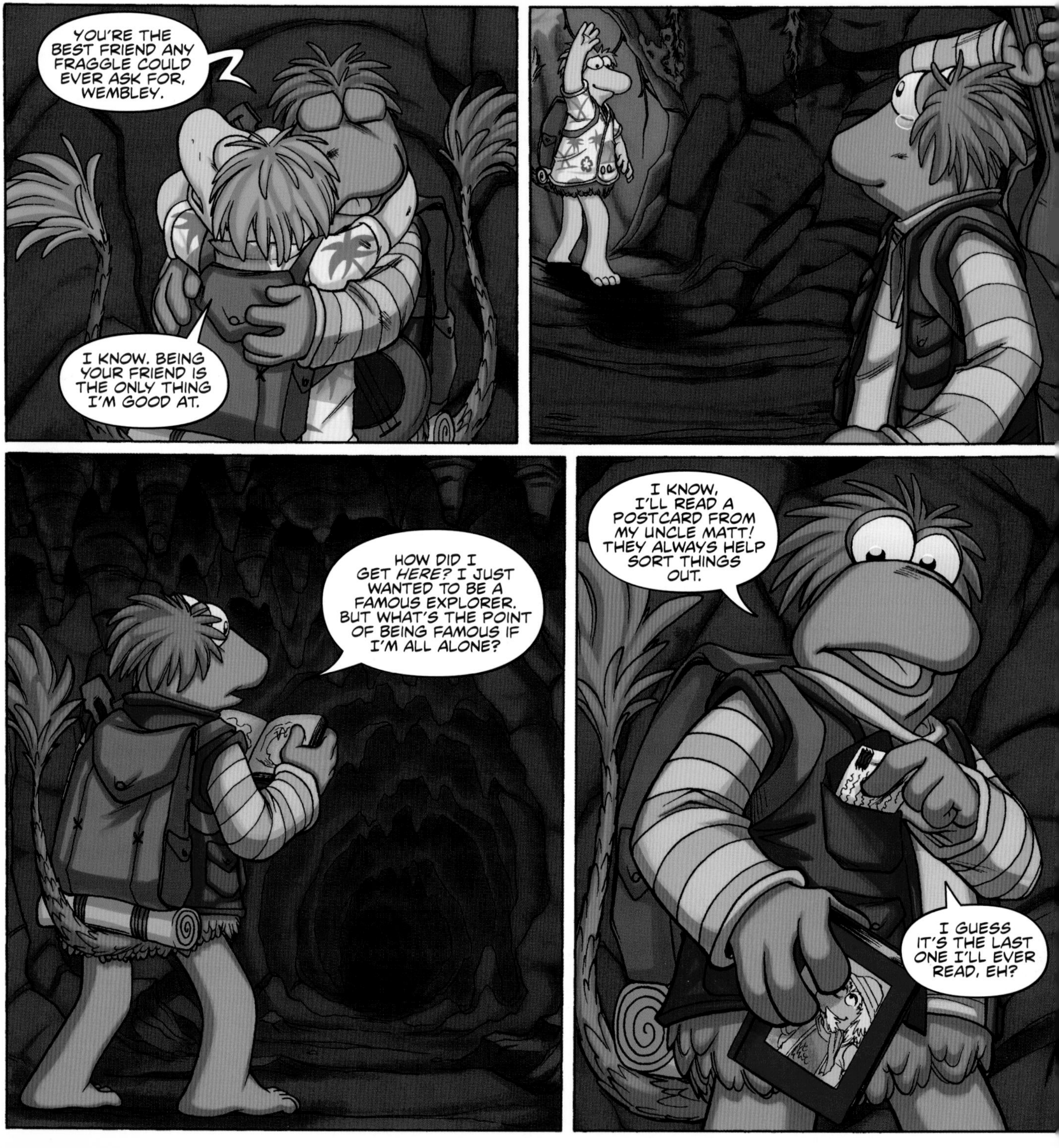
YOU'RE THE BEST FRIEND ANY FRAGGLE COULD EVER ASK FOR, WEMBLEY.
I KNOW. BEING YOUR FRIEND IS THE ONLY THING I'M GOOD AT.
HOW DID I GET *HERE?* I JUST WANTED TO BE A FAMOUS EXPLORER. BUT WHAT'S THE POINT OF BEING FAMOUS IF I'M ALL ALONE?
I KNOW, I'LL READ A POSTCARD FROM MY UNCLE MATT! THEY ALWAYS HELP SORT THINGS OUT.
I GUESS IT'S THE LAST ONE I'LL EVER READ, EH?

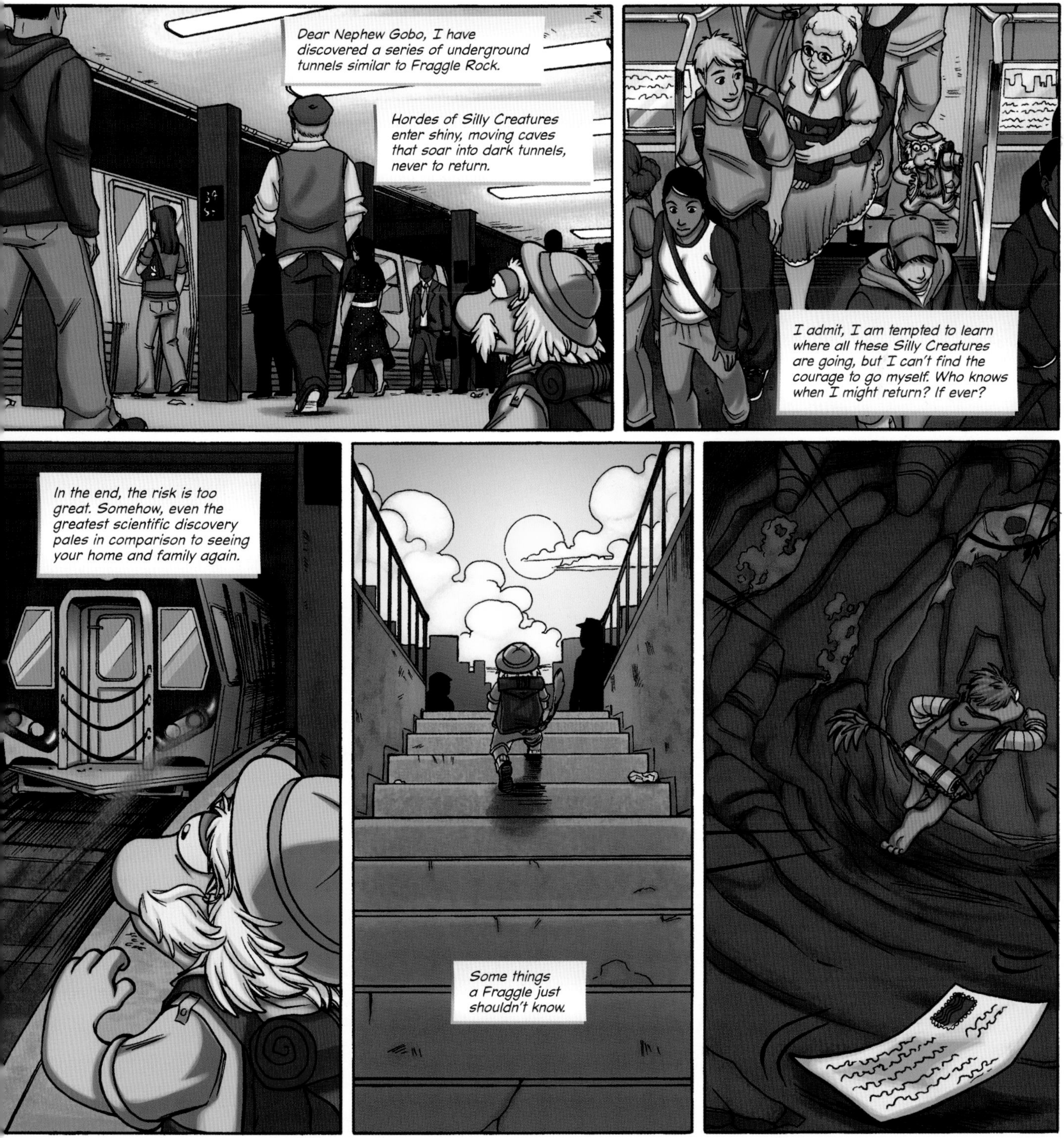
Dear Nephew Gobo, I have discovered a series of underground tunnels similar to Fraggle Rock.
Hordes of Silly Creatures enter shiny, moving caves that soar into dark tunnels, never to return.
I admit, I am tempted to learn where all these Silly Creatures are going, but I can't find the courage to go myself. Who knows when I might return? If ever?
In the end, the risk is too great. Somehow, even the greatest scientific discovery pales in comparison to seeing your home and family again.
Some things a Fraggle just shouldn't know.

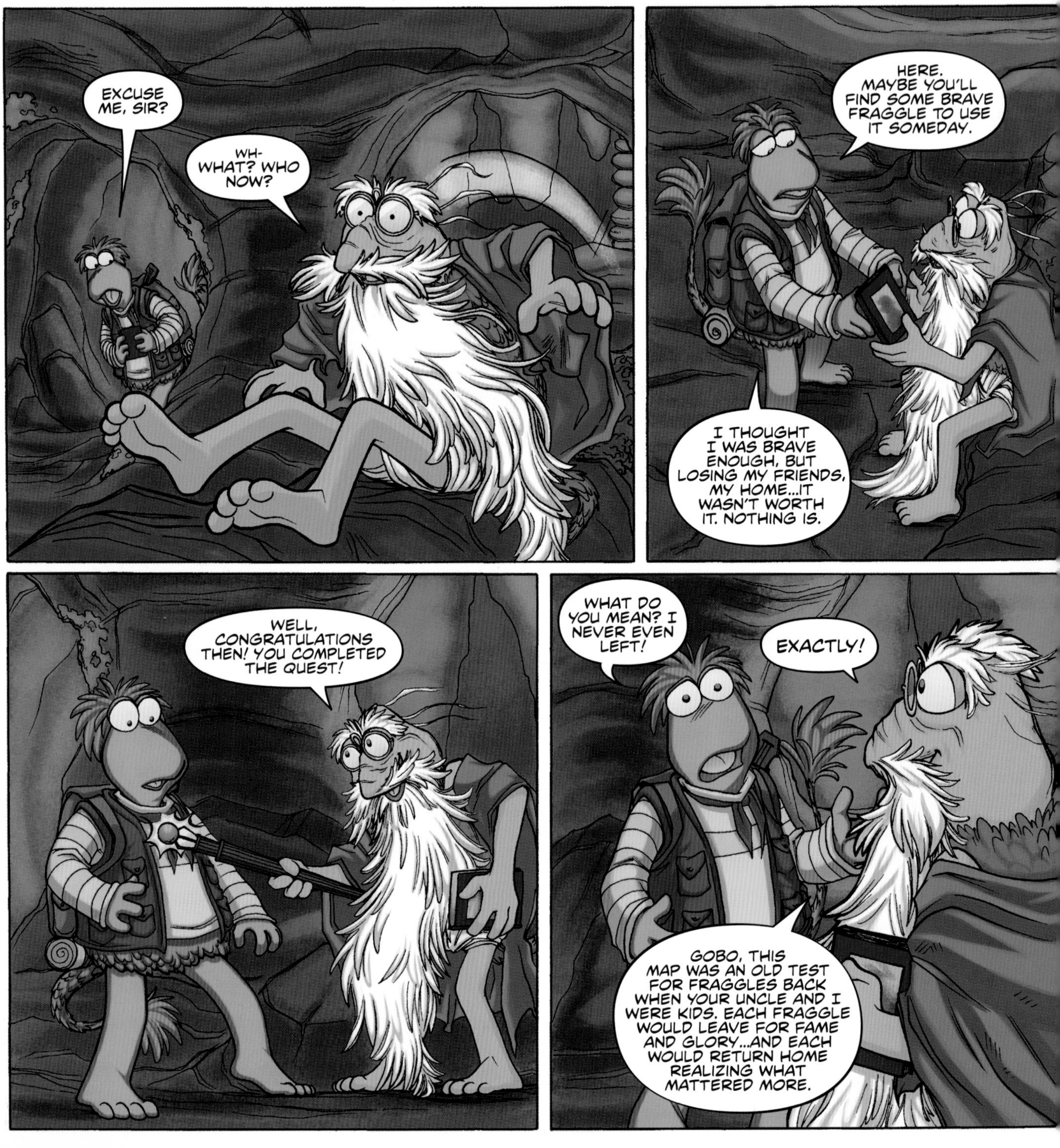
EXCUSE ME, SIR?
WH- WHAT? WHO NOW?
HERE. MAYBE YOU'LL FIND SOME BRAVE FRAGGLE TO USE IT SOMEDAY.
I THOUGHT I WAS BRAVE ENOUGH, BUT LOSING MY FRIENDS, MY HOME...IT WASN'T WORTH IT. NOTHING IS.
WELL, CONGRATULATIONS THEN! YOU COMPLETED THE QUEST!
WHAT DO YOU MEAN? I NEVER EVEN LEFT!
EXACTLY!
GOBO, THIS MAP WAS AN OLD TEST FOR FRAGGLES BACK WHEN YOUR UNCLE AND I WERE KIDS. EACH FRAGGLE WOULD LEAVE FOR FAME AND GLORY...AND EACH WOULD RETURN HOME REALIZING WHAT MATTERED MORE.

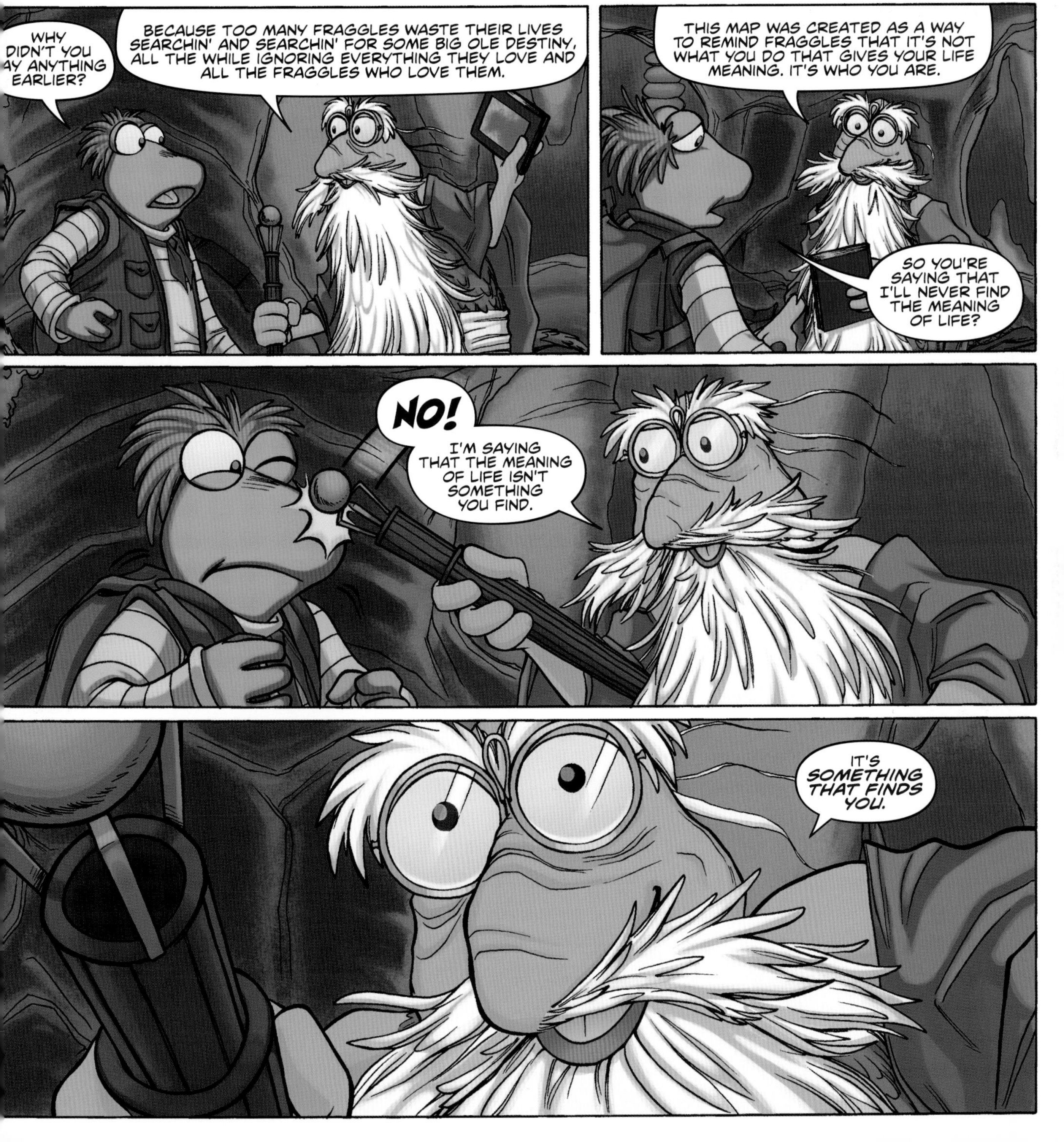
WHY DIDN'T YOU SAY ANYTHING EARLIER?
BECAUSE TOO MANY FRAGGLES WASTE THEIR LIVES SEARCHIN' AND SEARCHIN' FOR SOME BIG OLE DESTINY, ALL THE WHILE IGNORING EVERYTHING THEY LOVE AND ALL THE FRAGGLES WHO LOVE THEM.
THIS MAP WAS CREATED AS A WAY TO REMIND FRAGGLES THAT IT'S NOT WHAT YOU DO THAT GIVES YOUR LIFE MEANING. IT'S WHO YOU ARE.
SO YOU'RE SAYING THAT I'LL NEVER FIND THE MEANING OF LIFE?
NO!
I'M SAYING THAT THE MEANING OF LIFE ISN'T SOMETHING YOU FIND.
IT'S SOMETHING THAT FINDS YOU.

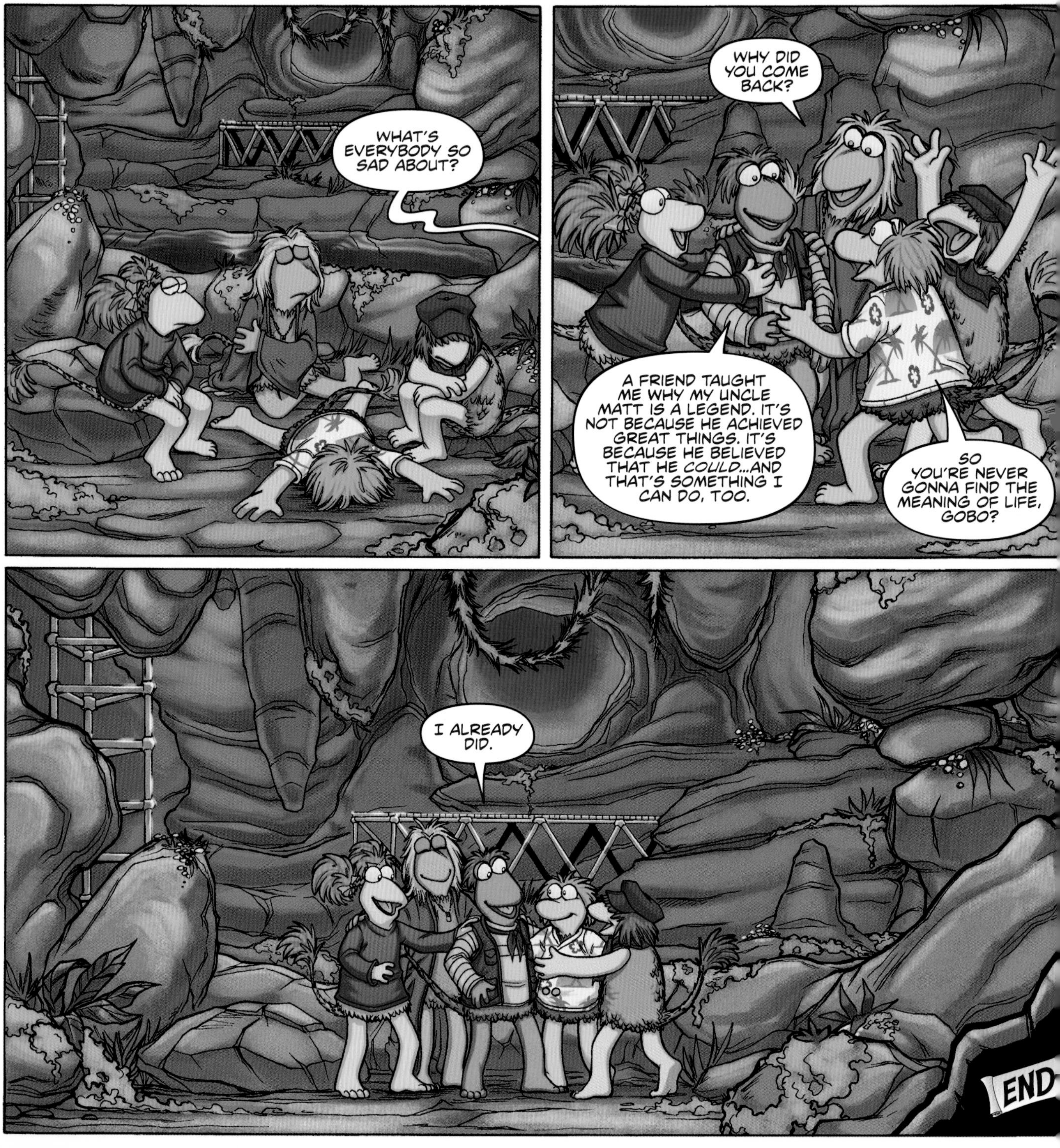
WHAT'S EVERYBODY SO SAD ABOUT?
WHY DID YOU COME BACK?
A FRIEND TAUGHT ME WHY MY UNCLE MATT IS A LEGEND. IT'S NOT BECAUSE HE ACHIEVED GREAT THINGS. IT'S BECAUSE HE BELIEVED THAT HE *COULD*...AND THAT'S SOMETHING I CAN DO, TOO.
SO YOU'RE NEVER GONNA FIND THE MEANING OF LIFE, GOBO?
I ALREADY DID.
END

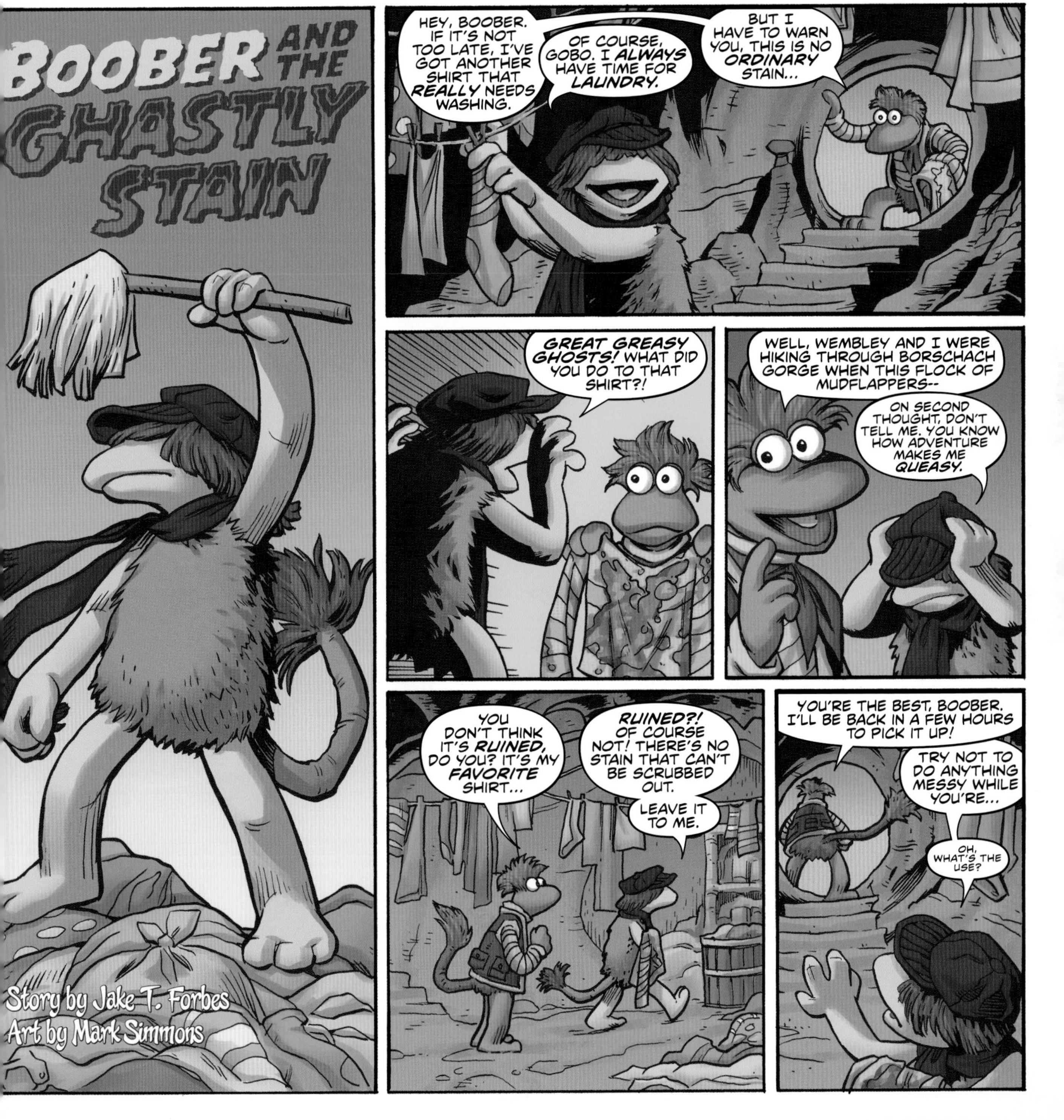
BOOBER AND THE GHASTLY STAIN
Story by Jake T. Forbes
Art by Mark Simmons
HEY, BOOBER. IF IT'S NOT TOO LATE, I'VE GOT ANOTHER SHIRT THAT REALLY NEEDS WASHING.
OF COURSE, GOBO. I ALWAYS HAVE TIME FOR LAUNDRY.
BUT I HAVE TO WARN YOU, THIS IS NO ORDINARY STAIN...
GREAT GREASY GHOSTS! WHAT DID YOU DO TO THAT SHIRT?!
WELL, WEMBLEY AND I WERE HIKING THROUGH BORSCHACH GORGE WHEN THIS FLOCK OF MUDFLAPPERS--
ON SECOND THOUGHT, DON'T TELL ME. YOU KNOW HOW ADVENTURE MAKES ME QUEASY.
YOU DON'T THINK IT'S RUINED, DO YOU? IT'S MY FAVORITE SHIRT...
RUINED?! OF COURSE NOT! THERE'S NO STAIN THAT CAN'T BE SCRUBBED OUT.
LEAVE IT TO ME.
YOU'RE THE BEST, BOOBER. I'LL BE BACK IN A FEW HOURS TO PICK IT UP!
TRY NOT TO DO ANYTHING MESSY WHILE YOU'RE...
OH, WHAT'S THE USE?

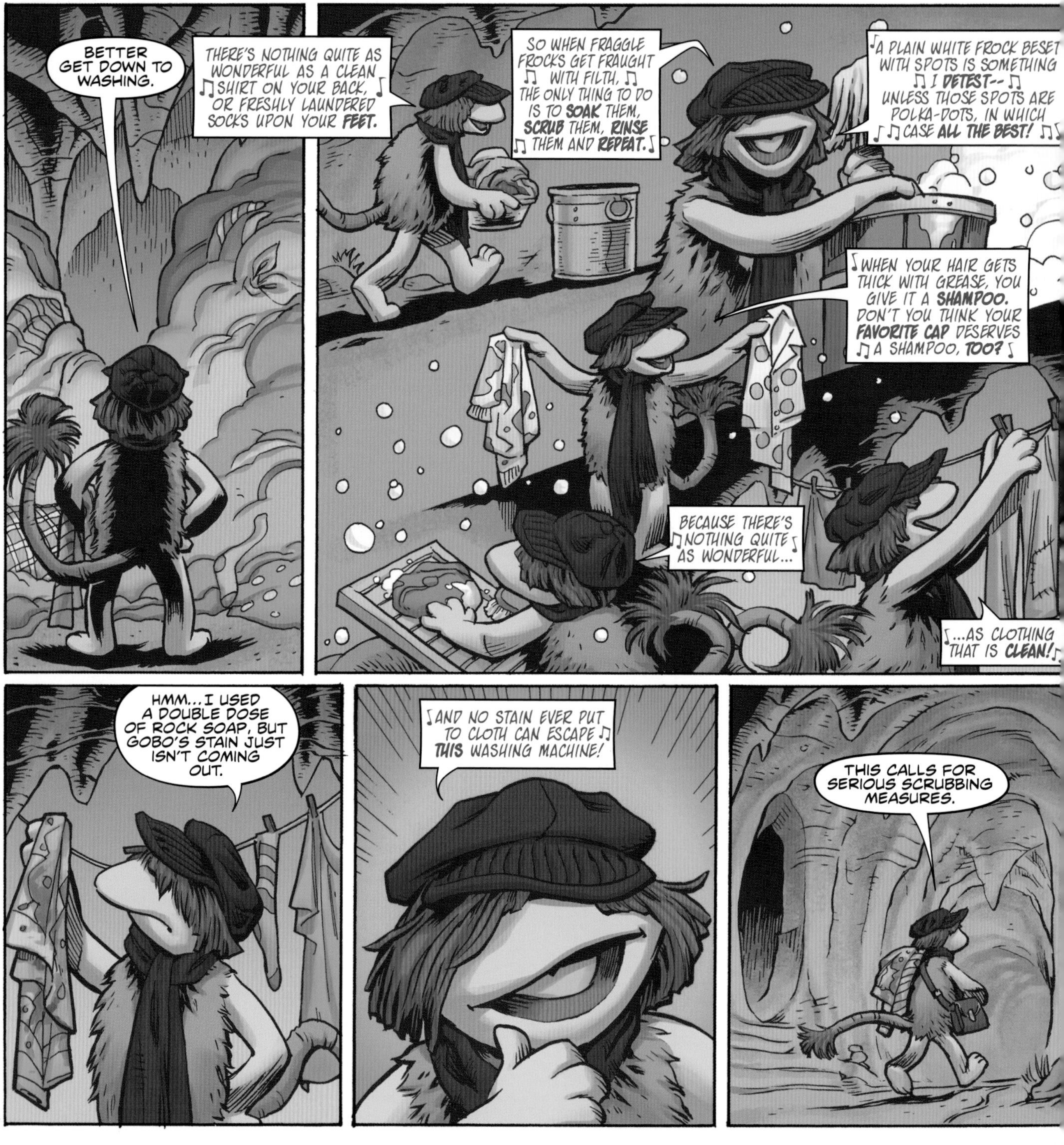

BETTER GET DOWN TO WASHING.
THERE'S NOTHING QUITE AS WONDERFUL AS A CLEAN SHIRT ON YOUR BACK, OR FRESHLY LAUNDERED SOCKS UPON YOUR **FEET.**
SO WHEN FRAGGLE FROCKS GET FRAUGHT WITH FILTH, THE ONLY THING TO DO IS TO **SOAK** THEM, **SCRUB** THEM, **RINSE** THEM AND **REPEAT.**
A PLAIN WHITE FROCK BESET WITH SPOTS IS SOMETHING I **DETEST--** UNLESS THOSE SPOTS ARE POLKA-DOTS, IN WHICH CASE **ALL THE BEST!**
WHEN YOUR HAIR GETS THICK WITH GREASE, YOU GIVE IT A **SHAMPOO.** DON'T YOU THINK YOUR **FAVORITE CAP** DESERVES A SHAMPOO, **TOO?**
BECAUSE THERE'S NOTHING QUITE AS WONDERFUL...
...AS CLOTHING THAT IS **CLEAN!**
HMM... I USED A DOUBLE DOSE OF ROCK SOAP, BUT GOBO'S STAIN JUST ISN'T COMING OUT.
AND NO STAIN EVER PUT TO CLOTH CAN ESCAPE **THIS** WASHING MACHINE!
THIS CALLS FOR SERIOUS SCRUBBING MEASURES.

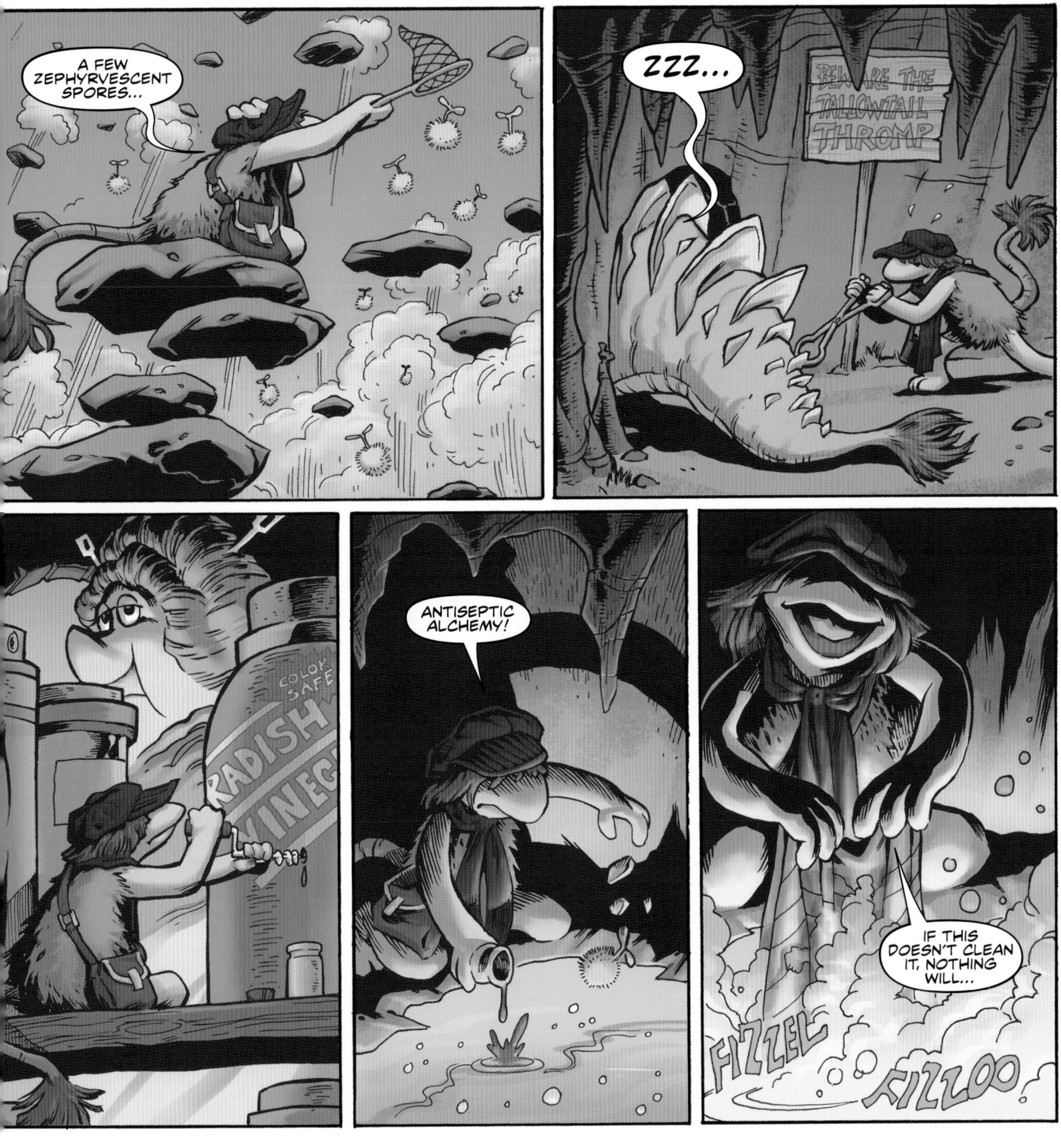
A FEW ZEPHYRVESCENT SPORES...
ZZZ...
BEWARE THE TALLOWTAIL THROMP
COLOR SAFE
RADISH
ANTISEPTIC ALCHEMY!
IF THIS DOESN'T CLEAN IT, NOTHING WILL...
FIZZEL
FIZZOO

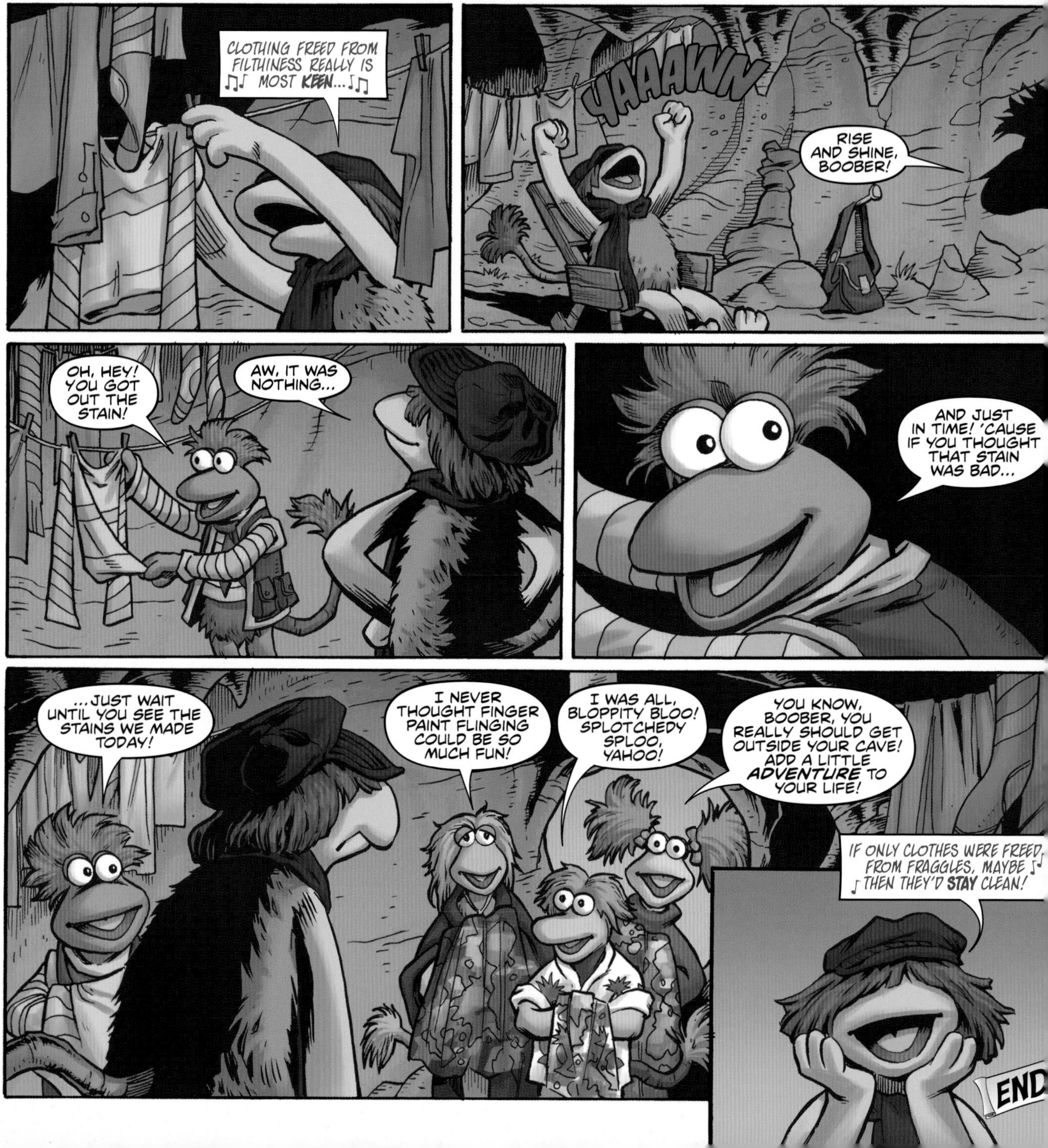
CLOTHING FREED FROM FILTHINESS REALLY IS ♫♩ MOST KEEN... ♩♫
YAAAWN
RISE AND SHINE, BOOBER!
OH, HEY! YOU GOT OUT THE STAIN!
AW, IT WAS NOTHING...
AND JUST IN TIME! 'CAUSE IF YOU THOUGHT THAT STAIN WAS BAD...
...JUST WAIT UNTIL YOU SEE THE STAINS WE MADE TODAY!
I NEVER THOUGHT FINGER PAINT FLINGING COULD BE SO MUCH FUN!
I WAS ALL, BLOPPITY BLOO! SPLOTCHEDY SPLOO, YAHOO!
YOU KNOW, BOOBER, YOU REALLY SHOULD GET OUTSIDE YOUR CAVE! ADD A LITTLE ADVENTURE TO YOUR LIFE!
IF ONLY CLOTHES WERE FREED FROM FRAGGLES, MAYBE ♪ ♪ THEN THEY'D STAY CLEAN!
END

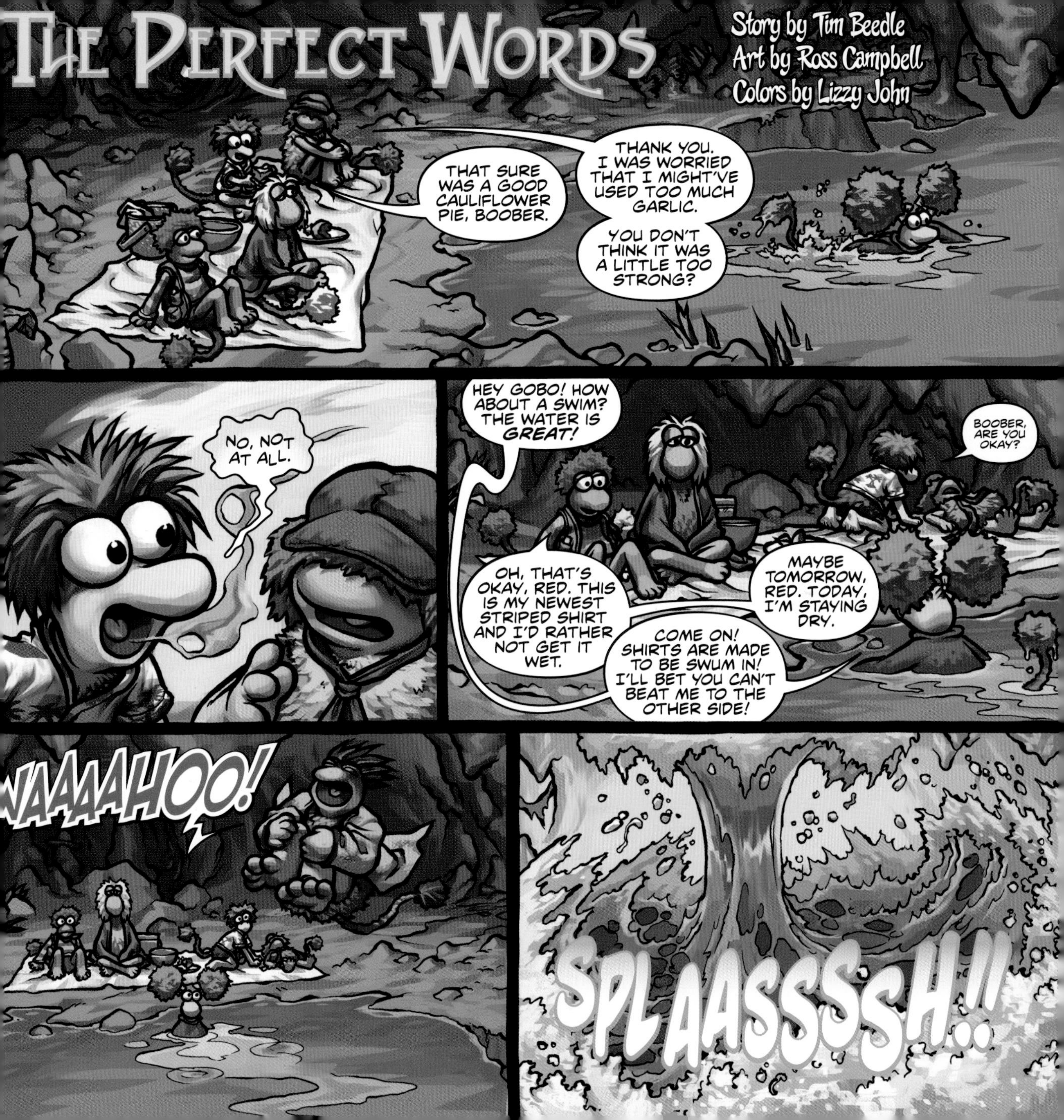
THE PERFECT WORDS
Story by Tim Beedle
Art by Ross Campbell
Colors by Lizzy John
THAT SURE WAS A GOOD CAULIFLOWER PIE, BOOBER.
THANK YOU. I WAS WORRIED THAT I MIGHT'VE USED TOO MUCH GARLIC.
YOU DON'T THINK IT WAS A LITTLE TOO STRONG?
NO, NOT AT ALL.
HEY GOBO! HOW ABOUT A SWIM? THE WATER IS GREAT!
BOOBER, ARE YOU OKAY?
OH, THAT'S OKAY, RED. THIS IS MY NEWEST STRIPED SHIRT AND I'D RATHER NOT GET IT WET.
MAYBE TOMORROW, RED. TODAY, I'M STAYING DRY.
COME ON! SHIRTS ARE MADE TO BE SWUM IN! I'LL BET YOU CAN'T BEAT ME TO THE OTHER SIDE!
WAAAAHOO!
SPLAASSSSH!!

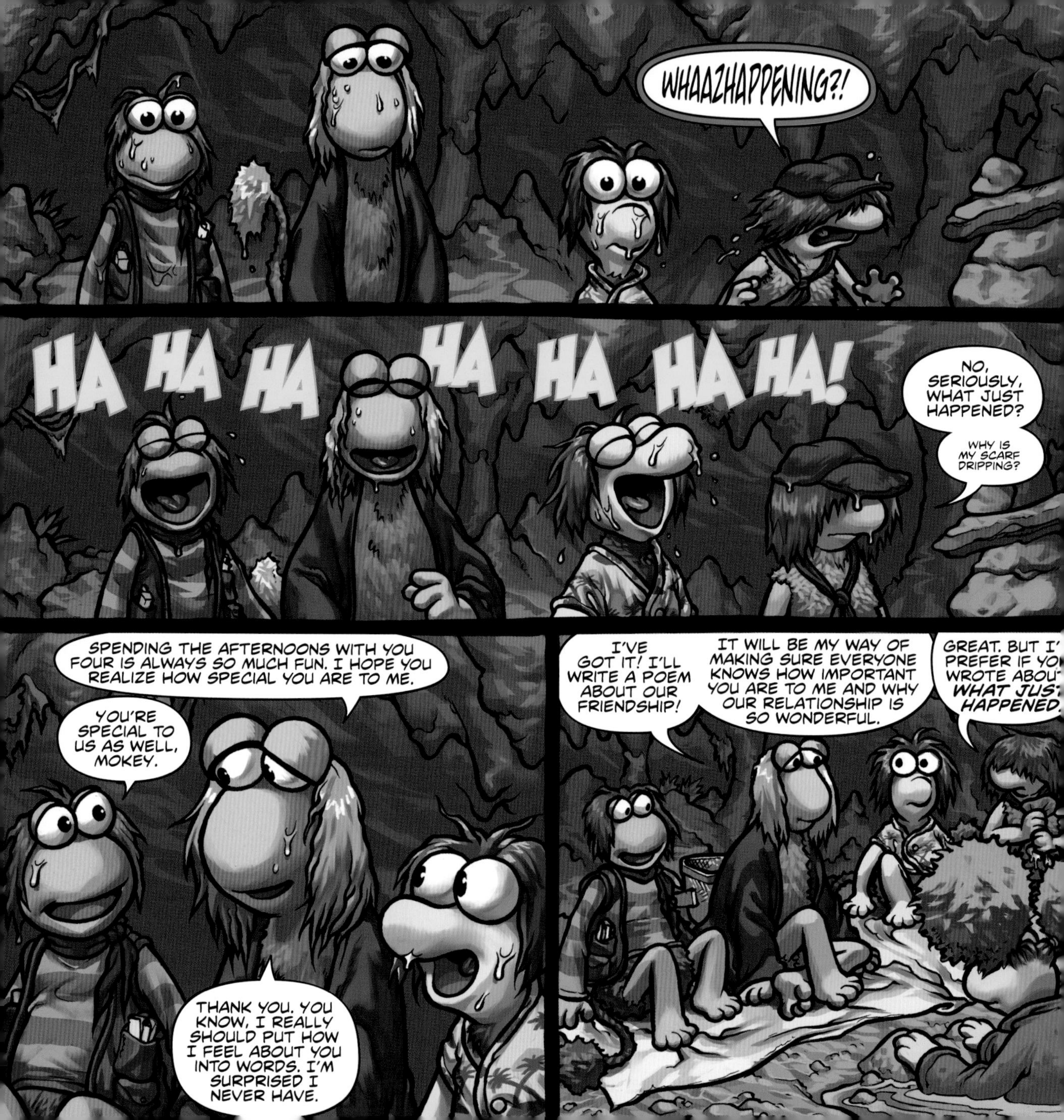
WHAAZHAPPENING?!
HA HA HA HA HA HA HA!
NO, SERIOUSLY, WHAT JUST HAPPENED?
WHY IS MY SCARF DRIPPING?
SPENDING THE AFTERNOONS WITH YOU FOUR IS ALWAYS SO MUCH FUN. I HOPE YOU REALIZE HOW SPECIAL YOU ARE TO ME.
YOU'RE SPECIAL TO US AS WELL, MOKEY.
THANK YOU. YOU KNOW, I REALLY SHOULD PUT HOW I FEEL ABOUT YOU INTO WORDS. I'M SURPRISED I NEVER HAVE.
I'VE GOT IT! I'LL WRITE A POEM ABOUT OUR FRIENDSHIP!
IT WILL BE MY WAY OF MAKING SURE EVERYONE KNOWS HOW IMPORTANT YOU ARE TO ME AND WHY OUR RELATIONSHIP IS SO WONDERFUL.

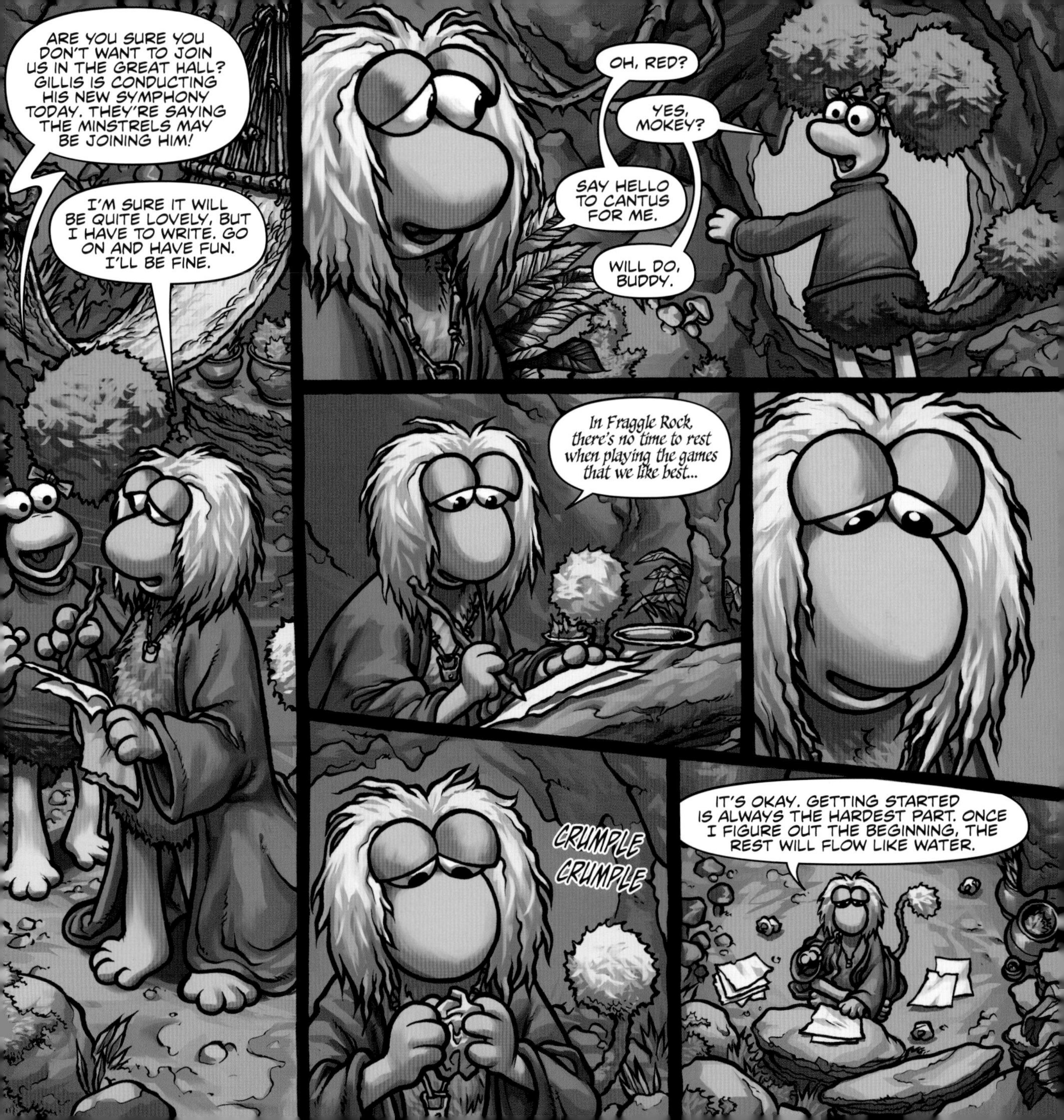
ARE YOU SURE YOU DON'T WANT TO JOIN US IN THE GREAT HALL? GILLIS IS CONDUCTING HIS NEW SYMPHONY TODAY. THEY'RE SAYING THE MINSTRELS MAY BE JOINING HIM!
I'M SURE IT WILL BE QUITE LOVELY, BUT I HAVE TO WRITE. GO ON AND HAVE FUN. I'LL BE FINE.
OH, RED?
YES, MOKEY?
SAY HELLO TO CANTUS FOR ME.
WILL DO, BUDDY.
In Fraggle Rock, there's no time to rest when playing the games that we like best...
CRUMPLE
CRUMPLE
IT'S OKAY. GETTING STARTED IS ALWAYS THE HARDEST PART. ONCE I FIGURE OUT THE BEGINNING, THE REST WILL FLOW LIKE WATER.

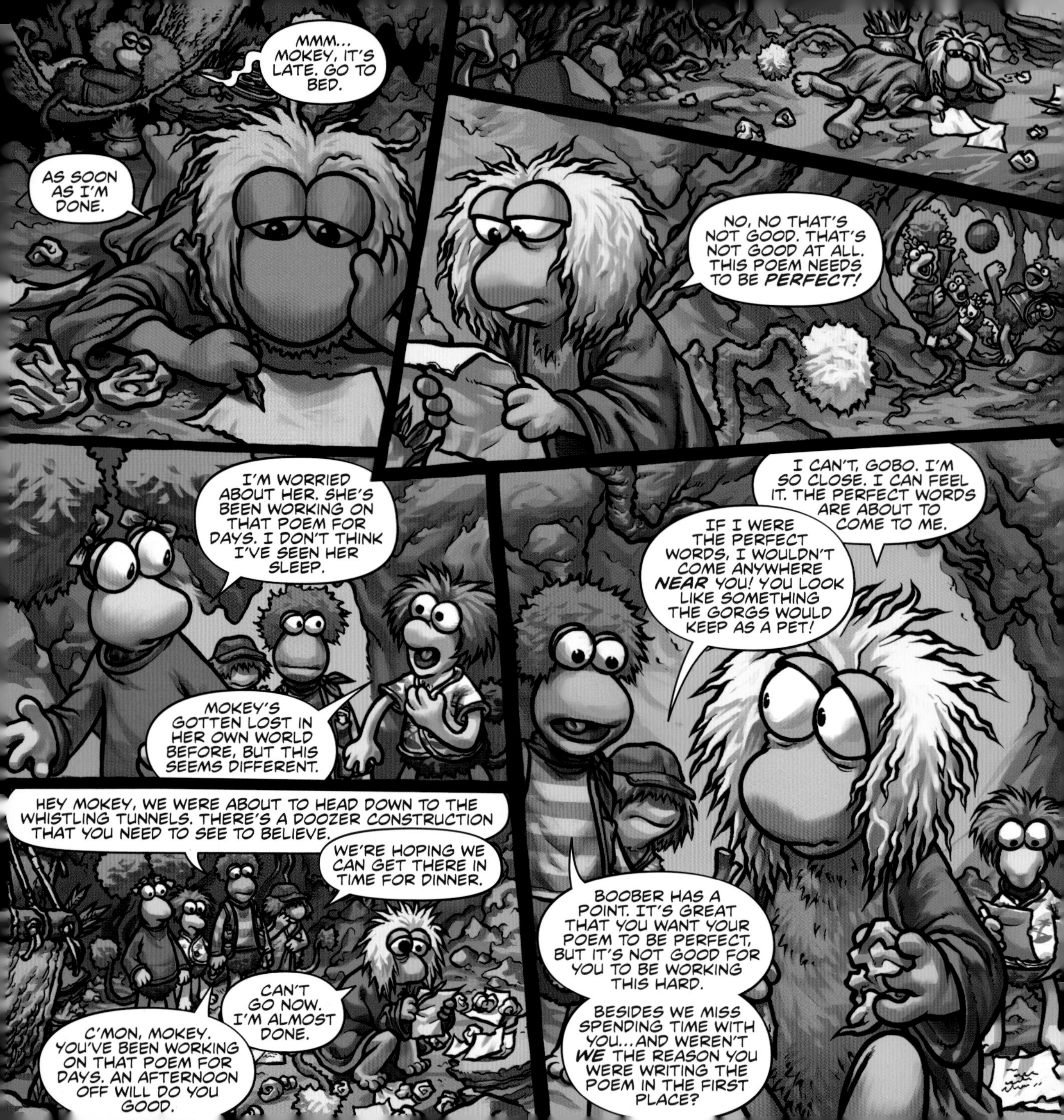
MMM... MOKEY, IT'S LATE. GO TO BED.
AS SOON AS I'M DONE.
NO, NO THAT'S NOT GOOD. THAT'S NOT GOOD AT ALL. THIS POEM NEEDS TO BE *PERFECT!*
I'M WORRIED ABOUT HER. SHE'S BEEN WORKING ON THAT POEM FOR DAYS. I DON'T THINK I'VE SEEN HER SLEEP.
MOKEY'S GOTTEN LOST IN HER OWN WORLD BEFORE, BUT THIS SEEMS DIFFERENT.
HEY MOKEY, WE WERE ABOUT TO HEAD DOWN TO THE WHISTLING TUNNELS. THERE'S A DOOZER CONSTRUCTION THAT YOU NEED TO SEE TO BELIEVE.
WE'RE HOPING WE CAN GET THERE IN TIME FOR DINNER.
CAN'T GO NOW. I'M ALMOST DONE.
C'MON, MOKEY. YOU'VE BEEN WORKING ON THAT POEM FOR DAYS. AN AFTERNOON OFF WILL DO YOU GOOD.
I CAN'T, GOBO. I'M SO CLOSE. I CAN FEEL IT. THE PERFECT WORDS ARE ABOUT TO COME TO ME.
IF I WERE THE PERFECT WORDS, I WOULDN'T COME ANYWHERE **NEAR** YOU! YOU LOOK LIKE SOMETHING THE GORGS WOULD KEEP AS A PET!
BOOBER HAS A POINT. IT'S GREAT THAT YOU WANT YOUR POEM TO BE PERFECT, BUT IT'S NOT GOOD FOR YOU TO BE WORKING THIS HARD.
BESIDES WE MISS SPENDING TIME WITH YOU...AND WEREN'T **WE** THE REASON YOU WERE WRITING THE POEM IN THE FIRST PLACE?

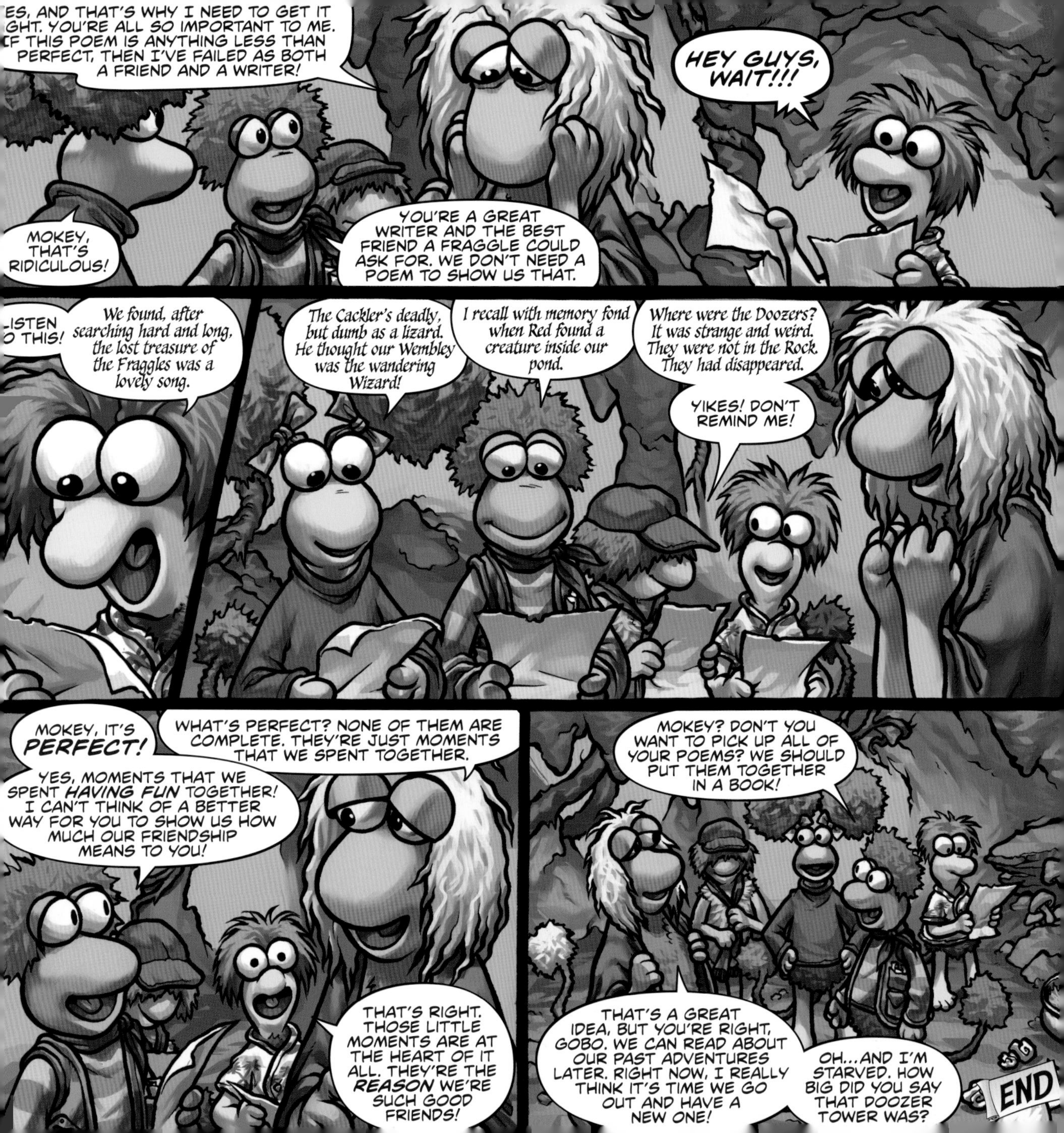

ES, AND THAT'S WHY I NEED TO GET IT GHT. YOU'RE ALL SO IMPORTANT TO ME. CF THIS POEM IS ANYTHING LESS THAN PERFECT, THEN I'VE FAILED AS BOTH A FRIEND AND A WRITER!
MOKEY, THAT'S RIDICULOUS!
YOU'RE A GREAT WRITER AND THE BEST FRIEND A FRAGGLE COULD ASK FOR. WE DON'T NEED A POEM TO SHOW US THAT.
HEY GUYS, WAIT!!!
LISTEN O THIS!
We found, after searching hard and long, the lost treasure of the Fraggles was a lovely song.
The Cackler's deadly, but dumb as a lizard. He thought our Wembley was the wandering Wizard!
I recall with memory fond when Red found a creature inside our pond.
Where were the Doozers? It was strange and weird. They were not in the Rock. They had disappeared.
YIKES! DON'T REMIND ME!
MOKEY, IT'S PERFECT!
WHAT'S PERFECT? NONE OF THEM ARE COMPLETE. THEY'RE JUST MOMENTS THAT WE SPENT TOGETHER.
YES, MOMENTS THAT WE SPENT HAVING FUN TOGETHER! I CAN'T THINK OF A BETTER WAY FOR YOU TO SHOW US HOW MUCH OUR FRIENDSHIP MEANS TO YOU!
THAT'S RIGHT. THOSE LITTLE MOMENTS ARE AT THE HEART OF IT ALL. THEY'RE THE REASON WE'RE SUCH GOOD FRIENDS!
MOKEY? DON'T YOU WANT TO PICK UP ALL OF YOUR POEMS? WE SHOULD PUT THEM TOGETHER IN A BOOK!
THAT'S A GREAT IDEA, BUT YOU'RE RIGHT, GOBO. WE CAN READ ABOUT OUR PAST ADVENTURES LATER. RIGHT NOW, I REALLY THINK IT'S TIME WE GO OUT AND HAVE A NEW ONE!
OH...AND I'M STARVED. HOW BIG DID YOU SAY THAT DOOZER TOWER WAS?
END

Cover & Activity Page Gallery

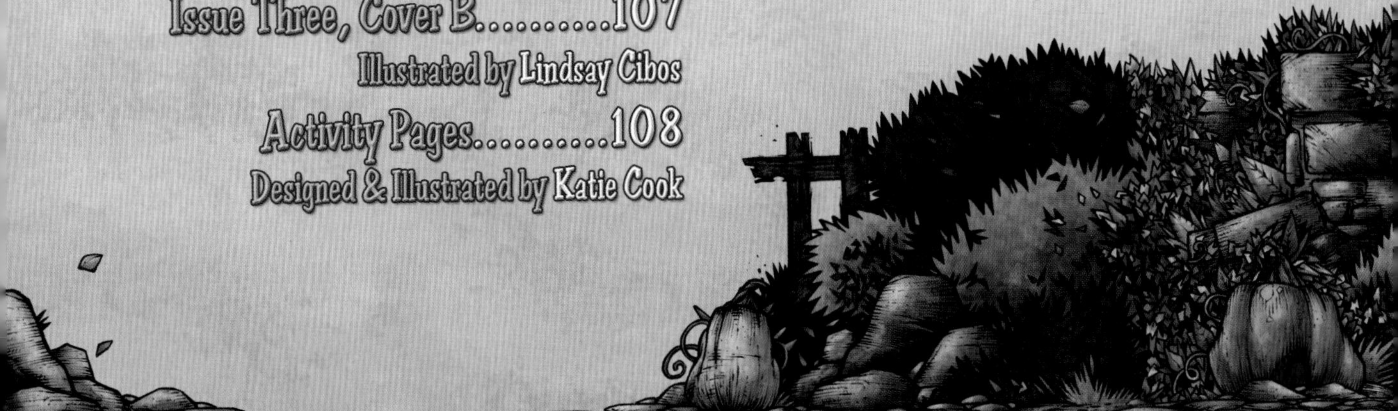

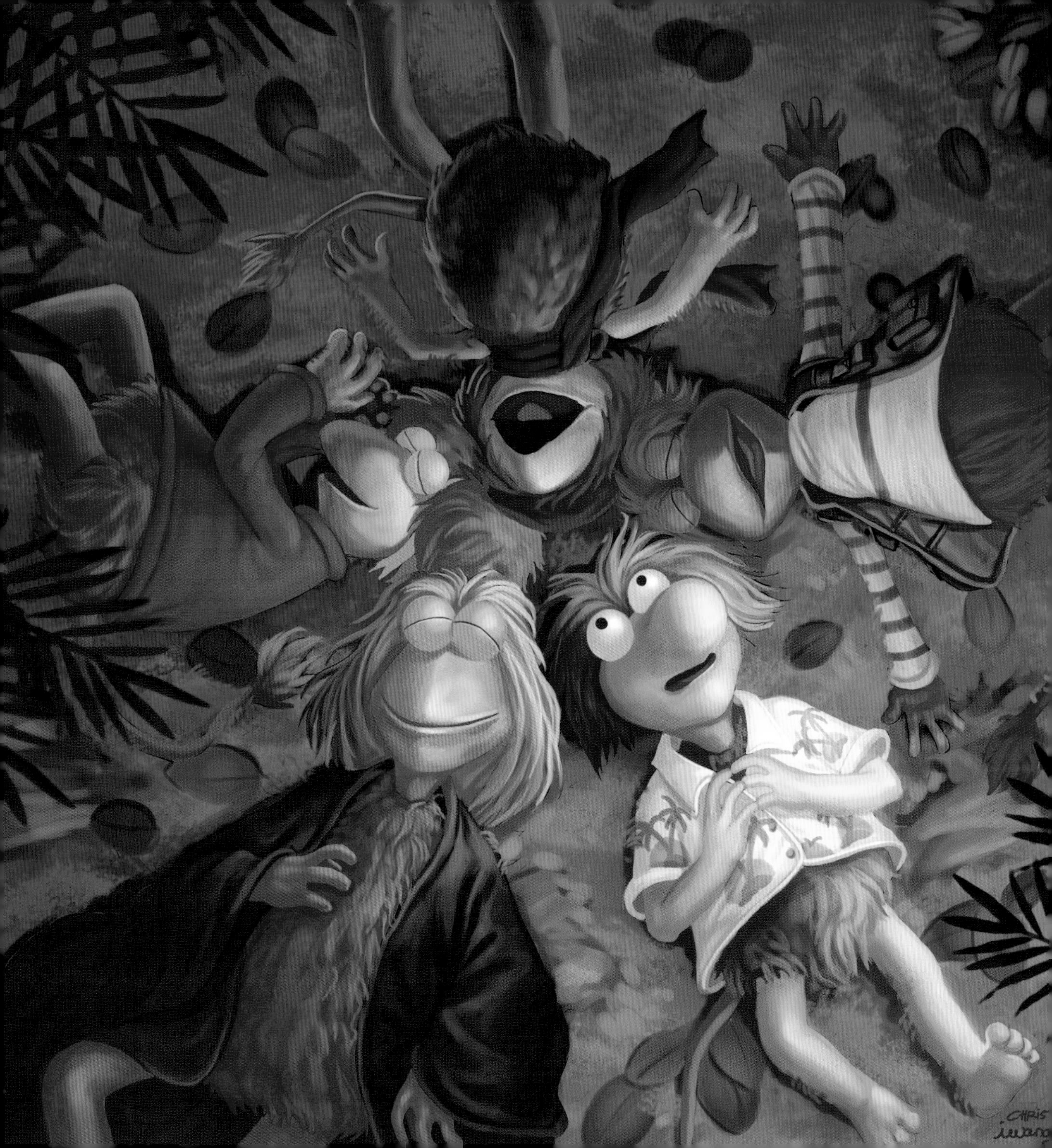

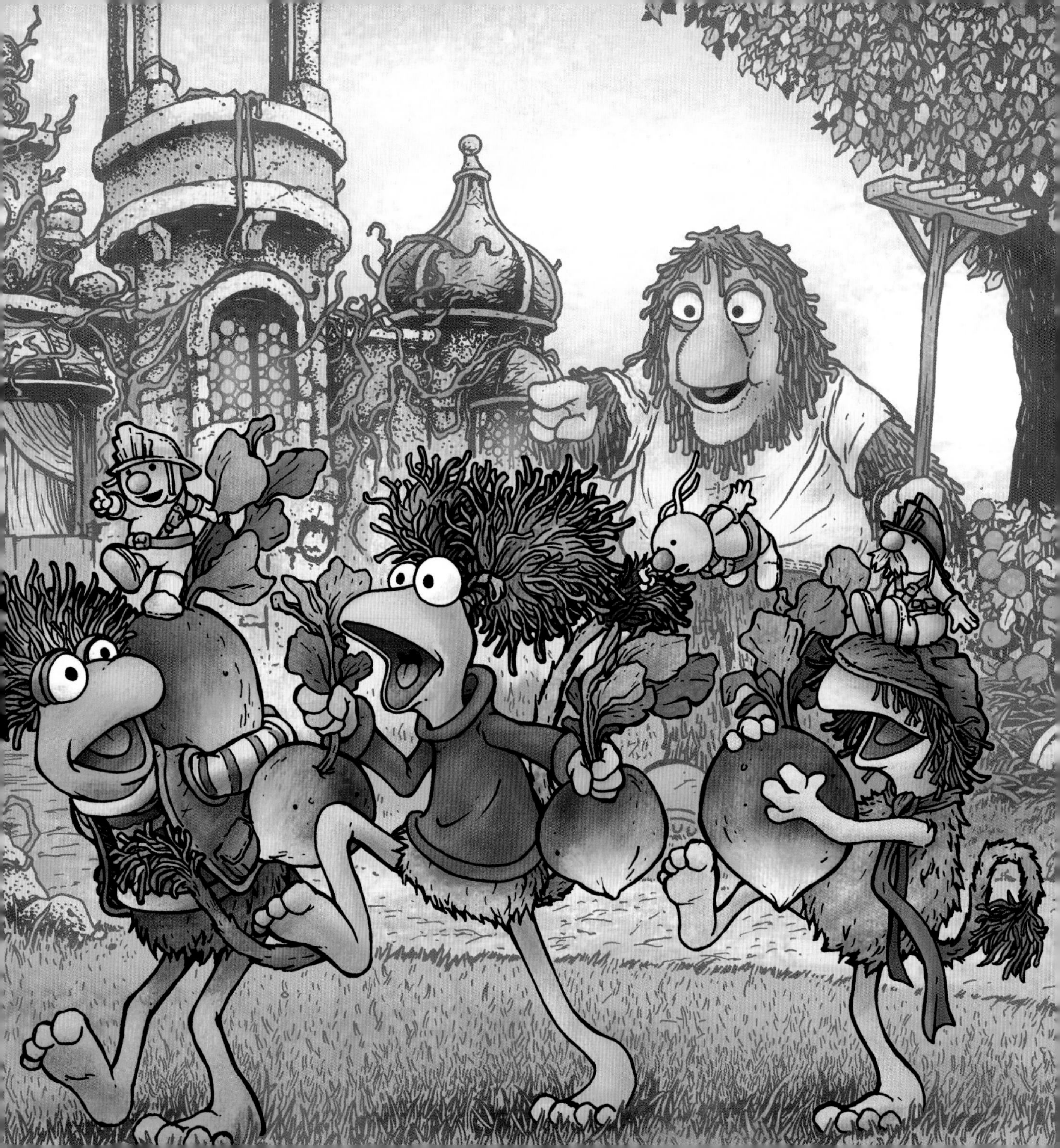

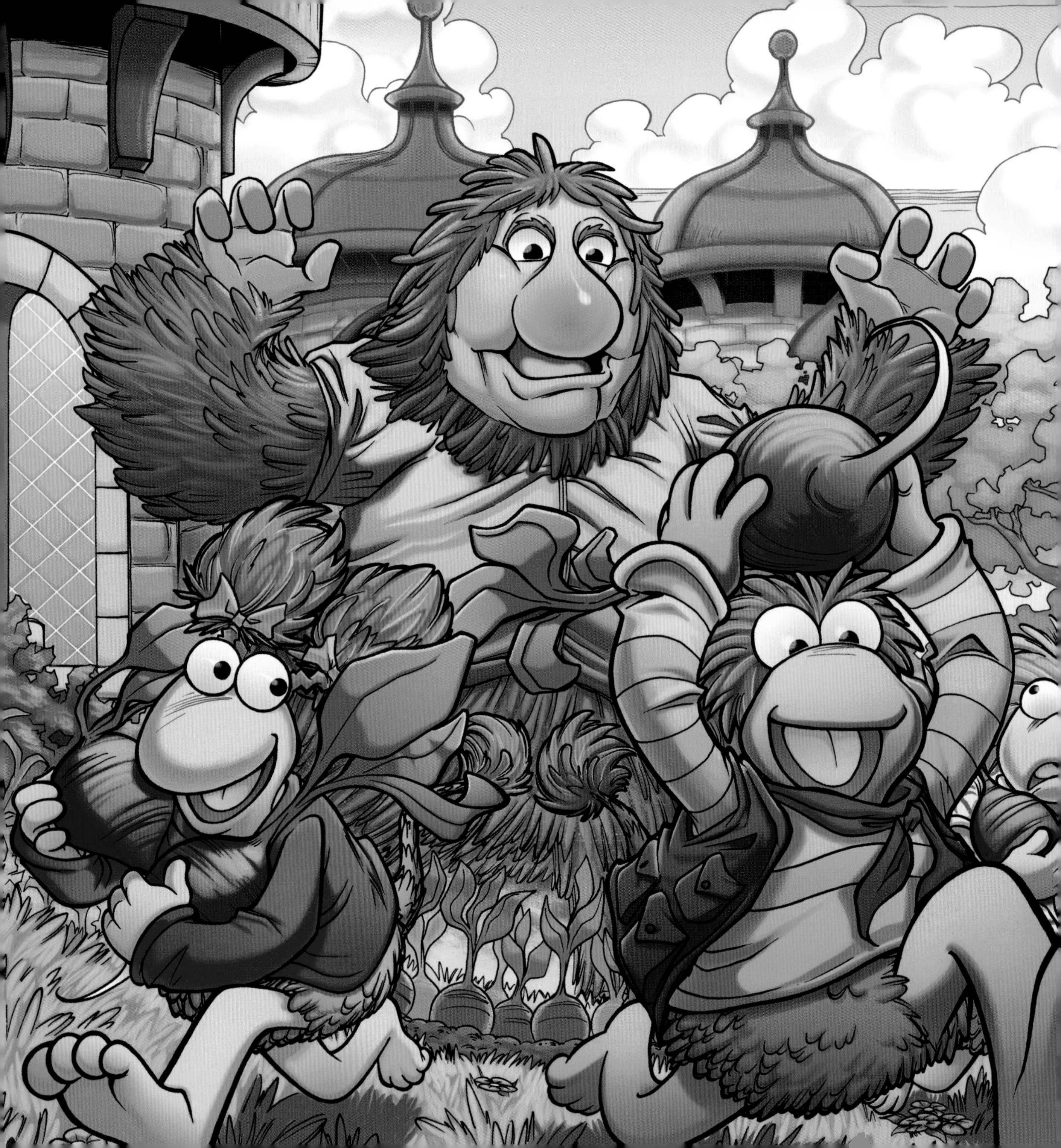

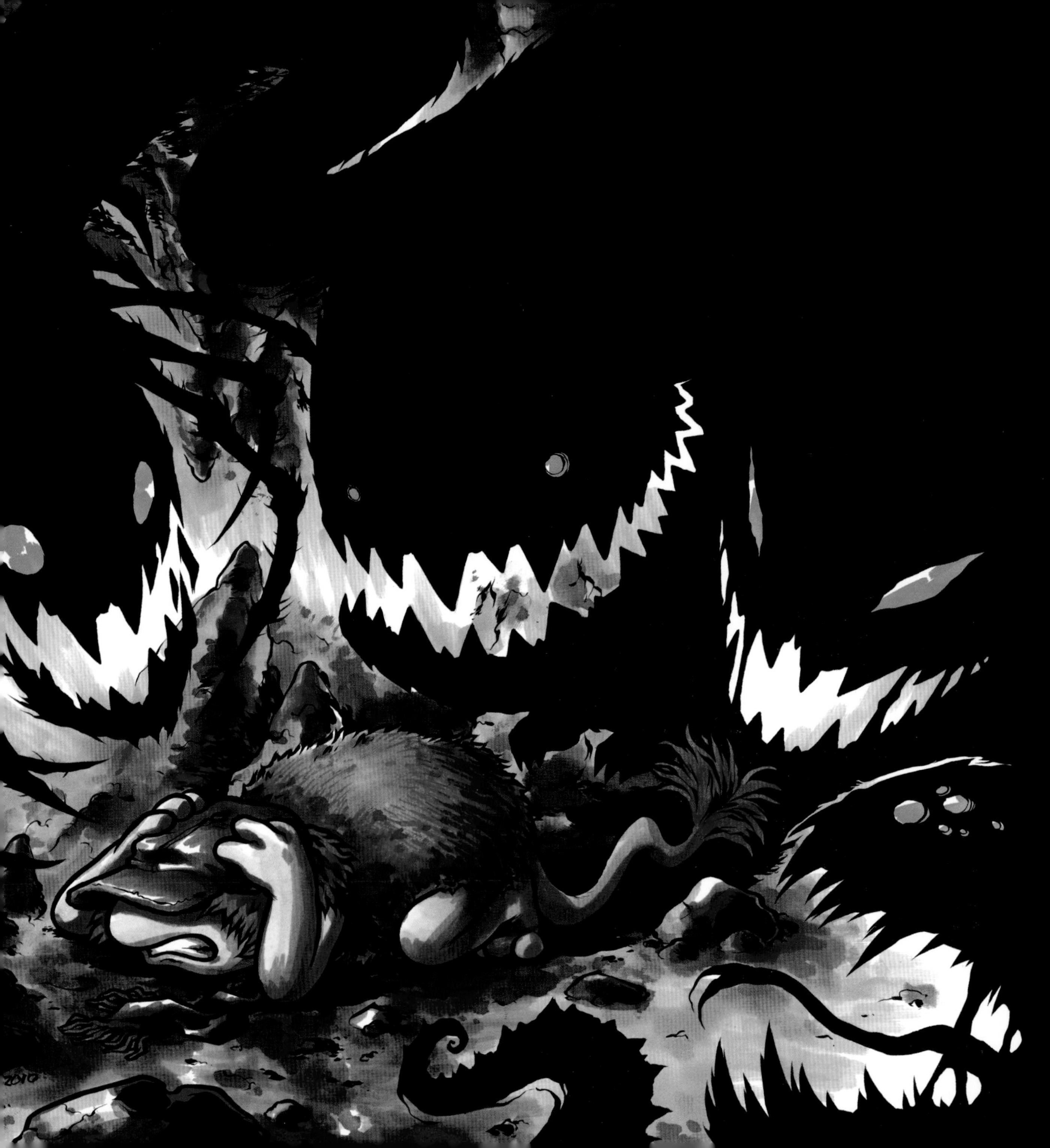

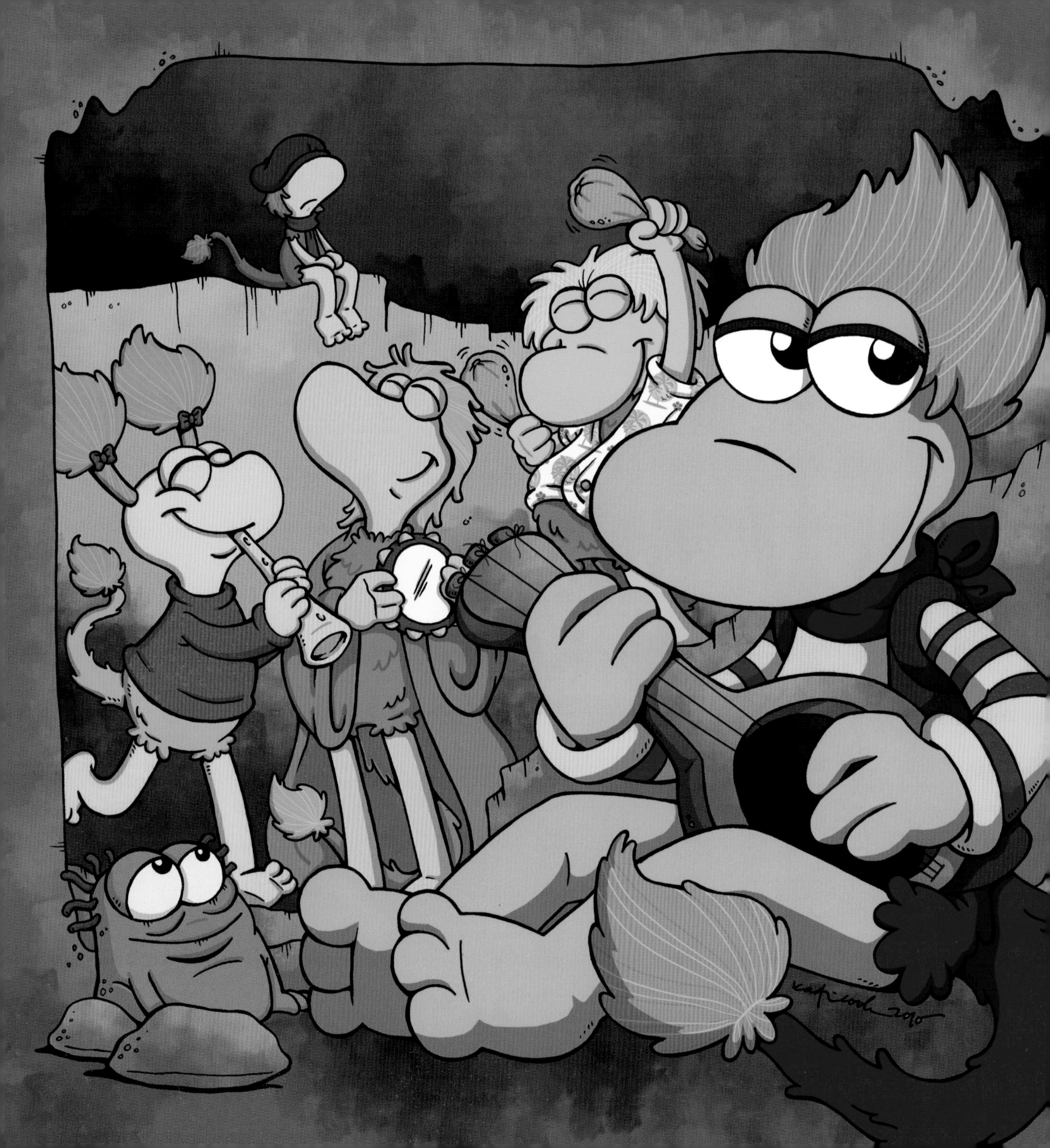

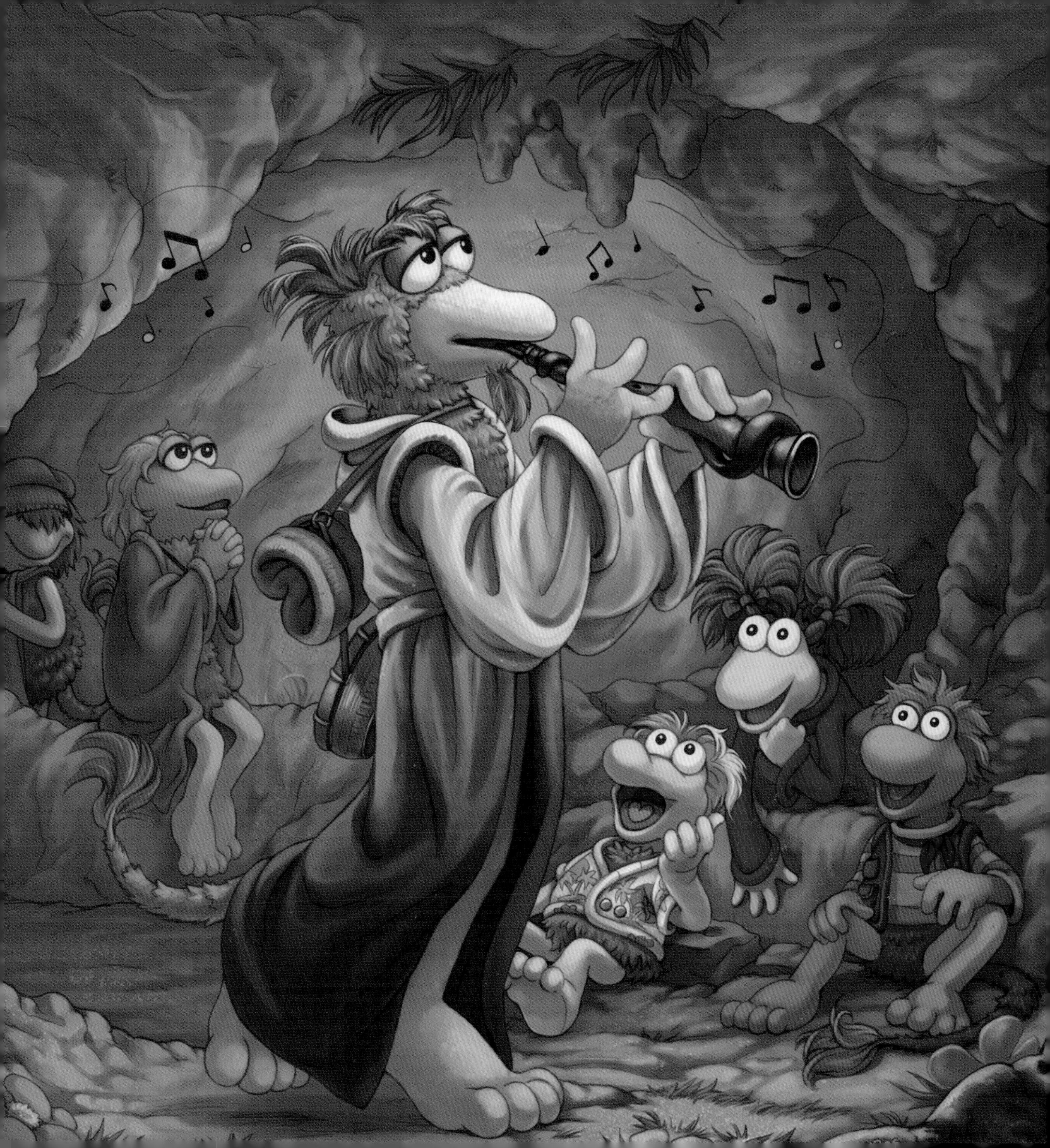

"how to stretch before exercisin
with RED FRAGGLE

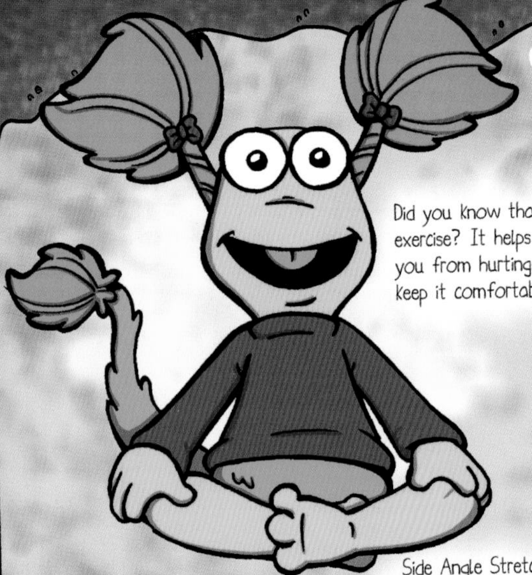

Did you know that you should stretch before you exercise? It helps your muscles loosen up and keeps you from hurting yourself while you play! Remember, keep it comfortable. Never stretch until it hurts!

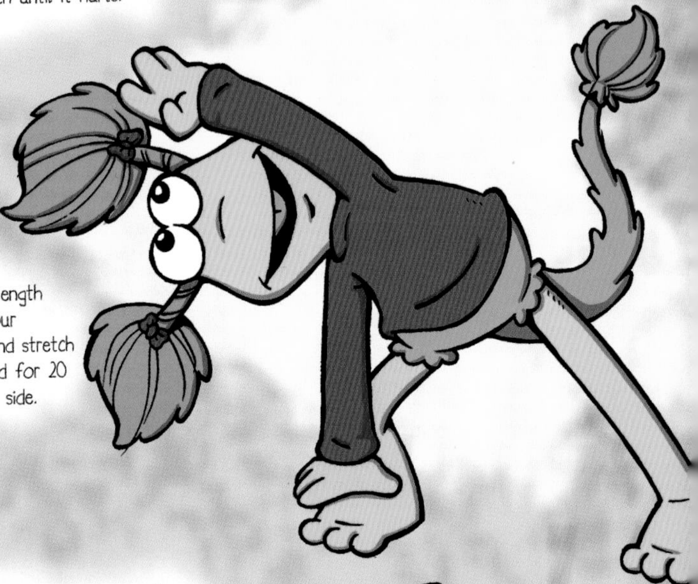

Side Angle Stretch:
Stand with your feet shoulder length apart. Lean down and touch your right hand to your right toes and stretch your left arm to the right. Hold for 20 seconds. Repeat on your other side.

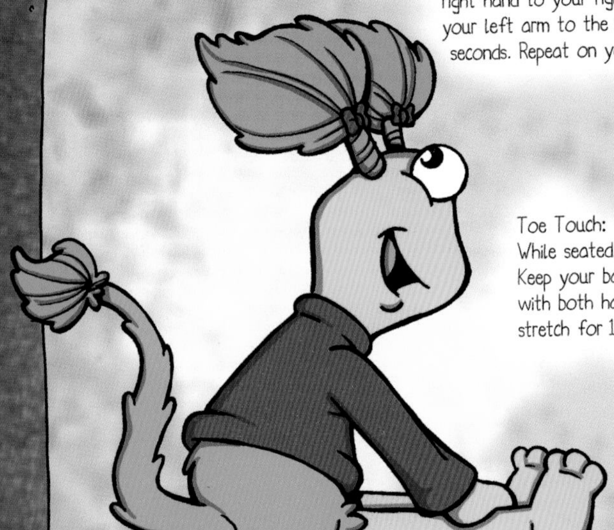

Toe Touch:
While seated, extend both legs in front of you. Keep your back straight and reach for your toes with both hands. Do not bend your knees! Hold this stretch for 10 to 30 seconds.

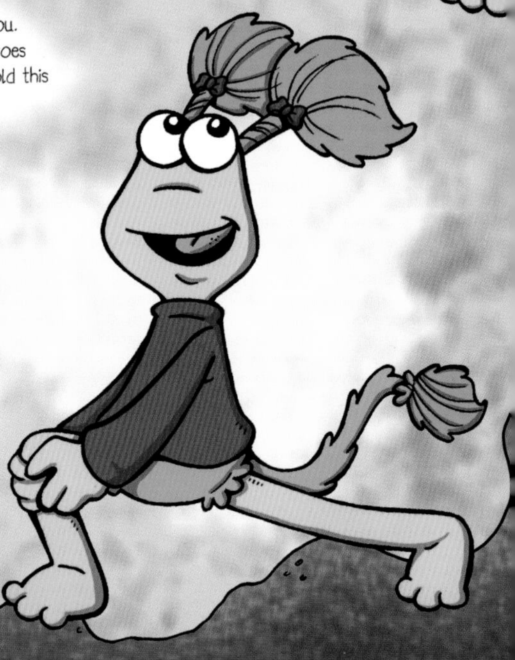

Lunge Stretch:
Stand with your feet shoulder length apart, make sure your toes are pointing forward! With your right foot, take a large step forward to create a "lunge" position. How far down can you lunge and still keep a straight back? Hold this stretch for 30 seconds. Repeat on your other side.

"how to make fingerprint art" with THE DOOZERS!

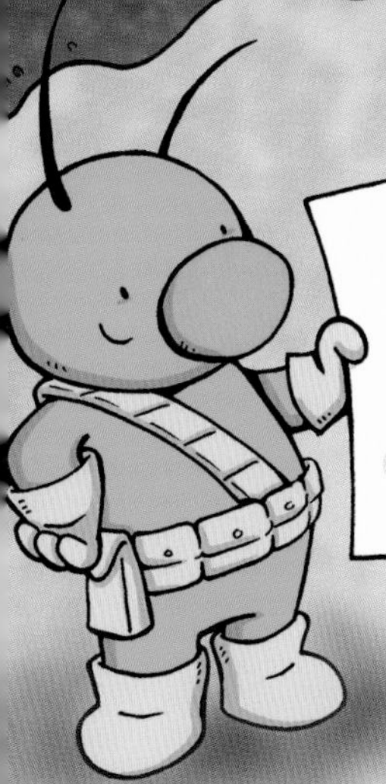

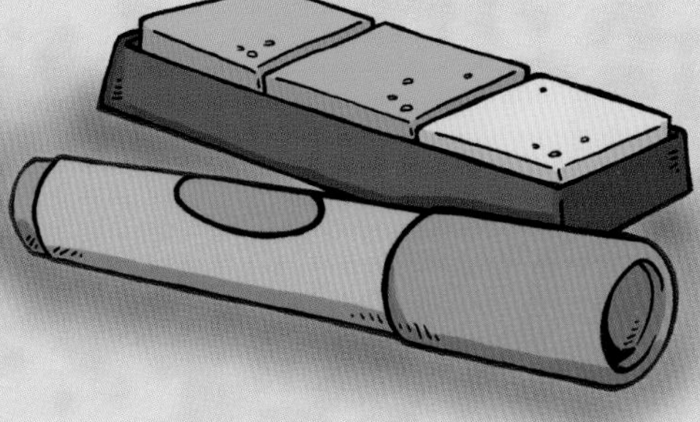

All you need is some paper and either a colorful ink pad or some markers!

Dab your finger in the ink pad...

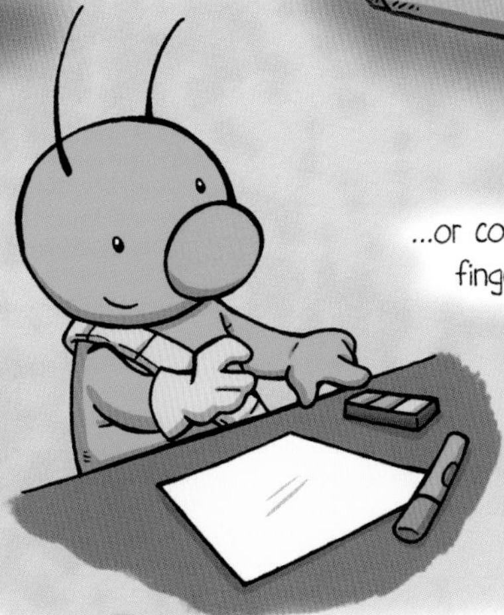

...or color the pad of your finger with a marker!

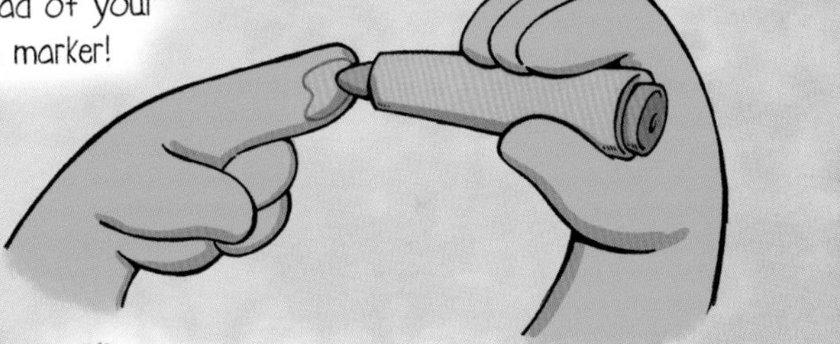

Then, use your finger to create a dot on the paper!

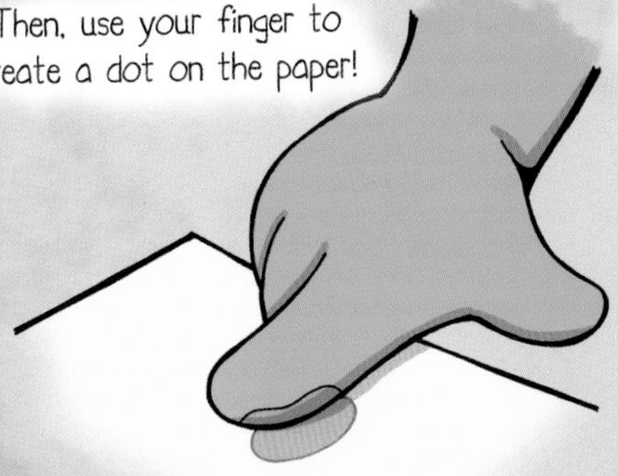

You can use this method to create all kinds of Fraggle Rock characters! Use a thin, black marker to add details.

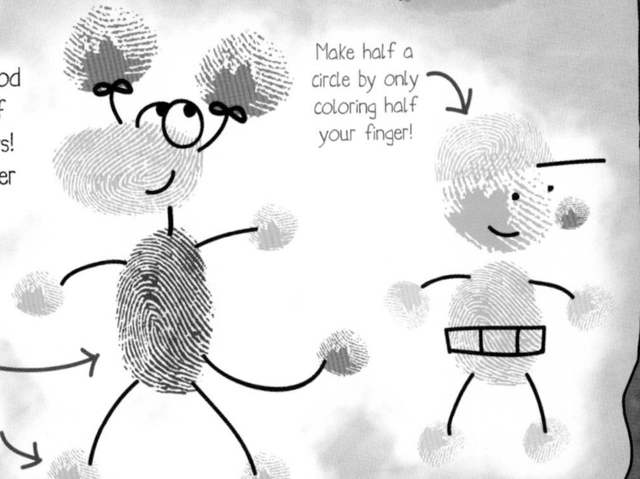

Make half a circle by only coloring half your finger!
Use the pad of your thumb!
Use the tip of your pinky finger!

Make sure you make your fingerprint creations on paper... not the wall! d wash your hands when you're done!

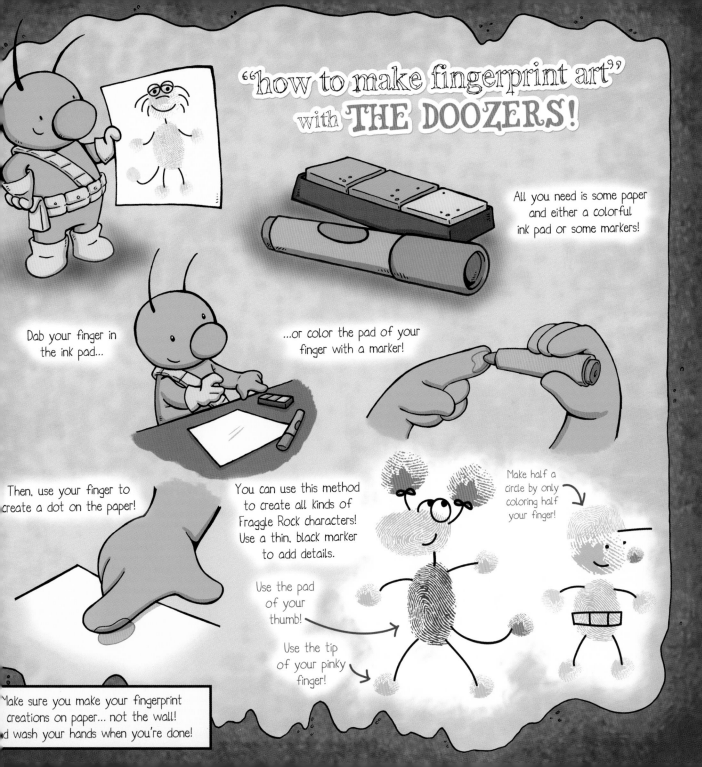

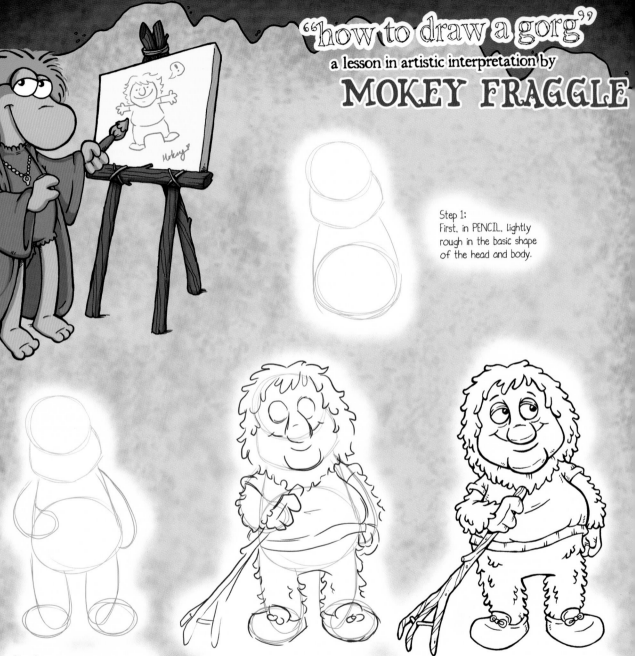

"how to draw a gorg"

a lesson in artistic interpretation by MOKEY FRAGGLE

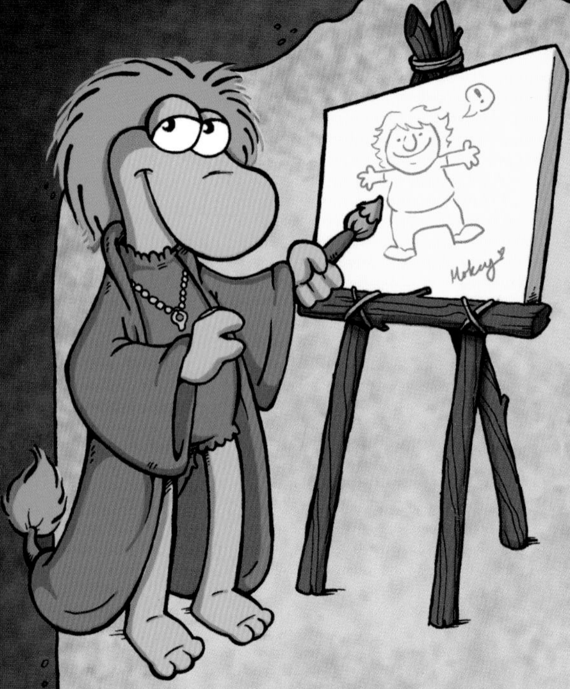

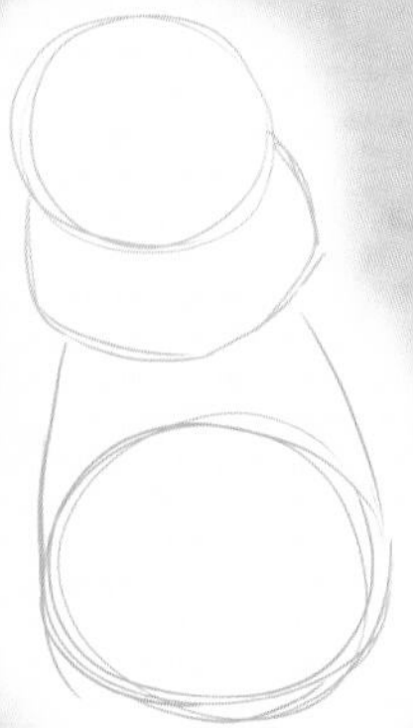

Step 1:
First, in PENCIL, lightly rough in the basic shape of the head and body.

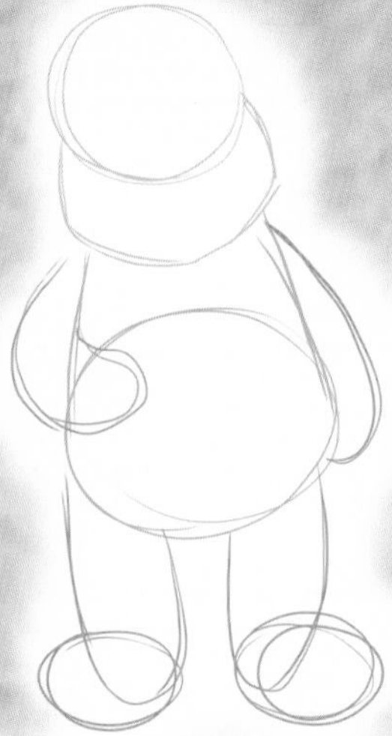

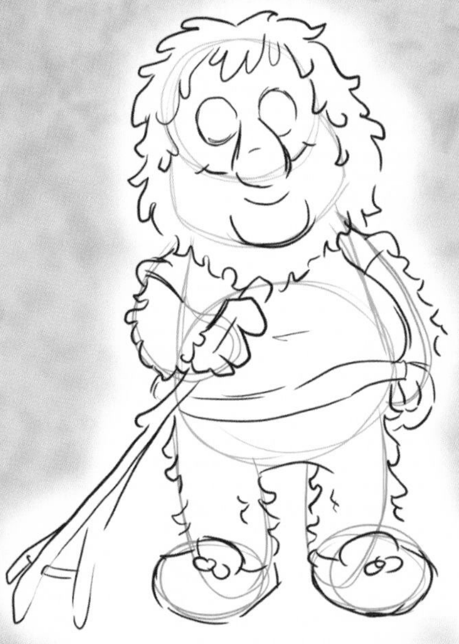

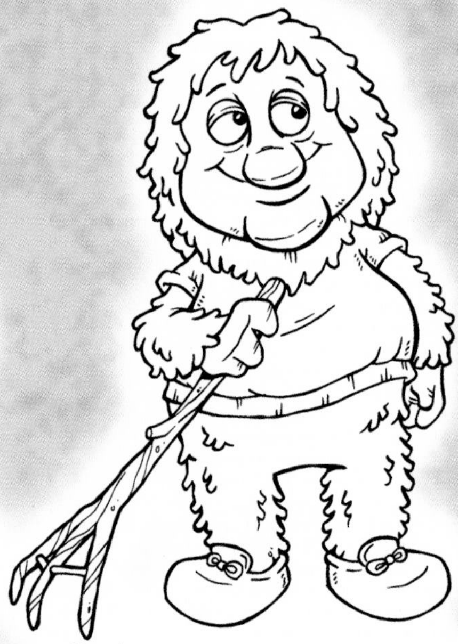

Step 2:
Next, still in pencil, add the details of the arms and legs.

Step 3:
Details, details! More details! Now it's time to pencil in some of Junior's features!

Step 4:
Now, with a black pen or marker, trace over your pencil drawing. Erase your pencil lines and you're done!

"how to make a radish flower"
with BOOBER FRAGGLE

You will need:
- radishes
- a small paring knife
- a cutting board
- adult supervision (knives are sharp!)

Step 1: Cut off the top and bottom tip of the radish with the paring knife. Throw them both away.

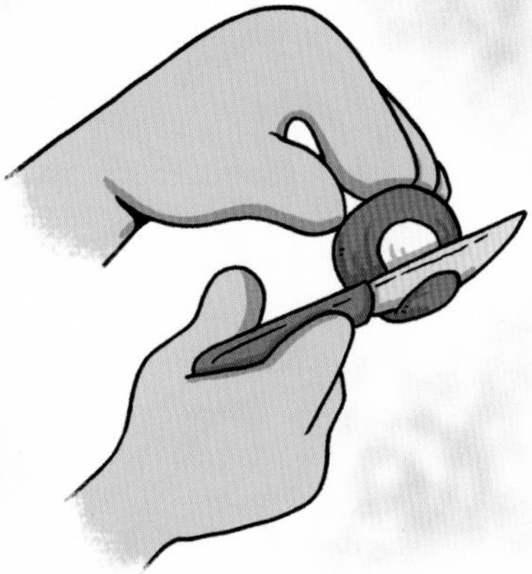

Step 2: Set the radish upright on the cutting board. Cut a thin, vertical slice down one side of the radish with the knife. You want to cut about 3/4ths of the way into it.

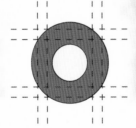

Step 3: Make one or two additional slices down all sides of the radish, spacing the slices evenly around. DO NOT CUT ALL THE WAY THROUGH!!!

Step 4: Place the radish in ice water until it opens slightly. Remove it from the water and drain it well.

Step 5: Garnish your radish flower with a leaf and you're done!

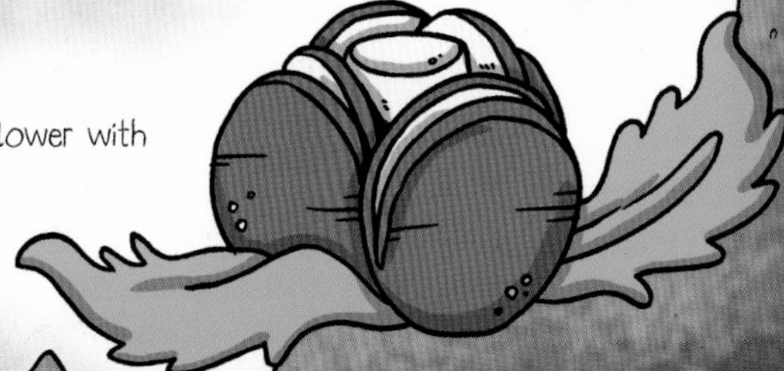

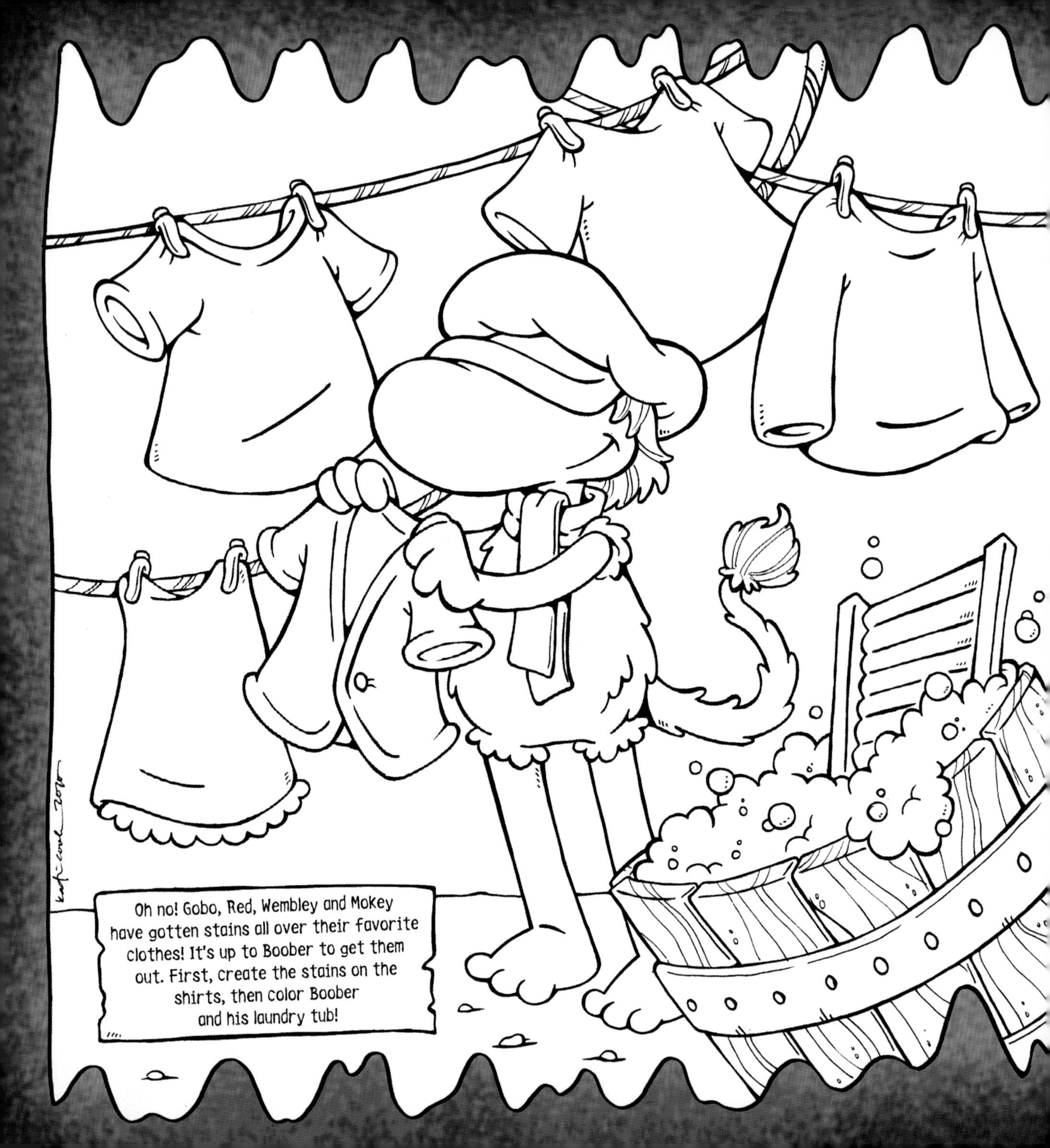
Oh no! Gobo, Red, Wembley and Mokey have gotten stains all over their favorite clothes! It's up to Boober to get them out. First, create the stains on the shirts, then color Boober and his laundry tub!

Fraggle Rock Sketchbook

I often compare editing an anthology project like **Fraggle Rock** to creating a new recipe. Much like when you're in the kitchen, it's all about achieving the perfect balance. Ultimately, you want every component to work together to deliver a result that's nothing short of delicious.

I certainly hope none of you have tried eating our Fraggle Rock comic, but the process really isn't much different. When looking for talented artists to contribute, we looked for men and women who brought something new, exciting and different to the mix. Every artist who has contributed to this collection brings their own distinct flavor to the book, and when you see them all side by side, it becomes clear that together they add up to something truly wonderful. *(At least, we hope so!)*

It would've been easy to have only worked with artists who possessed a similar style. But just like in a recipe, if you only choose similar ingredients, you end up with a very bland result. Sure, it may go down easy, but is it very memorable? Is it exciting? Do people talk about it afterwards? It was our goal to put together a **Fraggle Rock** collection that fans will hopefully be discussing for years to come. After all, the television show has proven to be remarkably enduring. We'd be doing it a disservice if we aimed for anything less!

What follows is a look at some of our early steps in putting together the **Fraggle Rock** comic book. While most of our contributors were fans of the show when it originally aired, many hadn't seen it in a while and hadn't drawn the characters in years…if they'd ever attempted to draw them at all. As with all comics, there was a little bit of a learning curve as artists experimented with drawing the characters, testing the waters to see how much of their style they could bring to them. As you've seen, in some cases, the answer was quite a lot!

You've enjoyed the final result, now take a peek at what went into what we hope was a truly tasty experience.

—**Tim Beedle**
Managing Editor

113

Chandra Free

Illustrator of "The Fraggle Who Cried Monster"

Chandra Free was one of the first artists to get involved with ***Fraggle Rock***. Her initial Fraggle sketches were actually less stylized than what ultimately wound up in the book.

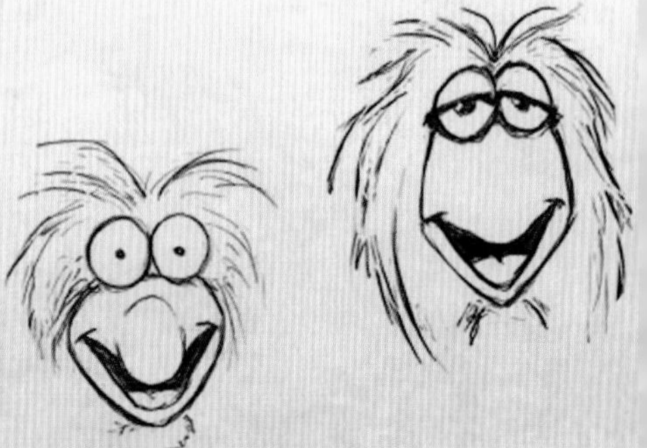

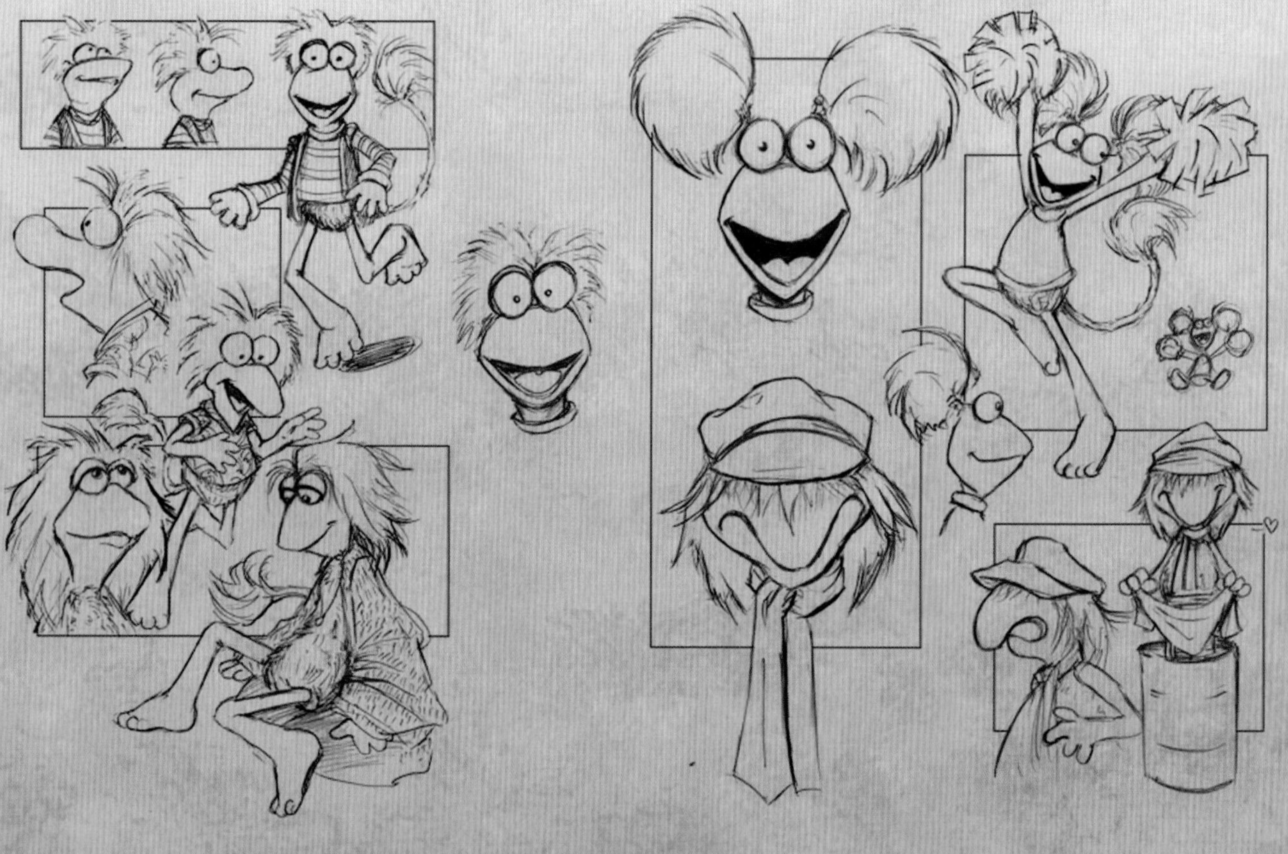

Katie Cook

Illustrator of "My Gift is my Song"

Katie Cook was one of the few artists chosen for this collection based on ***Fraggle Rock*** art she had already drawn. You can see some of her early Fraggle illustrations on her website!

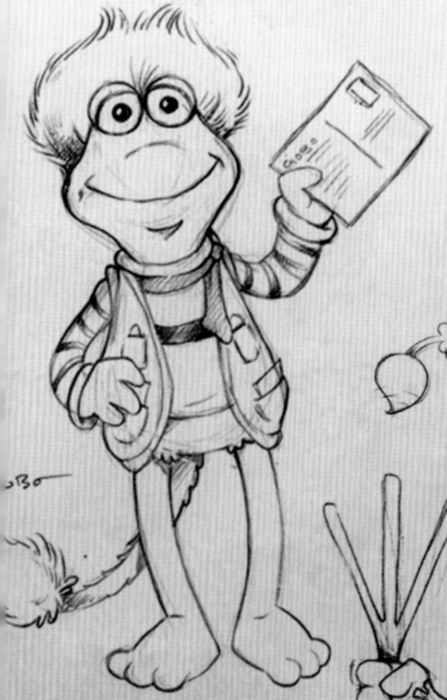

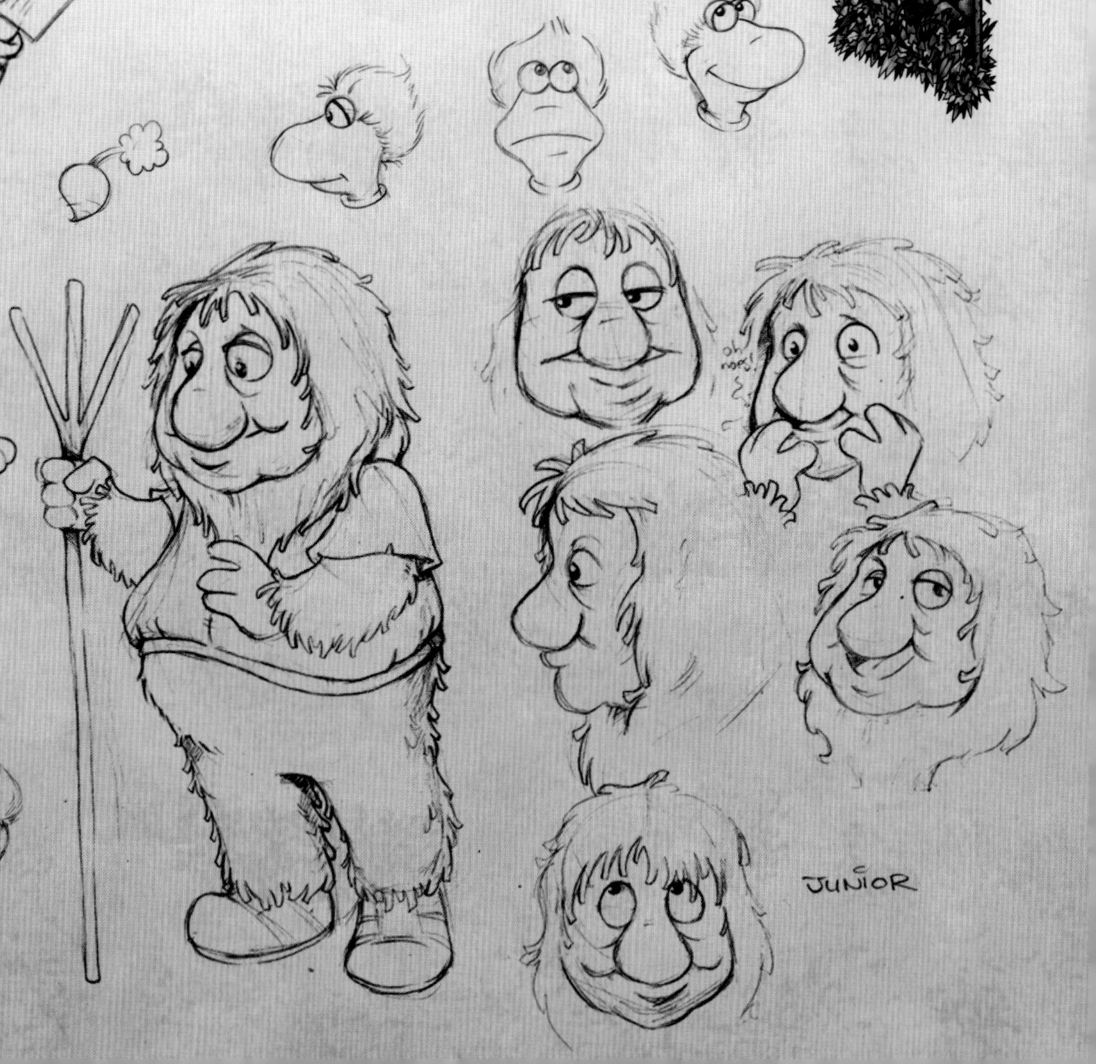
JUNIOR

Chris Lie

Illustrator of "Wembley and the Great Dream-Capade!"

As the illustrator of ***Return to Labyrinth***, Chris Lie had worked with The Jim Henson Company once before. However, ***Fraggle Rock*** provided Chris with a chance to draw Jim Henson characters in an entirely different style.

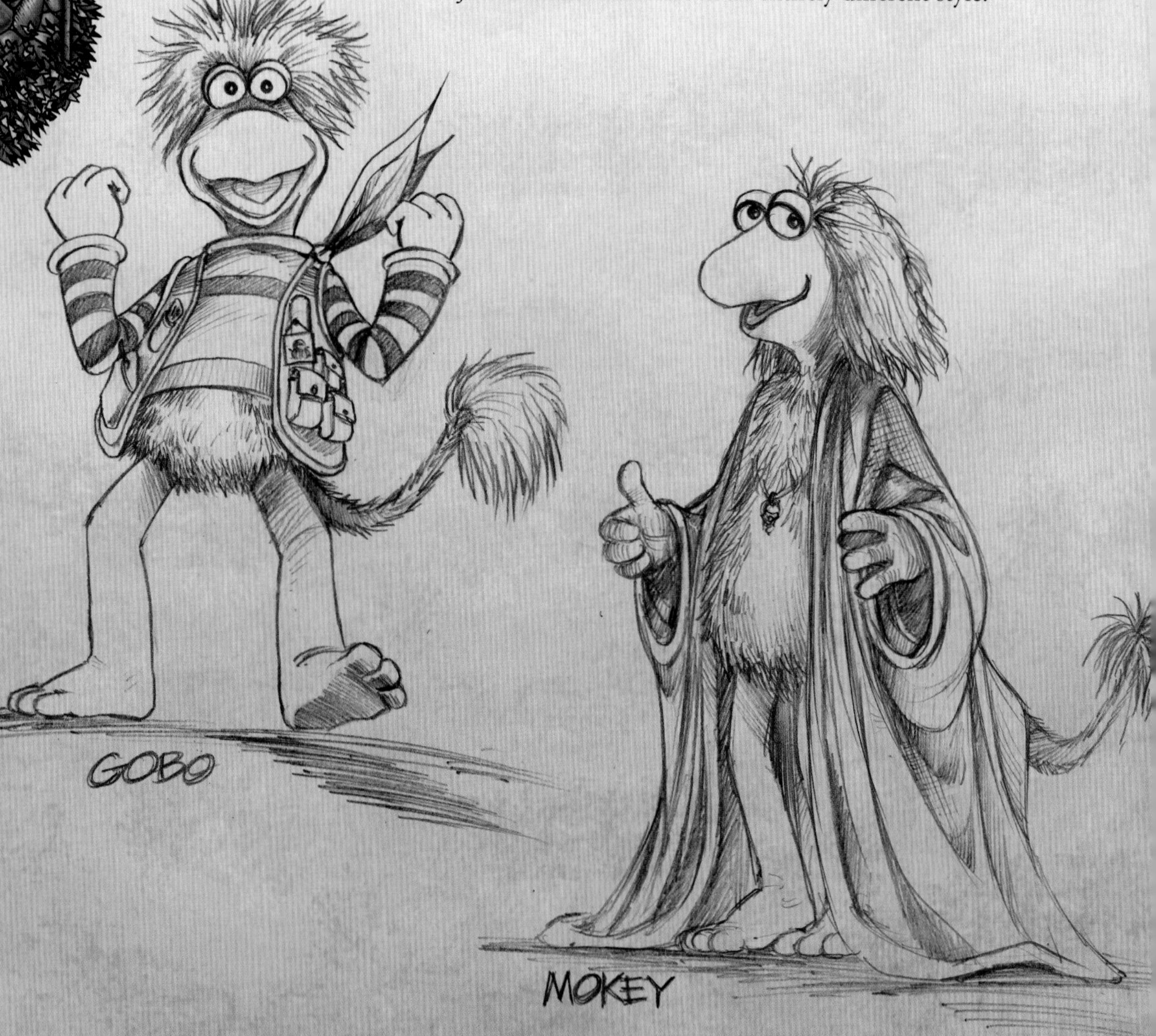
GOBO
MOKEY

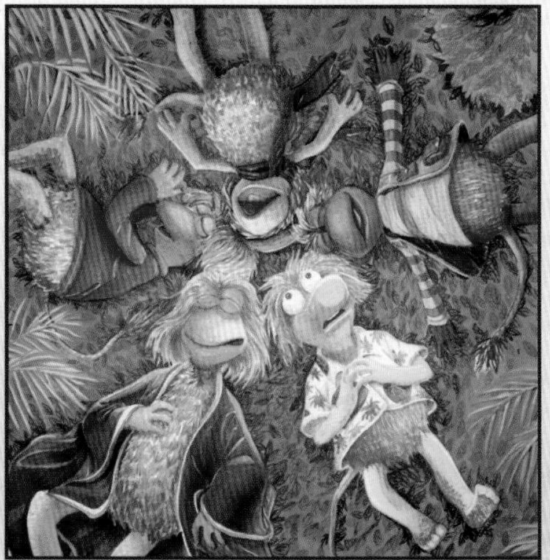

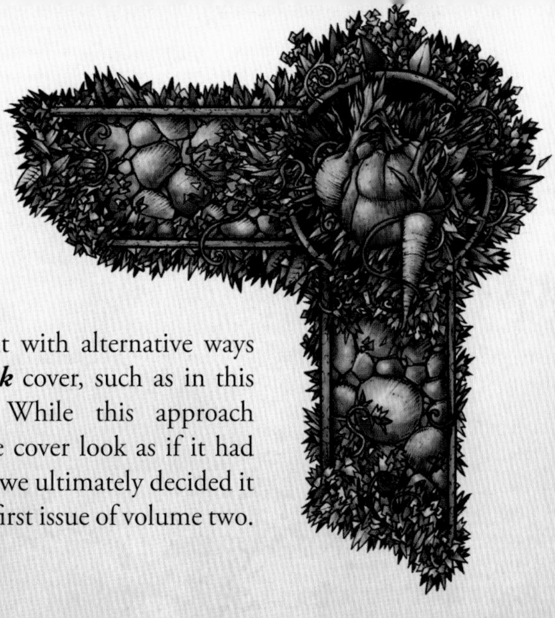

Chris wanted to experiment with alternative ways of coloring his ***Fraggle Rock*** cover, such as in this never-before-seen variant. While this approach added texture and made the cover look as if it had been rendered using pastels, we ultimately decided it wasn't the right look for the first issue of volume two.

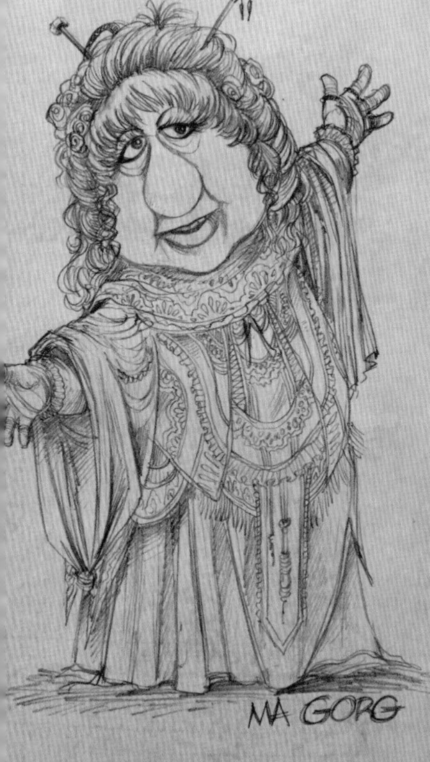
MA GORG

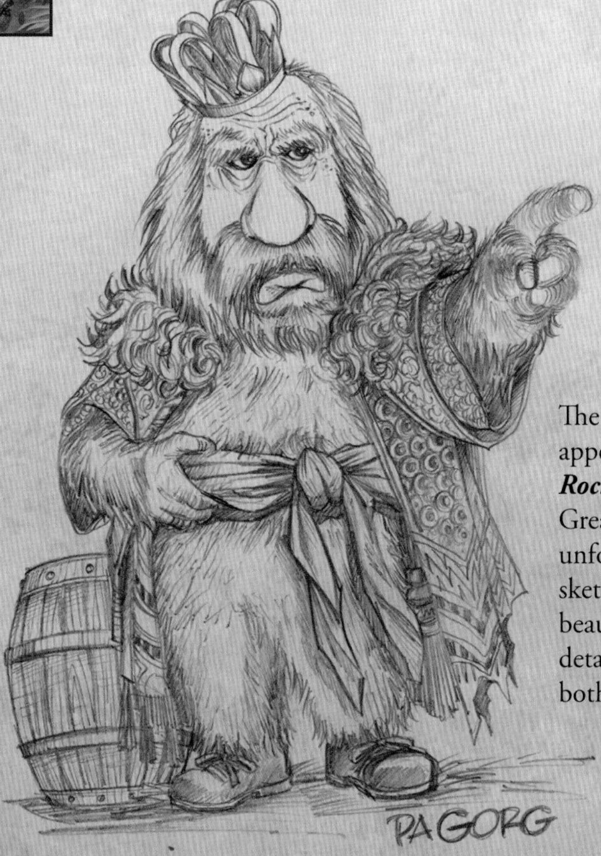
PA GORG

The Gorgs don't make an appearance in Chris' ***Fraggle Rock*** story, "Wembley and the Great Dream-Capade." That's unfortunate because these two sketches are nothing short of beautiful! Check out all of the detail and texture he brings to both of them.

Mark Simmons

Illustrator of "Boober and the Ghastly Stain"

One crucial component of ***Fraggle Rock*** that often goes unacknowledged is the look of the Rock itself. The environment the show is set within is crucial to the look and feel of the series, so it was necessary that any artist we brought to the book be capable of reproducing ***Fraggle Rock***'s distinct caverns and caves. To help ensure this, we asked the artists to draw sample environments as well as characters, as seen in some of these sketches by Mark Simmons.

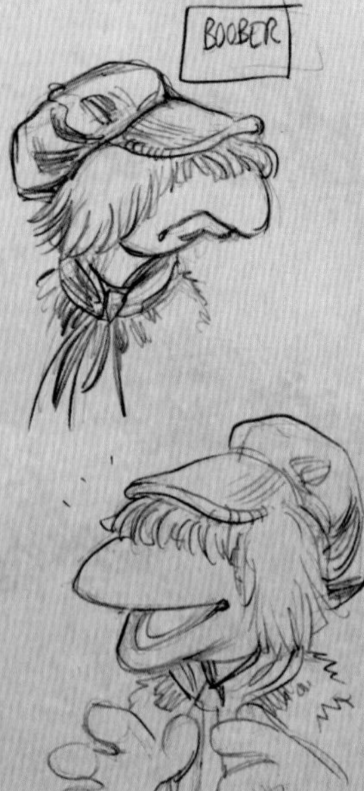
BOOBER

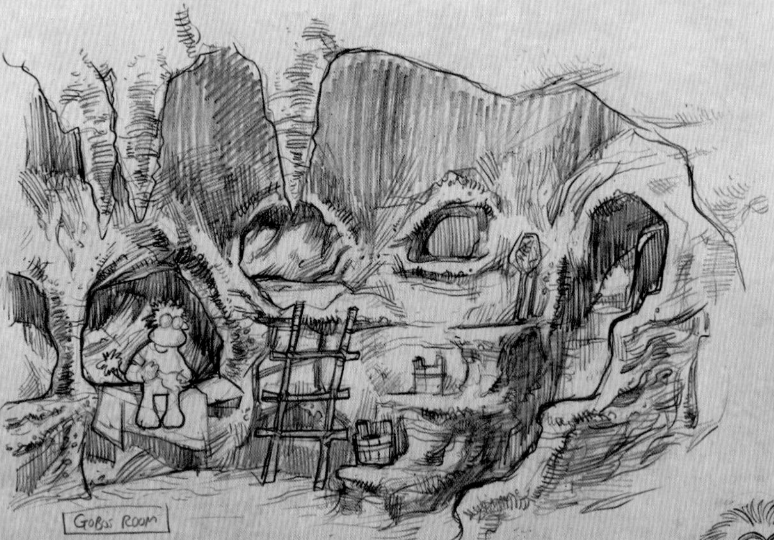
GOBO'S ROOM

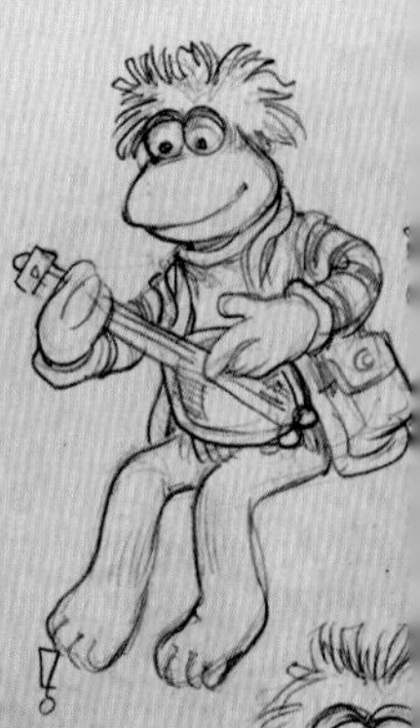

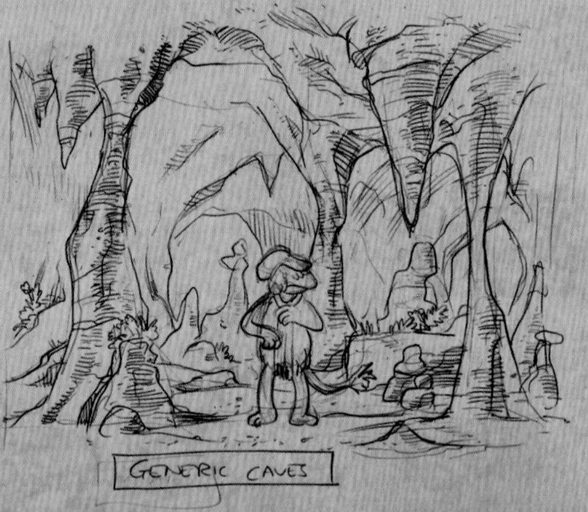
GENERIC CAVES

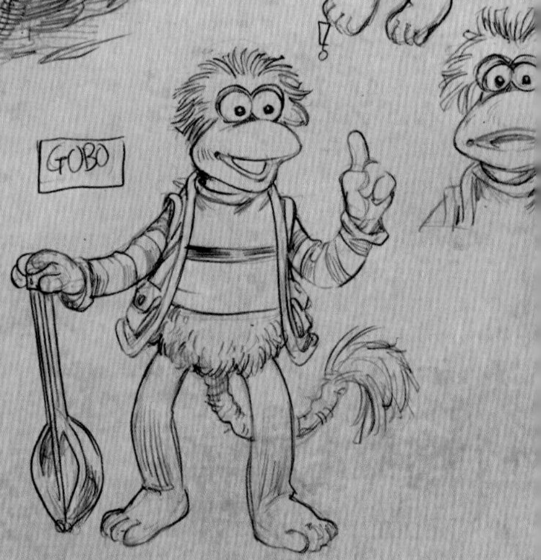
GOBO

Joanna Estep

Colorist of "My Gift is my Song"

If you're familiar with Joanna Estep's work, you know she's capable of drawing in different styles, so it was important to nail down what style she would use for ***Fraggle Rock***. Her Travelling Matt pinup is pretty close to what we ultimately went with. Joanna helped us out by coloring Katie Cook's story in this volume, but she illustrated two stories for us in volume one.

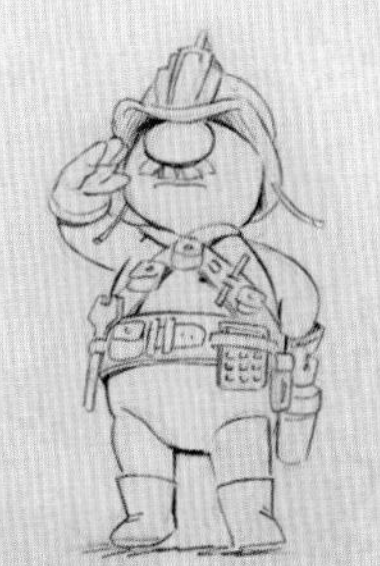

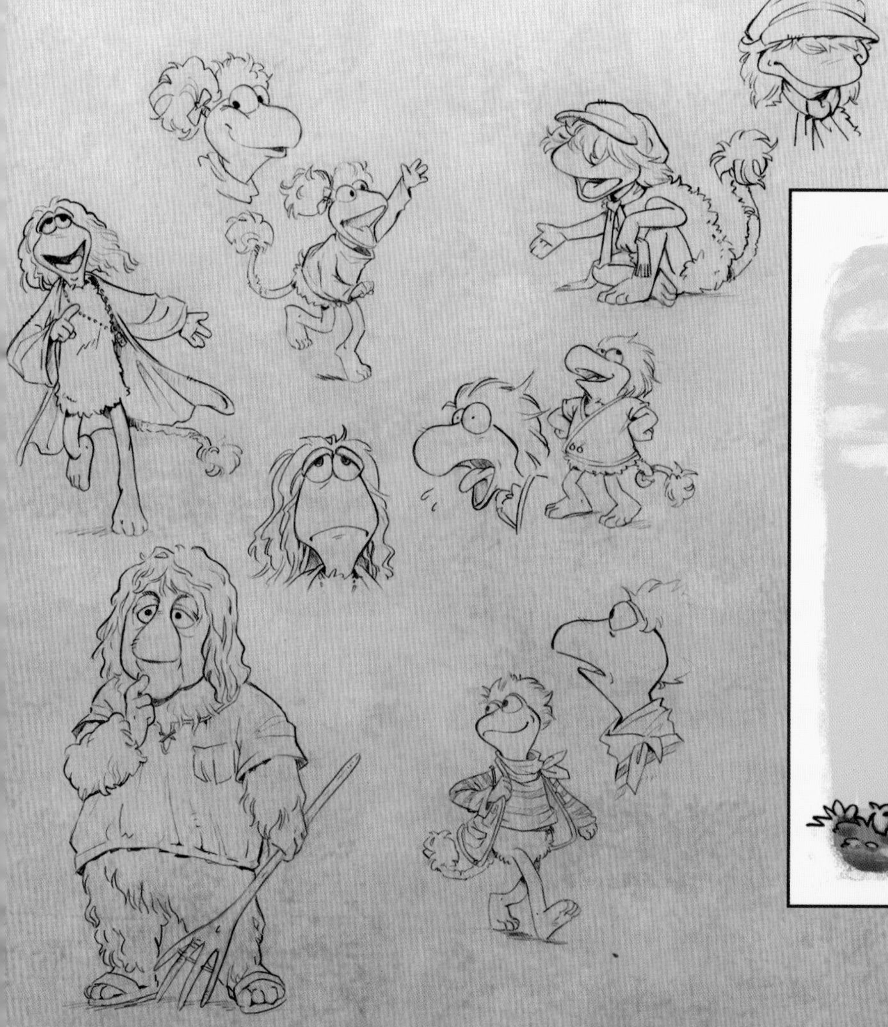

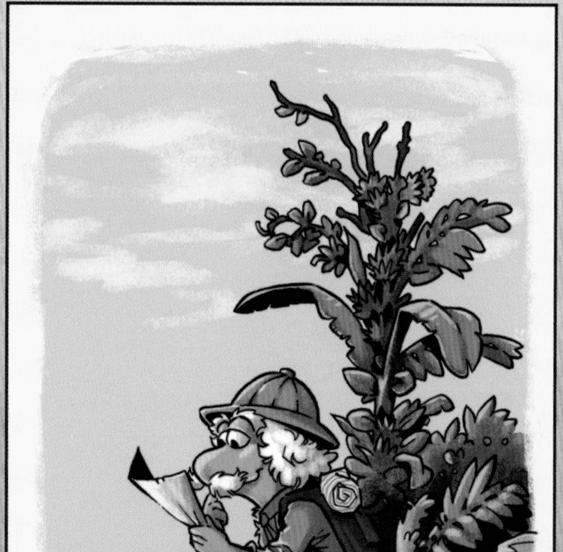

Cory Godbey

Illustrator of "Brave Sir Wembley"

Cory Godbey certainly has one of the more distinct styles in our collection. His tight, flowing pencils emphasize the natural textures of the characters while also bringing out their personalities.

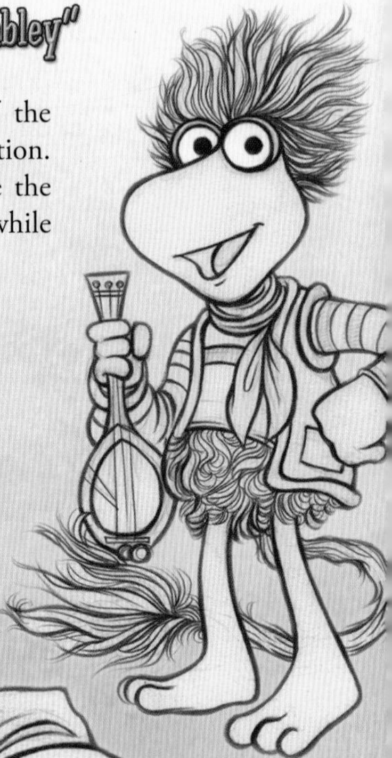

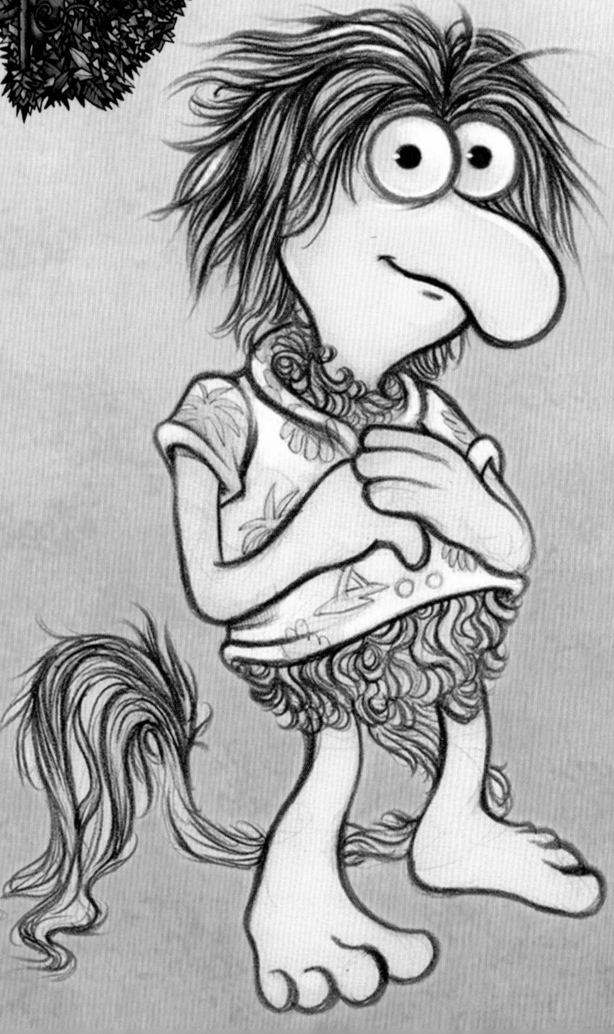

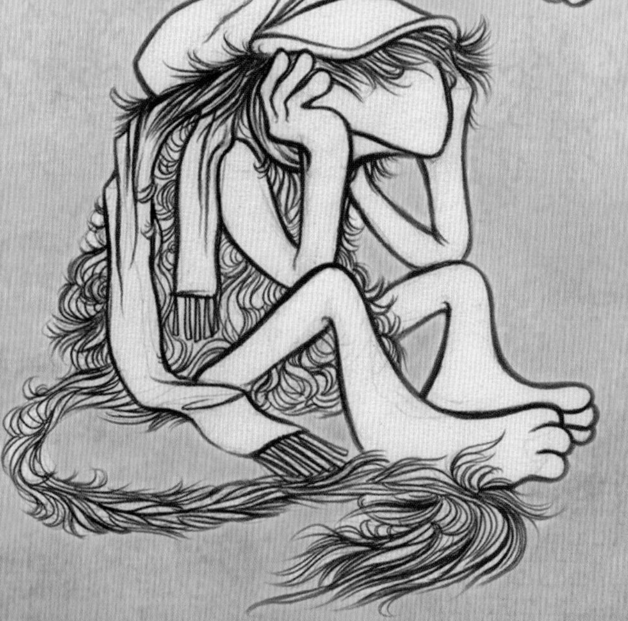

Heidi Arnhold

Illustrator of "The Meaning of Life"

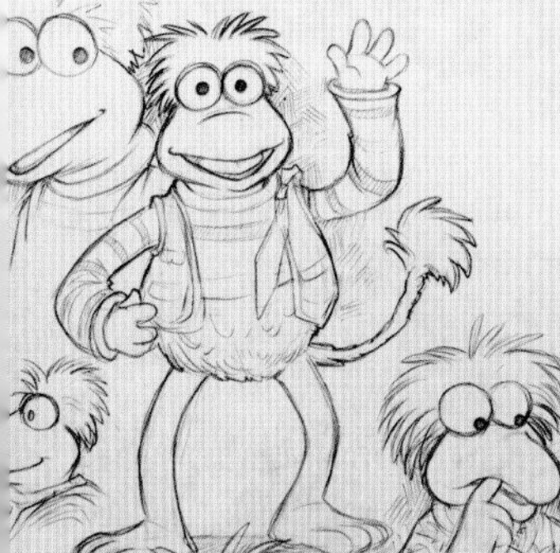

Like Chris Lie, Heidi Arnhold had also previously illustrated comic books for The Jim Henson Company. However, her prior series, ***Legends of The Dark Crystal***, was considerably different than ***Fraggle Rock***. Fortunately, Heidi proved to be as skilled at drawing Fraggles as she is at drawing Skeksis!

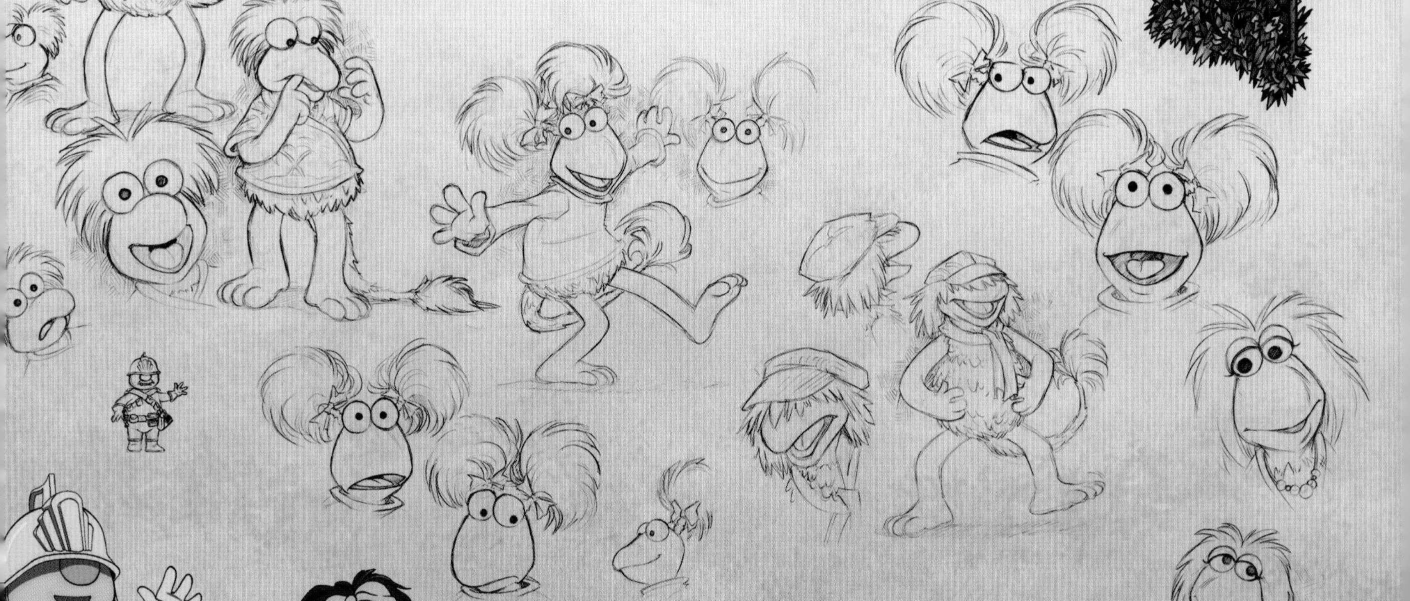

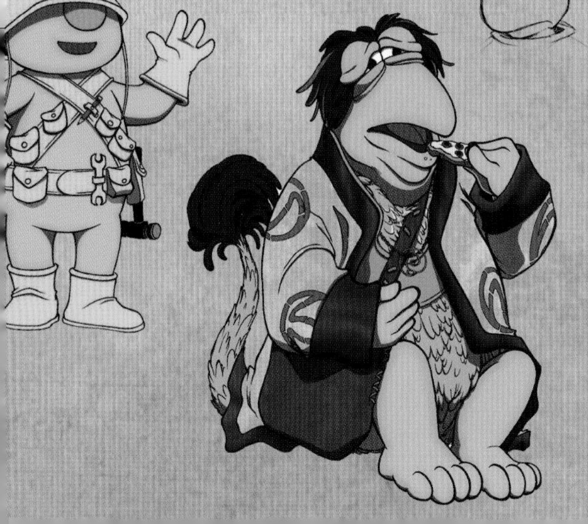

Initially, we tapped Heidi to illustrate "Red's Chomp-a-Thon," a backup story that ultimately was drawn by Nichol Ashworth. Since the Doozers and Large Marvin both figure prominently in that story, we asked Heidi to draw them before getting started. Again, it's another glimpse of what might have been since neither of these characters show up in the story Heidi actually wound up drawing.

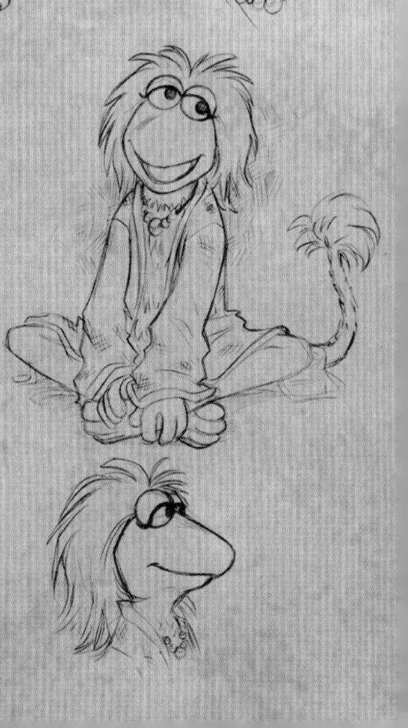

Nichol Ashworth

Illustrator of "Red's Chomp-A-Thon"

Nichol Ashworth was another artist we reached out to early on, but her first pass at drawing the Fraggles was a little too simple and cartoon-like. We saw potential in these early sketches, but they needed more detail and to be brought closer to model. We told Nichol to work on them a bit more, and brought on another artist to illustrate the ***Fraggle Rock* Volume One** story she had written, "Boober the Doozer."

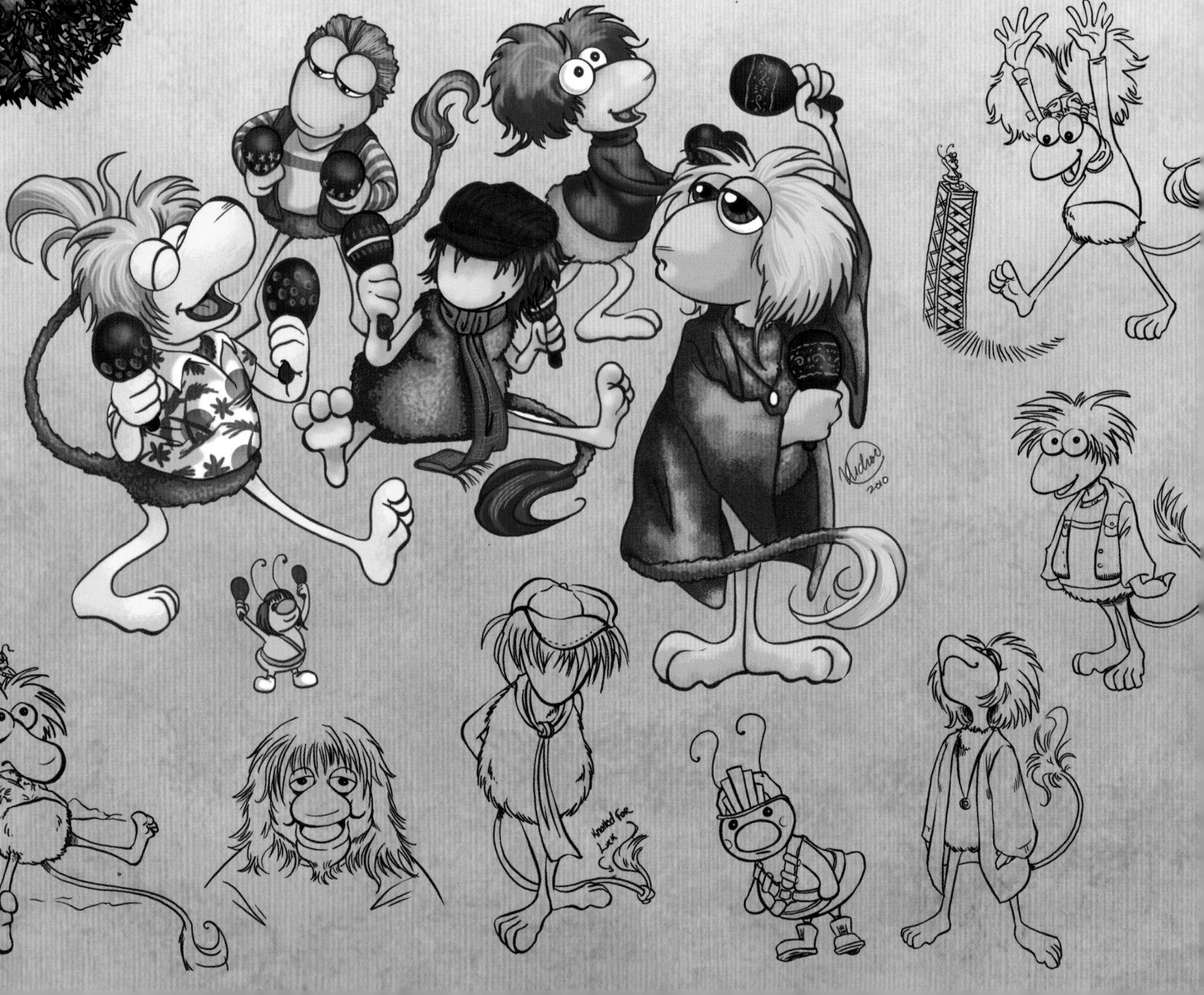
Knotted For Luck

After we finished up the first volume, we got back in touch with Nichol and she provided us with these revised sketches. This second pass was much closer to what we wanted to see from her and allowed us to work with Nichol on ***Fraggle Rock*** again—this time as an artist!

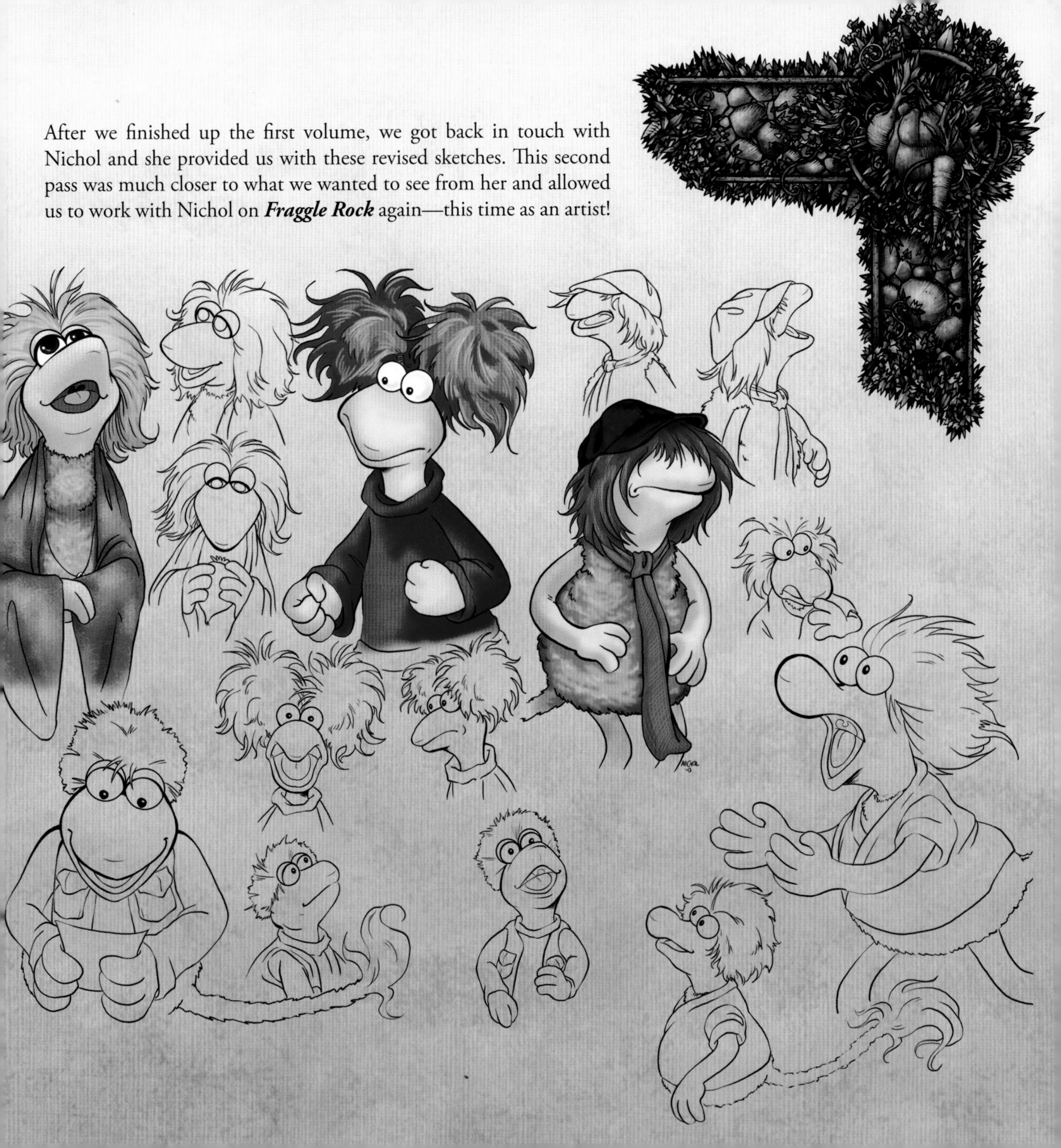

Lindsay Cibos

Illustrator of "Shopping with Silly Creatures"

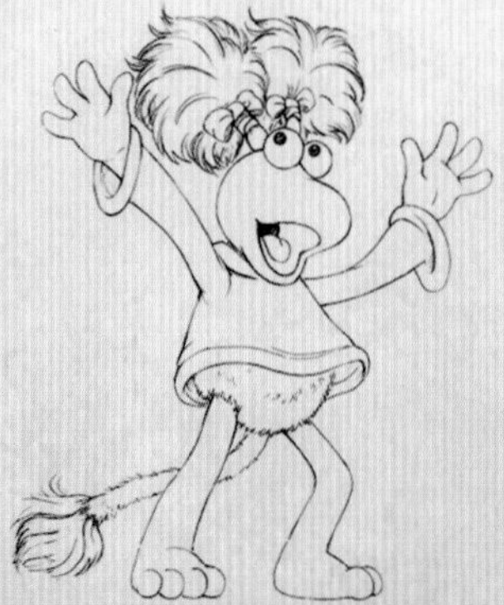

Lindsay Cibos was one of the last artists to come onboard this volume. While the fact that she was a huge ***Fraggle Rock*** fan didn't hurt, it was her stunning work on her webcomic, ***The Last of the Polar Bears***, as well as her tight sketches, that made us really want to work with her.

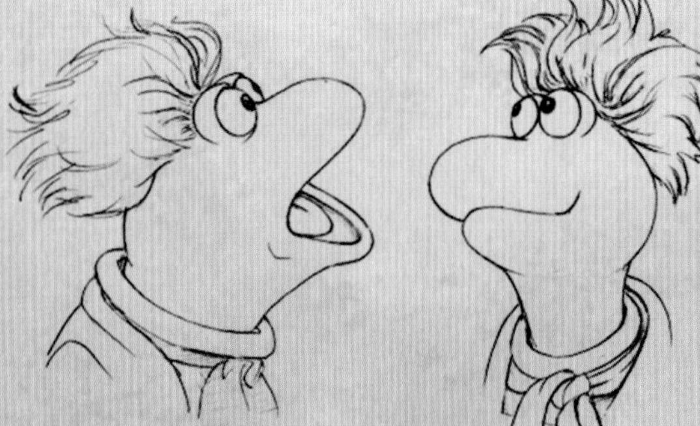

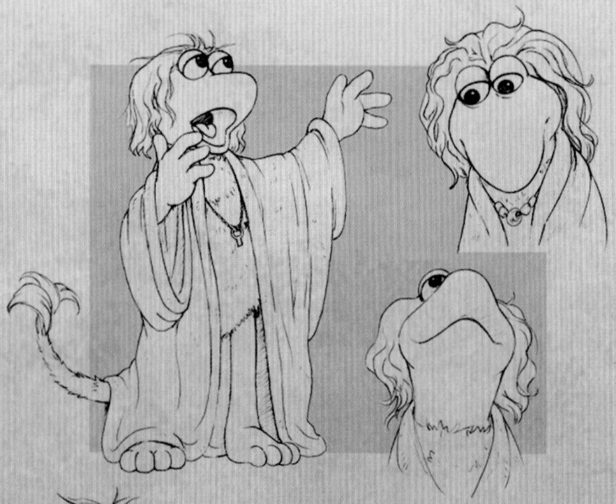

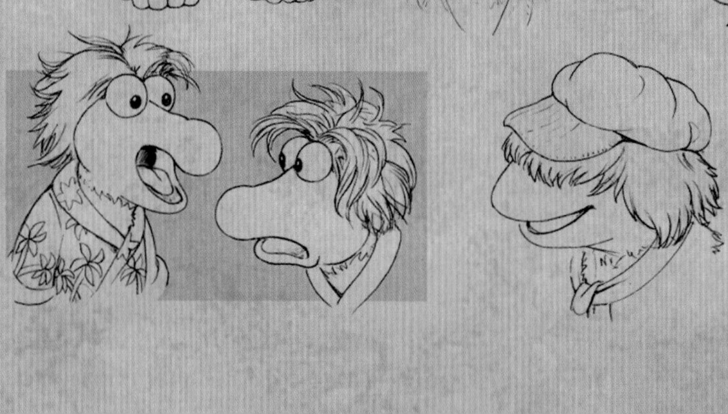

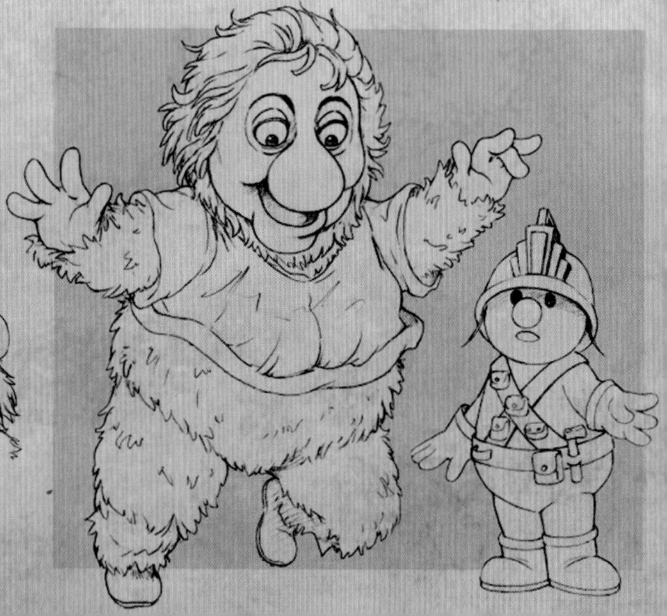

Ross Campbell
Illustrator of "The Perfect Words"

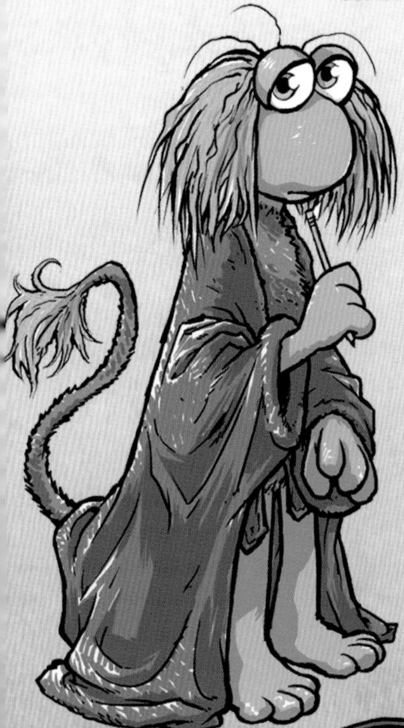

Fraggle Rock was a bit of a departure for Ross Campbell, who has made his name drawing indie comics like ***Wet Moon*** and ***Shadoweyes***, but that was what made working with him so appealing! His quirky take on the Fraggles was a lot of fun, particularly Red's giant hair!

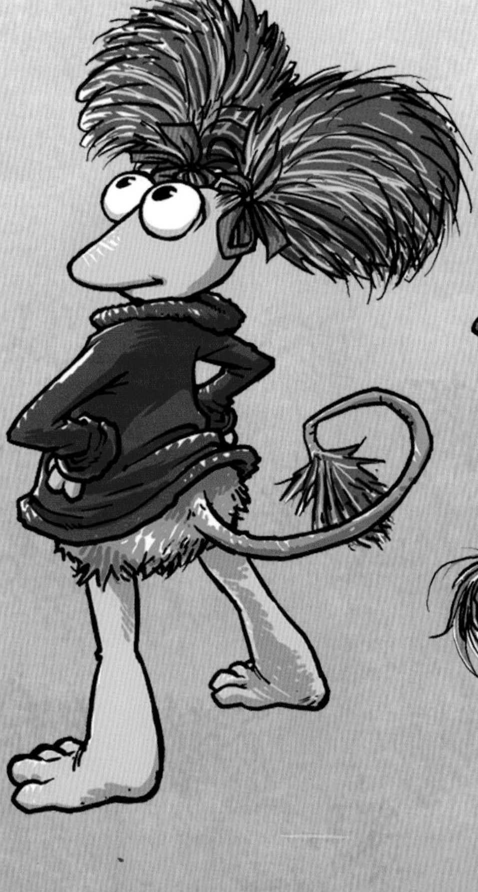

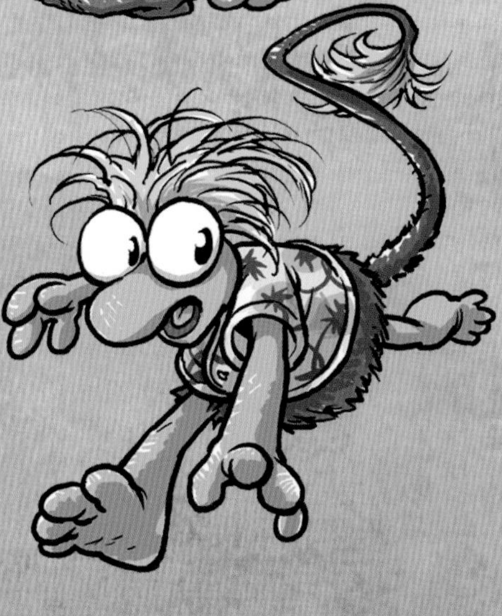

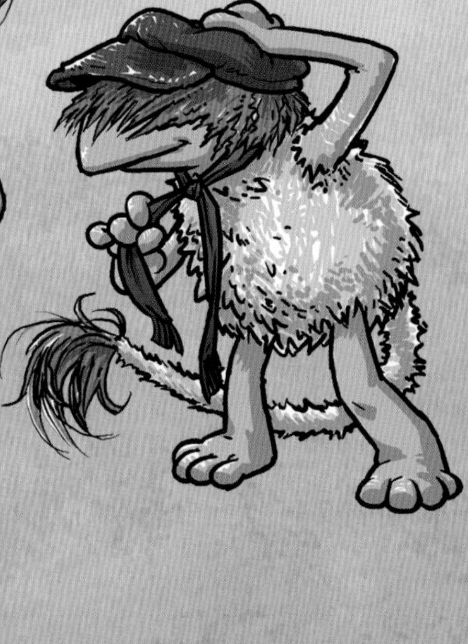

About the Creators

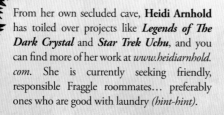

From her own secluded cave, **Heidi Arnhold** has toiled over projects like *Legends of The Dark Crystal* and *Star Trek Uchu*, and you can find more of her work at *www.heidiarnhold.com*. She is currently seeking friendly, responsible Fraggle roommates… preferably ones who are good with laundry *(hint-hint)*.

Nichol Ashworth is no stranger to the Fraggle crew. She wrote "Boober the Doozer" for the 2010 Free Comic Book Day issue and now she's Fraggle Rocking yet again, this time as an illustrator. Check out more of Nichol's projects on *www.nixcomix.com*.

Tim Beedle has written and edited many puppety comics including *Muppet Robin Hood* and the New York Times bestselling *Return to Labyrinth*. He's currently editing Archaia's forthcoming *Dark Crystal* graphic novel and posting occasional updates to his website, *www.wordsthatstay.com*.

Named Best Indie Writer of 2008 by the Project Fanboy Awards, **Jason M. Burns** separates his time writing creator-owned content (*A Dummy's Guide to Danger*, *The Expendable One*) and licensed comics (*Pocket God*, *Jericho*, *Kung Fu Panda*). For more information, visit *www.jasonmburns.com*.

Ross Campbell is the Eisner-nominated creator of a bunch of comic including *Wet Moon*, *Shadoweyes*, *The Abandoned* and *Water Baby* and he almost got to draw *Teenage Mutant Ninja Turtles* a couple o times. He likes cats, monsters and tea.

Lindsay Cibos is the creator of the graphic novel series *Peach Fuzz* as well as the author of several art instructional books. She's currently working on a new graphic novel called *The Last of the Polar Bears* which you can check out on her website at *www.lastpolarbears.com*.

Katie Cook is an illustrator and comic book artist currently best known for her work in the Star Wars universe and in our first volume of *Fraggle Rock*. Her work on many other popular licensed properties and her own artwork can be found at *www.katiecandraw.com*.

Joanna Estep is an artist, writer and accomplished whateverist. She ha illustrated such titles as *Roadsong*, the S.P.A.C.E. Prize-winning *Reflection* and her self-penned story *Happy Birthday, Michael Mitchell*.

Chandra Free is the artist and writer of the oddly dark and totally no for kids *The God Machine* graphic novel. She's been flailing her arms about in joy with the Fraggles and the Muppets since she was a wee thing back in the 80s. More of her work can be found at *www.spookychan.com*

Jake T. Forbes is one of the leading scholars of Goblinology After a visitation by the Goblin King himself, Forbes dedicated his days to translating the original notebooks of Sirs Froud and

Jones. The resulting scholarly works were published in four volumes as **Return to Labyrinth** and became New York Times Bestsellers, much to the chagrin of Professor Forbes. Burned by his experience, Forbes turned to Fraggropology, which sounds much dirtier than it is. He is currently working on an original graphic novel that has neither goblins nor Fraggles. His website is *www.gobblin.net.*

Cory Godbey seeks to tell stories with his work. He also likes to draw monsters. His short graphic novel stories can be found in the Eisner-nominated **Flight** anthologies. Cory's also animated stuff for Prudential, Microsoft and a documentary film, **The Last Flight of Petr Ginz**.

Lizzy John lives in Brooklyn and spends most of her days there drawing pretty pictures. Sometimes she gets paid for it.

Joe LeFavi is a silly creature who is indescribably honored to write comics and screenplays for a living, and cherishes every day that he wakes up as an obnoxiously passionate producer, story editor, and transmedia "geek for hire" in the entertainment industry.

Chris Lie founded Caravan Studio in 2008 and has since been working on various comic, illustration, toy design and concept art projects, such as **Marvel Ultimate Alliance 2**, **DC Universe Online**, **Magic the Gathering Tactics**, **GI Joe** and **Warhammer**. Caravan Studio's art can be seen at *www.caravanstudio.com.*

Paul Morrissey edits comic books and graphic novels. Paul oversaw the award-winning **Muppet Show** comic book for BOOM! Studios, along with a number of kid-friendly Disney comics, including **The Incredibles**, **Cars**, **Monsters Inc.**, **Finding Nemo**, **Wall*E** and **Toy Story**. He lives in L.A. with multiple video game systems.

Grace Randolph has written for Marvel, DC, BOOM! Studios and Tokyopop. She is also the host and creator of the web show **Beyond The Trailer**, as well as the new host and writer of Marvel's web show, **The Watcher**. To get a full rundown of her work, visit *www.gracerandolph.com.* Grace thanks you for taking the time to read her bio.

Mark Simmons is a recent art-school graduate and an expert on Japanese super robots. Visit *www.ultimatemark.com* to see more of his work, and see *toysdream.blogspot.com* for his latest news and doodles.

Katie Strickland currently resides in Mt. Jewett, PA, where she stays up much too late writing comic books and screenplays. She wants to thank her kids, Athena and Charlie, for watching hours of **Fraggle Rock** with her and for bringing so much fun and inspiration into her life.

Dance your cares away, worry's for another day.
Let the music play, down at Fraggle Rock.

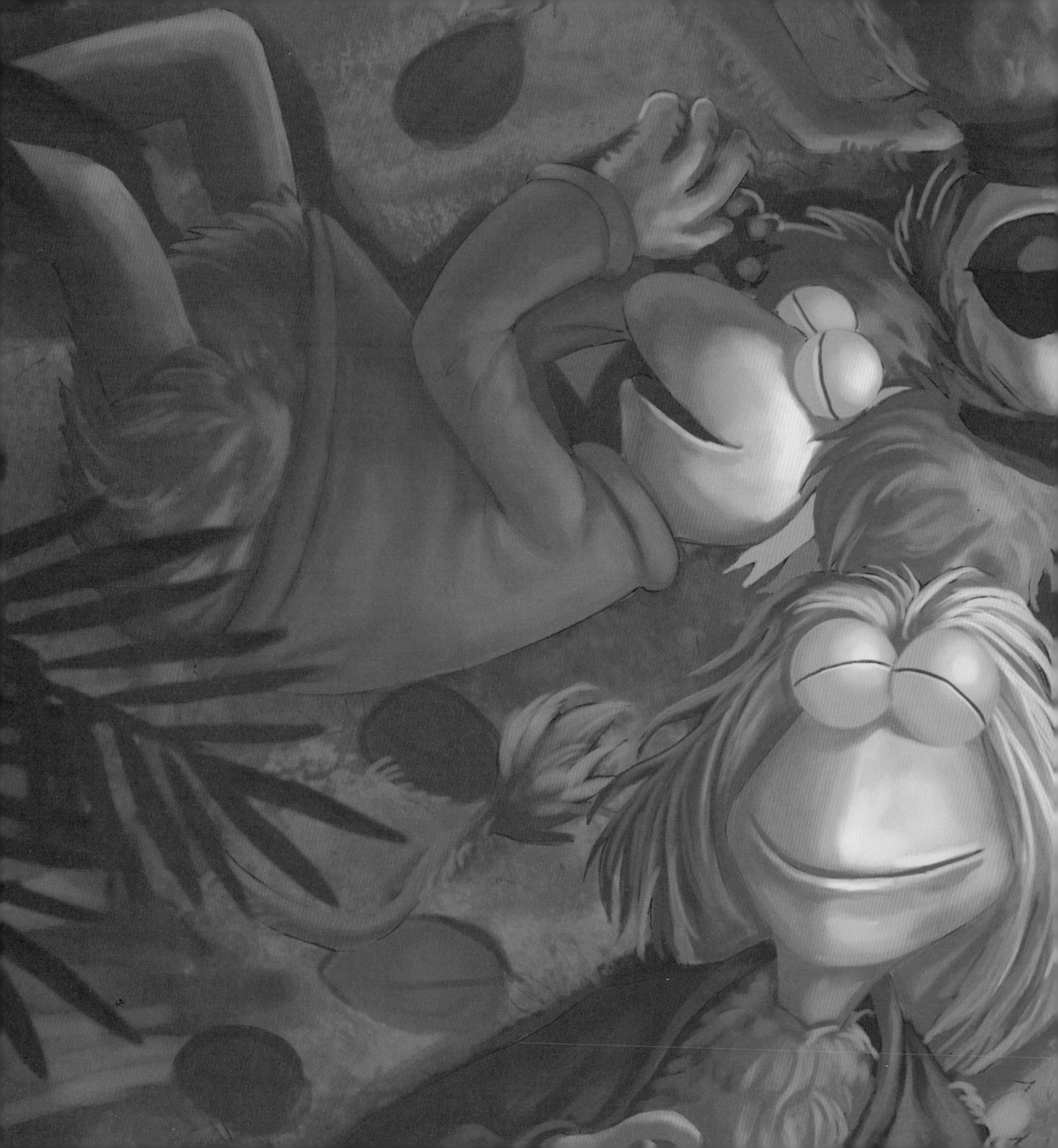